Praise for Elena Greene's Books

"*Lady Dearing's Masquerade* could have been a dark, depressing story considering its many tragedies: orphaned foundlings, throwaway babies, malicious gossip, years of abuse. But it's a tribute to Elena Greene that the story is poignant, and the admirable way in which Jeremy and Livvy deal with their trials endears them to readers and will have you rooting for them to unite."

— *Romantic Times Bookclub* (4 and 1/2 stars, Top Pick)

"The story (*The Incorrigible Lady Catherine*) gives fresh new twists to traditional Regency plotlines and introduces a well-drawn cast of characters, three of whom cry out for their own tales to be told—the notorious Lord Verwood and Catherine' two school friends."

— Jane Bowers, in *Romance Reviews Today*

"I consider *The Redwyck Charm* one of the best Regencies I've read in the past few months. Elena Greene is a reliable author who delivers the kind of story Regency readers love."

— Barbara Hume, for *Rakehell*

"Elena Greene writes an intriguing tale of hope, love and joy. In this clever story of just who rescues whom, the political intrigue and developing passion between the main characters neatly blend together to make it (*Saving Lord Verwood*) a highly pleasurable read."

— *Romantic Times Bookclub* (4 and 1/2 stars)

Fly
WITH A
Rogue

by

Elena Greene

Cherwell Cottage PRESS

Cherwell Cottage Press

ISBN-10: 1942328141
ISBN-13: 978-1-942328-14-8

Cover art by:

In loving memory of
Philip Ashley Greene
whose spirit soars

With thanks to:

Gail, Jeanne, Karen,
Kathleen, Mary, Teri, Wendy,
the Risky Regencies and
the Beau Monde

Part One

"We had been born to war, reared in war,
and war was our trade;
and what soldiers had to do in peace,
was a problem yet to be resolved among us."

— Sir John Kincaid, *Adventures in the Rifle Brigade*

Chapter One

Green Park, London
April, 1817

He was damned if he did, damned if he didn't.

Gilbert Manning, late of the 95th Rifles, watched the blue and yellow striped envelope of his balloon, Alcyone, sway in the stiff breeze. She'd been a hell-cat to fill, tugging one way then another with each gust, practically lying on her side at one point. Now she strained against the efforts of four park keepers holding her mooring ropes and Gil's regular crew holding down the car itself.

It would be one hell of an ascension. If he went through with it.

He glanced toward the mixed throng, some in open carriages, some on foot. Whether they'd purchased tickets for prime spots next to the enclosure or not, they'd be angry if he postponed. For now, they all seemed well entertained by the balloon's gyrations and by his crew: ex-sergeant Lund, his eye-patch the final touch to a naturally villainous appearance, red-haired Birkin hobbling about on his wooden leg, and Sancha, dark and exotic in the traditional tight bodice and voluminous skirts of her native Extremadura.

His new man Reed, recently plucked out of the gutter but now mercifully sober, was the only one who did not draw attention to himself. But Gil didn't like the frenzied look in his eyes.

"S-sir, are you quite certain you should go up? Is not the wind too strong?" Reed spoke politely, as befitted one who had once been an officer's servant, but there was a squeak in his voice. The fellow seemed unnaturally anxious. Perhaps hiring him had been a mistake, but Gil had a soft spot for any soldier down on his luck.

"*Capitán!* You are mad to fly on such a day!" Sancha's eyes flashed as she looked up from her place between Lund and Birkin.

"They don't call 'im Mad Manning for nought," said Lund, grinning as he looked up from his task.

"And you will go up with him? *Madre de Dios!* Do you wish to be killed too?"

"Don't worry, love. The Captain knows what he's about," Lund replied.

"That he does," Birkin corroborated.

"But I had a dream," she insisted. "I saw great danger!"

"Ye're just upset I won't be there to warm yer bed to-night," said Lund.

"Stubble it!" Gil commanded before anyone could continue. "There are ladies and children about."

Silent but still grinning, the men continued to hold the balloon while Sancha began the process of loading.

Gil looked up at the sky. It was blue and clear, only the occasional cloud scudding southward. Down at ground level, gusts continued to buffet his vessel.

He stepped away and bowed, assessing the crowd as he did so. Their mood seemed festive, but that could change. Green Park still showed signs of the ravages of three years ago. Rioters had burned down the Temple of Concord when the Prince Regent failed to make an appearance during the celebration of the Centenary of the House of Brunswick. The illustrious James Sadler had taken up a balloon that day. The lucky devil had gotten off safely well before the crowd turned ugly. Gil hoped to do the same. There was good reason that the gas swelling Alcyone's belly was called inflammable air; it would take no more than a smoking pipe thrown at her to turn the ascension into a disaster.

He circled the perimeter, stopping occasionally to bow and smile.

Several young ladies in a barouche coyly returned his smile. The wind molded their thin muslin gowns against their limbs and brought out the roses in their cheeks. Quite fetching, they were. Enough to remind him that he hadn't had a proper tumble in a while. But he didn't need the warning look from the chaperone sitting beside them to remind him that respectable young ladies were off limits.

A nice, round-heeled widow, that was the thing. Perhaps he'd meet one soon.

But now he'd a job to do. He made the ladies a deep bow and moved on, listening to snatches of conversation until one made him prick up his ears.

"If it were that young Sadler, he'd go up, wind or no," said one of a trio of young dandies sitting in an open coach near the edge of the enclosure.

"Maybe he'd try, but no one's better than Mad Manning! He'll do the trick."

Gil strolled casually closer to the group.

The third dandy, in a green coat with extravagantly padded shoulders and half-strangled by his high cravat, rolled his eyes. "There will be a put-off! Just look at that wind. Snatched the hat right off my head! Don't know why we bothered to come. No one in his right mind would fly on such a day."

"But I just might," said Gil.

"It's sheer lunacy!" The green-coated gentleman laughed. "Even if you manage to set off, you'll find yourself stuck in a tree or smeared all over the countryside!" He shuddered delicately.

"You are certain of that, I suppose?" Gil asked.

"I'd bet a hundred Yellow Boys on it!"

"Tilly, you're an idiot! He'll win, I tell you!" said the youngest.

The one called Tilly gave his friend a pained glance and introduced himself to Gil. "Augustus Tillingham. I am prepared to wager you a hundred guineas that you won't complete this flight and walk away to tell the tale."

When one lived hand to mouth, it was tempting to pluck the occasional pigeon. This was a fat one, too. If Gil wasn't mistaken, Tillingham was the son of a marquess with an allowance to match. He paused deliberately, as if weighing his chances.

"He won't take it, he ain't got the bottom!" said the first fop.

"If your friend is so certain of winning, he should offer me odds," said Gil.

"Five to one, then," Tillingham offered.

"You're a ninnyhammer, Tilly!" said his young friend.

The other shook his head. "You're sending a man to his death."

"I'll take it," said Gil, suppressing a grin.

He pulled his flight journal along with a pencil out of the pocket of his coat. Within minutes, he'd scrawled the terms of the bet onto a blank page, he and Tillingham had signed it and the friends witnessed the agreement. He whistled softly as he strode back to Alcyone, waving his hat to the crowd as he went. Now all he had to do was take off safely and make sure he *didn't* get himself smeared across the countryside.

"What have you been doing?" Sancha demanded.

"Making our fortunes. Five hundred guineas to be precise, if I complete the flight in one piece."

"A cool monkey!" said Lund. "Ye're bloody brilliant!"

"*Estúpido!* You will get yourself killed and my dearest Roberto along with you! You are all idiots. But I do not wish you to die!" Sancha stamped her foot.

A new gust blew up, causing Alcyone to tilt. Ladies shrieked and the crowd grew louder.

"I'm going up alone today," Gil decided. "With less weight, she'll rise quicker and I'll have a better chance of getting off safely."

"Damn it all, Captain, you promised me I'd go up!" Lund protested.

"Stop your poutin', ye big baby!" said Birkin.

"Enough! Hold tight. I'm going in," said Gil.

He climbed into the car of the balloon and eyed its contents. The barometer and compass would have to stay, as well as the cork jacket. It was light and who knew whether the winds might sweep him out over open water. The grappling iron would have to stay, fastened to its neatly coiled rope. He'd need it to anchor Alcyone on landing.

He made a few more mental calculations. "Take out all the sandbags but one."

"Just one sandbag?" Birkin asked. He and Lund frowned. They knew as well as Gil the risks of flying with too little ballast on a day when the wind might make it difficult to control his landing. But for now, he needed to make sure he would clear the crowd and surrounding buildings.

"Just the one sandbag," he said. Obediently, they removed the rest of them.

He picked up the basket of food and drink Sancha had packed and handed it out to her.

"*Capitán*, this is a very bad idea. I feel it, here!" She held the basket in one hand and pressed the other to her breast.

"Please, sir, I implore you, do not fly today!" said Reed frantically.

"Don't fret," said Gil, grinning. "God doesn't want me and the devil will wait."

All was ready, but a particularly strong gust of wind caused Alcyone to tilt again. "Let's wait until this passes," he commanded, as the keepers and his crew fought to hold the car steady.

After a moment the wind died down. "Release the mooring ropes!" he shouted.

The park keepers let loose the ropes that tethered Alcyone to the ground. She shifted again with another gust but Lund, Birkin and Reed managed to hold onto the car.

Gil waited until she settled again, then looked around to make sure no one was entangled in the mooring ropes. "All ready?"

"Aye," the men said as one.

And he gave the final command. "Let go!"

The men released the car. Alcyone sprang upwards before a fresh gust of wind sent her sideways, over the heads of the spectators. Horses shied. Ladies screamed. The crowd roared. But an instant later Gil was wafting upward again, spinning and rising at an oblique angle. The screams became cheers. He pulled off his hat and waved it at the crowd.

Now was the moment he loved: the upturned smiling faces, the cheering. It was magic and it never failed.

But he was rising very quickly. Too quickly, now that he was clear of the buildings. The gas inside Alcyone was expanding faster than it could escape through her neck; he had to release it before the pressure grew too great. He tugged on the valve-rope. Nothing happened. Frowning, he tugged again. This time it worked and the balloon dropped back toward the park.

He soared over the oblong reservoir at the north end, catching the fleeting reflection of Alcyone in the wind-ruffled water. She floated swiftly over Mayfair. London's parks spread out beneath him—Green Park, St. James's, Hyde Park—luxuriant green patches in the fabric of London. In the streets, carriages moved along like toys. The serpentine curves of the Thames sparkled in the sun.

Examining the barometer, he saw that the balloon had leveled off. He was floating along in a steady southwestern current at a little over a thousand feet. No need to go higher today and waste precious ballast. He hoped the valve would give him no more trouble.

Soon he passed over the fringes of town and into the countryside, dotted with villages. Below him lay England:

green with spring, serene and fertile, undulating with gentle hills like a woman's body. Alcyone's small, dark shadow passed over it like a swift caress. Serenity enfolded him; he'd worry about the landing later.

Tom Hill was squirming in his seat again.

Emma Westfield left a knot of older students for the group of younger children whom she'd set to practicing their sums in their place near the window. She couldn't blame them for fidgeting. It was a lovely day outside, bright and breezy. But surely they could get through a few more minutes.

"Tom, I see you have two more sums to complete," she said.

His eyes remained glued to the window. "There's something out there, Miss!"

"Two more sums and you will be free to go."

"No, truly, Miss, there's something there!"

The other children pricked up their ears. Emma went calmly to the window and peered out the dusty panes. There *was* something there. A dark speck in the distance, rather high for a bird and not moving like one either.

"Is it a balloon, Miss?" Tom joined her by the window.

The other children gathered around as she stared out at the object. It seemed a trifle larger already, with rounded contours.

"I think you are right," she said.

"May we go out and watch it?" Tom asked.

"Yes, may we? Please..." pleaded a chorus of high-pitched voices.

Memories surfaced of the first and only time she'd watched a balloon ascension. Papa had taken her to London when she was ten. How splendid it had been, but how long ago it seemed! Now twelve pairs of eyes begged her indulgence. How could she deny them this treat, these children of villagers and farm laborers who sometimes missed school because they were picking stones or scaring birds from the fields to earn a few pennies for their families?

"Of course we may go outside," she said. "We can see the balloon better from the pasture."

"Hurrah! We're going to see the balloon!" Tom shouted, starting a rush to the doorway.

"In order, please, not like a herd of cows!"

They slowed just enough to get through the doorway without trampling one another, while Emma snatched her bonnet from its peg and hurried after them. For a moment the sunlight dazzled her. The wind tugged her bonnet from her hand. Quickly she tied it on and followed the swarm of children down the lane toward the sheep pasture beyond the schoolhouse, keeping her eye on the approaching balloon. As she passed the low, thatched cottage that had been her home for the past two years, she thought of her brother. How Kit would love to see the balloon!

As if on cue, Becky, her maid of all work, poked her head out of the front window, eyes bright with curiosity. "What is it, Miss?"

"There's a balloon coming. Take Kit into the garden so he can see it. Quickly!"

Becky nodded, curls bobbing beneath her cap, and disappeared back inside the cottage.

The fastest children had already reached the stile that led over the stone wall into the sheep pasture and were swarming over it like so many ants. Emma lifted her skirts and broke into a run to catch up. The older children were already over; she gave a hand to some of the smaller ones, smiling at their eagerness to see the balloon. Of course, at two and twenty she was too old to be excited about such things.

She hoped the children would not be disappointed. Balloons were subject to the vagaries of the wind. Wayward creations, not to be relied upon.

They stopped again at the high end of the long sloping pasture, which afforded the best view. Below them, at the other end, grazed a flock of sheep. As they watched, the balloon came closer, looking like a huge upended pear on the opposite side of the village. Emma cast about in her mind to recall everything she'd ever read on the subject. Papa had been a naturalist, but their library had included a variety of books on subjects of scientific interest.

"Do any of you know what makes a balloon ascend?" she asked the children.

A boy raised his hand.

"Bill?"

"Hot air, like what lifts ashes from a fire?"

"Well done! Some balloons are raised by heated air. However, they cannot carry fuel for a long flight, so now most balloons use a gas derived from a mixture of . . . vitriolic acid and iron," she concluded, pleased she'd remembered. "It is called inflammable air."

"What's in-in-inflammable?" asked one of the girls.

"It means it can catch fire."

"Will the balloon catch fire?" Tom asked, eyes wide.

"No, of course not."

"It's coming down!" Bill shouted.

"No, it's not!"

"Yes, it is!"

"It's going to land *here*!"

"Hurrah!"

A gust tugged at Emma's bonnet again, almost lifting it from her head. She shivered. The hapless aeronauts would have their hands full trying to land on such a day. Unlike the children, who did not know the risks, she was not so sure she wished to see it.

"What in hell . . ." Gil frowned up at Alcyone. Aiming for the meadow he saw beyond the village below him, he'd given the valve rope the slightest of tugs. But the valve had reacted sluggishly, releasing too much of the buoyant gas before it closed again. What was the matter with it?

He was plunging down toward thick woods this side of the village.

Quickly, he tossed his lone sandbag overboard. Alcyone slowed her descent, and not a moment too soon, passing about ten feet over the woods and then over a lane leading into the village. But he was still descending, heading over cottages toward an enormous horse-chestnut tree in the middle of the green, just before a stone church whose spire dominated the scene.

He cast the cork jacket over, then the barometer and his compass, not without a pang, for they'd be expensive to replace. He'd lightened the load and felt the change in the balloon. She was no longer dropping so fast. But he needed her to rise. Quickly.

Villagers were staring and shouting up at him, but he ignored them. Hastily he shrugged off his coat and flung it out along with his gloves and hat. Then he dropped to the floor of the car to pull off his shoes. He'd no sooner tossed them than he passed over the horse-chestnut. Its top branches crackled against the wooden bottom of Alcyone's car. Below him was the churchyard; the spire was still some fifty feet away. He'd no time to guess whether he'd clear it. He'd only seconds to rip off his waistcoat, shirt and cravat like an impatient lover and send them fluttering down into the churchyard to land on the gravestones. A laugh rose in his throat. Pray it wasn't an omen!

He held his breath as Alcyone approached the spire, then missed it by inches. He exhaled as she rose still higher and, like the daughter of the wind-god she was named for, soared lightly over the church.

She passed over a small wooded area before leveling out high over the meadow. A small flock of sheep, new lambs among them, scattered as he came close. He heard children shouting. Looking down, he saw a group of them, jumping up and down around the taller figure of a woman. He waved.

A new air current was drawing him onward; he'd have to look for another landing spot. He gazed out over the landscape and decided to make for a level field about a half mile away. He gave a cautious tug to the valve rope. But instead of a short whoosh of the gas, Alcyone began to emit a steady whistling sound. He gave the rope a few quick jerks, but still the valve failed to close.

"Hell and damnation," he muttered.

He was out of ballast and Alcyone was plunging earthward. He started to unfasten the grappling iron, hoping to throw it overboard, but he was running out of time.

Perhaps the devil had decided to claim him, after all.

Chapter Two

The children screamed. Emma's heart turned over.

The balloon plummeted towards the earth, its brilliant blue and yellow striped envelope thinning from a pear to a mushroom. A fierce whistling sound filled the air. A child cried; some of the little ones clung to Emma's skirts. She couldn't look away.

The aeronaut was struggling to do something; she could not tell what. A moment later the boat-shaped car hit the ground. It bounded up ten feet or so, flinging the aeronaut upwards as if he were a doll. It struck the ground again, this time landing on its side with a horrible cracking sound. She could not see where the aeronaut fell.

The whistling ceased as the balloon expelled its remaining gas and slowly collapsed. All that could be heard was the bleating of the sheep, huddling in a frightened mass near the shallow brook that bordered the meadow.

For a moment Emma stood staring. Then she saw the children looking at her in a mute plea for reassurance. She heard voices in the distance. People were coming from the village to see what had happened, but for now, she was the only adult present.

"Stay here!" she commanded, her voice shaking. "I will assist the aeronaut."

She sped toward the fallen balloon, stumbling and slipping over the damp, uneven turf. She prayed the children wouldn't follow, because she feared what might lie beneath the wreckage.

Hell. Damnation. Unladylike curses she'd never voiced aloud ran through her head. *Let it not be a corpse.*

She reached the balloon, now a pathetic mass of netting and striped fabric. Somewhere beneath lay the broken car and its passenger.

"Are you injured, sir?" she called out.

There was no reply.

She lifted the edge closest to her and peered under. "Can you hear me?"

She bent down and raised an edge of the heavy varnished canopy. Light filtered through, dim and blue, illuminating the upturned car of the balloon. Its wooden floor was cracked; wicker-work protruded from tears in the painted canvas covering the sides. She couldn't see the aeronaut.

"Can you hear me? Are you hurt?" Her throat tightened with dread. She took a step forward, holding up the edge of the balloon, but stopped when she heard a low moan. He was alive!

There was a rustling, and a hand appeared atop the wreckage of the car. More rustling, a muttered curse, and she saw his face as he peered up at her over the ruined car. The odd light made it hard to see his coloring, but his hair was a bit longer than fashionable, framing a face with strong but handsome features. He blinked several times, as if struggling to bring her into focus. Then of all things, he grinned up at her. What fool smiled at such a moment?

Then she saw that his shoulders and neck were bare. He hauled himself up against the wickerwork. She could even see a faint trail of hair down his chest, his muscled contours, brown nipples . . . He was *naked.*

Hastily she averted her gaze. "I—I had better call for—" Words failed her; she turned to leave.

"Stay. Please."

Something in his voice—a command? a plea?—rooted her to the spot. But she didn't dare look back. Perhaps he was a madman.

He laughed softly. "You must pardon my improper state of dress. I had to lighten the load, else I'd be dangling off the church steeple."

He had a pleasant voice, the voice of a gentleman. But why would a gentleman fly a balloon? Despite herself she looked at him again. He was holding a hand to his temple while using the other to lift the fabric above him.

"Are you injured?" she asked. "I really should fetch someone to . . ."

"No. Just help me and I'll do."

"I can't possibly—oh!"

She turned away, cheeks burning, as he struggled to his feet.

"Don't fear. It's quite safe to look."

Slowly, she turned back around and let out a sigh. His nether regions were decently covered in a pair of dark trousers.

He chuckled.

"How can you laugh at such a time? You were nearly killed!"

"But I was not. I consider myself the luckiest of men. Not only alive, but attended by the prettiest rescuer I could wish for."

"Don't be silly! How do you feel?" she asked.

"As if a cavalry charge had just passed over me!" His smile became a grimace as he tried to take a step towards her. "I think I've sprained my ankle."

He staggered and tried to balance himself on the broken car. She heard the sound of cracking whicker, saw him stumble. Swiftly she went forward, raising her hands to fend off the canopy descending on them. The fold she'd lifted earlier fell behind her, leaving her and the aeronaut in something like a dimly lit tent. She had to step over what seemed like a snakes' nest of ropes, but she reached him before he fell and put a steadying arm around him. The feel of hard, warm flesh under her hand brought the blood to her face. She drew a ragged breath.

Dear God, what had she gotten herself into?

Gil felt the lady tremble as she helped him regain his balance. His ankle throbbed, his head ached even worse, and he was bruised all over. All in all, it was a vast improvement over what he'd expected in those final moments before Alcyone hit.

Besides the fact that a pretty woman had her arm around him. What a sight she'd been, peering cautiously under Alcyone's canopy at him. Large, frightened eyes in a heart-shaped face. A trim figure silhouetted against the sunny meadow. What a vision to greet a man who thought Death had finally caught up with him!

"Thank you, ma'am," he said. "Gilbert Manning, your most grateful servant."

She didn't look up; the brim of her bonnet hid her face. "I am—I am Miss Westfield."

Not a round-heeled widow, then. And unquestionably a lady.

"Can you walk?" the lady asked.

"If you help me." For five hundred guineas, he'd damn well manage it.

He put an arm around her shoulder and used the other hand to hold up Alcyone's folds. He took a cautious step, trying not to wince as his ankle protested.

"Not . . . too heavy for you . . . am I?" he asked.

"Not at all."

"Strong as well as pretty," he murmured.

"Save your energy for walking, Mr. Manning," she said sharply.

His head throbbed again and a faint buzzing started in his ears.

Miss Westfield lifted another fold of the balloon before them. "Once we are out, you must lie down while I fetch a surgeon."

"Not yet. I must—" He wasn't sure what it was he had to do, except keep moving. *Slow march. One foot in front of the other.*

The buzzing intensified, like the sound of a thousand bees. *A few more steps. Don't fall.*

He thought he heard voices. The whole village would turn out to see the fun; they always did. Together, he and the lady lifted the last fold and emerged into the sunlit meadow. The bright light hurt his eyes. He blinked.

"Someone fetch Mr. Hollis!" Miss Westfield's voice pierced the humming in his ears.

A sea of faces undulated before him. He tried to bow. He heard cheers, but the ground tilted beneath him.

"Help me, he's fainting!" Miss Westfield shouted, tightening her hold on him.

"No, I'm not," he retorted and planted his feet more widely.

An arm slipped around him from the other side. He heard more voices, loud yet indistinct. A young man said he'd fetch Mr. Hollis, whoever that was.

"Welcome to Tichbury," a new voice said.

Gil struggled to bring the face before him into focus. Brown eyes in a wrinkled face surrounded by white hair. A gentle smile. Sober garb. A parson, he guessed.

"Tichbury?" he repeated. He'd just heard the name, hadn't he? It was hard to think over the noise in his head.

"I am Mr. Grimshaw, the vicar," the man said. "We have summoned a surgeon."

"Gilbert ... Manning." He tried to smile at the vicar, though now there were two of the old gentleman. "Thank you."

"You must lie down, Mr. Manning," Miss Westfield insisted.

"Not yet." He looked down at her. Two pairs of large blue-gray eyes stared anxiously up at him. Entrancing as the sight was, there was still something he had to do. He tried to think, despite the humming in his ears, the host of faces in front of him and ground that swayed like the deck of a ship in high seas.

Then he had it.

"Has my . . . coat been found?"

"Indeed, Mr. Manning, we retrieved a number of items of your clothing from the village." The vicar's voice mingled gentle reproof with a touch of humor.

"I found it necessary . . . to discharge some ballast," he explained. "I think my coat fell in . . . a garden. My journal was in the pocket. I need it."

"If it will ease your mind, it shall be found," said the vicar soothingly. He raised his voice to address the throng. "Does anyone have Mr. Manning's coat?"

"I've got it!" someone shouted. A villager came to the front, holding Gil's coat out to the vicar.

"Please . . . bring it to me."

"Why does it matter?" asked Miss Westfield. "You should lie down and await the surgeon."

"My journal . . . and a pencil . . . are in the pocket. Mr. Grim-shaw . . . if you please . . . record that you saw me walk away from the landing . . . and then witness it . . . I would be most obliged."

"Good God, is it a wager?" said Miss Westfield.

He nodded. "Please . . . there's a considerable sum . . . riding on it."

"Very well, Mr. Manning," said the vicar in a disapproving tone, but he accepted the journal from the villager.

Gil's vision blurred as he watched the vicar record the landing.

"There, Mr. Manning. It is done," said the vicar.

He thanked him, his head so thick he couldn't tell if he shouted or whispered.

"And now will you lie down?" the lady—whatever her name was, somehow he'd forgotten it—insisted.

"Very well." Gil nodded, which was a bad idea. The thrumming in his ears grew louder. The ground heaved again.

The lady cried out, and he knew no more.

E mma staggered as the aeronaut sagged against her. Curse him! Why did men never listen?

The vicar's manservant, on the other side, got a better hold on Manning. Between them, they let the aeronaut down gently onto the turf. She dropped down beside him but instantly the crowd pressed around them.

"Stand back!" she ordered, using her schoolmistress voice to good effect.

"Oh dear, what is to be done?" Mr. Grimshaw exclaimed.

Emma stared down at the aeronaut. His chest rose and fell steadily. He was still alive but the injury to his head must have been far worse than he'd admitted. She carefully felt his head and found a sizeable swelling on one side. Idiot! Instead of resting like a sensible person, he'd fretted until they'd signed his journal. All for some stupid bet! He was a rogue and a flirt. But lying there barefoot and half-naked, he looked more vulnerable than roguish.

A sudden grief welled up inside her.

She started to avert her gaze when something caught her eye: a round, healed scar over his ribs. There was another much like it near his shoulder. A long, pale scar slashed across one arm.

"Good God . . ." she murmured.

"Let us lay his coat over him!" Miss Grimshaw, the vicar's sister, had edged her way through the crowd. The villager still holding the coat handed it to Emma. Miss Grimshaw bent down and helped her arrange it over Manning, who gave no sign of noticing. He looked so peaceful, almost as if he were . . .

"Let us try to revive him." Miss Grimshaw, always practical, held out her vinaigrette.

Emma opened the small silver box and waved the grill under Manning's nostrils, releasing the scent of lavender-infused vinegar.

"Wake up, Mr. Manning," she said. *Wake, damn you.*

He did not even flutter an eyelid.

She repeated her efforts, to no avail.

"Ought we to move him?" Mr. Grimshaw asked.

"We should wait for Mr. Hollis," Miss Grimshaw advised. "Do you not think so, Emma?"

"He took a blow to his head. I'm not sure—I think—"

"Make way! Make way, I say!" A masculine voice boomed from the back of the crowd.

Emma looked up and saw Sir George Chesmore, the local squire, making his way through the crowd. Villagers parted to allow the fair-haired, stout gentleman to pass, followed by his wife and sister, both in fashionable bonnets and pelisses and agog with curiosity. Emma frowned. If she knew those two, they'd find a way to make a farce of this calamity.

The ladies' eyes widened as they gazed down at Manning. Lydia Chesmore, seventeen, plump and fair-haired like her brother, let out a giggle. "He's handsome! But look at his feet! And his arms! Is he *na*—"

"What happened?" Sir George interrupted, giving his sister a warning look.

Emma recounted the events as concisely as she could. "We have sent for Mr. Hollis," she concluded.

"Oh, the poor man!" said Lady Chesmore, her dark, bird-like eyes taking in every detail of the aeronaut. "Do we know who he is?"

"He introduced himself as Mr. Gilbert Manning," supplied the vicar. "Odd, he spoke like a gentleman."

"I think he is a soldier," said Miss Grimshaw.

"Perhaps he is an officer!" said Lydia. "His coat seems rather fine, does it not?"

"It appears the foolish young man undertook this flight on a bet," said Mr. Grimshaw.

Lydia gazed at Manning. "He will not die, will he?"

"Of course he will not die, Lyddy," said Lady Chesmore. "We shall take him up to the Manor so he may be nursed properly."

"Yes, we must," said Lydia, her crimped curls bobbing as she nodded. "Our carriage is right there, in the lane, for we were just returning from a visit to the Hartleys."

Emma couldn't remain silent. "But it is nearly two miles by road! A blow to the head is a serious matter. To jolt him over such a distance might aggravate his injury."

"Our carriage is very well-sprung," said Lydia.

Sir George looked first to his wife, then his sister. "I don't know if we should—"

"We must help him, George!" insisted Lydia. "He is a gentleman, I am certain of it."

"I think it unwise to move him," said Emma, braving frowns from the two ladies. Not that the aeronaut was any of her business.

"Ahem," said the vicar. "I fancy Miss Westfield knows more of nursing than any of us."

"Surely you do not intend to keep him lying here like this." Lady Chesmore pouted. "Who knows how long it will take for Mr. Hollis to arrive!"

Emma stared back down at Manning, who lay oblivious to the struggle raging over him. What did she care? Let them take him away, make a pet of him over at Chesmore Manor. That is, if he survived the trip. Damn him, the last thing she needed was another charge on her hands. But she'd helped him and now she felt bound by something—honor, perhaps—to continue doing so.

She straightened her shoulders. "Let him be taken to Meadowcross Cottage then."

The Chesmores all stared at her. The surrounding villagers watched, curious at this turn of events.

"You cannot take him to your home. It would be most improper!" said Lady Chesmore.

"We could take much better care of him at the Manor!" cried Lydia.

Sir George frowned, unwilling to argue with the ladies.

Emma bit back the urge to scream at them. She didn't want the aeronaut in her care. She didn't want him to die, either. But she'd not considered the possibility of scandal, or how she was going to find time to care for him.

"You cannot have a man in your cottage!" insisted Lady Chesmore.

"She can if I come to stay as well," said Miss Grimshaw.

"An excellent notion, my dear!" said the vicar said to his sister. "You may help Miss Westfield care for the unfortunate man. While you are present as chaperone, there can be no impropriety."

"Well then, it is settled," said Sir George.

"Let us hope he revives," said Lady Chesmore, as if she doubted Emma's care would prove sufficient. "You shall keep us apprised of his progress." Head held high, she flounced away. Lydia followed, with a lingering backward glance at Manning.

Sir George shifted his feet for a moment before addressing himself to Emma. "Have Mr. Hollis send the reckoning to us. And don't hesitate to let us know if there's aught you need."

Emma murmured her thanks. As Sir George turned to follow his ladies, she looked down at her new charge. What had she just done?

Under her orders, several villagers picked Manning up. His head lolled helplessly against one bearer's chest. She warned them to be careful, then looked around. The children had all found their parents; no one seemed inclined to leave. It was no surprise. There hadn't been such excitement since Sir George's prize bull got loose.

The vicar and his sister were perusing Manning's journal to discover his address. They would catch up later, she supposed. It was time for her to go to the cottage and prepare to receive the injured aeronaut.

She set off at a run, her senses all in a whirl. That laugh, the sensation of a man leaning against her. The unmistakable air of a military man. Those wounds . . .

But it was time to be practical. They'd never get Manning up the stairs. The only choice was to put him on the sofa. But her desk was in the parlor, along with her manuscript, all her papers . . . Somehow she'd have to manage. She'd give Miss Grimshaw her own bed and set up a cot in the same room, so as not to disturb Kit.

Kit . . . He must have seen the accident. He would be frightened. She quickened her pace. By the time she reached the cottage she had a stitch in her side.

Becky stood in the doorway, eyes wide. At least she hadn't deserted her post.

"The aeronaut is"—Emma gasped—"injured. They are bringing him . . . here. How is . . . Kit?"

"He's nervous but well enough, Miss."

"Still in the garden?"

"Yes, Miss."

"Good. I'll go tell him . . . what happened." She drew another deep breath. "Fetch the spare bedding and make up the sofa."

Becky bustled up the stairs while Emma hurried through their small parlor, through the kitchen and into the garden. Kit sat in his wheeled chair under the large plane tree. As she rushed down the gravel path toward him, she nearly tripped over their gray cat, Pandora, who let out a yowl in protest.

Kit looked up, his shadowed eyes like holes in a face too pale and thin for a boy of eight years. There was a book in his lap, but she doubted he'd been reading.

"Dearest, there's been an accident," she called out. "The aeronaut is alive but he is injured. They are going to bring him here in a few minutes."

"Will he be all right?" he asked as she came up to him.

She leaned down to kiss his forehead. It felt cool and dry. "I am sure he will," she said, hoping it was true. "But he will have to stay with us for a bit."

Kit brightened. "May I meet him?"

Something inside her ached at his eager expression. She thought of the physician's warnings and hesitated.

Before she could reply, he burst out, "You won't let me, will you? You'll say it is too exciting!"

She clenched her hands. "Perhaps once he is well . . . but I doubt he will stay long. Now I must go and help Becky. Do you need anything?"

Kit shook his head sullenly. She hurried back to the cottage, hoping Manning's presence there would not overexcite her brother.

But a meeting between the two was the least of her worries.

"Forgive me, but I think it best that you ladies be prepared," said Mr. Hollis in a low voice, though they were in the kitchen and Manning now lay on the sofa in the parlor, dressed in a nightshirt borrowed from the vicar and attended by Mr. Grimshaw's manservant. "He has sustained a very severe blow. It is a bad sign that he has remained insensible."

"Heavens, what do you mean?" asked Miss Grimshaw.

Emma kept her eyes on the surgeon, an honest man with a reputation for knowing his business.

"What I mean is that if he awakens, he may no longer be in possession of his faculties, in which case do not hesitate to send for help. Or he may . . ."

"Go on," said Miss Grimshaw.

"He may slip away in the night."

Emma stared down at a knot in the oak table. So he might wake up a madman or an idiot. Or not at all. She was right to keep Kit away.

"But do not despair," the surgeon continued. "He may come to with a bad headache and recover fully. He appears to have a strong constitution. Strong indeed, to have survived the old wounds I saw when I examined him. A soldier, is he?"

"We think so," said Miss Grimshaw.

Emma lifted her eyes. "What can we do for him?"

"Apply cold compresses of water and vinegar to his head and ankle. After he wakes, send for me. If he is in pain, you may give him fifteen to twenty drops of laudanum. For now I recommend that you take it in turns to sit up with him."

She and Miss Grimshaw nodded.

"Does he have family?" Mr. Hollis asked. "They ought to be notified."

"My brother found a direction in his journal," said Miss Grimshaw. "For a gentleman living somewhere near Richmond. We will write to him."

"Good." Mr. Hollis rose from the table and gathered up his bag. "I shall return tomorrow morning. Do not hesitate to send for me if there is any change, for good or ill."

"Emma. Emma," a voice whispered. A hand touched Emma's shoulder. She started up from an uneasy slumber. Miss Grimshaw stood by the cot, holding a candle that shadowed the lines in her face.

"What is it?" Emma asked. "Oh yes, I remember . . . Has there been any change?"

Miss Grimshaw shook her head. "I am afraid not."

Manning hadn't roused all evening and now he'd slept half the night. He'd wake by morning, Emma thought fiercely. He had to. She pushed herself up, swung her legs over the side of the cot and grimaced as her feet hit the cold floor. She dressed quickly, leaving her hair in its thick nighttime braid, tossed on an old shawl, thrust her feet into slippers and left while Miss Grimshaw was still readying herself for bed.

Emma tiptoed past Kit's room and down the stairs, avoiding the creaky spots out of habit. She reached the landing and rounded the screen they'd set up between the parlor and the entry.

The clock on the mantel showed four o'clock in the morning. Manning lay in shadows, flat on his back, illumined only by the light of her candle. He was so still he reminded her of the effigies of Sir George of Tichbury and his wife that lay in the village church. She moved quietly toward the sofa. When she saw the slow but steady rise and fall of his chest, she let out a small sigh.

He was not gone. Not yet.

She sat down in the wing chair in the corner, setting her candle on the small table nearby. Manning slumbered on. For a moment she stared, in the grip of the feeling that she was seeing someone else. But that was a different time and place. She'd go mad if she continued. She eyed the papers on her desk but couldn't muster the resolution to deal with them. She had to do *something*. Her sewing basket stood close by. She pulled out one of Papa's old shirts she was making over for Kit and began to work. After a few moments she caught herself looking back towards the sofa. She gave herself a mental shake, but she hadn't set five more stitches before the urge to gaze at Manning seized her again. She gave up the struggle, poked her needle into the shirt and tucked it back into the basket.

She might as well study him, so she could move past the superficial resemblance that plagued her. It was time to convince herself that he was indeed a stranger and not the embodiment of a memory.

She tiptoed toward the sofa and then knelt on the carpet beside it. Shivering, she smoothed her dressing gown around her legs and feet. Now that she was close to him, she hesitated. But she forced herself to look, to take note of every detail of his face and form.

He was slightly taller and leaner than the image from her memory, but well made. Her throat tightened; she held back tears and forced herself to continue. His hair was a shade darker: a medium brown, wavy and in need of trimming. Lydia hadn't exaggerated when she'd called him handsome. His features were regular. He had a long, smooth forehead, now partly hidden under a damp compress, a longish nose, an angular chin. Manly, stronger features than . . . She closed her eyes to recall the color of this stranger's eyes: blue tinged with green, fitting for someone who moved between earth and sky. Eyes that laughed along with the rest of him.

He was a flirt and a daredevil, there was no doubt of that. A gambler. A gentleman, perhaps an officer sold out since Waterloo. She wondered if he'd known . . . but how likely was that? Yet how could she not think about it? She'd seen the scars, the result of bullets and swords piercing his flesh. Scars that did not obscure the beauty of a healthy male body.

She blinked away a tear. Lud! She hadn't cried in ages. What was the matter with her now?

She knew what was the matter.

It was the look of childlike innocence Manning wore in sleep, as he might in death. Had Charles looked so when he died? Had he thought of her? Perhaps, regretted . . .?

Charles . . . my love . . .

She caught herself whispering the words aloud. Now she *was* going mad.

But Manning did not wake. Perhaps his spirit was already beyond reach. Did he have a wife or a sweetheart who would mourn him?

Tears blurred her vision as she leaned over him. His mouth was surely made for smiling. For laughing. For kissing. Grief welled up along with the feeling that he might never do any of those things again.

She closed her eyes and pressed her lips to his. They were cool and unresponsive.

Then they parted.

She jerked back, saw his eyes flutter open.

"Don't stop now," he whispered.

Chapter Three

Emma jerked to her feet, her cheeks burning.

Manning looked up at her. "I thought the devil . . . had claimed me this time," he murmured. "But now I'm sure I'm . . . in heaven."

Lord, what must he think? "How are you feeling, Mr. Manning?" she said in as matter-of-fact a voice as she could muster.

"I'd be a great deal better . . . if you kissed me again."

"I did not kiss you!"

"Then I dreamt it." He squinted and then closed his eyes, as if even the candle light pained him. But he smiled faintly. "A shame that one wakes . . . just when a dream becomes most interesting."

She turned away, holding a hand up to cool her cheek. He was awake and in possession of what sense he had before. There was nothing to do but pretend she had never kissed him and hope he took the hint.

"You must be parched," she said. "I shall fetch you some water." She went to a pitcher on the side table and poured some water into a pap boat. As she turned back to him, Manning made a move as if to sit up.

"Be still, please." She laid a hand on his chest to stay him. He felt warm and solid, reassuringly so. She felt his intake of breath and quickly withdrew her hand. "The surgeon said you must keep very quiet. All you need do is open your mouth. I will help you drink."

He gave a slight nod and then winced. She tilted the spout of the vessel toward his lips. He parted them, eagerly taking in the trickle of water. "You're an angel," he whispered after he'd finished.

Her fingers trembled as she set the pap boat back down onto the table. She sat back down in the hard chair and clasped her hands in her lap. "How is your head?"

"Still attached. At the moment I'm not sure that is a good thing!"

"Do you remember who I am?"

"You are Miss ... Westfield. You helped me after my balloon crashed. I didn't dream that, did I? I *did* walk away from the landing?"

"You did indeed. Mr. Grimshaw wrote it all down in your journal. I have it here, along with your clothing and the purse that was in your coat pocket."

He looked relieved. It must have been a considerable wager.

"Alcyone ... my balloon. Is she much damaged?"

"I cannot say. Sir George Chesmore, who owns the pasture in which you landed, had everything put onto a cart and taken to his carriage house. But do not worry about that now. You should rest."

"Where am I?"

"Meadowcross Cottage, in Tichbury. You would have been taken to Chesmore Manor, but we thought it unwise to move you so far."

"You live here?" His eyes narrowed as he looked at her.

Her cheeks flushed again. "Yes. I am the parish schoolmistress. Sir George provided this cottage for my use."

"You're prettier than any schoolmistress I've ever seen."

"I would be flattered were I not well aware that you have suffered a severe blow to the head." She stiffened at his soft chuckle. "Miss Grimshaw, the vicar's sister, has come to stay with me and help me care for you until you are better."

"And to maintain propriety?"

She sat up straighter in her chair. "Mr. Grimshaw found an address in your journal," she said. "It was for Sir Colin Stanstead. Mr. Grimshaw took the liberty of writing to him of your injury. Is there anyone else we ought to inform? Family, perhaps?"

"No one." He frowned. For a moment she wondered if she'd erred or whether his headache had grown worse, then his expression softened. "I am afraid the Stansteads will worry."

"I will write tomorrow to inform them you are out of danger."

"Please tell them ... to inform my crew of my whereabouts, in case they have lost my trail. I flew ... further than I planned."

So he had someone coming to fetch him. "Yes, of course. But now I shall replace your compresses and then you should sleep."

"Thank you, Mistress," he said as she rose from her chair.

"You may call me Miss Westfield." She removed the warm, damp cloths from his forehead and ankle and carried them out to the kitchen.

A banked fire still warmed the room. Curled up nearby, Pandora slept, her coat silvery in the moonlight streaming in through the window. Emma leaned her forehead against the pane for a moment. She was happy he was better, but she'd have that daredevil in her care for days, perhaps weeks. He was a disturbing presence, dominating her small parlor, his feet dangling over the edge of her sofa, his words designed to make her blush.

How could she have been so foolish as to kiss him?

She straightened up. All she could do was be more careful. She moistened the cloths again with cool water from a jug near the door. She returned to find Manning lying in the same still pose, eyes closed. For a moment it seemed as if she'd imagined his reawakening. But as she drew back the blanket to replace the compress on his ankle, he rewarded her with a faint smile. She placed the second cloth over his head. Gently, she felt the lump. She thought the swelling might have decreased a little.

"Thank you ... Mistress."

"You should rest now. Do you wish for more water?"

"Please."

"Mr. Hollis said you should take some laudanum if you are in pain."

He grimaced. "Must I?"

"It will help you rest."

"Yes, Mistress," he said meekly. "Perhaps I can recapture that dream I had earlier."

"You are outrageous." She poured more water into the pap boat and added laudanum from the bottle Mr. Hollis had left. She brought the lip of the vessel up to his mouth.

"Then you should cane me ... That *is* what you do with troublesome pupils ... isn't it?"

Before he could say more she tilted the liquid down his throat.

Alcyone hurtled earthward with a whoosh of escaping gas. The wind shrieked in Gil's ears like the ungodly sound of Congreve rockets. He was out of control. He had nothing left to do but prepare to meet his maker.

A pity he couldn't remember any prayers.

Then he felt ground beneath his feet, heard the sounds of musketry, men shouting. Cannon fire reverberated through his head. Smoke obscured the late afternoon sunshine, wreathed the sandpit where he and his men exchanged fire with wave after wave of French skirmishers. The bodies of fellow Riflemen lay about, their dark green uniforms stained with darker blood. Corpses of French cavalrymen and their horses lay under the steep bank of the Brussels road. Ahead, the ominous red glow of fire raging through a burning farmhouse, still held by a few stalwart defenders against droves of Frenchmen.

He heard shouting ... no, it couldn't be. Dryburn and his company were fixing bayonets to their rifles, preparing to charge to the farmhouse's defense. Dryburn shouted to Gil, gesturing. Damned fool! He wanted Gil's company to support him. It was hopeless; they hadn't the numbers. Dryburn knew it as well as Gil did. Their duty was to survive and keep fighting, not die in one death-or-glory charge.

"It's no use!" he shouted, his voice thick with the smoke. "Stay back!"

But Dryburn turned and yelled to his men to come on. Some hesitated but in the end, discipline won, and they followed their captain. Gil's own men turned to him, grim questions on their faces.

Damn Dryburn.

"Stay where you are!" he snarled.

Dryburn and his men made it up to the outlying kitchen garden but no further; the French had spotted them and began to shoot. Dozens of Riflemen reeled and fell, death cries mingling with the roar of weapons. Gil's head pounded in time with each shot. He and his lads couldn't fire without hitting their fellow Riflemen; they could only watch.

Dryburn was struck. He staggered a few steps onward toward the farmhouse before falling heavily in the road.

The new second lieutenant—a Johnny Raw if Gil had ever met one—tried to organize a retreat. Gil caught a brief glimpse of his surprised face as he too fell, blood spurting from a hole in his chest.

The remnants of Dryburn's company—perhaps half—ran back toward the relative safety of the sandpit. But now a new wave of *voltigeurs* advanced to their left. Gil hoisted his rifle, aimed along with his men. Frenchmen fell but shots continued to come their way. A musket ball shrieked past Gil. From the other direction. Bloody hell, they were being surrounded! If he didn't get his company and the survivors of Dryburn's back to rejoin the battalion at the crossroads, none of them would live to tell the tale.

"Back to the knoll!" he shouted. All around him, Riflemen scrambled up the knoll behind the sandpit. Gil turned to follow but was knocked gasping to the ground. Strangely, he felt nothing but the pounding in his head. But when he looked down, he saw the hole the musket ball had made in his chest.

"To the crossroads!" he tried to say, but his voice failed him.

Sergeant Lund hesitated and come towards him. Others slowed, seeing he'd been shot. Fear gripped him. He'd called the retreat too late. The slaughter wasn't over.

He tried again to shout but his lungs constricted. He couldn't breathe.

"Wake up."

Cannon-fire reverberated in his head. Musket balls roared by. He still couldn't draw breath, couldn't make himself heard.

"Mr. Manning?" A soft feminine voice. A hand on his shoulder. He grasped it, bewildered. It was a woman's hand. A woman's slender fingers ... He gasped for breath and this time, miraculously, his lungs filled.

"Wake up, Mr. Manning." She sounded worried.

He gripped her hand and the ghastly scene slowly receded. The artillery fire dwindled to a throbbing echo in his head. He opened his eyes. The outlines of an unfamiliar, dimly lit room shifted and tilted sickeningly. He closed his eyes again. He couldn't remember where he was or what had happened.

"You were having a bad dream," said the sweet voice.

Slowly he reopened his eyes to the dark room. Though his head still spun he perceived the outlines of a woman leaning over him. He licked parched lips and called out to her. "Maggie?"

"I am Miss Westfield," she said. "You are at Meadowcross Cottage."

He clutched her hand. After a few moments, the room steadied and with a surge of sorrow and relief, he returned to the present. He and his men had rejoined their battalion, Lund and Birkin dragging him along with them. He'd survived.

But Maggie had already been dead, two years before Waterloo.

His eyes adjusted. Miss Westfield's face was pale and drawn. He let go the death-grip he had on her hand. "I'm sorry. You reminded me of ... someone I once knew."

She pulled her hand away and stared down at it, flexing her fingers. "Do you recall what happened to you?"

No doubt he'd seemed a lunatic, shouting commands in his sleep. "Yes ... I crashed ... in the meadow nearby." He cleared his throat. "You helped me."

"I'll get you some water." She got up and moved out of his sight. He didn't dare turn his head for fear of sending the room spinning again. But it was strange. He hadn't dreamt of Waterloo in a long time. He no longer wasted time trying to think of a way to stop Dryburn. The poor devil was dead, too.

Perhaps it was the laudanum, bringing him these dreams.

The room brightened; Miss Westfield must have lit another candle. Then she reappeared over him with the small vessel she'd used before. Gratefully he swallowed the cool water. The horror was over, once again. He'd survived and he was in good hands. The very best sort.

"Are you better now?" Her voice shook and her face was too pale. He'd frightened her, though the last thing he wanted to do was draw her—or any other innocent, goodhearted person—into that particular hell.

He summoned up a smile. "Much better ... now that I can look at you."

What a sight she was to banish morbid thoughts: brown hair hanging down over one shoulder in a disheveled braid, wide, anxious blue eyes in the heart-shaped face he remembered from yesterday. If it weren't for a dozen blacksmiths pounding away in his head, he'd think he was in paradise.

"I'd be even better if you kissed me again."

"You are mistaken. I did not kiss you last night. I was—I was merely assuring myself that you were still breathing." A charming blush colored her cheeks.

"Don't hesitate to do it again... anytime you are in doubt."

She bit her lip back on what was likely a blistering retort.

Gil relaxed. Better she thought him a flirt than a raving lunatic.

"Do you think you could eat some breakfast?"

His stomach was none too steady but he nodded. "If it would please you. But first..."—now he was really going to make the pretty schoolmistress blush but there was no help for it—"...I need a chamber pot."

"I expected you would," she said. She bent down and reached under the chair. Meanwhile he tried to shift onto his side, but the room roiled around him again.

"Don't move," she said. "I'll help you."

Like hell she would. "Nonsense. I can do it myself." He tried to shift again but had to give it up.

She set the chamber pot on the floor next to the sofa and leaned over him. "If I can just lift you on your side... no, let me do the work."

He gave in, helpless against the spinning of the room. She was strong, though. He wasn't a small man but she managed to turn him onto his side. She arranged the pillows to support him as if she did it every day. But he needed her to leave. Bad enough that he'd gripped her hand like a frightened child; he wasn't about to relieve himself in front of her. He'd rather burst.

"I can manage from here."

"Are you quite certain?" Her voice faltered.

"Yes." He took several deep breaths. The room had righted itself again and the chamber pot was well placed. He'd manage.

"Very well. Ring this bell when you are finished." She placed a small hand bell within his reach and left him.

A few minutes later Gil shook the bell lightly. Miss Westfield came quickly to take away the chamber pot, her expression matter-of-fact. When she left him again, he closed his eyes, quelling an ingrained impulse to familiarize himself with his surroundings. At present his surroundings had too great a tendency to spin around him.

Muffled sounds came from somewhere nearby; she was making him breakfast. Though clearly respectable, she was no soft lady, this one. She was more like the army wives and camp-followers he'd known. Like his friend Colin's wife, Susan. Like Maggie. Strong and as capable as she was comely ...

Skirts rustled softly. Gil reopened his eyes. His head still ached. It was lighter in the room now; perhaps he'd dozed. Miss Westfield reappeared from behind the screen, bearing a tray. She was wearing the same faded gown and shawl as before but now her hair was coiled neatly high on her head.

"Mr. Hollis said you were not to have anything stronger than gruel," she warned him.

"I have an especial fondness for gruel," he lied. Truth be told, he was feeling queasy, but knew he should try to eat.

"Indeed," she said, with the glimmer of a smile. She set the tray down on the table and then drew the chair closer.

"Are you going to feed me like a baby?"

"Yes, I am. Resign yourself to it, Mr. Manning." She seated herself and gathered up the bowl and spoon. She'd spoken as if she were dealing with a tiresome child, but she looked strained. Which wasn't surprising, if she'd been up half the night watching him.

"I'm still thinking about that caning, Mistress," he murmured, igniting a spark of indignation in her eyes. "I—"

She silenced him with a mouthful of gruel. Bland stuff, but he'd eaten far worse on campaign. Willing his stomach to settle, he swallowed spoonful after spoonful. She fed him efficiently, as one accustomed to feeding children or invalids. But the flush remained in her cheeks. Probably she'd never nursed a grown man before. Or perhaps he'd gone too far reminding her of the kiss she'd given him. She'd said something before that kiss, but his head throbbed when he tried to remember what it was.

She paused. "Is that enough for now?"

"Yes. Quite." He felt less queasy but the mere effort of eating had drained him. "Thank you. For everything."

"There's no need for thanks. The sooner you recover, the sooner you will be off my hands."

Wishing he could do more to thank her, he let out a mock sigh. "Ah, I should have known. You only wish to be rid of me. But I intend to be a model patient, I promise."

"I am not sure I agree with your notion of a model patient," she retorted. "Are you never serious, Mr. Manning?"

"Not if I can avoid it."

She gave him an intent look, then busied herself rearranging the tray. "I shall be leaving in a few minutes. Miss Grimshaw will care for you today. I suggest you try to sleep again; it will do you good."

"Yes, Mistress."

Despite his misgivings, he submitted to another dose of laudanum. She replaced the compress on his ankle and began to bathe his head. His headache began to fade under the effect of the drug and the cool water. He smiled up at her in gratitude. What a lucky dog he was. Not only to have survived but to land practically in the arms of a pretty female. How Lund and Birkin would laugh over his luck when they saw him. He wondered what her Christian name was . . .

Chapter Four

A cold compress on his forehead roused Gil from another uneasy dream. He kept his eyes closed, giving himself up to the blissful numbing coolness of it.

"Ah . . . that's almost as good as a kiss," he murmured.

"Just as well, since you won't be getting one of *those* from *me*," a high-pitched feminine voice replied.

Damn.

It wasn't his ministering angel from the night. He opened his eyes and blinked in the dim light. Once his eyes adjusted, he saw a woman with a lined face surrounded by a pristine white mob-cap, frowning at him in disapproval. The vicar's sister, no doubt.

"Nor from Miss Westfield," she added. "We are gentle-women here and while you are amongst us, you will behave like a gentleman."

"Yes, ma'am," he said meekly.

"Hmph. I am Miss Grimshaw. I have come to help Miss Westfield care for you."

And to keep things proper, no doubt. He ought to reassure her he was no threat to Miss Westfield. His head still ached but he managed a smile. "I'm fortunate to be in such good hands."

She hmphed again. "How are you feeling, Mr. Manning?"

He felt ridiculously weak, his head ached when she stopped bathing it, and he suspected any sudden move would bring on vertigo.

"Better than yesterday," he said.

Miss Grimshaw was a disapproving dragon but she proved to be a capable nurse, replacing the compress on his ankle, fetching the chamber pot without fuss, helping him to water and more gruel, which he just managed to keep down. As she bustled about, a large gray cat followed, supervising her activities. Gil relaxed. Though Miss Grimshaw lacked his younger nurse's charms and was clearly suspicious of his intentions, she had a motherly air, though in a different style than the sweet, elusive memories he had of his own mother.

"I would offer you some laudanum, but Mr. Hollis—the surgeon, you know—will be coming to see you in a little while," she said, setting down the spoon. "I think he will wish to speak to you."

"I hope he'll tell me I can rise from this sofa soon."

"Don't get any foolish notions. You must not risk further injury. You should rest until Mr. Hollis arrives."

"I would rather talk."

She settled herself back in the chair beside the sofa. He felt her sharp-eyed gaze upon him. "We have sent a letter to Sir Colin Stanstead. It was posted this morning, as you requested."

"Thank you."

"It was Miss Westfield who dispatched it this morning on her way to school," she said in her chirping voice. "This Sir Colin . . . he is a friend of yours?"

"Yes, an excellent fellow. My crew and I stay in a cottage on his estate when we are not traveling."

"You know him from the army?"

Perhaps she'd seen the scars. Gil realized he was under interrogation. "Yes."

"You fought at Waterloo?"

"Yes."

She looked at him keenly then but he would not be drawn on such a subject.

"I've a favor to ask you, Miss Grimshaw," he said, hoping to divert her.

"Do you wish me to write another letter?"

"No, merely to send the latest page of my journal to the Honorable Augustus Tillingham. His direction is on the previous leaf."

She picked up the journal from the side table and turned to the current page. She raised her brows.

"Please feel free to make use of the contents of my purse," he added. "I don't wish to put you or Miss Westfield to any additional expense."

"Mr. Manning, I shall do as you request," she said in frigid tones. No doubt she didn't approve of gambling. It was no use explaining the circumstances that led him to accept the bet. Five hundred pounds, managed carefully, would keep him and his crew in comfort for some time.

"Is there anyone else you wish me to notify of your circumstances? Family, perhaps?" Miss Grimshaw asked.

"No one, thank you."

"Come, everyone has family."

"None with whom I have ties."

"Where were you born?"

He smiled wryly. "In Jamaica."

She gave a slight shake of her head. "But your parents . . . they are English, of course?"

"They were."

She paused and her voice softened. "And where did they hail from, Mr. Manning?"

"Norfolk."

Her brows drew together and she looked off into the distance, as if an idea had occurred to her. He wasn't sure he liked her look. Perhaps he should just say his headache at returned. Or raise a much more interesting subject.

"Miss Westfield . . . she is the schoolmistress here?" he asked.

"She not only teaches; she is also writing a book on English birds, continuing her father's work. He was an eminent naturalist as well as vicar here at Tichbury, before my brother. His death left Emma and her brother, who is a cripple, in straitened circumstances."

Emma ... A nice, round name, like a woman's breast or bottom, something you could cup in your hand and hold onto. Just saying it was like a kiss.

But he was sorry for her circumstances and said so.

"She has had many sorrows, Mr. Manning. Her brother was not born as he is; he fell ill with a mysterious disease. The physician feared he'd not last the night. Poor old Mr. Westfield sat up, fretting with worry, and his heart gave out. It was Emma who found him, cold in his chair. With no family who would own them, it was left to her to fend for herself and her brother." Miss Grimshaw looked at him sternly. "So you see she has more than enough burdens to bear already."

"I shall trouble her as little as possible."

Miss Grimshaw shot another steely look at him. "Be sure that you do. Allow me to remind you that though Emma is poor, she is not without friends to protect her."

He couldn't mistake the warning. "Of course."

"You should rest now, until Mr. Hollis arrives."

She turned her attention back to her book. Gil was glad she'd ended her interrogation. He couldn't blame her for being protective of Miss Westfield ... Emma ... but he didn't need her warnings. He knew the rules regarding unmarried ladies. Flirt all you wish, but touch more than her hand and you risk getting caught in the parson's mousetrap. Besides, he wouldn't hurt his pretty schoolmistress for the world.

Miss Grimshaw cleared her throat. "There is one thing I should perhaps tell you, Mr. Manning. I am a *very* light sleeper."

K it closed *An Exposition of English Insects* with a slap. It was his favorite sort of book but it still wasn't half so interesting as what was going on in the parlor. Mr. Hollis had come to see how the aeronaut was faring, but Kit was stuck in the kitchen, sitting in his chair with the book he'd been told to amuse himself with, as if he were a troublesome baby. At this rate, he'd be the last person in Tichbury to see the aeronaut. Even Becky had managed a peek at him, while he was sleeping, but all she could say was that Mr. Manning was ever so handsome. What rubbish!

Emma was still at the parish school, and Becky and Miss Grimshaw were busy preparing tea for Mr. Hollis. Over the clink of dishes, Kit could just hear the surgeon's voice alternating with a lower-pitched one that must belong to the aeronaut. He wished he could make out what they were saying.

"Don't you like your book, lamb?" Miss Grimshaw looked up as she finished filling the teapot.

He only scowled. She *would* keep calling him that. But he heard a movement, footsteps coming to the door. Mr. Hollis came in and Kit stuck his nose back in his book. People talked so much more freely when they didn't think he was listening.

"Well, how is he?" Miss Grimshaw asked in a lowered voice.

"Better than one might have expected," said the surgeon after he'd closed the door. "It's a good sign that he remembers what happened to him. Color's good, pulse is steady. He'll suffer headache and dizziness for some time, but I expect he'll do."

"How long do you suppose he will have to remain here?" Miss Grimshaw poured out cups of tea for herself and Mr. Hollis.

"A few weeks, most likely."

"So long?"

Sneaking a look at her from the corner of his eye, Kit saw Miss Grimshaw was frowning.

"It would be most unwise of him to risk the jolting of a carriage before the injury to the brain has healed," said Mr.

Hollis. "For now he should remain perfectly quiet. Do not allow him out of bed yet. However, once the dizziness has gone off he may sit up if he wishes. Perhaps in a week or so he may be able to move from his couch. Indeed, with his constitution, I expect he will soon regain his strength."

"Indeed. Let us hope he makes a rapid recovery." Miss Grimshaw had a dry note in her voice that made Kit wonder if she liked Mr. Manning.

Mr. Hollis shot a glance at her that Kit did not understand. "At least it should become easier for you and Miss Westfield to care for him."

"Emma knows she may depend on me," Miss Grimshaw replied.

Another incomprehensible glance passed between the two, then they talked of compresses and laudanum and such things until Mr. Hollis took his leave. Kit lowered his gaze to his book, wondering gloomily if Emma would allow him to see the aeronaut even once before he left. He stole a glance at Miss Grimshaw. She probably wouldn't let him talk to Mr. Manning either. Her brows had drawn together and she looked as if she'd just made some sort of decision.

She caught him staring at her and set down her tea. "Kit dear, I must be off to the vicarage. Since that unfortunate man may be here for several weeks, I must make some arrangements. My brother *cannot* be trusted to manage the household in my absence!"

As always, she wasn't telling him everything. "But what about Mr. Manning?" he asked.

She looked a little guilty. "I expect he will wish to rest again after the examination. Becky, please look in on him now and then. If he wishes it, you may give him twenty drops of the laudanum."

"Of course, Miss."

After Miss Grimshaw left them, Kit tried to absorb himself in his new book while Becky washed dishes, humming all the while. When she'd finished, she tiptoed into the parlor to check on the aeronaut. She'd just returned with the report that he was asleep when Kit heard a cheerful shout. Ned, one of the footmen from the Manor, leaned into the window and grinned at Becky. Kit thought he looked like a dolt but Becky smiled back, looking just as foolish.

"You'll be all right for a few minutes while Ned and me have a chat in the garden, won't you, poppet?"

Kit nodded. *Poppet* was even worse than *lamb*, but he wasn't going to complain. Becky had left the door to the parlor slightly open and he was getting an idea. Emma would be in a stew if she knew what he was planning. But she hadn't caught him practicing, so perhaps he could manage it without her finding out.

Even if she did, it was worth it.

As soon as Becky had stepped out, he leaned down and put his hands on the wheels of his chair. He hated his fingers: sickly, wormy looking things compared to the callused ones of the village boys. His arms were pathetic and skinny, but they worked better than anyone thought.

He grasped the wheels tightly and pushed, the way he'd done a few times before. At first the chair only creaked. Pandora, dozing by the hearth, lifted her head and stared at him with her orange eyes. He tried again and this time the chair moved a few inches. Crookedly, but it was a small victory. He pushed again and the chair lurched a few feet over the uneven stone floor. It would be easier once he reached the parlor.

He gave a few more shoves, straining until his muscles protested. At some point he realized Pandora had arisen and was following him. He hoped she'd be able to stay out of his way. When he reached the door to the parlor, he paused. His heart raced and he could barely breathe. If anyone saw him now, they'd think he was having convulsions or something. He could practically hear Emma reciting Dr. Procton's rules. How appalled she'd be to know he was propelling the chair by himself!

But she probably wouldn't scold him. She was too afraid that it would upset him and he'd die just like Papa. Sometimes Kit wished she'd just give him a proper tongue-lashing like the mothers of the village children did.

Becky's laughter drifted in through the window. Good. She and Ned wouldn't hear the creaking. Giving the wheels another big push, Kit cleared the entrance to the parlor. Now all he had to do was steer around the screen. The gap between it and the wall was just wide enough. He tried to make the turn, but at the last moment, a wheel caught against the screen. He froze, terrified it would all come tumbling down, then he backed up and came forward more carefully. He cleared the screen and grinned. He'd made it!

Then he heard the sound of the screen clattering, tumbling down behind him. Pandora yowled, her claws scrabbling on the floor. He twisted around. The screen had tipped over to lean against the far wall. There was no way to hide what had happened. A new fear twisted his insides. What if Mr. Manning was angry at the noise? And why would a soldier-turned-aeronaut want to talk to a puny cripple like him anyway?

Kit looked nervously toward the man on the sofa. He was tall, with legs so long his feet hung over the end. His face was lean and tanned; there was a darkish stubble on his chin. He stirred; his eyes opened. He shifted his head and closed his eyes tight again as if in pain. He reopened them more slowly and gazed at Kit for a moment as if trying to focus.

"Who are you?" His voice was friendly.

"Christopher Westfield, s-sir. But they call me Kit."

"Ah. Miss Westfield's brother. Miss Grimshaw told me about you."

Kit nodded, letting his breath out. "You're not—not angry with me for waking you?"

"Of course not. I like visitors. Will you stay and chat?"

"W-would you tell me what it's like to fly?"

"Of course." Mr. Manning smiled.

Kit dared to smile back and drew his wheeled chair closer to the sofa.

Emma stumbled over a stone in the road and cursed the pain in her toe. She was already tired to the bone, between little sleep and the effort of teaching children who could not think of anything but the aeronaut. She'd finally set them to practicing writing words like "balloon" and "ascension"; she rather wished she could have done the same with everyone else in the village. She'd had to dispel a number of wild rumors—mostly concerning the aeronaut's supposed demise—and the ladies from Chesmore Manor had all but ambushed her outside the schoolhouse, eager for news.

Now Emma longed for a cup of tea, bed and the chance to stop thinking about the man lying on her sofa. She flexed her hand, remembering how tightly he'd grasped it as he woke from whatever hell he'd been wandering in.

She almost preferred it when he was flirting.

Laughter echoed from the garden. Over the low stone wall, she saw Becky sitting on the bench and chatting with Ned from the Manor. There was no harm in it, of course, except they might wish to get married some day and then Emma would be hard-pressed to find another maid as kind and reliable as Becky to watch over Kit. She paused at the front door, wondering how Manning was faring and whether Kit still sulked about her refusal to allow him to meet the aeronaut. Tea and bed would have to wait.

She opened the door and was startled to see that the screen dividing the parlor from the entrance had tumbled over somehow. She heard voices in the parlor.

"I dropped my coat and it landed on a tombstone," Manning was saying. "But Alcyone was still on course for the church spire."

"What did you do then?"

It was Kit. How had he gotten there? Someone had disobeyed her instructions! She began to shake with a sudden surge of anger. But she could not allow exhaustion to overpower her self control. She squared her shoulders, stepped past the screen and into the parlor. Kit sat in his wheeled chair, next to the sofa. He and Manning went quiet as they saw her.

"I trust you are feeling better today, Mr. Manning," she said.

"Yes, thank you. I'm enjoying your brother's company."

She looked from Manning to Kit. "Where is Miss Grimshaw?"

"She—she had to go back to the vicarage for a bit," Kit stammered.

"So Becky brought you here?"

"Er ..."

Clearly, Kit was afraid she'd be annoyed with Becky. She was, but there was no use making a scene.

"Never mind," she said. She kissed his forehead and felt him stiffen. "How are you feeling, dearest?"

"I'm well enough."

"Kit! Kit!" Becky shouted from the direction of the kitchen.

Emma turned her head. Becky came dashing around the screen and stared at Kit. "Oh, thank goodness! You are here." She turned to look at Emma, eyes wide at Emma's questioning look. "But Miss, I thought you ..."

"You thought *I* brought him here?"

"Didn't you, Miss?"

"I thought *you* did."

"No, I promise you, Miss, I didn't!"

They both turned to stare at Kit. Emma's mind reeled. It was impossible. Kit couldn't have ...

She drew a shuddering breath. "How did you get here, Kit? Who brought you?"

A guilty flush colored his pale cheeks. He averted his face.

"Kit," she said, her voice breaking. "Look at me. Did you push your chair here by yourself?"

He looked up at her defiantly and nodded.

"I didn't leave him but for a few minutes, Miss!" Becky exclaimed. "I left him with his book. I didn't dream he'd ..."

"Hush, Becky, I do not blame you," she said, not taking her eyes off her brother. "You—you pushed yourself here?"

"You don't think I can do it, do you? But I can!"

Anxiety knotted her insides. "How could you? You know what Dr. Procton said. What if you'd done yourself a serious injury?"

Kit glared back at her; Manning looked away, no doubt wishing he could be anywhere else. She softened her voice. "Becky, take Kit to the garden, please."

"I'm all right, Emma," Kit said. "I'm stronger than you think!"

"Yes, well, we shall talk about it later." She touched his shoulder gently but he just scowled.

Emma restored the screen to its proper position, making room for Becky to wheel Kit out, and returned to Manning.

"I am sorry," she said awkwardly. "I should have shown more self control."

He gave her a sympathetic look. "You suffered a shock. Besides that, you sat up half the night with me. You must be tired."

She felt tears prickle her eyes and averted her face. "I'll fetch you some fresh compresses," she said and turned to leave.

"No, stay a bit," he said. "You don't wish the boy to talk to me, do you?"

"Mr. Hollis said you were to keep quiet."

"I can't always be sleeping. Besides, I like Kit. That's not why you're angry, is it? Do you think I'm a bad influence?"

She hesitated. "His physician warned me that Kit should avoid excitement at all costs. He—he has a weak heart."

"Is this the first time he has propelled his own chair?"

"I don't know!" There *had* been a few times she'd wondered if he and the chair were quite where she'd left them ... A familiar, sick anxiety clutched her insides. She didn't know Kit as well as she thought. She didn't know if she'd been too careful or too lenient. It seemed she didn't know *anything*. "Dr. Procton said any overexertion could be dangerous. What if he had lost control of the chair? I cannot bear to think ..." She sank into the chair beside the sofa and covered her face with her hands.

"He doesn't seem the worse for it," Manning said. "And I don't think it would harm him to speak to me."

She lowered her hands, straightened up, drew in a breath. "I suppose I shall have to allow it."

He did not reply.

"You think I am coddling him?"

He winced and she realized she'd raised her voice again. Idiot! She knew better than to scold an invalid. She opened her mouth to apologize but he spoke first.

"I did not say that," he replied. "I think you're a good sister and it is only natural that you should worry."

She averted her face again. She didn't want his understanding. "Mr. Hollis visited today. What did he say?"

"That I must remain abed for a little while longer, but he expects a full recovery within a few weeks."

"Excellent."

He closed his eyes again but smiled faintly. "You will not miss me? At least a little?"

"I have better things to do than nurse injured aeronauts."

He gave a mock sigh, but his brow had furrowed. She glanced at the note on the side table and saw he hadn't had any medicine since morning. "Your headache is worse, isn't it?"

"Like the devil," he admitted.

"You should have another dose of laudanum."

He hesitated.

"It is only a very small dose," she said. "It will help you sleep."

"Very well, Mistress."

She measured out the drops into some water. As she leaned over him, his lips parted. As she held the pap boat up to it, her eyes were drawn to his mouth. Suddenly she became aware of the stubble on his chin, his bare throat undulating as he swallowed, the faint trail of hair just visible at the neck of his nightshirt. No, he was not like any invalid she'd ever cared for.

She got up and went to the kitchen to freshen his compresses. She looked out the window. Kit and Becky were in the garden. As Manning had said, Kit didn't look the worse for wear. But what he had done... She shivered. Pandora stared up at her from the hearth with eyes of molten copper. Emma knelt down and stroked her, sliding her fingers through the short, soft fur, eliciting a robust, comforting purr. Yet she felt the tears well up again. *The devil.* She hadn't cried in ages, but ever since Manning had arrived she'd been fighting tears. And now she could not stop staring at him, forgetting decorum. Perhaps it was just the lack of sleep that was disordering her senses. As soon as Miss Grimshaw returned from the vicarage, she'd have a bite to eat and seek her bed.

But for now she had to face Manning and maintain her composure.

She straightened up and returned to the parlor. Manning's eyes were closed, but when she started bathing his forehead, he looked up at her with a hazy smile.

"A man could fall into... those eyes of yours... Mistress," he murmured.

His words triggered an almost-forgotten ache inside her. How long had it been since anyone looked at her so? It meant nothing, of course. She gave her head a slight shake. He was in her care; she could not think of him as a man.

His breathing slowed; his pupils contracted to tiny points in his blue-green eyes.

"Save your pretty words, Mr. Manning. It is time for you to sleep." She dampened the cloth again and continued to bathe his forehead.

"Thank you."

His eyes closed; the lines of pain around his eyes and jaw slowly relaxed. She thought he'd fallen into sleep. But he spoke again, so softly she had to lean over him to hear.

"Ah... I think I am... in love..."

"Indeed," she said dryly, but her hands shook as she smoothed the cloth onto his forehead.

The sooner he was gone, the better.

Chapter Five

C annons roared in the distance. Smoke obscured Gil's vision and filled his lungs. He struggled to breathe, but just as he started to lose consciousness, he drew in a breath of miraculous fresh, cool air. His vision cleared and he saw her: Maggie, red curls haloing her rounded face, her rosy complexion dusted with freckles. Her smile was serene and sad all at once. She held something. He reached for her.

The cannons spoke again, smoke writhed around her and she faded. He called her name several times and then he remembered. She was dead.

"Mr. Manning."

His mind slowly came back to the present but his heart ached as it hadn't for years. God, she'd been so vivid. So real, as if she were trying to tell him something . . .

"Mr. Manning!"

The pretty schoolmistress gazed down at him, candlelight revealing her heart-shaped face, her eyes wide with concern.

"Em-Miss Westfield." He tried to sound reassuring but his throat was too parched.

"You were dreaming again." She patted his shoulder.

He resisted the urge to cling to her as he had the previous night. Model patients did not frighten their nurses. "I know. I am sorry."

"Don't be. How is your headache?"

He summoned a smile. "There aren't... twenty blacksmiths pounding in my skull anymore. Perhaps only ten."

She smiled. "Let us see if we can silence them."

As she bustled about, making him more comfortable, he tried to focus on the present. Yet the vision of Maggie lingered, as vivid as his dream of Waterloo the night before. Such visions he'd seen in his sleep before—yet those visions had faded over the years along with the grief. What had brought them back now?

"Are you quite certain your headache is better? Do you wish for more medicine?"

Emma's voice recalled him. He realized he'd been frowning. As a slim shaft of light illuminated the bottle on the nearby table, he thought he had the answer to his question.

"Thank you, no. I am much better," he said, watching the dawn light creeping around the edges of the curtains. "In fact, I'll be eternally grateful if you opened those curtains. I'd like some sunshine."

She hesitated, then did as he asked. He found he could bear the soft light. As long as he moved slowly, he could turn his head and watch Emma move about, admire her quick yet graceful movements, try to imagine the slim figure beneath her dark gown and enveloping shawl. That was the thing. Stay firmly in the present day and take what innocent pleasure he could in his present company.

Soon enough, he'd be back with his crew and flying again.

When she left him to make breakfast, he took the opportunity to study his surroundings, which he'd been too dazed to look at before. The room was modest in size and simply furnished with the sofa, several oak tables and chairs that were dark with age. A desk in one corner bore an inkwell and several piles of papers, weighted down with an oddly-shaped stone. Dark beams punctuated whitewashed walls hung with sketches of birds and insects, all manner of flying creatures. Emma's work, he guessed, drawn in loving, meticulous detail and tinted with watercolors. Miss Grimshaw had spoken of a book, too.

Emma reentered the room with another steaming bowl of gruel. In the bright light he could more easily see the dark circles under her eyes.

"Gruel! I feel as if I could eat an elephant," he said.

She brightened. "I am afraid Mr. Hollis would not approve. Besides, we are quite out of elephants."

She drew the chair close and he submitted to the humbling yet pleasant act of being spoon-fed by a pretty woman. But remorse tugged at him. Despite her cheery facade, Emma looked ready to drop from fatigue. Once his crew was here, they could take over the night watches, but he wished there were some way he could repay her kindness. He'd gladly offer her part of his winnings from Tillingham, but he suspected she would refuse. If pride didn't keep her from accepting it, propriety would. Respectable young ladies did not accept money from gentlemen.

She set the bowl and spoon aside when he'd finished. "I am sure you are longing for something stronger, but Mr. Hollis warned us that you should be kept on a low diet to avoid a brain-fever."

"I promise you, gruel is one of my favorite dishes."

She raised an eyebrow. "Don't tell me you are not longing for a beefsteak and ale!"

He grinned. "While on campaign, we used to subsist on stringy beef and biscuits so hard they could turn a musket-ball. That is, when the supply train didn't get lost, in which case we had to forage for acorns or shoot hares. So you see, Miss Westfield, soldiers learn to take comfort and pleasure where they can."

He'd meant to make her smile but she looked away from him. "Miss Grimshaw told me you had been an officer," she said in a voice drained of expression.

"Yes."

"Which—which regiment?"

"The 95th Rifles."

Was it a trick of his eyes, or had she gone pale?

"Do you know someone in the 95th?" he asked.

"No, of course not. It—it was merely an idle question."
She rose from her chair but he saw her hands shake. "It is
time I set out for school. Miss Grimshaw will be here soon."

He was left to stare at cracks in the ceiling and ponder
her interest in the 95th. After a moment his mind sheered
away from the question. He was not sure he wanted to
understand. He liked Emma, felt grateful to her, and already
knew he'd miss her clever tongue, her gentle hands, the ease
with which he could make her blush.

She was right; it was better for all of them if he left as
soon as possible.

E mma opened the cottage door carefully, willing her
hands not to shake. Since the morning, her nerves had
been stretched thin, her mind wracked with the questions she
dared not ask. Now she would have to face him again and
pray she did not betray herself.

She heard a rustle of skirts and Miss Grimshaw emerged
from behind the screen, as if she'd been on the watch for her.

"Is something amiss?" she whispered.

"Not at all," said her older friend with a reassuring smile.
"I did not mean to alarm you!"

Emma let out a sigh.

Miss Grimshaw's expression sobered. "Emma dear, there
is something I wish to discuss with you. Perhaps we may go
into the garden? Becky could sit with Mr. Manning for a few
minutes."

Emma nodded. "How is he?"

"He is asleep, though he refused to take any more laudanum. He says he is much improved."

"And Kit? Is he well?"

"Perfectly. He is in the kitchen, studying. Mr. Grimshaw
left a short time ago."

"Oh, I'd forgotten it was his day to give Kit his lesson,"
she said, following the older woman into the cottage. They

tiptoed past the screen and into the kitchen, where she gave Kit a kiss on the forehead and bade Becky go into the parlor.

"Your brother has not had an opportunity to speak with Mr. Manning," Miss Grimshaw said as they walked down the path toward the garden bench. "I did promise him that he might do so later, if Mr. Manning is up for visitors after dinner. I hope I did not do wrong?"

"Of course not. But is that all you wished to discuss?"

Miss Grimshaw seated herself and began to fidget with the fringe of her shawl. "No," she said at length. "It was something I wished to tell you earlier, but you looked so tired last evening that I thought it best to wait."

"Whatever it is, I can bear it," said Emma, trying to ignore the anxious flutter in her stomach.

"I shall not mince words, my dear. I am concerned about Mr. Manning's attentions toward you. Yesterday he said something about wanting you to *kiss* him, before he realized it was I who was tending him."

Emma clenched her hands in her lap, staring down at the gravel of the path. What exactly had Manning revealed? "He is a shocking flirt," she said lightly, "but surely you do not think I would encourage him?"

"No, of course not."

She let out a sigh. At least he hadn't betrayed her midnight folly.

"I have every confidence in *your* virtue," Miss Grimshaw continued. "But I have none in his sense of propriety."

"He can do no harm in his present state."

"He is getting stronger every day, dear."

"I doubt he has any intention of crossing the line. He merely enjoys saying things to put one to the blush. If he were not confined to a sickbed, I doubt he would take much notice."

"You do yourself an injustice. You are only two-and-twenty, after all, and still very pretty."

"It is kind of you to say so." Emma made allowances for the partiality of a friend. But she knew the past few years had taken their toll, that she had grown thin and wiry, that the strain of her responsibilities showed in her face.

"Once Mr. Manning is safely away," said Miss Grimshaw, "you ought to put aside your mourning clothes."

"It is wiser to save my earnings than buy dresses. What I have is sufficient for my needs."

Miss Grimshaw sighed. "It is, since you continue to refuse all invitations. It was very natural that you did not wish to be in company after your poor father's passing, but it has been nearly two years. It would do you good to go about in Tichbury society. You and your father were so well-liked I am sure you would be welcome in the homes of many good families in the neighborhood."

"I am content," Emma replied. Miss Grimshaw would never know all the reasons she had chosen to withdraw from society.

"But you have no chance of meeting any respectable gentlemen this way!"

She gave a small laugh. "But you know that I am shockingly ineligible. Do not be making matches for me, please."

"I am certain there are gentlemen who could overlook your lack of dowry in light of your other virtues," her friend insisted. "I quite long to see you comfortably established. You know it would be the best thing for you and Christopher."

Emma could not argue the logic.

"Mr. Grimshaw says we should trust in divine providence," the older woman continued. "But I believe in helping providence along."

Emma summoned up a smile. She had long since given up on divine providence. "I've a better chance of securing our futures by writing more books. In fact, I had better get back to work now." She rose from the seat.

Miss Grimshaw gave her a sharp look. "At least promise me you will be on your guard regarding Mr. Manning. It would be dreadful if gossip were to destroy your chances with other gentlemen."

"Of course I will be careful."

They walked back to the cottage in silence. Emma knew it was useless to insist that the aeronaut was no danger to her. Not that he was a threat in the way Miss Grimshaw suspected. Emma didn't fear Manning so much as herself.

She feared she was neither as virtuous nor as wise as she pretended.

17. Your description of the courtship behavior of the male pheasant could be misleading to young readers. They must be assured that character is of greater importance than mere physical display.

E mma groaned inwardly, reading the cramped writing on the paper before her. She scanned down the rest of Erasmus Blodgett's long list of suggested changes to *A Child's Introduction to English Birds* and rolled her eyes. She'd rashly promised she would complete the changes by the end of the month. What had she been thinking?

The sofa creaked. Manning stirred and mumbled something. Was he wandering in a nightmare again?

Quietly, she rose from her chair and took a step closer. His breathing steadied and he settled into what looked like a deeper sleep. The covers had slipped, revealing enough of his throat and chest to unsettle her. She stared down for a moment, knowing she should smooth the covers over him, dreading even that slight intimacy. It was warm enough in the room, she decided.

She seated herself again, dipped her quill in the inkpot and tried to find words to express the indicated moral. She couldn't think; her eyes kept darting toward Manning.

Desperately, she fixed her gaze on her sketch of the male pheasant, hanging across the room. Papa had called him a handsome fellow, with his chestnut plumage, emerald green head, brilliant scarlet wattle and long tail designed to attract the female of his species. Papa had seen the Creator's hand in all that was interesting or beautiful in nature. Once she had seen it too. Papa would never have stooped to twist the truth to support Blodgett's stodgy morality. Just as well that *she* was the one finishing the book, then. She could not afford scruples.

She bent her head to her work and dutifully glossed over the pheasant's mating dance. As she moved on to Blodgett's concerns over the cuckoo's improper notion of motherhood, she heard a horse trotting down the lane. A moment later, Sir George passed the window on his dun cob. The hoof beats slowed and she frowned. Arabella and Lydia had probably sent him to check on Manning's progress.

She set the fossil Papa had bought in Lyme Regis on top of her pile of papers and then rushed to the door. She opened it just as Sir George was dismounting. She greeted him in a whisper.

He missed the hint. "How is Manning doing? Up for visitors, is he?"

"He is sleeping now. I think it unwise for you to see him at present."

"You're quite certain of that?" His face darkened but she sensed he was frustrated, not angry. No doubt he'd been sent with orders to learn as much about Manning as possible.

"Mr. Hollis says he must rest as much as possible."

"He is better, isn't he?"

"Yes, but the injury to his head was severe. Mr. Hollis recommends complete quiet."

"How soon *will* he be able to see visitors?"

"I cannot say."

He kicked his boot against a stone on the path. "The thing is, Arabella and Lydia are most anxious to make his acquaintance."

Anxious to fawn all over him. "I am afraid you must all await Mr. Hollis's permission."

"Oh, very well, I suppose that is best."

She said nothing, hoping he would take himself off so she could return to work. He continued to stand there, kicking at loose stones.

"Is there anything else I can do for you?" she asked.

"Well, er, is there more you know of him? Is he a gentle-man?"

"He was an officer," she offered. "In—in the 95th Rifles."

Sir George didn't notice her stutter. "Ah, that new-fangled regiment with those odd green jackets. Isn't that the regiment Hartley's second son joined?"

She could only nod.

We wear green to blend in with cover while skirmishing, he'd said proudly. And our rifles may take longer to load than muskets, but a good marksman can hit a target over two hundred yards away!

"Did you hear me? Are you unwell?" Sir George's voice broke her reverie.

"Oh, I am sorry, Sir George," she said quickly. "I confess I'm rather tired. What did you say?"

"I was saying Manning must be quite the dashing fellow. How are his manners?"

He continued to look at her oddly. She tried not to blush.

"They seem pleasant enough," she replied.

"Is he on half-pay? Or sold out?"

"I cannot say."

"Odd that a gentleman would take up flying. Was it for a wager?"

"I believe so."

"But you have been with him for several days now. Surely you and he have conversed."

"He sleeps a great deal. We have spoken very little."

Sir George took off his hat and fidgeted with it. "I'm afraid Lyddy has taken quite a fancy to him."

"No doubt he seems intriguing to a seventeen year old."

He gave her a searching look. "He's not crossed the line with you, has he?"

Lud! She wondered if the entire village was speculating on the possibility. "Of course not. He is an invalid and besides, Miss Grimshaw is always nearby."

"I am relieved to hear it." He remounted his horse. "Well, do tell me if there is anything you need or if you have any trouble with Manning."

She nodded and turned away before her face could betray her. Sir George, like Miss Grimshaw, had no idea of the real danger Manning posed to her.

He hadn't been here three days and already her defenses were crumbling. He roused all the feelings she'd hidden for nearly two years, the grief, the folly. The longing to be held close, to desire and be desired... Which was the maddest part of all. He was an invalid in her care. In his sleep he had even called out another woman's name. Yet he made her *feel*, made her *remember*. This morning, after she'd asked him about his regiment, she'd almost given in to temptation and let loose a torrent of questions.

She reminded herself that no good could come of reopening old wounds.

Chapter Six

Gil stared at the ceiling. Rain pattered against the windows but a modest fire in the hearth kept the small parlor cozy. A short while ago, Miss Grimshaw had given him a dinner of toast and broth and promised him that they would all come to sit with him later. His headache had subsided. Though any large movement still brought on dizziness, he'd had enough of sleeping. He wanted visitors. He hadn't seen Emma since morning.

He turned his head, hearing the creak of Kit's wheeled chair. Emma pushed her brother into the room; she avoided looking at Gil as she moved her brother next to the sofa. Miss Grimshaw seated herself in a nearby chair and took up some mending, her posture rigorously upright, her expression watchful. The cat Gil had seen earlier came in after them and curled up near the hearth.

Kit gave him a shy smile. "Emma said you could talk to me about balloons!" he said. "Can you finish telling me how you came here? Or start at the beginning. Emma and Miss Grimshaw will want to hear it, too!"

Gil watched Emma as she seated herself at the desk and spread out the papers upon it. Her eyes were shadowed.

"It was a windy day at Green Park . . ." He launched into the account, recounting as many details as he could, only omitting reference to his bet with Tillingham. Kit listened eagerly and even Miss Grimshaw glanced at him now and then with bright eyes. Emma sat writing, but her pen paused as he reached his troubles with the valve and his subsequent crash.

"Then your sister helped me out from under the wreckage," he concluded. "You know the rest."

"What do you think happened to the valve?" Kit asked.

"I don't know."

"Did you go very high? Maybe it froze up."

"A clever notion, but I did not go high enough this time. I don't know what happened. Perhaps the springs wore out. I'll have my crew look at it."

"You'll fly again, won't you?"

"Of course. I have already arranged to ascend from Greenwich Fair and several other fairs through the spring and summer."

"Is that wise, Mr. Manning?" Miss Grimshaw paused in her work. "Should you not consider a safer occupation?"

Gil caught Emma looking at him. She flushed and looked away.

Before he could reply, Kit burst out, "He ought not to give it up! Do tell me, Mr. Manning. What is it like to fly?"

"Imagine the highest hill you've ever climbed," he said. "Think how small buildings and animals look from there. Then imagine yourself even higher, everything spread out below, villages like toys, rivers and ponds shining like silver."

"Oh, I wish *I* could fly!"

Out of the corner of his eye Gil saw Emma's hand close tightly around her quill.

"How did you become interested in balloons, Mr. Manning?" Miss Grimshaw asked, continuing to ply her needle.

"I was stationed in the south of France in 1814, after the Battle of Toulouse. There I met a charming old gentleman who'd once worked at the Meudon workshops, near Paris. You see, Boney had toyed with the notion of using balloons for surveillance during battles; it's said the Battle of Fleurus was won using observations from the *Entreprenant*.

But the military experiments were discontinued and Monsieur Durand was left to fly on his own. He was kind enough to take me up with him a few times before we returned to England. I learned that he died soon after Waterloo, of grief. He lost a son there."

He paused, thinking of kind old Durand and his fascination with all things mechanical. "He hoped that in the future, balloons would be used only for peaceful purposes. He bequeathed Alcyone to me in his will." And gave Gil a new direction in the aftermath of all the bloodshed.

Miss Grimshaw peered at him over her spectacles. "So then you sold out and took up flying. Or do you remain on half-pay?"

He couldn't blame her for prying. As Emma's friend and self-appointed chaperone, she had the right to know what sort of man he was. Yet the turn of her questioning made him uneasy.

"I sold my commission. There is little for a soldier to do in peace-time."

"There were no other occupations that interested you?"

"I know little besides soldiering."

She tied off a thread and snipped off the end. "When did you join the army, Mr. Manning?"

"You could say I was born into it."

"Your father was an officer? Where did he serve? Jamaica, was it?"

He nodded.

Miss Grimshaw looked grave. Emma gave him a swift, intent look.

"Jamaica? I have never traveled. What is it like in the West Indies?" Kit exclaimed.

At eight years of age, he couldn't know that the West Indies were known as the graveyard of Englishmen. Gil suppressed dim images of brilliant skies, exotic scents, hordes of stinging insects. Yellow fever and the stench of death.

"I've little memory of Jamaica," he said. "I left when I was five years old."

"Your parents died there?" asked Miss Grimshaw, more gently than before.

He nodded.

"I am sorry. Were you brought back to England?"

"For a few years. Then I went to India with my father's friend, Captain Forsythe." He looked toward Kit. "Would you like to hear about the time I rode an elephant?"

"By Jove, yes!"

"It was during the expedition to fight Sultan Tippoo," he began.

"Tippoo?" Miss Grimshaw interrupted. She'd abandoned her work basket and now looked at him with a skeptical expression. "That had to be, oh, 1799 or so. You were only a boy then, surely too young to go on such an expedition!"

"I was twelve years old. I traveled in the rear with the women and children. That is, when I wasn't roaming around and getting underfoot."

"This Captain Forsythe, was he in the East Indian army?"

"No, he was in the regulars. He helped me to my first commission, in the 74th."

"That is a Highland regiment, Mr. Manning, is it not?"

"You are quite right. Captain Forsythe was Scottish. But how did you know?"

"I had a cousin in the East Indian Army. He used to correspond with me about his experiences. If you were an ensign in 1803, perhaps you were present at Assaye?"

Did she know what a bloodbath it had been? Gil clenched his jaw. "I was."

"The 74th sustained heavy losses there, did they not?"

He nodded. "Captain Forsythe died there." Emma was still watching him. But she said nothing, leaving it to Miss Grimshaw to ask all the questions.

"May I ask how you came to be transferred to the 95th?"

"The 95th was just then forming at Shorncliffe, in Kent. Though I made some friends at the 74th, it was thought that as an Englishman, I'd fit in better elsewhere." Though there'd been plenty of Scottsmen in the 95th too. Gil smiled as he thought of his friend, Johnny Kincaid. No matter what, they'd always be like brothers.

"So you must have been in the Peninsula and Waterloo. I imagine you distinguished yourself in that battle."

A breeze brought rain sheeting against the windows. The cat raised her head lazily and then dropped it, lulled by the warmth of the fire. Gil's head began to ache anew. It seemed wrong to speak of such things here.

Emma radiated tension, no longer pretending to continue her work.

"Many distinguished themselves," he said finally.

Emma staggered to her feet. "I—I think I shall take my work to the kitchen."

"You should take yourself off to bed, my dear," said Miss Grimshaw. "You look positively haggard. We cannot have you making yourself sick!"

Emma wavered. Gil was not sure that exhaustion was all that troubled her.

"Between us, Becky and I can carry Kit to bed," Miss Grimshaw insisted. "Go run along, do, before you drop!"

"Very well. Just be sure to wake me at midnight, please."

She practically fled the room. Gil's unease deepened.

"Now will you tell me about the elephant?" Kit asked.

Gil started the tale, glad to be on safer ground.

Emma jerked awake, her shoulder gripped by bony fingers. She blinked up at Miss Grimshaw, whose face looked drawn in the light of a single candle.

"My dear, I am sorry to wake you," Miss Grimshaw whispered. "You looked so tired last night. But Mr. Hollis does not wish us to leave Mr. Manning unattended and I'm afraid I'll nod off."

"It's no matter." She heaved herself up with a massive effort of will. Even the shock of the cold floor against her feet didn't quite pierce her exhaustion.

"He refused laudanum again. He seemed to fall asleep well enough without it," Miss Grimshaw sank down onto the bed, looking thoroughly worn out. A moment later she was snoring. Emma smiled as she smoothed the covers over her friend. It was so uncharacteristic of Miss Grimshaw to fall asleep in her clothes.

She glanced at the clothes she'd laid out for herself and decided not to bother. Manning would probably sleep longer now that he felt better. She'd have plenty of time to dress when morning came. So she pulled her dressing gown on over her shift, thrust her feet into slippers, took up the candle and tiptoed out. She paused by Kit's door. All was quiet and yet the usual sick fear twisted her insides. She opened the door and slipped in. She set her candle on the washstand and stared at her brother for a moment. He'd listened so eagerly to Manning's tales. Now he lay curled up, looking like any other boy, his twisted foot hidden under the quilt. He smiled in his sleep. Kit's old nurse had said he smiled at the angels, a sign he was not long for this world. But thus far he'd survived.

Emma kissed him lightly on the brow and went silently from the room.

In the parlor, the fire still glowed but the rain had stopped. Manning slept as peacefully as Miss Grimshaw had described. He looked like a ruffian, the stubble of several days adorning his chin. She tiptoed close and watched him for a few moments, unable to turn away. She wished she could stop thinking about his lean, muscular figure, hidden under the bed-clothes. And his scars . . .

All evening he'd tried to evade Miss Grimshaw's probing. Though there were gaps in his tale, what he'd revealed was disturbing enough. It was nothing short of a miracle he was alive and breathing there on her sofa.

Though Emma did not believe in miracles, she found it hard to take her eyes off him.

She set her candle down on the desk. Erasmus Blodgett's ponderous morality ought to give her mind a more proper direction.

25. The mute swan should be used as an example of matrimonial fidelity. You have neglected to mention that when one swan dies, its mate will die of grief.

Emma grimaced. Papa had burst that particular myth; he'd taken her and Kit to see that the widowed pen at the lake at Chesmore Manor had taken up with a new cob. But humans were not swans.

She sighed and leafed through her manuscript to the offending passage. After several attempts, she still could not bring herself to express the desired sentiment. She gritted her teeth, tried again and then gave up in disgust, crumpling up the sheet and tossing it to the floor.

She glanced toward Manning. She wished she could sleep, too. He looked so blithe, so unconcerned. It was maddening. He dominated the room, smiling as if coaxing her to rest from her work and . . . what?

She bent her head to the section on the mute swan but her attention faltered. Perhaps if she closed her eyes for a moment she'd be able to think more clearly. No, she'd fall asleep. She had to continue. Perhaps she ought to get up and move about. In a bit, she promised herself . . .

She found herself kneeling next to the sofa. Manning was so still, she could barely see him breathe. She placed a hand on his chest and felt the reassuring rise and fall. It was warm in the room; the fire threw flickering shadows on the walls. Surely nothing could wake him. She placed a hand on his cheek, stroked the stubble. She drew her hand down his neck, lightly tracing its indentations and curves, his Adam's apple. She stopped a few inches from where his chest hair began. She was tempted to touch it and terrified that she might. Then his eyes opened.

Her head bobbed and she came to with a start. Her heart beat a mad rhythm. She was still in her chair. Manning lay asleep, untouched. Relief swept over her. She hadn't committed another stupid indiscretion.

She needed a cup of tea. A strong one.

She picked up the crumpled papers and went to the kitchen. Pandora lay curled up on the wooden seat next to the hearth, basking in the warmth of the banked fire. Emma knelt down and brushed through the ashes. Deep within the gray mass, embers still glowed brightly. Using the ruined papers for kindling, she blew the embers back to a flame.

She put the kettle onto the hob and sat down. Pandora raised her head. While she waited for the water to boil, Emma stroked her fingers through the cat's thick fur, listening to her loud, contented purr that rivaled the crackle of the fire. Her head bobbed and she caught herself back from the brink of sleep. She ought to go sit by the table, but she didn't want to move. Instead, she opened the front of her dressing gown. She felt a bit cooler, but sleep continued to tug at her with velvet fingers.

A loud crash from the direction of the parlor jerked her upright again.

Emma sprang from the bench and ran to the parlor, skidding as she rounded the screen. Manning lay face-down on the floor beside the sofa. He'd knocked over the nearby table. The pitcher lay in shards on a soaked patch of carpet.

She fell to her knees beside him. "Mr. Manning! Are you hurt?"

He had his head to one side and his eyes were closed. "Sorry." His voice was low and hoarse. "Tried to get water . . . by myself. Bad idea."

"Are you hurt? Did you hit your head?"

"No. Just . . . room's spinning . . . like a top."

"Are you going to be sick?" She cast her eyes about for the chamber pot and found it, just a few feet away.

"No. I'll be all right . . . in a moment."

She waited. All was silent except for Manning's breathing.

"I think I can get up now," he said after a moment and began to raise himself onto his hands and knees.

"Here, let me help."

She put her arms around his torso and helped him to sit up on the floor against the sofa. He paused to fight another attack of vertigo. She tried not to stare at the hairy, muscular legs exposed by the vicar's too-short nightshirt.

He turned toward her and as his eyes focused, he grinned. "I'd have fallen out of bed sooner . . . had I known it would bring you in such a fetching state." His gaze lingered on her, brashly admiring.

She flushed to the roots of her hair as she realized her state of deshabillé. Her dressing gown was hanging from her elbows; above it her thin cotton shift revealed bare shoulders and arms and hid little even where it covered. Lud! She still had an arm around him.

"Don't make game of me!" She tried to pull her dressing gown back up, but it was caught beneath her.

"You don't think you look fetching?"

She stumbled to her feet and refastened her dressing gown. "It is very improper of you to say so. I—I was merely too tired to dress. I didn't think that you would wake and I went to make some tea. Anyway, what a fool you were to try to get the water! You know Miss Grimshaw and I would not leave you unattended for long."

"I was only trying to spare you the bother."

"You have been a bother since you arrived!" She tried to compose herself as she watched him get his legs under him. He stopped for a moment, closing his eyes, perhaps fighting another attack of vertigo. He would never get up by himself.

"I see I shall have to help you," she said. "Are you ready to get back into bed now?"

He reopened his eyes and grinned again. "Ready indeed. Will you join me?"

"That is *not* what I meant!"

He gave her a mock sigh.

"You had better behave yourself or I shall leave you there on the floor." She eyed him anxiously. Although she'd had plenty of practice lifting Kit, this was going to be very different. For one thing, Manning probably weighed fourteen stone. For another . . . there was no way to do this that would not be infinitely mortifying.

"Listen to me and do as I say," she commanded. "Can you get your legs under you?"

He nodded. Bracing himself with his arms, he rose to a kneeling position.

She turned to face him, placing a foot on either side of him. Then she bent her knees and put her arms around him.

He beamed up at her. "I like your methods."

"Do be quiet! When I say the word, try to stand. I'll help you up."

"I'm in your hands."

Manning gripped her waist, bringing back memories of what it felt like to be in a man's embrace. Emma forced herself to concentrate on the task at hand.

"Now." She pulled up with all her strength. Manning surprised her by carrying more of his weight than she expected. She lost her balance and they stood swaying, nightshirt against flimsy dressing gown and shift, heart to heart. A treacherous heat spread through her; a pleasant ache tugged in her belly; she couldn't let him go for fear he'd topple over. *Nurses were not supposed to be aroused by invalids.*

She'd forgotten how tall he was.

He gazed down at her, looking nothing like an invalid. His eyes glowed, blue-green, their centers dark and beckoning. She stared, not believing what she read in them. He pulled her closer, let out a long breath like an airy kiss on her cheek. He lowered his face, his mouth a mere whisper from hers.

She trembled, but did not pull back.

Chapter Seven

"Ahem."

Gil raised his head. Across the room he saw Miss Grimshaw, swathed in a dressing gown. Her face was rigid with disapproval. Emma stiffened and looked around. His rational mind told him it was all for the best, but part of him—the most wicked part—protested the interruption.

Emma backed away as far as she could without quite letting him fall. "M-Mr. Manning fell out of bed," she stammered. "I was just helping him get up."

He stifled a grin. She didn't quite realize the truth of her words but he dared not give a saucy reply, not with Miss Grimshaw looking daggers at him.

Time to fall on his sword, as it were.

"I made the mistake of trying to get some water for myself," he said penitently. "I am very sorry I broke the jug."

Miss Grimshaw glanced at the overturned table and the remains of the broken jug, then resumed her dragon-like scowl. "You were very foolish to attempt such a thing. I trust you have learnt your lesson."

"I have." He bowed his head, but Miss Grimshaw did not look appeased.

"Let us get you back into bed," Emma said. She held him as he sank to a sitting position on the edge of the sofa. Screened by her body, he winked at her. She glared at him.

He composed his face as Miss Grimshaw came forward to help Emma get him back down onto his pillows.

"That kettle must be boiling," Emma said, darting away as soon as he was settled. "I'll fetch a broom to tidy up."

Miss Grimshaw gave Emma a meaningful glance. "Just make the tea, dear. There is no need to rush back."

As Emma left, the older woman righted the table, aligning it precisely in its original position, then sat down in the chair beside the sofa. "That was most foolish of you, Mr. Manning," she said in a lowered voice.

He nodded.

"But you are not, in fact, a fool. You know I am not speaking of your attempt to get out of bed by yourself."

He decided to remain silent rather than incriminate himself further.

"While under this roof, you will comport yourself as a gentleman."

"Miss Grimshaw, I assure you I'd not harm Miss Westfield for the world."

"Then remember that the next time you are tempted to cross the line!"

"It won't happen again."

And it wouldn't. He'd been taken by surprise. That was what it was. Who would have expected it, given his headache and the lingering dizziness? But a part of him that hadn't been injured in the crash had come to life, roused by the sight of Emma in her shift, the feel and smell of her as she held him in those strong, supple arms. Next time, he'd be more prepared.

"See that it does not!" said Miss Grimshaw. "Emma could lose everything if a scandal broke out. She would not be able to continue her position as schoolmistress, let alone that it would ruin any chance she might have of contracting a suitable marriage. She deserves better than that."

"She does indeed." He closed his eyes and the image of Emma filled his mind. She'd trembled in his arms a bit, but she hadn't pulled back. Lud, she'd seemed *willing*, his prim schoolmistress who kissed strange men in their sleep.

"It is bad enough that she will not put off her blacks and refuses every invitation."

He stole a glance at Miss Grimshaw and was shocked to see a tear roll down one sunken cheek.

"She does not go about in local society?" he ventured.

"Not since her father died," she replied, half to herself. "Emma says she does not wish to be pitied. She is very proud. Too proud, I think."

He wondered if there was more than pride in it.

"I don't wish to see her dwindle into an indigent spinster," Miss Grimshaw continued. "She is not as lucky as I; she cannot expect her brother to provide for her."

Gil turned his face to the wall. If Emma continued her present course, she'd never be kissed, never be loved the way she was made to be loved. What he'd give to be the man to initiate her into the pleasures of the marriage-bed!

But he wasn't the man. There was nothing he could do for her or her brother. He could only avoid making matters worse.

Emma left the tea brewing, snatched up a candle and hurried up to her room. Setting down the candle, she caught sight of herself in the mirror. Her cheeks were still flushed, her eyes bright. Idiot! To invite Manning's kiss like a hussy. No, a pathetic, lonely spinster. Only a thin barrier of respectability lay between the two, she mused. But respectability was all she had now. What might be a casual diversion to Manning could prove disastrous for her.

She pulled off her dressing gown and stared at her reflection, seeing herself as Manning must have seen her. Her cheeks burned as she saw how her nipples shone darkly through the thin cotton of her shift. Quickly she snatched up her stays, the front-lacing ones she'd adopted since she'd begun to live alone with Kit. She fastened the stays around herself and laced them up tightly, trapping the breasts that were the only soft bit left of her. After she'd pulled on her petticoat, all that showed was her arms bulging with unlady-like muscles, the result of hours of work in the garden and carrying Kit about.

She should have been a man. It would have been so much easier to care for herself and Kit. She'd have more opportunities and no need to preserve her reputation.

Grimly, she pulled on a brown dress. She re-braided her hair and pinned it up in its usual tidy knot. She paused, still missing something. Then she knew what it was. She opened up the small jewelry casket on her dressing table and pulled out a small oval locket. No one else knew who'd given it to her, or whose hair it contained. But she did. She'd worn it under her clothing every day in the year following Waterloo, but lately she had fallen out of the habit. She put it round her neck and tucked it under the high bodice of her gown. The cool oval settled against her skin, a talisman to protect her from folly.

Now she was ready to go down. She'd have some tea, tidy up the mess and get back to work on her manuscript. She'd think about the tidy sum Mr. Blodgett had promised her for it and ignore the man on her sofa.

G il woke with a start. He couldn't move his legs. He stared up at the cracked ceiling, thinking that the strange dreams should have ended with the laudanum, but he still felt a weight pressing on him. Then he saw the gray cat curled up on his legs. Only the sight of Emma, slumped in the wing chair and fast asleep, kept him from laughing out loud.

She was fully dressed. He'd dozed off before her return, after Miss Grimshaw had scolded him as he deserved.

Though as he watched Emma sleep, he remembered how she had looked in that deliciously revealing shift. Surely that was some excuse; there was only so much temptation an unsuspecting man could withstand.

But he hadn't lied when he said he wouldn't hurt her for the world. Emma was a darling and he was deep in her debt. Slumber had smoothed her careworn look; her heart-shaped face was achingly sweet, eyelashes resting delicately on cheeks that he could make flush so easily. She looked younger and more vulnerable, making him remember all of the concerns Miss Grimshaw had poured out to him.

He didn't want to think about them.

Her clothes were a bit rumpled and wisps of soft brown hair escaped her prim coiffure. Just as she might look after a proper kiss. He almost wished that Miss Grimshaw hadn't interrupted them, but under the intoxication of those wickedly teasing nipples, he might have taken leave of his senses. Those pretty breasts weren't the only enticing bit of her, though. It was all of her, her face, her scent, her strong arms. What it would be like to have those arms and those long legs wrapped around him . . .

She stirred in her sleep and murmured something he couldn't catch. Then she straightened up, her eyes widening as she caught him staring at her.

"I am sorry," she said. "Have you been awake long?"

"Not at all. Don't fret, you needed the rest," he said. "I expect my crew will arrive today and relieve you of further nightly duties."

She colored up as she rose from the chair, muttering something about gruel before leaving him alone. She returned some twenty minutes later, her complexion cool and her manner distant.

"If you wish, you may sit up and feed yourself, Mr. Manning," she said briskly.

"I suppose I must," he said. "I cannot always be spoon-fed by a lovely woman. I'm afraid my man Reed would not be a satisfactory substitute."

A dimple quivered in her cheek. "Let me help you sit up."

Then she leaned over him, innocently placing those sweet breasts practically in his face. If he were fool enough, he would have reached for one. Instead, he closed his eyes and tried to master himself as she slid her arm beneath him. It wasn't merely the sight of her that tantalized. It was the smell of her, womanly with a hint of violet-scented soap. He tried to think of military maneuvers, mentally reviewing the drill for deploying from files into skirmish order. But nothing could compete with the reality of the woman holding him in her strong arms.

"Ready?" she asked. "Let's get you up."

He stifled something between a chuckle and a groan as she helped him slide into a semi-reclined position and arranged the pillows behind him. An ache that had nothing to do with his injuries came over him. He hoped she wouldn't notice what she'd done to him; his prim schoolmistress might swoon away from the shock. But as she straightened up, her pink cheeks went beet-red. She stared down, right at the tent he'd just made.

He hoped she wouldn't faint.

Emma tore her gaze away. Folly! Looking at what no respectable female ought to even be aware of ... She hurried to the table where she'd set the breakfast tray. But now she'd have to bring it to him. She'd have to look him in the face. She couldn't do it.

"Miss Westfield ..."

Lud! He'd seen her looking. She wished the floor would swallow her up.

"My wayward physiology wishes to apologize for its indelicate behavior."

Was *that* what he called it? She covered her mouth, stifling a most unseemly giggle.

"I may be a rogue, but I'm not a rake," he continued softly. "You've nothing to fear from me or my, er, friend."

If he was a rogue, then she was a brazen hussy for wanting to laugh. She squared her shoulders. It was nothing, just one of those reactions men could not control, perhaps, when in close proximity to a reasonably attractive female.

She drew in a deep breath, picked up the tray and turned around. He smiled as she brought him the food, his teeth gleaming in contrast to his tanned, stubbled chin.

She handed him the bowl and the spoon and pushed the table closer to the sofa. "Will you need anything else for a bit? I would rather not rouse Miss Grimshaw again so soon, but Kit is likely to be awake."

"You are not going off to the school?"

She smiled. "It is Saturday, though you may be excused for losing track of the time."

"In your presence, Mistress, I lose track of everything."

She choked back another giggle; he was amusing, but it would not be wise to take his flirtation too seriously. Briefly, she touched her locket before hurrying upstairs. Miss Grimshaw was snoring. As Emma had suspected, Kit was awake and anxious to come down for breakfast and see Manning again. She helped him dress and brought him downstairs. After he'd eaten breakfast—a good one, for him—he begged her to let him sit up with Manning.

"If he is awake, you may," she said.

He was still awake when she wheeled Kit in.

"Good morning, Mr. Manning," Kit said shyly. "Are— are you feeling better today?"

"Much better."

There was a wicked glint in Manning's eyes. Emma decided to ignore it as she gathered up the remains of his breakfast.

"Oh, I am so glad!" said Kit. "I was hoping you would tell me more about India. Did you ever see a real tiger?"

As Manning replied, Emma watched Kit's face, hero-worship written all over it. A pang went through her. Kit would take it hard when it was time for Manning to go.

She picked up the tray to leave and heard the clatter of hooves in the lane. Was it Sir George again? No, judging by the noise, there was more than one horse. She thought she heard several voices. She set the tray back down and drew the curtains. Up the lane she saw two sturdy piebald horses drawing a wagon with a number of passengers, who all seemed to be shouting.

"By Jove!" exclaimed Kit. "Is it gypsies?"

Emma listened.

"*Estúpidos!* He is near death's door, I know it." It was a woman's voice, deep and musical and strongly accented.

"No, the Captain's like a cat, he'll land on his feet every time. You'll see!" a masculine voice replied.

Manning laughed. Emma gave him a questioning look.

"Not gypsies," he explained. "My crew."

"Birkin, you've gone and got us lost!" shouted a new male voice.

"No, I 'aven't. Meadowcross Cottage, they said," the first man retorted, loud enough to be heard in the next county. "That's the meadow, ain't it? So this be the place."

"Mutton-brain! Ye couldn't find your arse with both hands!" said the second male voice.

Manning smiled wryly. "They're a villainous rabble but they're harmless. They take their orders from me."

She nodded and hurried to the door. She had just opened it when the wagon pulled up in front of the cottage. What had sounded like a mob turned out to be three men and a woman. A lanky, red-haired man held the reins, with a thin young man with an anxious expression beside him. Behind them sat a most interesting pair: a buxom, dark-haired woman in a red shawl and a burly man, also dark-haired but sporting an eye-patch. They continued to argue about whether they had found the right place.

"Quiet, please." She used her best schoolmistress voice. "There is an invalid here."

All four stopped to stare at her.

"We were told Captain Manning'd been brought to Meadowcross Cottage," said the man with the eye-patch, scowling. "This be it?"

She nodded, noting the use of Manning's military title. "Yes, he is here. I am Miss Westfield. Miss Grimshaw, the vicar's sister, and I have been taking care of him."

"In the village they told us he's at death's door. I'm trusting it ain't so?" His voice was rough with worry.

"Not at all," she said reassuringly. "He sustained a severe blow to his head and his ankle is sprained, but the surgeon is satisfied with his progress."

"Thank ye, Miss!" He and the man holding the reins both gave the woman I-told-you-so looks before turning their attention back to Emma.

"May we see him, Miss?" asked the man with the eye-patch.

"Of course. Only remember that the surgeon said Mr. Manning is to be kept very quiet. His head still pains him and he cannot bear loud noises."

The man nodded, climbed out of the wagon and gave a hand to the woman. Then he made Emma a clumsy bow. "Lund's the name, Miss. Bob Lund. And this ere's Sancha."

The woman glared at him.

"Sancha López Romero," he amended in a grudging tone.

"I am delighted to meet you," said Emma, using as friendly a tone as she could, though wishing she knew the correct form of address expected by Spanish ladies.

"And I you." Sancha lifted her chin and scrutinized Emma. Beneath her shawl, she wore a tight bodice that set off her ample bosom and small waist; a voluminous skirt spread over womanly hips. She looked exotic and proud. Was Sancha Manning's mistress? It would account for the challenging look.

Not that it mattered to her.

"And this is Will Reed. He's the Captain's bâtman, er, valet, that is," Lund continued, waving toward the nervous looking young man who had just jumped down from the box. He gave her a jerky bow before going to the horses' heads.

Meanwhile, the red-haired man climbed more slowly down from the wagon. A moment later Emma saw that he had one wooden leg.

Definitely soldiers. Waterloo veterans, she guessed.

"And this here's Jack Birkin," Lund continued the introductions.

She summoned a smile. "Please follow me. Your captain is sitting with my younger brother."

All except Reed joined her. "I'll stay and mind the horses," he said gruffly.

She led the group into the parlor, but they remained in a group just inside the screen, shuffling their feet and looking anxiously toward Manning.

"Why so hangdog?" he asked, laughing. "One would think you'd come to a funeral! Come in!"

In a rush, they ran towards the bed. Sancha was the first to reach him. She cast herself on Manning's chest, crying "*Capitán!*" Emma gritted her teeth.

"Now, Sancha, give over!" said Lund. "Remember the poor Captain's been hurt." He pulled her off.

Sancha did not fight him, but her eyes flashed as she looked toward Manning. "I told you bad things would come of that flight, did I not? But you did not believe me!"

"I beg your pardon for ever having doubted you," said Manning, smiling.

"*Idiota!* You might have been killed."

"But I was not," Manning said. "The surgeon says I shall be right as rain in another week or two."

"What went wrong, Captain? Was it the wind that gave you trouble?" Birkin asked.

"The valve stuck," Manning replied. "I don't know why."

"I checked it before the ascension. Reed checked it, too," said Birkin, shaking his head. "But they're tricky things, valves. Rather like women."

Sancha glared at him.

"We'll have to look at it," said Manning. "Alcyone's been taken to—ah, good morning, Miss Grimshaw."

Emma turned to see Miss Grimshaw next to the screen, her cap askew as if she'd donned it in a hurry.

"Good morning, Mr. Manning," Miss Grimshaw said, trying not to stare at the newcomers.

As Manning introduced his crew to her, Miss Grimshaw glanced over toward Emma, flashing the silent question that had been plaguing Emma since their arrival. What were they to do with all these people?

"There's an inn in the village, am I right?" Manning asked, as if reading her thoughts.

"Yes, the Hare and Hounds," she replied.

"You can put up there," he said, addressing his crew. "Then go see Sir George Chesmore at Chesmore Manor. He's got Alcyone in his carriage house." They nodded. "Is Reed here?"

"Out with the horses," Lund replied.

"Well, have him come back here once you're settled. He can relieve Miss Westfield and Miss Grimshaw of their nursing duties. Besides, I need a shave."

They took their leave soon after, Sancha giving Emma a dismissive look before she flounced out.

Manning closed his eyes briefly, as if the scene had taken a toll on him. But when he reopened them he was smiling. No doubt he was glad to see his crew—and his mistress, Emma thought caustically. It was just as well she'd no longer have to sit up with him. If she got some decent sleep, she'd regain her sanity.

She'd be wise enough not to care if another woman threw herself onto him.

"Do they—your crew—ever get to fly, Mr. Manning? Or should I call you Captain now?" Kit asked, breaking in on Emma's jumbled thoughts.

"It's no matter, lad. I've sold out; it's just a habit with my men to call me 'Captain'. And yes, they take it in turns to go up with me."

"How lucky they are," Kit breathed. Then he colored up. "I mean, I should have said . . ."

"Missing an eye and a leg isn't so lucky," Manning said. "But in truth, they are more fortunate than many."

Fortunate to have survived, Emma thought. And to have an occupation. Too many common soldiers now begged on the streets. She could not help but esteem Manning for giving them employment. No wonder they were so devoted to him.

"They must be very brave and strong," said Kit. He glanced down at his leg and Emma wondered if he was thinking about Birkin's wooden one.

She cleared her throat. "Miss Grimshaw, perhaps you could take Kit out into the garden for an airing? I should like to work some more on my writing this morning."

The older woman nodded and wheeled Kit out, leaving Emma alone with Manning. A sudden awkwardness came over her; she'd acted on impulse, sending Kit away, not realizing it would look as if she wanted a tête-à-tête with Manning. She went to her desk and started sorting her papers, hoping a show of diligence would keep him from speaking. It did not.

"Is something troubling you?" he asked before she could begin her work.

She raised her eyebrows. "Not at all. I merely have a great deal of work to do."

"Do you dislike soldiers?" he asked, undaunted.

"Not at all."

"Does the sight of missing eyes and limbs offend you?" His tone was teasing yet she sensed steel beneath it.

"Of course not! I am only concerned that their presence might excite Kit. They might make him think he can do things he should not."

"Do you think it would harm him to try?"

"You don't understand," she said. "We dare not take any risks. Kit has a weak heart, like his father."

"I am sorry. I've no wish for the boy to come to harm."

"He's becoming too fond of you," she blurted out. "Making a hero of you."

"Would you rather separate us?"

"I cannot. He'd be even more upset. But please, do not fill his head with ideas! Within a week or so, you'll be able to get up from that sofa and walk out of this cottage. Kit will never be able to do that. Have you thought how he'll feel then?"

He paused for a moment. "Perhaps he'll miss me. Will you?" He regarded her quizzically, the rogue on her sofa with his teasing ways and his Spanish mistress.

She turned away, blinking back a foolish dampness in her eyes. "Not a bit."

Chapter Eight

37. The behavior of female blackbirds in fighting over their territories could prove a bad example to readers of the weaker sex.

Emma gritted her teeth, but the recurring image of Sancha flinging herself onto Manning made it difficult to concentrate. Shaking her head, she buckled down to reword the offending passage.

A barely audible knock on the door brought her to her feet. She hurried to the entrance and opened the door to Manning's servant, Reed.

"How is he?" he asked in a low voice. He looked as if he'd not had a wink for days. She knew the feeling.

"Resting peacefully," she said.

"Is it not wrong for him to sleep so much?"

"The surgeon says it is not unusual in such cases. Come in. I don't know how soon he will wake. Would you like something to eat?"

Reed swallowed then shook his head. "I would like to sit with him, please."

She led him into the parlor, where he stood for a moment just staring at his master. He seemed so ... distraught.

"Pray sit down," she said kindly.

He sat on the edge of the chair closest to the sofa.

"Shall I make some tea? I am longing for a cup myself."

Reed hesitated, then gave a quick nod before turning his hollow-eyed gaze back to Manning. She retired to the kitchen and put on the kettle, thinking about Reed's strange behavior. When the tea was ready, she returned to the parlor and found him in the same position, his lips moving as if in silent prayer. She beckoned him to follow her back into the kitchen.

She glanced outside and saw that Becky and Kit were out in the garden. All was well enough there. She handed Reed a cup. Seeing his shaking hands, she smiled. "Please do not fret. We will hear the captain if he wakes."

Reed nodded. "Thank you, Miss."

"Have you been with him long?" she asked.

"N-no, just a month or so."

Only a month and already he was so devoted to Manning?

Reed swallowed some tea, then stared moodily into his cup before continuing. "What you do not know is how we met. I was lying drunk outside an inn, singing a song we used to sing in the 95th. He recognized it and questioned me. As soon as he'd learned I'd been an officer's bâtman, he offered me a position."

He let out a sound like a groan or a laugh, filled with self-loathing.

"Many soldiers took to drink after Waterloo," she said gently. "It is understandable."

"My brother died there."

So many losses ... Her heart warmed to the poor young man. "I am sorry," she said, wishing she could think of something better to say.

They drank their tea in silence for a few moments, then Reed set his cup down. "Miss, are you certain Captain Manning will recover?"

"Quite certain."

"Do you think he will fly again?"

"He says he will. He talked of ascending at Greenwich and other fairs." She clasped the handle of her cup, willing the image of his horrific crash in the meadow out of her mind.

Her dismay was mirrored in Reed's face. Of all the soldiers in Manning's crew, he seemed the only one to recognize the danger.

Then they heard a creaking from the direction of the parlor. Manning must have woken up again. Reed went out of the kitchen ahead of Emma, but stopped dead at the threshold.

Manning grinned. "Ah, Reed! Here to make me look like a gentleman again, I see. Come here, you look as if you'd seen a ghost! Didn't they tell you I was out of danger?"

"I—I'm sorry, sir. But I cannot forget . . . we heard reports that you'd . . ."

"Serves you right for listening to rumors. I'm only a bit battered and in need of a shave."

Reed bowed and went to the valise he'd set down near the sofa.

Emma went to her desk and began to gather her materials, thinking to take them into the kitchen with her. Manning interrupted her. "There's no need for you to leave, Miss Westfield. Reed is only planning to shave me today. Though perhaps tomorrow I might beg the luxury of a bath?"

His eyes glinted wickedly. Emma glared at him.

She returned to her work as Reed went to fetch water, but she was uncomfortably aware that Manning was watching her.

"Do you always stare at ladies when they are at work?" she asked.

"Only when they're as captivating as you are," he said. "But I shall stop if you wish."

With the air of a martyr, he contemplated the ceiling. She tried to return to her work, but neither the habits of birds nor Blodgett's endless moral commentary could occupy her mind.

Reed soon returned. Emma kept her eyes on her papers but could hear him mixing shaving paste and wetting the brush.

"Did you see Alcyone? Has anyone taken a look at the valve?" Manning asked.

Reed's voice quavered. "I'm sorry to tell you, sir, but—but—"

"But what?"

"It's too smashed to tell anything, sir."

"Smashed? How can that be? It would have been the last part to hit the ground, as the balloon deflated."

"I'm sorry, sir. It seems that one of the men bringing her from the meadow to Sir George's carriage house stepped on it. The springs are flattened and one of the clacks is split clear across."

Manning cursed softly.

"I'm so sorry, sir!"

"No use fretting about it. Though I wish we could tell why it failed."

"We—we checked it before the flight, Birkin and I," Reed stuttered. "I promise you we did."

"No one's blaming you."

"Sir, I implore you, do not fly again. It is too dangerous!"

"Nonsense!" Manning replied.

Emma clenched her pen. If he wished to kill himself, what did it mean to her, after all? He'd be gone soon enough, back to his devil-may-care life and his mistress.

"You will not feed him this—this *basura*, fit only for pigs!"

Gil winced as Sancha's strident tones echoed from the entrance to the cottage. She must have intercepted Emma, who'd just gone to fetch him his usual dinner of boiled chicken and toast.

"I am sorry, but the surgeon cautioned us most particularly not to give Captain Manning any strong food or drink."

"Oh, you English, with your bland foods and your tea! No wonder he languishes on the sofa. He shall have some of my *cocido* and you will see how it will strengthen him."

"We must abide by Mr. Hollis's orders. Please take it away."

"Do not snub your pale English nose at me. I made this for him and he shall have it!"

"Do not shout! You will aggravate his headache."

"*Madre de Dios*! Do you wish him to starve?"

"Do you wish to bring on a brain-fever?"

He heard a scuffle. A savory aroma of garlic and peppers wafted toward him and his mouth watered. Sancha's stews were famous, even though she never told anyone exactly what she put into them.

An instant later she appeared from behind the screen, carrying a covered pot. Emma followed, bearing his dinner tray. He should have told her she might as well reason with a hurricane as with Sancha.

"Kind of you to visit, Sancha," he murmured.

"*Pobrecito*!" she crooned. "I have brought you something to give you strength."

"Mr. Hollis expressly forbade you to have anything spicy," Emma warned.

He looked from one angry face to another, unsure whether to duck under his covers or laugh. "Do you really think it would harm me?"

"Mr. Hollis says heating foods could bring on a fever," said Emma, her voice as tight as her ramrod-straight posture.

He sighed, taking in one last sniff of the enticing stew. He doubted it would hurt him, but he hadn't the heart to worry Emma. "I'm sorry, Sancha. I'm afraid we must follow the good surgeon's orders."

"*Ingrato*! I made this especially for you!"

"It smells heavenly. I'm sure the lads will enjoy it."

Sancha glared first at him, then at Emma, then back at him. "You will take the advice of this—this—"

"Sancha," he said, giving her a look that his soldiers rarely saw but always heeded.

Her mouth snapped shut. "Very well, I shall go, then." Lifting her chin, she marched out of the cottage.

He drew a breath of relief. Her anger wouldn't last long. It was more important to appease Emma. He had a shrewd idea of what troubled her, but didn't know whether to be flattered or dismayed.

"I'm afraid this must seem dreadfully bland, if that stew is what you are accustomed to," she said as she set down the tray.

"Not at all, but having two pretty women fight over me lends an additional spice."

She paused in the act of reaching for his dish. "I was not fighting over you!"

The spark of anger in her eyes belied her words. Lud, he was right. She *was* jealous. He couldn't help enjoying it.

"No, of course not. To fight over me would imply you thought me something more than a mere nuisance."

"I do not! If you thought I was ... jealous, you are mistaken. I cannot—I mean, I am ..." She turned away, lifting a hand to her flushed cheek.

"A good nurse," he said. "You've no need to feel jealous, you know."

"Of course not. I have no intention of—of usurping Sancha's place."

"I trust not." He chuckled.

"How dare you laugh?"

"Because I have no interest in Sancha, nor she in me. She fell in love with Lund while we were quartered in her village one winter and has been with him ever since. She refuses to marry a heretic and he refuses to convert, but they are quite devoted to one another. Are you shocked?"

She stood for a moment, facing away from him. "No, of course not. I am sorry. It just ... it seemed ... She is very fond of you."

"Of course she is. She cares for all of us." He paused, deciding just how much to reveal. "She saved our lives after Waterloo."

Emma turned back to him. "She was there? Women were permitted on the battlefield?"

Now he was back on dangerous ground. But having begun, he had to go on. "They were not supposed to come with us at all on that campaign, but that didn't stop Sancha. She was there when Lund dragged me to a cottage where the regiment's wounded were being treated. Later she helped Lund bring Birkin to safety after he'd taken a load of grapeshot in his leg. She held Lund's hand as they cauterized his eye. If she hadn't been around to nurse us in the following months, I doubt any of us would be here to tell the tale."

"I did not know. I am sorry."

"Don't be ashamed. You would have done the same, just like any of the wives or camp-followers who searched for their husbands or sweethearts on the battlefield."

She clasped her hands tightly in front of her. "Like ... Maggie?"

So she remembered. With his refusal of the laudanum, the vivid dreams had ceased. But the memories lingered. But when he looked at Emma's pale face, he knew he was not the only one visited by ghosts.

She looked away. "I am sorry, I should not have said that. You should eat your chicken before it is entirely cold."

She'd been about to say something else. He took a bite, deciding it was best not to think about it. "I can't remember when I've had such delicious boiled chicken."

She laughed. "Better than Sancha's *cocido*?"

"I dare not answer for fear of my life."

She snorted and went back to her writing while he devoured the rest of the chicken and toast. He was getting stronger every day. It was a good thing, for it meant he could leave soon.

What he hadn't expected was the wrench he felt at the prospect.

She looked up and gave him a solemn look. "You are a liar, you know," she said.

"I have a great fondness for boiled chicken!"

She took the empty dish away from him. "No, you are a liar when you say you have no family to speak of."

He tensed. "I don't."

"Oh, but you do. I have met them today." She gathered up the tray and left.

Gil settled back onto his pillow. She was right. His crew was his family. Which was lucky for him, for he was cut out for no other.

E mma hurried out of church, hoping to evade Lady Chesmore and Lydia, who'd been eyeing her throughout the service. Her plans for a speedy escape were frustrated by Miss Grimshaw, who stopped to talk to her brother. An instant later, the two ladies were upon them, skirts rustling and the plumes on their bonnets nodding.

"My dear Emma," cooed Lady Chesmore. "How delightful to see you take a respite from your nursing duties. How is Captain Manning?"

So Lady Chesmore had got wind of his military title.

"He is making satisfactory progress."

"Oh, the poor, poor man!" exclaimed Lydia. "He must require the most careful nursing. You must be so tired, Emma. I so wish I could be there to help you!"

"With the arrival of his valet, Miss Grimshaw and I have very little to do."

"Since he is so much improved, perhaps we may visit him now?" Lady Chesmore ventured.

Miss Grimshaw rejoined them in time to reply. "Mr. Hollis has given strict orders that Captain Manning should be disturbed as little as possible."

"Surely our visit wouldn't be a disturbance!" Lydia protested. "Mr. Hollis, Mr. Hollis!" She waved toward the surgeon, who had just emerged from the church.

Lady Chesmore beckoned him over. "Miss Grimshaw tells us that Captain Manning is still too sickly for visitors. I trust that is not true?"

Mr. Hollis glanced from her to Lydia and smiled indulgently. "Eager to meet the adventurous hero, are we?"

Lydia blushed and averted her face.

"Of course we are," said Lady Chesmore. "You know we are dying for lack of amusement. Our aeronaut is the perfect antidote."

"Well then, I shall call on him tomorrow and if I deem him well enough for company, I shall send word to the Manor," Mr. Hollis suggested. "Will that do?"

Lydia beamed.

"An excellent plan," concurred Lady Chesmore. "I am sure Captain Manning is lucky to be in your care."

"Miss Westfield and Miss Grimshaw deserve most of the credit."

"I daresay, spinsters are the best nurses!" said Lady Chesmore. "After all, they have little else to occupy them."

Emma returned smile for smile. "Now if you excuse us, we spinsters must return to our charges."

"What an abominable woman!" Miss Grimshaw exclaimed as soon as they were out of earshot. "What a fool Sir George was to be caught in her net. And that silly creature, Lydia, mooning over Captain Manning like a perfect wigeon! Pay neither of them any mind, Emma. You are not an old spinster like me. And if you mind my advice, you need not ever be. You are looking very pretty today. Did you notice that agreeable gentleman, Mr. Newhall, who has just taken Ashford Place? He was looking at you with some interest. Or perhaps the Olneys' younger son. Or—"

As they returned to Meadowcross, Emma allowed her thoughts to drift, only nodding now and then out of politeness.

A thrush twittered somewhere in the high hedges around Emma as she walked down the lane toward home. She inhaled deeply, catching the elusive sweet scent of the violets that grew in the hedge's understory. She must find time to gather some for making soap. She'd had two uninterrupted nights' sleep and felt alive again, but restless. Filled with foolish yearnings.

In just a few weeks the nightingales would sing again.

She quickened her pace. As she reached the cottage, Manning's laughter rang out through the open door. Her heart skipped a beat. If she didn't watch herself, she'd end up as silly as Lydia Chesmore.

She stepped into the cottage. Manning was on his feet, supported by Mr. Hollis on one side and his man Reed on the other. Clean-shaven, fully dressed and over six feet tall, he dominated the small parlor. As she came closer, she saw his hair was damp. Reed must have helped him bathe.

"I see you are better today," she said.

"An achievement, isn't it, to totter between two other men?" He looked pleased to be up and about.

"An excellent recovery indeed, considering the degree of your injury," said the surgeon. "You must not be impatient. Your ankle needs time to heal as well as your head."

"It hardly bothers me, I promise. Perhaps tomorrow I could manage with Miss Westfield's support alone."

"Or that of a cane," she suggested coolly.

"Can you believe it, gentlemen? My kind nurse tires of me."

Mr. Hollis chuckled.

"A cane is an excellent idea," said Miss Grimshaw, coming from the direction of the kitchen. "I shall send Becky to fetch my brother's second-best one, if Mr. Hollis approves."

"Very well, but I must impress upon you the importance of avoiding a fall. You may walk, but I implore you not to ride or drive for at least another week."

"I'll be careful. I dare not take any risks, with such faithful dragons guarding me."

To Emma's surprise, Miss Grimshaw beamed at him in a motherly way. "Emma, there is a matter which I must discuss with you. Shall we step into the kitchen?"

She nodded and followed her friend, who sat down by the kitchen table with an air of suppressed excitement. Emma peered out the window, saw that Kit and Becky were in the garden, and rejoined Miss Grimshaw at the table.

"I have the most amazing news, my dear," she began, her eyes bright.

"Let me guess. Sir George's prize sow has given birth? A regiment is going to be quartered at Tichbury?"

"Nothing like that." Miss Grimshaw picked up a paper Emma hadn't noticed before from the table. The single sheet was crossed over in a small, neat hand. "I have a letter from my cousin Charlotte."

"How very pleasant. I trust she is well?"

"Yes, of course. The important thing is, she used to live near Swanham, in Norfolk, and she knows all about Captain Manning's family!"

Emma stiffened. "I cannot think it right for us to pry into his background."

"Rubbish! While he is here and I am your chaperone, it is my duty to learn as much about the young man as I can. And I cannot see the harm in your doing the same. Do you wish to read the letter?"

Emma stared down at the letter Miss Grimshaw held out to her. "I ought not. I am sure I ought not."

"Come, are you not the least bit curious?"

She could not lie to herself. There was no good reason to learn more about Manning. He disturbed her enough already and soon they would go their separate ways. Despite all that, she was intrigued.

"I suppose I *am,* just a tiny bit." And she took the letter.

Chapter Nine

*D*ear *Amelia,*

How surprised I was to learn that you have met Mr. Gilbert Manning! I trust he is making a swift recovery from his injuries.

It has been seven years since I lived near Swanham, but I can tell you what I know from having spoken to Mrs. Wycke, who kept house for the Mannings at Lynnford Abbey.

Lord Manning, whom I believe to be your aeronaut's uncle, succeeded to the barony as a young man. His younger brother James fell in love with a young woman of great beauty but no fortune or connections. His elder brother would not approve the match and since James had no fortune of his own, he sought a commission in the army. It was unfortunate that he was posted to such an unhealthy climate as Jamaica. His poor wife was rash enough to follow him there. Sadly, both succumbed to the yellow fever but by some miracle their young son survived.

The boy was brought home to Lynnford Abbey and lived there for several years, but Lord and Lady Manning found it difficult to manage him. He was always running off or fighting with his cousin. So when Captain Forsythe, one of his father's friends, offered to take the boy on, the Mannings agreed. Captain Forsythe had just transferred to the 74th Regiment and took young Gilbert to India with him.

I know no more of what happened to the boy. Several years ago, I heard from Mrs. Wycke that Lord Manning's son had been killed in a curricle race, leaving Mr. Gilbert in line to inherit. But he never returned to Swanham. How odd of him to give balloon exhibitions! It is an unusual pursuit for a gentleman. Perhaps he does it for sport. One never knows about these young bucks!

The rest of the letter contained only family gossip. Emma straightened up and met Miss Grimshaw's expectant gaze.

"What do you think, Emma?"

"It is all very interesting."

"You don't doubt that our Captain Manning is the same person my cousin wrote of?"

"No. The tale matches everything we already knew of his history. But I fear he will be annoyed to learn we are all gossiping about him. He does not like to speak about his family."

"But you do not realize what this means? Captain Manning stands to inherit a barony and a handsome estate!"

"I fail to see what significance it can have to us."

"You cannot have failed to see how attracted he is to you!"

"You cannot be thinking... it is preposterous!" She laughed.

"Do you not like him?"

"I do like him. But I do not believe he is interested in marriage, nor is he the sort of man I could imagine marrying."

"Surely you don't believe those reports of his wildness? There must have been bad blood between his father and his uncle, but I see no signs of an evil nature in *him*."

"The charms of a barony certainly change your opinion of him!"

"Indeed not," Miss Grimshaw insisted. "Even before I received my cousin's letter, I had come to the conclusion that Captain Manning is a gentleman, who will not take advantage of you. No matter how sorely he is tempted." She winked.

Emma ignored the hint. "He ought to be learning the management of his future estate and getting to know his dependants rather than flying about the country."

"He could become more settled, given the right influence. A lady of good character, of whom he is very fond."

"Please do not be making matches for me. He is only indulging in a little flirtation to pass the time."

"I see the way he looks at you, dear. You are a fool if you do not make a push to secure him!"

Emma shook her head and forced a laugh. "I should make a great fool of myself if I did. Please, I beg you not to even hint at such a thing to him!"

"I would never say anything so tactless," said Miss Grimshaw, getting up from the table and going to the half opened door. "Becky!"

The maidservant appeared quickly at the door. "I was just pulling some weeds, ma'am. Is there aught I can do for you?"

"Please go to the vicarage and bring back Mr. Grimshaw's second best cane."

After Becky had gone back out, Miss Grimshaw turned to Emma, smiling. "At least now Captain Manning may be able to walk out with you. Won't that be pleasant? What is the matter, Emma?"

She smiled ruefully. "I am wondering if Becky overheard us."

"Gracious! I should have been more discreet. Becky! *Becky!*" the older woman shouted several times.

"I am afraid she is gone," said Emma. "You know you cannot keep secrets in a neighborhood like this."

Miss Grimshaw frowned. "Now it will be all over the village, I daresay, and that silly Lydia Chesmore will be setting her cap at him!"

Emma shrugged. "Better she than I."

"Emma dear, why don't you lend Captain Manning your arm for a turn about the garden? It is a lovely evening."

Gil saw the accusing look Emma gave Miss Grimshaw and wondered what was afoot.

"Reed will be back from the inn in an hour," Emma replied. "Surely Captain Manning can wait for his support."

"If you are busy, I can wait," he said.

"Nonsense!" said Miss Grimshaw. "It will be nearly dark by then. Go, while it is still pleasant."

"Yes, Emma, why don't you go out?" Kit chimed in.

Gil glanced at Kit, his eyes narrowing. He wasn't surprised the boy had noticed something between him and Emma—Kit was no fool—but if he hoped it would lead to a lasting connection he was doomed to disappointment.

"You work too hard, Emma," Miss Grimshaw continued. "An outing will do you good."

"Better than wasting the evening on Mr. Blockhead's book!" added Kit.

"You are not to call him that!" Emma protested.

"Very well, I promise not to. But only if you will go take a walk with Captain Manning!"

A gentle wind ruffled the curtains, as if beckoning them outside. Gil sensed Emma was wavering. Despite the inexplicable currents of matchmaking in the air, Gil hoped she would relent. They'd not have many chances to be alone again before he left.

"Very well, then," she said, still reluctant.

But she gave him her arm and he limped out with her. As they passed out of the kitchen into the garden, Gil took a deep breath, inhaling the scents of damp earth and newly planted herbs. The breeze fanned his cheek and brought the fragrance of the bluebells that grew mingled with daffodils around the base of the plane tree at the back of the garden. It was his first time out of the cottage in a week.

Everything was perfect, except for Emma's obvious embarrassment.

"What troubles you, Mistress?" he asked as soon as they'd gotten out of earshot of the kitchen window.

She straightened her shoulders. "There is something I must confess."

"What dire sin have you committed?"

"Not I. It was Miss Grimshaw, but you must excuse her. She did it for the best."

"And what did our dear dragon do?"

"She wrote to her cousin, who used to live in Norfolk, to learn more about you and your family history. Please do not be angry! She meant well."

"I'm not angry. As your chaperone, it is her duty to discover just what sort of rogue I am."

She sighed. "I'm afraid there's more. Her cousin wrote back. I do not know if her information is correct, but she wrote that you are the nephew of a lord and stand in line to inherit."

"That is correct," he said grimly.

"I do not want to pry, but this is not something you wish to be known?"

"It is of no consequence."

"We think Becky may have overheard us. If she did, it will be all over the village by tomorrow. I hope you do not mind too much."

He realized he'd spoken brusquely before. "Will I be besieged by eager young ladies and matchmaking mamas?"

She relaxed. "You would enjoy that, wouldn't you?"

"Not at all. I count on you to protect me."

"I think you are very well able to protect yourself," she said. "You do know that *I* am not so foolish as to think you are looking for a wife?"

"You are far too wise, Mistress Westfield." He hesitated, weighing his next words. "The truth is I'm not as eligible as I might seem."

"I am not on the catch for you, Captain Manning!" she retorted.

Good; she did not pry into details he would rather not share. He smiled. "I am glad of it, for then I may safely continue trying to flirt with you. Your set-downs are good for my soul."

She laughed. A sweet, throaty sound. He wished he could hear it more often. They walked on, arms linked, the awareness

99

of her slender body beside him a pleasant torture. He'd enjoy it while he could. Though he'd had a few brief affairs, not since Maggie had he walked with a woman in such a companionable fashion.

"It must be pleasant not to be cooped up anymore," she said.

"I prefer to be out of doors whenever possible." He gazed ahead, past the stone wall that surrounded the garden, to the sheep pasture and wooded hills beyond, blue-gray against the backdrop of rosy clouds. After a week of restriction, the open sky and the beauty of the rolling hills were a welcome change. He paused to drink them in.

"You are not dizzy, are you?"

He shook his head. "Just taking in the view."

"You must have seen many places more picturesque. I've heard the Pyrenees are magnificent."

"Yes, if one were not freezing from the cold or being scorched black by the sun, one might find them magnificent! I like England best."

"Even though you have not spent much time here?"

"Just a few years in Norfolk, when I was a boy." He bit his lip; he hadn't meant to bring that up. But perhaps she knew that part of his history.

"I've never been there," she said. "It is quite different from Sussex, is it not?"

"Quite different." Memories flooded him: watching swans on the Bure, the windmills used to drain the marshes. Running away from the tutor to trail around after Farmer Colby and his sons. Mrs. Colby feeding him shortcakes ... They would be sowing spring wheat about now, and preparing to send some of the fattest sheep to Smithfield Market. But it was no use dwelling on scenes he'd likely never revisit.

He shook off the mood, looked down at her and grinned. "Don't worry. In truth, *this* is my favorite sort of view."

"Poor man, you have been confined for too long." Her ready blush belied her sharp words.

He loved both. "I knew something was up when Miss Grimshaw threw us together, but I can't find it in me to complain. We'll not have many chances to be alone again."

The sun had slunk lower; the clouds glowed rose and salmon. In silent agreement, they stopped at the far end of the garden to watch. Gil's inner devil pointed out that they were out of sight of the kitchen and the lane. He could take her in his arms and no one would see. The urge took hold of him to kiss her and make her forget whatever unspoken sorrow she harbored within. Despite her staunch disavowal of any interest, he knew she was becoming fond of him.

Perhaps too fond. But he was not cut out for matrimony, as she'd said herself, and she deserved nothing less. Yet if she continued her present path, she'd never know the caress of a lover, the warmth of a shared marriage-bed. What a cruel waste that would be.

He turned to face her, took her hand in his. She stared up at him, eyes deep blue in the evening light. Her breath quickened and he knew she wanted it too, sensed how delicious their kiss would be. Making rash vows—*keep it just a kiss, fool*—he lowered his face to hers.

And she moved back a step, alarm in her face.

He beat a quick retreat. "I'm sorry, Emma. I meant no insult. You know that?"

She briefly touched something under the high neck of her bodice. "I know. But I don't want your kisses. There *is* something else I do wish you could tell me."

It was as if she'd raised an invisible wall between them.

"What is it?"

"Captain Manning, you have seen things ... I can never imagine. At Waterloo ..."

"It's better not to think about it."

A distant rumble sounded. Thunder, or an oncoming carriage?

"I can't help it. I want to know what it was like. You see, I had a ... friend ... who died there."

"I am sorry." He gave her hand a squeeze, while burning inwardly. God, he wished he could embrace her, caress those pretty breasts, kiss her senseless. Anything but talk of war. Of her *friend*.

"His name was Charles Hartley."

Charles Hartley. The name sounded familiar. And then it came to him: Charles was the name she'd spoken as he lay on her sofa that first night, seemingly close to death. Just before she'd kissed him.

"He was in the 95th," she continued. "First battalion. Captain Dryburn's Company."

And his memory cast up not only the name but an image. Of a young second lieutenant, trying to organize the retreat after Dryburn had fallen. Falling in the road with a hole blown through him.

Hell and damnation.

Emma made a small protesting sound; he released his convulsive grip on her hand, murmuring an apology. She pulled away.

"Sorry, I should not have said it. I—" She turned her head. The rumble sounded again: horses' hooves and carriage wheels. A coach drawn by a team of matched bays hove into sight.

"It is Sir George's carriage," she said.

Lydia's head dipped out of a window and back again.

Emma stiffened. "You can stay here, but I must meet them." She met his eyes briefly before turning towards the cottage.

The moment was lost, but Gil had a feeling it would come again.

Emma trembled as she ran into the cottage. What demon had prompted her to ask such questions? Fear of his kiss, of the feelings it revived, the memories ... She'd revealed far too much, told him more than anyone else in

Tichbury could even guess. And to what purpose? His face had turned quite grim upon her questioning and it was her fault, for reminding him of the ordeal that had haunted his dreams not many nights ago.

She reached the kitchen door but had to jump back to avoid a collision with Lydia Chesmore, who burst out, followed by her brother and his wife.

"Mr. Hollis said we could visit you, Captain Manning," Lydia shouted as she ran past Emma, her bonnet ribbons streaming behind her. "We are so happy to see you so much recovered!"

Manning had sat down on the bench. Lydia bounded over and took a seat on one side of him. Lady Manning followed a little more sedately and sat on the other side. By the time Emma reached them, Sir George and the ladies were introducing themselves. She stood quietly by while Manning spoke to them as if nothing had just happened. Perhaps she had imagined the stricken look on his face. Perhaps she ought to just leave them and go back into the cottage. But she saw lines of strain around his eyes and decided to stay, in case the visitors tired him.

"Thank you for allowing my crew to take over your carriage house," he said to Sir George. Emma had heard that his crew had begun repairs to the balloon.

"Happy to be of assistance," said Sir George.

"Of course we are," added Lady Chesmore. "You must know, Captain Manning, that your arrival here has been a great source of amusement in our small circle."

"How thrilling it must be to fly!" exclaimed Lydia. "I should love to try it. Would it not be exciting if you held an ascension here, in Tichbury? Would you take me up with you, Captain Manning?"

"I am sorry but I can make no promises. I am not certain the balloon can be repaired in time," Manning said.

Lydia pouted. "George, tell him he must give an ascension!"

"But Lyddy dear, think of the danger!" Sir George exclaimed.

She tilted her chin. "I would not care a snap of my fingers for it!"

"It would distract the laborers from their work," Sir George added hurriedly, as one casting about for an excuse.

Lydia looked ready to dispute this, but Lady Chesmore forestalled her. "In any case, we must allow Captain Manning time to recover his health before making such requests. Enough talk of balloons! You must know we are all agog to know you better. We hear you hail from Norfolk. Quite the agricultural county, is it not?"

Manning inclined his head. "I could just as easily be said to hail from Jamaica, or India, ma'am."

"How exciting to meet someone so well-traveled," Lydia breathed, edging closer to him. "I cannot wonder that you have taken to the skies. It would be excessively dull to return to England only to take up farming."

Sir George shook his head. "Caring for his land and his dependants is the first duty of any landowner."

Lydia rolled her eyes. "Oh, what a bore you are, George! Please do not be talking of crop rotations, or seed drills and such! You'll give Captain Manning a headache!"

"Yes, let us speak of something more amusing," said Lady Chesmore. "Captain Manning, I am thinking of holding a party once you are fully recovered."

"Let it be a ball!" cried Lydia. "I should dearly love that. George, if we cannot have a balloon ascension, at least let us hold a ball!"

"We shall talk about it later," said Sir George.

"Oh pooh, what is there to discuss?" said Lydia. "You would not be such a monster as to deny us such a little treat?"

Manning half-closed his eyes.

Emma took his cue. "Captain Manning must rest now. Mr. Hollis said he must not tax himself too much," she said quickly, earning an indignant look from Lydia.

"Very well, we must not go against Mr. Hollis's orders," said Sir George. He held out his arm to his wife, who reluctantly rose from her place.

"Can we not stay longer?" Lydia pouted.

But Sir George was adamant and so Emma saw them out. Relief gave way to dread as she realized she must face Manning again. She returned to the garden and found him still sitting on the bench, staring out toward the hills.

He forced a smile as she came up to him. "I suppose my secret is out. Thank you for protecting me, Mistress!"

He rose from the bench, wincing as he did so. But she guessed more was troubling him than just his ankle.

"I am sorry if I gave you pain by asking . . . what I did," she said. "I shan't speak of it again."

"Don't be sorry, Emma. I know you have suffered, too." His voice was rougher than she'd ever heard it.

He looked around, perhaps making sure the Chesmores' carriage was gone, and pulled her close. She stiffened and then relaxed, when he did nothing more than hold her. He seemed to be seeking consolation as much as giving it. How wonderful it felt to be pressed against a man's warm, solid chest! She could not withdraw, not yet. On impulse, she put her arms around him. His expression was sober, but his eyes glowed with a sincere, direct sympathy that brought tears to hers. He pressed her head to his shoulder and they stood, leaning against each other. She relaxed, basking in the shared solace of their embrace. Finally she felt strong enough to look back up at him.

Comfort gave way to something more potent. The kiss hung between them again, like a promise. She drew in another slow breath but it did nothing to calm her. The mildness of the air and the scent of bluebells were a sweet reminder of another spring when she'd felt wild and foolish. Warmth spread like sap through her limbs, urging her to commit new follies.

She withdrew from his embrace. "Let us get back inside, so you may rest."

Her marketing basket weighed down Emma's arm as she approached home the following day. She'd felt uneasy all day, wondering if it had been wise to try to confide in Manning. Certainly it had been wise to evade his kiss—yet that made her uneasy, too.

Peals of laughter echoed down the lane. Curious, she reached the stone wall surrounding her garden and peered over.

Captain Manning and her brother sat together under the tree, surrounded by a group of her pupils, all laughing and scrambling around in the grass. One handed a small red ball to Manning while others brought him blue and yellow ones. He winked at the children and began to juggle. Fascinated, she watched as he succeeded in keeping the three balls aloft for several rounds and then finally lost control of them. With more shouts and laughter, the children raced to find them in the grass.

Kit was beaming.

She looked toward Manning. They had exchanged few words since last night's embrace. Perhaps he sensed, as she did, that they'd come close to a boundary it was safer not to cross. He seemed his usual self now, cheerfully entertaining the children. He had the knack of making people around him happy.

Perhaps it was his way of fending off grief.

He started another round, this time keeping the balls airborne for perhaps half a minute before they all tumbled down again. One bounced her way, pursued by Tom, who stopped in his tracks when he saw her over the wall. Within seconds, all of the other children, including Kit, froze and stared. Manning quirked an eyebrow at her, as if daring her to break up the party.

"That was brilliant!" She smiled broadly until the children relaxed. "Wherever did you learn to juggle, Captain?"

"India. Though I'll admit, I'm out of practice."

"May I try?" Kit ventured.

"Of course," Manning replied. "We'll take it in turns."

As he began to teach the children, Emma came around to the front of the cottage. As she reached the kitchen, she found Becky there, her apron dusted with flour and in the act of removing a batch of gingerbread from the oven.

"I thought you would not mind if I made the children a treat, Miss."

"Quite right, Becky," she replied, breathing in the spicy aroma. "Is Miss Grimshaw here?"

"She went to see her brother, Miss, but said she'd be back in a few hours."

Was it another ploy by Miss Grimshaw to throw her and Manning together? Fortunately, the bevy of children out in the garden was as good as a chaperone.

Emma gathered up the gingerbread and a pitcher of milk and took the tray out into the garden. This time, as the children saw—and smelled—what she brought, they pressed around her eagerly. She set the tray down on the bench and began to serve the children. One hung back. It was Tom, who looked to be holding something behind him.

"Is something amiss?" she asked him.

He came forward reluctantly. "I—I broke one of your daffodils, Miss." He held up the blossom.

She laughed. "Is that all? Don't fret." She took the flower from him and on impulse, tucked it behind her ear.

"Pretty!" said one of the younger girls.

Manning's eyes twinkled wickedly as he gazed at her. She ignored the warmth kindling inside her and busied herself handing out second helpings of gingerbread. She ought not to feel so flattered by his interest, but she couldn't help enjoying it. As she carried the tray back to the cottage, she caught herself humming.

She continued to hum as she helped Becky tidy up, so that she barely heard a carriage pull up, followed by a rap on the door.

"I'll see who it is," she said. Not even another invasion by the Chesmores could ruin this day. Nothing could. Or so she thought until she opened the door and saw the man standing there.

Erasmus Blodgett.

Chapter Ten

The man standing on Emma's doorstep was of average height and slightly plump. He was garbed in sober black and wore an unfashionable, broad-brimmed hat. Not an alarming figure, but one look at him and Emma's day clouded over.

"M-mr. Blodgett, what an—an unexpected pleasure it is to see you here," she stammered.

"I trust I find you and your brother well." His tone was kind but his smallish eyes were sharp with curiosity.

She plucked the flower out of her hair. "Yes, very well. Do come in. My brother is in the garden at present, so we may speak without interruption."

She led him into the parlor, wishing she'd had time to remove the bedclothes from the sofa.

"Pray take the wing chair; it is most comfortable," she said, taking the seat by the desk. "I must apologize for the state of the room; we have had an unexpected guest."

"Yes, I heard that an aeronaut came to grief and you were obliged to receive him here," said Blodgett. "I was quite dismayed. Given his occupation, I fear he cannot be a man of steady character."

"He has done nothing unbefitting a gentleman," she replied, aware she was under close scrutiny. "But you could not have come all the way from Bath just to inquire about him. I can tell you that I am making good progress on the manuscript. If you wish, I can show you the changes I have made so far."

"That will not be necessary. I place complete confidence in your abilities. That is not what brought me here."

"What is it?"

"Dr. Procton has compounded more of your brother's medicine and as I am on my way to London, I thought I would deliver it myself." He withdrew several small bottles with squared-off sides, filled with dark liquid, from his greatcoat pockets and set them upon a side table.

"It is very kind of you to go out of your way for us."

"You know you may always count on me." There was something rather smug about his smile. "And where is your brother?"

"He is outside, with Captain Manning and a few friends."

Outside the children laughed, loud enough to carry all the way into the parlor.

"Are you wise to allow him to associate with other children? He might take an infection from them."

"There is no illness in the village at present," she replied.

"And this aeronaut—I fear he cannot be a good influence."

"The surgeon says he will be able to leave us within a week or so."

"I trust that his presence in your cottage has not given rise to any injurious gossip."

"Miss Grimshaw—the vicar's sister, you know—has come to stay with us while Captain Manning is here."

"I am glad to hear it. May I see your brother? And I suppose I ought to meet this aeronaut, if only to impress upon him that he is in a respectable household."

"That will not be necessary, I assure you. But you are welcome to see Kit if you wish."

She hoped Kit would remember his manners. She also hoped Manning would not try to flirt with her.

He was helping Kit juggle, but he stopped as he saw them approach. The children quieted and Manning rose to his feet. Emma performed the introductions and as she watched them bow, she thought no two men could be more unlike.

"Pray sit down," Blodgett said. "You must not tax yourself after sustaining such a blow to the head."

Manning stayed on his feet. "Thank you, but I am very nearly recovered."

Emma remained standing, so as not to encourage Blodgett to linger.

"Christopher, I am delighted to see you looking so well," he said. "But are you quite certain you ought to be playing with the others?"

"I like juggling," said Kit.

"But my dear child, you must—"

"Look, a butterfly!" Manning interrupted, pointing toward the bole of the tree. "Quick! Someone catch it!"

The children, released from their nervous silence, converged noisily on the tree to hunt the insect.

"When you've got it, bring it to Kit. He'll tell you all about it," Manning advised them.

Emma flashed him a grateful look as the children gathered around Kit's chair.

Blodgett frowned. "My only concern was for the child's wellbeing. Young men with excellent constitutions cannot be expected to understand that others are more delicate."

"I see," said Manning.

"Now I must offer you my wishes for a rapid recovery from your accident, and the wisdom to avoid such dangerous pursuits in the future."

"With such nurses as Miss Westfield and Miss Grimshaw, my recovery is assured. As to wisdom, I'm a hopeless case."

"My dear friend Hannah More believes there is something of blasphemy in the notion of a balloon *ascension*. No feeling person could fail to be concerned about the risk to life and limb. There are things men were never meant to attempt. Besides, it is a frivolous display devoid of moral value."

"You must enlighten me," said Manning, in a voice that was far too earnest. "What other amusements do you find objectionable?"

Emma wished Manning would stop. Even Blodgett might realize he was being baited.

"Gambling, of course, is wholly to be deplored."

Manning nodded gravely. "And dancing?"

"The waltz is certainly to be avoided but even a country dance can produce a certain laxity of virtue. Frivolous diversions can only distract us from our higher purpose."

"Diversions such as juggling?" Manning looked down at the brightly colored balls he still held in his hands as if assessing the moral hazards they embodied. Then with a laugh, he sent them through the air again. "I am sorry, Mr. Blodgett. I find I am hopelessly addicted to the pursuit of pleasure."

Emma glared at him, but he only grinned back.

Blodgett's pale complexion deepened to a dull red. He opened and closed his mouth several times before speaking. "I see I have been wasting my efforts here. You mock that which you do not understand. Good day, Miss Westfield."

She followed Blodgett toward the garden gate. "I am sorry he gave offense."

"I am appalled to think you and your brother are subjected to the pernicious influence of such a scoundrel."

Emma bit back the urge to defend Manning. Blodgett would never understand; Manning was the one who should have known better.

"He will be gone soon. We will take no harm, I assure you, but I am grateful for your concern."

"It gives me great satisfaction to aid the deserving. You may always rely on me to be your friend." As they reached the gate, he took one of her hands and pressed his soft, round fingers around it.

"Thank you." She slipped her hand back out of his grasp as soon as she could.

As Blodgett's carriage rolled away, she breathed a sigh of relief.

That did not mean she was ready to forgive Manning.

Leaning on his cane, Gil limped toward Emma as she returned from the gate. The children were clustered around Kit with a new find, which was just as well. He was ready for a scold from Emma, but he would do it again, to anyone who stole the smile from her face the way Blodgett had. She'd even removed the flower from her hair.

Now she looked magnificent, stalking across the grass towards him like a tigress, her eyes glittering with anger.

"Are you quite determined to ruin everything for us?" she hissed in a low voice as he came to meet her.

"I'll tell you, but let us get out of earshot of the children," he whispered back.

She bit her lip and nodded. They set off together along the southern wall of the garden. When they'd gone far enough, she let loose. "Well? What possessed you to bait poor Mr. Blodgett so? Do you not realize how much my income depends on his good will?"

"Don't tell me you and Kit are happy to see him!"

"He is a good man. Of course I must be happy to see him."

"I've never met anyone with so little sense of humor." As he said the words, he knew he was wrong. The image of Captain Dryburn flashed into his mind; the poor devil had never understood why Gil strove so hard to keep up morale in the regiment with games and jokes and the like.

"Kit and I owe a great deal to Mr. Blodgett. He has done much to help us."

"Yes, and with what motives?"

"What can you possibly mean?"

"It's plain as daylight. He lusts after you. Didn't you know?"

"Rubbish! He prides himself on being married to his charitable works."

He gave her a skeptical look. "So he is too proud of his virtue to act. I'd be careful if I were you. That might change."

She grimaced. "If you must know, there is a rumor that he has been pursuing the daughter of a wealthy philanthropist."

He laughed. "However did you get yourself involved with such a prosy hypocrite?"

She lifted her chin. "Through my father. Though Papa was not one of the Clapham Sect, he sympathized with many of their goals: the abolition of slavery, prison reform, improvements in education."

"I doubt your friend is one of their more exemplary members. Perhaps it was his notion to form a Society for the Suppression of Vice? You're a sore temptation to him, Mistress. *That* I can understand."

Her cheeks flushed. "He's been kind to us and has never asked for anything in return. You have no notion what it was like, after Kit's illness! Papa was dead and I was alone. Mr. Blodgett brought his mother's own physician to examine Kit. I could never have afforded such services, but he paid every one of Dr. Procton's bills!"

"The same Dr. Procton who wants you to wrap your brother in cotton-wool? Do you still believe Kit needs all that coddling, and all those potions?"

She glanced over toward her brother and his friends, a sudden painful yearning in her expression. "He is much improved of late. I am happy to see him with the other children. He has been so self-conscious about his leg; it seems to matter less now. But I can't forget how ill he was. Or how Papa died."

"Are you quite certain that Kit shares the same malady?"

"Dr. Procton says so."

She pulled her shawl more closely around her.

"You are not sure?"

"I cannot afford to seek another opinion."

"Is that why you're slaving over that book of yours?"

"What do you know about my book?"

"Your brother showed me the manuscript. I saw Blodgett's comments. Indecent pheasants? Disorderly blackbirds? What rot!"

"Perhaps," she said dryly. "I am being paid for that rot and if I fail to complete it, I will never be able to take Kit to see another physician. If I cannot earn an independence, we will never be able to remove from Tichbury."

"Leave Tichbury? You've lived here all your lives."

"It carries too many memories." They reached the end of the garden. She leaned against the wall, gazing out over the pasture where he'd crashed barely a week before. Then she spoke again, almost as if to herself. "I hope that when Kit is older, we can remove to Oxford or Cambridge and find a small house or lodging there, so he can pursue his studies. He is quite clever, you know."

"And you?"

The breeze fluttered her shawl, a few stray wisps of hair around her face. But the blush in her cheeks had faded.

"I will write more books and keep house for him."

Would that he could take her in his arms again! He'd show her there was more to life. But he couldn't. Respectability was important to her. And she might not welcome his comfort, if she knew the truth. Like Dryburn, she might blame him for Charles Hartley's death. Yet part of him raged at the prospect of her consigning herself to quiet spinsterhood.

"Is that the life you want?" he challenged her.

"What I want is none of your concern."

She turned on her heel and left him leaning on his cane, still too lame to give chase. She was right. Her problems were none of his business.

For the next few days, the children converged on the cottage after school, while Emma carefully avoided any further private conversation with Manning. But on the third day after Blodgett's visit, she returned home under cloudy skies, to find the cottage unusually silent. In the parlor she found Kit and Miss Grimshaw sitting with Manning. No one looked happy. Manning got up from his seat as she entered, moving with ease but without his usual smile.

"Captain Manning is leaving us!" Kit blurted out before she could say anything.

Her heart turned over. All she could think was that it was too soon; she was not ready for him to go. But she kept her thoughts to herself, sat down near Miss Grimshaw on the sofa and forced a smile. "So Mr. Hollis says you are ready to travel? That is excellent news."

Manning sat back down in the wing chair. "Not precisely. He advises me not to ride or drive for another week. However, now that I can walk with ease, I have accepted the Chesmores' invitation to stay with them at the Manor."

"I see." She clasped her hands in her lap. What could prompt Manning to go where he was clearly being hunted?

"I couldn't ask for better care than I've had here," he said, "but I don't wish to continue to be a burden on your household."

"You're no bother!" said Kit. "I don't want you to go. Tell him he must stay, Emma!"

"I'll visit you every day," Manning said. "It will be just the same, except that Miss Grimshaw may go back to her brother and your sister can have her parlor back."

Emma moistened dry lips. "When are you going?"

"In a few hours, Reed will come to escort me. Hollis insists he go with me, just to be sure I do not fall or swoon on the way, I suppose!"

Miss Grimshaw got up. "Kit, let us go into the garden while we may. I shouldn't be surprised if it rains in another hour."

"It doesn't look like rain yet," Kit protested. But he brightened. "But if it does, then Captain Manning will have to stay another night, won't he?"

"Who can say what will happen, pet? But let us go out while we can."

Emma flushed at this last-ditch ploy to throw her and Manning together. As Miss Grimshaw wheeled Kit out, he moved to take a seat on the sofa beside her.

"I will visit every day," he said.

"Kit will enjoy that."

"It's little enough to repay you for your kindness to me. I'd like to offer you more."

She stiffened.

"I've just received a draft on the bank account of a young gentleman who was foolish enough to bet against my surviving the ascension from Green Park. I've given part of it into Mr. Grimshaw's care on your behalf. Once I'm gone, he'll give it to you so you can take Kit to Bath or London and consult another physician. Mr. Grimshaw promised to send his manservant with you to help you on the journey."

Her mind whirled. She got up from the sofa and went toward the window. His offer was generous and yet so . . . final. A parting gift.

"I did not help you with the expectation of being paid."

"Of course not." His voice sounded close behind her. "Will you take it? I hope you will."

She wrapped her arms around herself. What if she subjected Kit to such a journey and then learned nothing new . . . or even received a more serious prognosis? Yet a new physician might offer them hope. She could not refuse.

"I will," she said, her voice breaking. "Thank you for all your kindness."

"It's nothing," he said harshly. "Nothing compared to what I owe you."

She turned around and was shocked to see his grim expression.

It changed to a wry smile. "So it ends, Mistress. I hope you are not *too* happy to be rid of me."

She blinked, fighting a rush of tears.

"I shall miss you," he said.

"You will have other ladies to console you."

"Jealous, are you?"

"Not a bit. I am only delighted to have my parlor back."

"Shrew! So cruel, when you know I'll be pining for you."

She couldn't bear any more. "Save your silly speeches! I don't need any more of your pity."

His eyes narrowed. "You think I've been flirting with you out of *pity*?"

He took a step toward her, more outraged than she'd ever seen him. She backed away. "I think you feel sorry for me, for my situation. While I do not think you find me ... unattractive, I—"

She broke off, finding herself with her back against the wall and Manning just inches away. He glanced around, took her hands and pressed her against the wall.

"What are you doing?" she asked, heart racing.

"Showing you just how much I *pity* you."

He kissed her, gently at first. Dear heaven, it was sweet, the intimate taste of lips, the press of bodies together. Sweet, familiar and yet different somehow ... Was she disloyal to allow it? Yet she did allow it, a hungry ache spreading through her. *Just a little more ...*

His tongue explored her mouth, a sensation that was unfamiliar and shocking. He released one of her hands and began to caress her waist, then slid his hand up slowly to cup her breast. She gasped in surprise. No one had ever touched her there. Undeterred, he circled his thumb, seeking her nipple through the protection of cotton gown, stays and shift, another new and shocking sensation. Her nipple strained against her stays; heat spread through her core. She longed for a more direct touch, skin to skin.

She ought to stop him. She ought not to behave like a lonely spinster desperate for any touch, any crumb of affection. But the traitorous voice within her continued to whisper. *Just a little more ...*

She moaned and put her free hand around him. It felt natural, even right to pull him closer. Natural and right to join in his tongue play, to feel a thrill of power as he groaned and hardened against her belly. *Just a little more ...*

Then he broke the kiss and took a step back. His breath echoed in the quiet room. She sagged against the wall, flushed and breathless, bereft of the ability to speak or even stand on her own.

She was mortified by her weakness.

His voice was so rough she barely recognized it. "Now do you understand why I must leave you?"

She could only nod.

Chapter Eleven

Emma did not see Manning for several days. His visits to Kit were carefully timed to end well before she returned from the village school. She was glad of it, for every time she thought of their kiss, she was shocked by her own behavior. She'd only thought briefly of Charles before losing herself to wanton pleasure. If she were wise, she'd try to forget all about it.

But she was not wise.

When she returned home on the third day, she found Manning sitting in the parlor with Kit. A guilty blush stole over her as she inquired after his health. As he replied, a glimmer in his eyes betrayed that he, too, was thinking of their kiss.

At least Kit seemed unaware. "Emma, Captain Manning is going to hold a balloon ascension. Here! Next Saturday, if the weather is clear!"

Emma sat down, feeling off balance. A flight . . . had Lydia persuaded him to it? How could he risk his life again so soon? *Mad Manning*. That's what she'd heard his men call him, chatting outside the blacksmith's. An apt name.

"May I go up with him, Emma? May I?" Kit continued.

"You? Go up with him?" she asked blankly. She met Manning's eyes and realized he must have invited Kit. Without consulting her!

"It is just a tethered balloon ascension," he said, with a wary look. "Much safer than a free flight."

"Yes, it's perfectly safe," said Kit. "Everyone is going to do it. May I, Emma? Please?"

Emma clenched her hands, forced a lid down on her anger. "Kit dear, I am not convinced it would be safe."

"We would only go up if the weather is perfect," Manning offered. "My crew will haul down the balloon at the slightest sign of a problem."

"See, Emma? It will be all right," Kit said, eyes wide and pleading.

She felt like an ogre. "Dr. Procton would disapprove."

"That prosy fool! He's just like Mr. Blockhead. How can you be in league with him, Emma? You know I'm stronger now. You should—"

"We must give your sister time to think about it," Manning interrupted. "Shall we go into the garden and speak privately, Miss Westfield?"

She glared at him. He wouldn't succeed in changing her mind, but she was loath to argue with him in front of Kit, so she nodded.

Having wheeled her brother into the kitchen so Becky could watch him, Emma and Manning stepped out into the garden. He was not such a fool as to offer her his arm.

"Forgive me for not having asked you first," he said as soon as they were out of earshot of the kitchen window.

"How *could* you raise Kit's hopes so?"

"He'd already heard about the ascension. When he asked me, all I could do was say it was your decision. But I would very much like to take *both* of you up with me."

"I have no desire to fly with you." She caught the look in his eye. "Or do anything else with you, for that matter!"

"You slay me, Mistress," he said with a mournful look, trying to cajole her.

She glared at him.

"A tethered ascent on a calm day is nothing like a free flight, where the landing is the most dangerous part."

"Of which we have ample proof! No, I can't trust you where safety is concerned. I don't even know how the altitude would affect Kit's heart."

"We won't go above a few hundred feet," he persisted.

"My mind is made up. You may kill yourself if you wish, but I can't risk Kit!"

"Will you at least come to watch? It will be quite the spectacle."

"So you can try once again to coax us into flying? How will Kit feel, seeing others go up when he cannot?"

"I was hoping you might both enjoy it!" A hint of anger tinged his voice, startling her.

"Thank you, but I intend to keep us both safely on the ground!"

His jaw tightened. "So Miss Grimshaw was right."

"What do you mean?"

"She told me you never accepted any invitations. Is it true?"

"I cannot see how it is any of your business."

"Except that I . . . like you. And I like Kit. You're both in danger of forgetting how to enjoy yourselves. Someday you'll regret the opportunities you allowed to pass by. Think about it, Emma."

The caress in his voice tugged at her. She turned away and kept her voice cold. "I made the mistake of letting you kiss me, but I have not given you leave to use my name."

He came closer. She felt his breath on her cheek and turned to look at him. His eyes were glittering, his mouth inches away. For a few heartbeats, a new kiss hovered between them.

Then he straightened. "Then I bid you good-day, *Miss Westfield*." He strode off toward the garden gate, whistling as if he hadn't a care in the world.

Damn him.

Emma made several rounds of the garden before she felt calm enough to tell Kit her decision. He said nothing, but looked away so she couldn't see his tears. He did not speak to her the rest of the day. She endured the silence, though it felt like a dark weight pressing upon her. He was all she had.

As she picked him up to carry him upstairs, Kit put his arms around her neck. "I'm sorry, Emma," he said gruffly. "I shouldn't have been such a baby. I should know I can't do what everyone else can."

She held him close, feeling the dark weight lessen. But as she carried him upstairs, her muscles strained and worry gnawed her. He was growing, which was a good thing, but what would she do when she couldn't carry him by herself?

As she set him down on the bed and brought him his nightclothes, he asked, "Are you angry with Captain Manning?"

There was no way to explain her feelings to a child. "I was, but now I know he meant well."

"Do you think he'll visit again?"

"I'm sure he will." She would make it happen, whatever it took.

Kit pulled his nightshirt over his head. "Emma?"

"Yes?"

"I wish—I wish I could at least be there to watch them fill the balloon."

He sounded so wistful, her brother who used to shrink from crowds, not wanting to be stared at, mocked or pitied. Now he wanted to go. He looked up at her with bright eyes. He knew she was wavering; he always did.

She raised her hands in a helpless gesture. "Very well then, we shall go."

"But how will I get there?"

"I'll manage it somehow, dearest. I promise."

The doors to the carriage house were opened wide, admitting fresh spring air and a stream of sunlight. Gil stared at the wood and metal device in his hands but his thoughts were far from the intricacies of springs and clacks. At the sound of fabric rustling in the doorway, he glanced up warily.

But the female figure silhouetted against the bright sunlight was not Miss Lydia Chesmore. It was Emma and the sight of her in her sober gown and bonnet, an anxious but not unfriendly look on her face, was enough to lift him from the doldrums.

"Emma, what is the matter?" he asked, setting down the valve and coming forward to greet her.

"Nothing," she said, flushing. "I wish to apologize for my rudeness yesterday. I know you meant no harm."

"Don't fret, Mistress! You've had too many troubles." He took her hands and gave them a squeeze, searching her face. There were faint circles under her eyes. "Am I right in thinking there's more?"

"Not a trouble, precisely. But I should like to ask you a favor."

"Come in and tell me about it." He took her to the bench, waited until she sat and then took a spot near her, close but not dangerously so. What he'd give to continue what they'd started with that one kiss ... but he'd already taken things too far.

He wanted them to part as friends.

"Is that the new valve?" she asked, staring at the device on the table as if it were a dangerous creature.

He nodded. "I have just been checking it over."

"Do you think it will work properly?"

"I expect so, but I won't need it for the tethered ascension."

"I hope everything goes well." Her voice sounded tight. Was it anxiety over his safety?

"What can I do for you?" he asked.

"Kit would like to see the balloon filled and watch the ascension. I was too harsh yesterday; I don't think it will harm him to attend."

"Excellent!" His heart lightened; she'd taken at least a small step, his grief-bound schoolmistress who'd forgotten how to enjoy herself.

"But I don't know how—"

"How to convey him here?"

She nodded.

"That's easily solved. I can send one of my men with the wagon. There's plenty of space for Kit's chair and room enough on the box for three."

She let out a sigh. "Thank you! I suppose you are wondering why I did not ask Sir George, but—"

"No need to explain," he said, thinking how awkward it would have been for her to ask for Lady Chesmore's carriage.

She let out another sigh. "Ah, you understand. Thank you again. Not just for this, but everything you have done for Kit."

Her smile was sweet, pricking his guilt. Not for Hartley's death—he could not blame himself for that—but for not telling her what she had asked about Waterloo. What she needed to know, perhaps, about that young man she'd called her "friend". She'd had no one to tell her the details. No one to help her grieve.

He owed her that much, even if she despised him after.

She was on the point of rising to leave, but he took her hand. "No, stay a bit."

She sat back on the very edge of the bench.

"A few days ago you asked me a question, about your . . . friend, Charles Hartley," he said.

"Did you know him?" Her voice was bright. Brittle.

"Not very well. There was not time. But I met him and I was there when he died. Do you want me to tell you about it?"

She looked straight forward, her profile tranquil. "Yes," she whispered. "I want to know everything. What happened . . . how he died . . ."

God, this was going to be harder than writing any letter of condolence to a soldier's bereaved family. But she deserved to know.

"You know Hartley was a second lieutenant in Dryburn's company," he began.

She nodded.

"Dryburn's company and mine were posted around a sandpit on a farm called La Haye Sainte, ahead of the junction of the roads to Brussels and another town, Ohain. There was another company, under Captain Johnston, on the knoll behind us. The farmhouse itself was being defended by a battalion of the King's German Legion, under Major Baring. Together we were to prevent the French from gaining control of the road."

He went on, suffering the images of the flaming house, the echoes of artillery and musket-fire that arose as he spoke. "Baring's fellows were a brave lot, but too few, and they were running out of ammunition. Dryburn, Johnston and I talked of going to their aid, but we didn't have the numbers. We'd have been shot to pieces."

He moistened his lips—God, he could almost taste the smoke—and continued. "The hours wore on. It seemed for every Frenchman we killed three others sprang up in his place. The farmhouse was on fire. We knew Baring and his men couldn't hold out much longer. Dryburn called upon me to join him in a charge to defend the farmhouse."

"So you joined him in the attack?"

Her hand was cold in his grasp; perhaps she'd soon pull it away. "I did not. I tried to stop him. Our men would have been slaughtered, to no purpose."

She said nothing, almost as if she had not heard.

"Our duty was to survive and keep fighting. I don't regret my decision. I only wish I'd knocked Dryburn over the head. Instead, I believed him when he pretended to agree with me. Then he ordered his own men to charge."

"His plan ... did not succeed?"

He shook his head. "Within moments, Dryburn was wounded and several other officers fell. Lieutenant Hartley called for a retreat."

"And that was when he ... fell?"

"Shot through the heart. I'm sorry. All I can say is that it was quick. He did not suffer long." *His last thoughts were probably of you.* But he couldn't say it, so he pressed her hand. It lay still and lifeless in his. "I wish to God I could have prevented it."

She spoke again, in that same unnaturally calm voice. "If things had gone differently, he might have lived?"

"No one believed the attack could succeed."

"I did not mean that. But if—if—"

"If I'd been able to stop Dryburn? Perhaps I should have guessed what he would do. He'd made several blunders during earlier campaigns, trying to prove to everyone that he was worthy of the rank he'd bought, but none so ghastly as this. Afterwards, he insisted that his plan would have succeeded if I had joined him."

"He survived?"

He nodded, remembering his last meeting with Dryburn, in London, some months after the battle. "His wounds continued to pain him, but he was also in disgrace over the needless loss of so many men. He kept blaming me, but perhaps he knew the slaughter was his fault. Last winter, I heard he'd been drowned off the coast of Northumberland, close to his home. His family called it an accident."

She sat quietly for a moment, then spoke again. "I don't blame you for Charles' death. Perhaps he would have been ... killed anyway."

"Many more were killed or wounded before it was over."

She nodded. She'd seen him half-naked. She'd seen the scars.

Then she pulled her hand away and stared blindly at the work table. Her frozen look frightened him. He put an arm around her. Perhaps she'd hate him later, but meanwhile he would do what little he could to comfort her.

"Charles died bravely, trying to save his men." He wished he could say more.

She shivered.

"Are you all right? Do you want some water, or ...?"

"No. Thank you for . . . telling me. Somehow it all seems more real now. I must accustom myself."

He pressed her head to his shoulder. She neither accepted nor resisted. "Brave Emma. Cry if you want to. It can help."

At least she didn't object to his use of her name. She drew in a shuddering breath and he thought she was on the verge of softening into his embrace. Then voices outside pierced the quiet.

"He must be in the carriage-house."

Lady Chesmore. What damnable timing. Emma stirred and Gil had to release her.

"Oh yes, of course!" Lydia said. "Let us tell him the good news at once!" Her voice sounded close by.

Emma blinked and looked toward the doorway.

He got to his feet. "Do you wish me to try to keep them out?" he whispered.

She shook her head "I can manage."

He offered his hand to help her up. Though pale, she had already regained her composure. She was good—too good— at hiding her feelings.

He braced himself to deal with the Chesmores.

Chapter Twelve

"Ah, there you are, Captain Manning!" shrieked Lydia from the doorway. "You would not believe what my dear brother has agreed to. Now that you are fully recovered, we are to have a ball! Is it not the most delightful thing?"

Emma blinked, barely comprehending the shrill stream of Lydia's babble.

Then the girl noticed her. She pouted. "Oh, what are *you* doing here, Emma?"

Her mind froze. Before she could manage a reply, Manning spoke.

"We were just discussing how to convey her brother here for the balloon ascension."

Lydia frowned but Lady Chesmore darted one of her predatory glances at Emma. "What a pleasure it is to see you. Had we known you were interested in coming, *of course* we would have offered our carriage for your poor brother."

"Thank you, ma'am," Emma said. "Captain Manning has offered to send one of his men with the wagon, which will have more room for Kit's wheeled chair." Her voice sounded perfectly normal; amazing how habits of politeness could come to one's rescue.

"How kind of him!" said Lydia, looking not at all pleased as her eyes flicked from Manning to Emma and back again.

Lady Chesmore scrutinized them both; the air in the carriage house felt stuffy. Emma needed to get away from their prying looks as soon as possible.

"Yes, very kind," she echoed. "But now I must leave you. I see you all have much to discuss."

"No, stay a moment, Miss Westfield," Manning said, ignoring her protesting look. "If it is indeed a ball, I'm sure the kind ladies will not wish to exclude you from the invitation list."

The other ladies cast appalled looks at each other. Emma wished she could stop Manning. No doubt he meant well; he couldn't know how many ways a ball could be her undoing.

"I had not imagined you would wish to come, but of course we will send you an invitation," said Lady Chesmore, forcing a smile to her face as Lydia pouted beside her.

"Thank you, but I do not dance anymore."

The other ladies visibly relaxed. "I am sorry to hear that," said Lady Chesmore. "Are you *quite* certain there is nothing that could induce you to change your mind?"

"Nothing. Thank you for your very great kindness. Now I must bid you all a good day."

She curtseyed and left. Once out of the carriage house, she sighed and briefly touched the locket beneath her gown. It was time to think about all that Manning had said, to make peace with it. To rebuild her defenses.

She would take the longest path home.

Gil swirled his glass, watching waves of port wash its sides as he imagined himself dancing with Emma.

Sir George cleared his throat with a loud rasp. Gil braced himself.

"Manning, it's been a pleasure having you here."

"I could not ask for kinder hosts."

Sir George took a sip of his port. "Begging your pardon, I was a bit worried when the ladies persuaded me to invite you.

To be giving balloon exhibitions—it is not what one expects of a gentleman. But I've made inquiries. You're well spoken of in military circles. Quite the hero."

Gil kept his face expressionless.

"Now that you're home, have you no thought of learning the business of your estate? It is not all merely collecting rents, you know."

Sir George's tone was friendly. Gil knew he was a good landlord, up to date in his farming methods, kind and honest with his tenants. He couldn't be angry with the line of questioning, even though he knew what prompted it. Even though it roused a dark anger far older than his acquaintance with the good squire.

"There are reasons why it has not been convenient for me to do so."

"Sorry if I seem to pry, but ..."

"No, it is no secret," he said, keeping his voice level. "My uncle quarreled with my father. He told me he'll not see me at Lynnford Abbey while he is alive."

"But you're his heir! He should make you an allowance, teach you the ropes."

Gil shrugged. It was better than saying he wished to be at Lynnford Abbey as little as his uncle wanted him there.

"Yet you will inherit one day."

"Which may be far distant. My uncle is only in his fifties and has always enjoyed excellent health." There. It was out and Sir George and his family could make what they wished of it.

Sir George frowned and took a large gulp of his port. "Let me be honest with you. My sister has developed quite a fancy for you. Perhaps you've noticed?"

Gil nodded. "Your sister is a very amiable girl, but she is too young for me, even were I in a position to seek a wife." He gulped some port. "I have tried not to encourage her."

Sir George gave him a thoughtful look and then nodded. "Well then, I thank you for your honesty! You are a gentleman. The ladies had this notion in their heads but I agree,

Lyddy is still a giddy young miss." He sighed. "She'll be disappointed."

"She is young. Once I'm gone, she will find a new object for her affections."

"Too true! At least her taste is improving. The last man she fancied herself in love with was a *poet*." Sir George guffawed.

Gil joined politely in his host's laughter, then took another long swallow of the strong, sweet wine. Sir George's talk of marriage had stirred up too many memories. A woman's hair splayed across the pillows, her body curled up against his ... He could picture Emma just so, her lips swollen from kisses, her body languorous, her expression sated and serene.

The devil was that he knew he could satisfy her that way, but not in any other.

"Emma dear, I should like a word with you!" Lady Chesmore sat in her carriage, smiling condescendingly at Emma over the garden wall.

"Of course. Becky will show you in and I shall join you shortly." Reluctantly, Emma got up, wishing she could have been left to her weeding and her thoughts. Manning had given her much to think about yesterday. But if Arabella Chesmore, from her elegant barouche, deigned to smile at the village schoolmistress, on her knees in a cabbage bed, she must want something. Since Emma owed her present position to Sir George, she would probably get it.

While the carriage drove around to the front of the cottage, Emma hurried into the kitchen and stripped off her gardening gloves and apron. She made a face when she saw the mud on the hem of her skirt and then shrugged.

She found Lady Chesmore lounging elegantly in the wing chair, her maid standing nearby with a large package in her hands. She lost no time coming to her point. "Dearest

Emma, perhaps you are wondering why I called. I have come to tell you that Sir George and I have decided that we cannot—simply *cannot*—allow you to refuse our invitation to the ball."

"That is very kind of you, but—"

"Hush! I will hear no more objections." Lady Chesmore raised a gloved hand. "You have been in mourning long enough, my dear. Although you hold the post of schoolmistress, everyone knows you are a gentlewoman of a good family. You must not keep hiding yourself."

Emma blinked. Was Manning behind this? The tale he'd told yesterday had been painful to hear, yet she'd felt comforted. But this was too much. She was not ready for a ball. Not now, perhaps never. "I thank you, but I am content."

Her visitor tilted her head. "No, how can you be? Oh, I can guess why you don't wish to come. You dyed all your dresses black, did you not? I am prepared to repair that problem! Harriet, show Miss Westfield the gown, please."

The maid opened up the outer wrapping of muslin and held out a lustrous silk gown the color of violets.

Emma stared, captivated by the play of light on the shimmering fabric. As a young miss, she'd always worn pale colors, never anything so boldly seductive. The bodice appeared to be quite shockingly low-cut. She felt a sudden rush of longing to let Manning see her in it. She could show him exactly what he was leaving in just a few days . . .

Folly!

"You are very kind, but I could not possibly accept it."

"Rubbish! I cannot wear it any more, not since I learned that I am in a delicate situation." Lady Chesmore tittered and placed a hand on her belly. "And it is far too mature for Lydia, so you positively must have it for your own. Harriet can measure you and make any necessary alterations."

Emma forced a smile. "Please believe me when I say I cannot take it."

A spark of annoyance flared in Lady Chesmore's eyes. "Harriet, do go into the kitchen and sit with Becky."

After her maid had bobbed a curtsey and left the parlor, Lady Chesmore beckoned Emma to a nearby chair, as if she owned the cottage. Which she did, in a sense. Emma submitted, uncomfortable but curious.

"Emma, I had not thought you would be so ungrateful," Lady Chesmore complained.

"I did not mean to be ungrateful. I confess I do not understand why this is important."

"Sir George and I truly feel for you in your lonely situation, but since you are being honest, I will be so as well. We need your help."

"My help?"

Lady Chesmore nodded. "Perhaps you have noticed that our foolish little Lydia has developed quite a *tendre* for Captain Manning. Sir George and I think her too young to be married. However, we cannot convince her of that."

More likely, they had discovered what Manning had told her earlier, that he was not the catch he seemed. Now they wanted *her* to help wean Lydia from him?

"Depend upon it," Lady Chesmore continued, "if she sees him showing a preference for an *older* female, she will realize she is only making a fool of herself."

Nothing could prevent Lydia making a fool of herself, but Emma kept that observation to herself. "And you believe I could be that older female? Is Captain Manning aware of this plan?"

"Of course not! There is no need. He admires you and I am certain he would very much enjoy dancing with you on Saturday. And you, unlike our poor Lyddy, are too clever to mistake his gallantry for anything serious."

"Of course, but—"

"Then it is settled. Harriet can take your measurements, and—"

"I am most sorry to disappoint you," Emma interrupted. "But I don't wish to dance anymore. I cannot accept."

"Cannot? Or won't? You are foolish beyond anything! How many such opportunities will come your way? At our ball there will be other gentlemen, some who might be willing to overlook your lack of fortune. You cannot wish to remain a spinster forever!"

When Emma said nothing, Lady Chesmore rose from her chair, pressing a hand to her belly. "Harriet!"

Her maid popped back into the parlor.

"Let us go. Miss Westfield is not disposed to be measured today." She gave Emma a pointed look. "We will be back tomorrow."

Emma tried to hand the gown to Harriet, but Lady Chesmore interposed herself. "No, keep it, and think about all I have said." She swept out of the room, her maid trailing her, leaving Emma still holding the open package containing that shimmering silk.

Tentatively, she stroked it with the back of one finger and then gave a hopeless laugh. Her hands were too work-roughened to even touch such delicate fabric. She was not the same person she'd once been. If she were wise, she would not repeat that younger Emma's mistakes.

"Lawks! How lovely!" Becky's eyes widened as she caught sight of the gown. "Just the thing for you, Miss."

Emma shook her head. "I can't wear anything so brazen. Please take it back to the Manor on your way home."

"You're not going to the ball? That would be a shame, after Lady Chesmore brought you this fine gown. Harriet said once it was made over, you'd look prettier in it than her mistress! You really should go, Miss. You'd get to dance with Captain Manning."

"I don't wish to go."

Becky stuck out her chin. "Well, I shan't return it until tomorrow, to give you a chance to think about it."

Emma decided to let it pass. She shrugged and went into the kitchen to see Kit.

There was an angry gleam in his eyes. "I heard what you said, Emma. Why won't you go to the ball?"

"I am too old for such things."

"Only two-and-twenty, Miss!" said Becky, coming into the room. "Hardly past your prayers. Why shouldn't you dance? The fine folk at the Manor dance and the rest of us get to dance at harvest time and at fairs. Why shouldn't *you*?"

"Captain Manning will be there," Kit offered. "*He'll* dance with you."

"There will be plenty of ladies for him to dance with."

"But he likes you best!"

Emma just shook her head.

"You do like him, don't you?" Kit asked. "You're not still at outs with him about the balloon ascension?"

"Not at all."

"So you will go?"

Why was everyone conspiring against her? "I don't wish to, dearest."

"You said it was good for me to be with the other children. Isn't it the same for you?"

"It's not the same. I have resp—" She stopped, seeing the stricken look on his face.

"Responsibilities," he finished. "You won't have any fun because of *me*."

She could not explain her reasons. He was too young to understand; she could not tell him what had happened the last time she'd gone to a ball.

"If you won't go, then I don't wish to go to the balloon ascension," he declared.

"But you wanted to go so badly!"

"So? You used to like dancing."

"It's not the same. I don't wish to dance anymore."

"You're just pretending because you're afraid to leave me. But Becky will stay with me, won't you?"

"Of course I would, poppet." Becky patted his head approvingly.

Kit tolerated Becky's caress and turned a pleading gaze on Emma. He was deliberately tugging her heart-strings. She knew it was crushing him to think she denied herself on his account.

She thought again of the violet silk lying on the sofa in the parlor. What harm would it do to wear it, to take a few turns on the dance floor with Manning? It would only be a few dances, after all. It was not as if it would lead to anything else. Manning didn't want to cause a scandal any more than she did. Perhaps this night would be different.

You'll regret the opportunities you let go by . . .

He would think her a coward if she didn't go. This was her chance to show him she was no such thing. He'd seen her sad and wounded. She could show him she was strong and beautiful, too.

She drew in a deep breath. "Very well. I will go."

Becky clapped her hands. Kit shouted "Hurrah!"

She smiled at them both, though she felt as if she had just jumped off a cliff with no idea what sort of landing awaited her.

E mma sat in the bathtub, violet-scented water swirling around her as a fire crackled in the kitchen hearth. She'd hoped a long soak would calm her nerves before the ball. But it was no use; her mind kept circling round all the things that could go wrong.

What if the Hartleys were invited? Could she maintain her composure around them? No one knew of her and Charles' attachment. She was a poor match for him by worldly standards, so they'd agreed to keep it a secret until he'd earned his father's respect. She lifted her chin. It would remain a secret forever now.

Was she betraying Charles' memory by going? She thought he would not wish her to be forever mourning. But what would he think if he knew she'd allowed Manning to kiss her? How foolishly she looked forward to dancing with him?

She was not so stupid as to think they were anything but friends. Not even that, for he was leaving soon and made no hint he'd ever visit again. Whether he really was not in a position to marry or just wished to pursue his daredevil occupation did not matter. There was nothing between them other than a fleeting passion. It would pass, but she would enjoy it for what it was.

A pleasant diversion.

"Are you ready to get out, Miss?" Becky called from the parlor.

"Yes," she replied and climbed out. Despite the fire, the air felt cool against her skin. Her nipples tightened as she reached out for the towel hanging nearby. Her pulse beat with the memory of how Manning had touched her breast the day he'd left the cottage. The day he'd kissed her. Quickly, she wrapped herself up, uncomfortably aware of a tingling, an expectancy in her body.

"What time is it, Becky?" she asked.

"About seven, Miss," said Becky, coming into the kitchen.

The Chesmores had arranged for their carriage to fetch her at eight. There should be enough time for her to prepare. She went upstairs and allowed Becky to help her into her best chemise and lace her into stays and petticoat. As Emma pulled on her one pair of silk stockings, a lump came to her throat. She hadn't worn them in nearly two years, but the glide of silk over her leg brought back such memories . . .

"Is something wrong, Miss?"

She shook her head and briskly tied her garter, then pulled on the other stocking. She got to her feet and stood quietly as Becky lowered the gown over her head, its silken folds settling around her with a swish, and shivered as Becky fastened the cords inside the bodice to fit it snugly around her bosom.

"It fits you a treat, Miss," said Becky.

Emma studied what she could see of herself in the small, spotted mirror over her dressing-table. The altered dress did fit well, but she grimaced as she caught sight of her muscular arms, revealed by the short sleeves of the gown, a reminder of how the years had changed her.

She'd grown stronger, she reminded herself. And wise enough not to repeat earlier mistakes.

"Where are my gloves, Becky?"

Becky handed her the long evening gloves, resurrected from wrappings of silver paper along with her stockings. After pulling them on, Emma looked back in the mirror and shifted to get a more complete image of herself. Somehow, covering her arms made her more conscious of her décolletage, which dipped to a fashionable low both front and back. The sleeves were cut wide on the shoulders, seemingly ready to slip off at a touch. She'd never worn anything so revealing. What would Manning make of it?

He would like it very much, she guessed. A tender, sweet pleasure, almost a pain twisted deep inside her as she remembered the feel of his lips, his hands . . .

That was a line they would not cross again. She had better stop thinking about it.

Tonight, she would maintain her composure. She would smile and dance and enjoy herself and make sure Gilbert Manning never forgot his last evening with her.

"Hurry, Miss. The carriage will be coming soon!"

"Yes, of course." She seated herself at the dressing table and Becky arranged her hair, coaxing damp ringlets to curl around her face.

"There, Miss! You'd best get downstairs now."

They heard a carriage come down the lane; the coachman called out.

Emma took one last look at herself in the mirror. Her cheeks were flushed, her eyes bright. A thrill went through her as she imagined Manning's reaction to her transformation. *Folly*.

Could she really do this without making a fool of herself?

"Miss, the carriage is here!"

Instead of going, she could send a note with her regrets, saying she'd fallen suddenly ill.

But that would be craven. She had to go, if only to show Manning he meant no more to her than she meant to him.

"Not yet. I need something." She opened her jewelry box, pulled out her locket and put it on.

"Well, you ought to have diamonds, but it is quite nice," said Becky. "Is it gold?"

Emma merely smiled. It was pinchbeck, the sort of trinket a younger son on a modest allowance could afford. Its value lay in the memories it held. Perhaps she would put it away tomorrow, with her other keepsakes. Tonight, it would serve as a reminder not to take matters too far with Manning.

"Emma! You look rather pretty," Kit pronounced as soon as she arrived in the parlor.

"High praise from a brother!" She laughed, feeling as if she'd drunk three glasses of wine.

She put on her cloak, bade her brother and her maid good-bye, then headed out toward the carriage and Heaven knew what else.

Chapter Thirteen

Gil secretly watched the entrance as he stood in the receiving line with the Chesmores. Ever since he'd got word that Emma planned to come, he'd been wondering what had changed her mind. He hoped local society would welcome her back, that she wouldn't be a wallflower. He'd do all he could to help her enjoy herself.

He was going to miss her damnably.

"You look so handsome this evening, Captain!" Lydia cooed beside him. "But I so wish you could have worn your regimentals!"

Dodging Lydia's advances was one thing he would not miss. "Now that I have sold out, it would be improper of me to do so," he replied.

"No matter! You are still by far the handsomest gentleman here, even with the militia officers coming! Captain Manning, you—"

She broke off, staring toward the entrance as the butler intoned "Miss Westfield."

The buzz of conversation in the hall quieted. Gil caught his breath as Emma walked toward the receiving line. There was a shy, doubtful look on her heart-shaped face, but her eyes glowed blue-violet, catching the sheen of her gown. Her hair was elegantly tousled. She wore a glittering pendant that flashed in the candlelight with every breath, drawing his eyes to the creamy swells of her breasts, half revealed by a deep neckline. Her sleeves sat low on her shoulders, ready to slip off at a touch.

And he wanted to make love to her right there.

Her expression brightened as she curtseyed, giving him an even naughtier view of her décolletage. "Do you not recognize me, Captain Manning?" she asked, her voice husky and tinged with humor.

He closed his mouth and made a desperate effort to recover. "How could I not? I see I was right to want to see you out of your blacks."

And now he wanted to see her out of anything at all.

Then Lydia let out a high-pitched giggle. "Oh, Emma! Arabella's gown looks pretty on you but—those arms! You are quite the Amazon! I vow I'm half-frightened of you!"

Gil reminded himself it was bad form to throttle the host's sister at a ball.

But Emma needed no help from him. Before he could think of a polite set-down for Lydia, Emma tossed her head. "Indeed Lydia, I promise you I have left my long-bow at home." She laughed; it was a sound to drive men mad.

Gil laughed back, suppressing the urge to kiss her right there. No fear she would be a wallflower tonight; he'd better claim some dances before anyone else got sight of her. "Then I need have no fear in asking you for the second country dance. And may I have the honor of taking you into supper?"

"You may." Her smile told him she knew the effect she had upon him, and that she was enjoying it.

"And the first waltz after supper?"

"Greedy, Captain?" She arched her brows, the minx.

"Can you blame me for stealing a march on the others?"

"A clever strategy indeed. I—"

Just then the butler announced the next group of guests. "Lord and Lady Hartley. Mr. Hartley. Miss Hartley."

Emma paled. She murmured an assent, dropped another curtsey and hurried out toward the ballroom.

"What is the matter with *her?*" Lydia asked. "She must be nervous. Poor old thing, I imagine she hasn't been to a ball in years! It was so kind of you to offer to dance with her."

Gil ignored her babbling. He braced himself to speak to the Hartleys about their son. It was never easy to console families of fallen officers, but honor demanded he do his best.

But it was all he could do not to pursue Emma.

Shaken, Emma found an empty seat in the corner of the half empty ballroom. The musicians were busy tuning up; no one among the small groups of guests noticed her. A moment later, Lady Hartley entered with her children, who went to join some friends in one corner. But Lady Hartley herself, diamonds flashing at her ears and throat, headed straight toward her. Emma rose and curtseyed, vowing not to be intimidated. The Hartleys belonged to an adjacent parish, so she'd had little acquaintance with Charles' parents. She did not know much about them, except that Charles feared they would not approve of his interest in a vicar's daughter.

"I am delighted to see you here, Miss Westfield," said Lady Hartley, her expression kinder than Emma had expected. "I was told you've not been out much in society since your father's death."

"I have not, ma'am."

"A very sad thing, your father's passing. My poor Charles did so enjoy their rambles together. He was always telling us about some rare bird or plant they'd found and how much he learned from your father's discourse. I believe you may have accompanied them at times?" Lady Hartley eyed her closely.

"I did, along with my brother Kit." It was not a lie. There was no need to say that her father had often allowed her and Charles to wander off on their own for a bit. Or how Charles

sometimes came to see her in the garden, before the appointed time of his visits, or lingered afterwards when Papa went
to rest after their long walks. But perhaps Lady Hartley had
guessed.

"He was quieter than his older brother. But such a dear
boy ..."

"He was very gentlemanly."

Lady Hartley brushed her eye. "Forgive me, I am becoming melancholy. Captain Manning just spoke to us so kindly
about poor Charles. He fell at Waterloo, or perhaps you had
not heard?"

"I ... had heard, ma'am. I am most sorry for your loss."

"Thank you, Miss Westfield. I am glad he was able to experience so much happiness in visiting you and your papa."

Emma could not think of a reply.

Lady Hartley looked toward her surviving children. "Ah
well, I trust you will enjoy yourself this evening. It is not
good for young people to mourn for too long."

With a friendly nod, she departed. Emma let out a sigh of
relief. She'd kept her composure, although Lady Hartley had
probably guessed the truth.

She fingered her locket, now warm from contact with her
skin, and then let it go. The grief it carried had softened. Lady
Hartley was right; the time for mourning had ended. She might
never have the romance she'd once dreamt of, but that was
no reason to deny herself whatever joys life still held for her.

She remembered how Manning had looked at her. As she
guessed what he'd been thinking, something inside her
twisted, a sweet pleasurable pain. She blushed, wondering if
she glowed like a beacon.

A moment later, she was approached by a young officer
in the scarlet uniform of the local militia. At the same time,
Miss Grimshaw arrived, looking eager to assume the role of
chaperone.

"Lieutenant Smythe, at your service," said the officer,
with a bow to her and Miss Grimshaw. "May I beg the
pleasure of an introduction?"

"Indeed you may." Miss Grimshaw's eyes sparkled as she introduced them.

Lieutenant Smythe asked for the first dance and Emma accepted. More officers came forward, along with several of the Cox brothers, members of a family whose property bordered on the Chesmores' land. They were soon joined by an elegantly dressed gentleman of middle age and medium height, with curly hair and pleasant smile, who introduced himself as Mr. Newhall, the new tenant at Ashford Place.

As the room filled up, Emma promised dances to them all. But her heart beat fastest as Manning entered with his hosts and his eye caught hers. As the musicians played the opening strains of the first dance, her feet began to tap.

O nce again, honor placed demands on Gil. As the guest of honor, he danced the opening dance, an antiquated minuet, with his hostess. Further down the room, Emma danced with a young militia officer, resplendent in gold braid and all the swagger of one who'd never seen action and probably never would.

She looked happy.

More than he could say for himself, stuck dancing the following country dance with a simpering Lydia, while Emma took the hand of a gentleman he'd met in the receiving line but whose name he could not recall, a dandy with pomaded hair and a cravat that must have taken him hours to tie. Gil did not like how the man's eyes lingered on Emma's bosom.

As the dance began, Lydia batted her eyelashes up at him. "It is so dreadful to think you will be gone in a few days. Could you not stay longer?"

"It is time I planned my next ascension."

The movement of the dance separated them briefly. Out of politeness, Gil smiled at the other ladies in their group, but out of the corner of his eye he watched Emma linking arms with several militia officers in turn. Lucky devils.

"Could you not come back and visit us?" Lydia asked at the next opportunity.

"I cannot say." He tried to imagine seeing Emma again, on terms of mere friendliness. He couldn't do it.

"I know! George and Arabella have told you not to come back!" Lydia pouted.

"I assure you they have not."

Emma and the fellow with the wayward eyes were still far down the set. It would be a while before she and her partner progressed back toward him.

Lydia's petulant voice intruded on his thoughts. "Don't let them stop you, I pray! I am not one who cares about uncles and estates and rubbish like that."

He forced his attention back to her. Lord, the chit was more infatuated than he thought. "You are too young to bestow your heart on an old soldier like me."

"I am not too young! And you are not old at all!"

They parted for a moment but Lydia soon resumed the onslaught. "Is there nothing that could induce you stay?" she said, coyly squeezing his hand.

"I am afraid not," he said.

"The gardens are so beautiful in the moonlight. Let us go there, so we may speak freely!"

There was only one woman he'd like to take into the gardens. "That would be improper, Miss Chesmore."

"How noble of you, but I do not care for such silly conventions!"

"But I care about the night air. It might aggravate my . . . gout."

Lydia's mouth gaped as they approached the bottom of the set. She was forced to take the outstretched hands of the dandy while Gil claimed Emma. As they turned together, he breathed in the scent of violets and Emma. She danced well, as he should have expected, rousing fantasies of holding her strong, lithe body in a place more private than a ballroom.

"I hope you appreciate the sacrifices I've made on your account," he murmured.

"What can you possibly mean?"

The quiver of laughter in her voice was nearly his undoing. He nodded toward Lydia. "Removing from your cottage to here, where I must fend off Miss Chesmore's advances, all to preserve your virtue."

The wild color came into her cheeks and he knew he'd made her think of their kiss, just as he was thinking of it. The taste of her lips, her soft breast in his hand, her moan of pleasure . . .

He cleared his throat. "And who is your partner?"

"Mr. Newhall, the new tenant at Ashford Place."

Reluctantly, he released her and rejoined Lydia, poor child. Her sullen silence gave him time to remember that he'd heard that Newhall was considering purchasing Ashford Place. A widower with several children, he was said to be seeking a new mother for them. The man did not look as if he were thinking about his children at the moment.

Gil told himself he ought to be glad for Emma. But it was all he could do to bide his time until the next country dance, the one Emma had promised to him.

Emma withdrew her hand from Mr. Newhall's lingering clasp. Out of the corner of her eye she saw Manning making his way toward them and her pulse quickened.

"My dance, Miss Westfield." Though he smiled, something in his expression caused Mr. Newhall to sketch a speedy bow and promptly disappear.

She took Manning's arm, raising an eyebrow. "If I did not know better, I might imagine you were jealous."

"I am jealous of every other man who dances with you tonight. Can you not see I am in agony?"

She laughed, but felt that foolish thrill in her belly. The light in his eyes was unmistakable. He desired her, though he would do no more than flirt. The temptation rose within her to show him two could play such a game.

The music began. They started the first figure together and she met his eyes boldly, a half smile on her lips. "I did not know my presence would torment you so. Perhaps I should not have come."

"That would have been a great shame," he murmured. "To miss the sight of you in that gown would have been far worse."

She felt the heat rise in her cheeks as he released her. She joined hands with yet another militia officer—those scarlet uniforms were beginning to all look the same!—and exchanged conventional nothings with him until Manning reclaimed her.

"That poor lad!" he said, watching the departing officer. "Another innocent victim of your charms. Have you no remorse?"

"I daresay he will forget me by tomorrow."

"You don't know your own power, Mistress," he said in a lowered voice.

The figures of the dance separated them again and yet several times she caught Manning watching her. When they came together again, he took her hands and led her into another turn.

"And what power is that, Captain Manning?" she asked.

His gaze lingered on her as they completed the figure; she felt it down to her toes. Finally, before relinquishing her again, he said gruffly, "Of making a man forget himself."

She joined hands with the next gentleman in the figure, her body still thrumming with awareness of Manning.

"Is anything amiss?"

George Cox looked puzzled; she must have missed something he said. She mumbled an excuse about the heat of the room. Lud! Manning was addling her wits. This would never do. He might act as if he hungered for her, but she ought not to forget he had no intention of going further. Tonight, they would dance. Tomorrow, he would risk his life in his damned balloon and then he would be gone for good.

"Is all in good order for your ascension?" she asked when they came together again.

He nodded. "Birkin assures us we will have a fine day. He claims to sense inclement weather in his leg. The missing one, I might add! Yet he is rarely wrong."

She laughed. "In any case, I hope all will go well."

"I still wish you would let me take you up."

The earnest note in his voice tugged at her, but she was determined to maintain her composure. "I should warn you not to get your hopes up too high," she said, reverting to her schoolmistress's voice.

"Too high—what a wretched pun! You are lucky you are so beautiful."

"I did not mean that!" she said, laughing. "But flattery will not convince me to fly with you, or allow Kit to do so."

He released her to Mr. Newhall. This time she remembered to be polite and respond amiably to his elegant attempts at flirtation, aware that Manning was watching them even as he danced with the others in the group.

There was a dangerous glint in his eyes as he recaptured her hands. Whatever happened later, tonight she could make him jealous. Tonight he desired her. The tightness of his grasp sent another thrill of nervous pleasure through her.

"Shall I tell you what I really wish," he asked, his husky voice a temptation in itself. "Even though I know it is impossible?"

She succumbed and met his gaze. "Can I stop you?"

"What I really wish is that once the ascension is over and everyone else has gone home . . . that I could take you up with me. Alone."

Again she felt that sweet pulling inside her, the desire for what she ought not to want. Again, she reminded herself that this was no more than a game, that he would leave without a second thought for the spinster schoolmistress he'd flirted with.

She straightened her back and kept her voice matter-of-fact as she replied. "Thank you, Captain Manning, but I prefer to keep my feet on the ground."

od's head! Gil cursed himself, watching Emma revert to her schoolmistress manner. How could he bring back the woman he'd just glimpsed: the Emma who loved to dance, who knew how to flirt? Who enjoyed being kissed?

But no teasing could bring her back; they danced the rest of the set with an awkward sort of consciousness between them. He made light conversation, plagued all the while by the sense that time was running out. He wanted to say goodbye properly, yet for once he did not know how. Well, he knew how he would *like* to say goodbye, but that would be the devil of a way to thank her for all she'd done for him.

As he took her into the supper room, one of the Cox girls invited them to join their table, and any chance he had to speak to Emma was swallowed up in the flow of local gossip. All he could do was bear his part politely, all the while conscious of her every movement, the graceful tilt of her arm as she lifted her champagne glass, the subtle, sensual ripple of her throat as she drank.

He didn't doubt every man at the table felt her power; perhaps it was her destiny to marry one of them. He ought to want that for her. He ought to content himself with what was left to him: a single waltz.

S he shouldn't have had that second glass of champagne, Emma thought as she accepted Manning's arm out of the supper room. She wasn't used to it and she needed her wits about her. As they progressed slowly along in the crush of couples heading back to the ballroom, she glanced at Manning and caught him looking at her. There was no hint of lazy flirtation in his eyes now; only something darker, more ominous.

She stumbled and decided to keep her eyes forward. Even surrounded by others, she was sharply aware of him. Without looking, she knew he still watched her with that intent gaze. He was going to miss her after all. She couldn't doubt it. Maybe she meant something to him, though she would soon become no more than a memory.

They entered the ballroom as the musicians were tuning up; phrases of the waltz they were going to play fluttered through her consciousness, stirring memories of another ball. But memories were not what she wanted.

Manning took her hand, the warmth of his clasp penetrating her glove. His hand was warm against her waist; as she laid her arm over his, he drew her slightly closer. Not enough to be scandalous but enough to make her aware of the short distance that separated them. His expression hadn't changed; if anything, there was a fierce intensity about him, something usually hidden under his carefree gallantry.

They began to dance. She hadn't waltzed in two years, but somehow it was easy as he guided her into each new movement. How quickly it all came back: the surge of desire, the exhilaration, the urgency. The sense of spinning out of control.

Perhaps it was just the champagne.

"I hope I didn't offend you earlier." Manning pitched his voice low enough not to be heard by the other dancers.

"I was not offended."

"The last thing I want to do is hurt you, after all you have done for me."

"What I did for you, I would have done for anyone."

"I know. You deserve every happiness."

He twirled her, brought her back into position and again she felt that urgent awareness of him, the wish that they were in some far more private place. As well that they were not. She wasn't sure she had the strength to resist his kisses or any other ways he might choose to pleasure her . . .

"I am glad you came here and put off your blacks, even though I must endure seeing other men admire you as I do," he said. "Better men than me."

Any more of this damned nobility and she might scream. It seemed he was in no risk of giving way to lust. She ought to be grateful. Instead, something raged inside her. She covered it with a laugh. "So which of these gentlemen would you choose for me?"

"I wish you to choose someone you can love."

"Love? I thought you knew better. I doubt anyone is besotted enough to offer for me in my penniless state, but let me tell you, if someone like Mr. Newhall were to offer for me tomorrow, I would be a fool to refuse!"

"You believe you won't love again, but I promise you—"

Lud! He thought she was still wearing the willow for Charles. Idiot!

"Who are you to tell me what to do? You, who would rather risk killing yourself than mind your duty to your family and your future dependants?"

"You don't know anything about it." he said, in a harsher tone than she'd ever heard from him.

"Of course not! You pry into my life, but will not reveal anything of yourself."

His eyes darkened. "I am sorry, Emma. If my circumstances were different . . ."

"No, don't say it! Don't pretend!"

"Emma . . ."

She couldn't bear the soft intimacy of his voice, the way he'd tightened his grip on her back, pulling her closer. Any more of this and she'd be begging him to stay.

"To hell with you!" She said in a low voice, and wrenched herself out of his arms.

She staggered away, nearly colliding with a surprised pair of dancers. People stared as she crossed the floor. She muttered something about feeling unwell and fled the ballroom.

Chapter Fourteen

A heartbeat later, Gil started after Emma. Several dowagers in turbans moved closer together, perhaps to comment on Emma's abrupt departure. His way blocked, he skidded to a halt. They stared at him with raised brows.

"Miss Westfield has taken ill," he explained. "You must let me pass, so I can make certain she is cared for."

He bowed and darted through the gap between the ladies, hoping he could catch up with Emma before she drew any more attention.

Inwardly seething, he made his way through the crowd and out into the front hall. Sir George and Lady Chesmore were bidding farewell to the Grimshaws. Emma was not with them, so he turned towards the supper room. Perhaps she'd gone there or to the back parlor currently in use as a ladies' retiring room. He cursed silently as he entered the supper room; Lydia and a friend were near the entrance, giggling.

She skipped up to him and cooed, "Oh, Captain Manning, did you save a waltz for me?"

He caught a flash of violet through the window and knew what he had to do. "I am afraid I have a . . . headache," he said. "I must retire if I wish to be in good form for tomorrow's ascension."

"Do you need some laudanum, Captain? I shall—"

"I thank you, no."

He beat a retreat, wishing all the Chesmores to the devil. But when he reached the hall, Sir George and his wife were still there, with a maidservant.

"Miss Westfield said she felt warm from dancing and wished to walk home, ma'am," the maid was saying. "I gave her her cloak. I hope I did right."

Gil stayed in the shadows, listening.

"Did she not ask for a carriage?" Sir George asked.

"She said she did not want to be a bother."

Sir George frowned. "If she is unwell, we should send someone after her."

"Of course not," said Lady Chesmore. "It is nothing, half a mile through the woods. She is probably home by now."

"Oh, very well," Sir George agreed.

As Lady Chesmore directed the maidservant back to the ladies' retiring room, Gil tried to slip by, but she noticed him.

"Is anything amiss, Captain Manning?" Lady Chesmore eyed him sharply.

"Only a slight headache. Everything has been splendid, but I must retire if I'm to fly tomorrow."

"Shall I get you some brandy?" Sir George offered.

"I thank you, but no. I need nothing."

He climbed the stairs, curbing the urge to take them by twos. As soon as he was out of sight, he dashed to his room. It was empty; luckily he'd told Reed not to wait up for him. The window was partly open. He widened the gap and looked out. Someone was moving through the gardens, heading toward the lake.

He swung over the sill. Ivy grew all over the wall; it would serve, he hoped. Holding onto the ledge, he lowered himself, grasping the ivy. It held for a moment, then started to peel away. As he dropped, he grabbed another handful and descended a few more feet, until he was low enough to jump. He fell a few more feet and landed with bent knees. Looking up, he saw the strand of ivy hanging down the wall. He reached up and tucked it behind another strand, then set off toward the shrubbery.

E mma could no longer hear the music or laughter from the ballroom. She'd run through the gardens, but now she walked slowly between the trees that dotted the edge of the lake, toward the wooded path that led home. She longed to be back at the cottage, where she could sit by the fire and berate herself properly. But she dreaded having to deal with Becky's questions. What a fool she'd been!

She stubbed her toe on a root and stumbled. "Damn you!" she cursed the tree, Manning and the entire male sex.

She caught her balance and leaned against the tree, waiting for the throbbing in her toe to subside. Then she stiffened, hearing the crunch of shoes on gravel. Someone was coming through the shrubbery. It was Manning.

She pressed herself against the tree trunk, then cursed the revealing moonlight as he turned and strode briskly across the lawn in her direction.

"Emma?" he called out.

Reluctantly, she stepped out of the shadow of the tree. "I am sorry I made a scene."

He took her hands into a firm clasp. "I told them you were unwell. But why did you run away?"

"I'm tired and I wish to go home."

"So why didn't you ask for the carriage?"

"I want to walk. The moon is bright and it is not far."

She withdrew her hands and turned to go, but he blocked her path. "You're still upset. At least let me go with you."

"Do you think I shall fling myself into the lake if you are not here to stop me?"

"No, but you should not be alone."

"I'm perfectly well."

"No, you're angry. Is it because I am leaving?"

"Of course not."

"You will not miss me?"

She resisted the urge to succumb to the half-joking, half-wistful tone in his voice. "I shall endeavor to survive. Now, if you will please let me by..."

She backed away and found herself against the tree trunk.

He came closer. "I can't let us part this way," he said softly. "Tell me what is wrong."

"Nothing," she said, barely getting the word out.

"Liar," he said in that same soft voice. "If it wasn't me, then who? I didn't think seeing the Hartleys overset you."

"It did not."

"It brought up memories, didn't it? Lady Chesmore said the last time they held a ball here was in the spring, the year of the Waterloo campaign."

"That is right," she said stiffly.

"And you danced with him—with Hartley?"

"I did. We even stole away for a short time into the gardens. No one knew of our attachment. His parents would not have approved. There. I have admitted it. Are you done prying now?"

"So our dance reminded you of that night? Is that what upset you?"

"A little, but I am perfectly well now. I do *not* need company."

"You're lying to me again." With one hand, he lifted her chin.

Her heart raced as he pressed closer, clasping her waist with his other hand. She knew she should try to pull away. He would not force himself on her; he would let her go if she insisted. But when he kissed her, pressing his lips gently against hers, she didn't move. When he kissed her again, her mouth parted. Just a little more, she thought desperately, welcoming his tongue, the faint scrape of his chin against hers, the heat of his breath.

She should have struggled; she should have run. Instead, she allowed him to kiss her, his lips roving from her mouth to her cheek, then to her neck. A nightingale began his liquid song somewhere nearby. She melted against the tree, sighing as Manning pushed open her cloak and began to caress her shoulders. Sweet, sharp memories flooded her.

Desperately, she reached for her locket.

Manning pulled away and stared at her. "What the devil are you doing, Emma?"

"Nothing. I must go."

In one swift movement, he lifted his hands to her neck. She heard a faint snap as he rent the chain apart. She blinked in shock, then caught the movement of his arm as he tossed the locket toward the lake. It spun, catching the moonlight for a few seconds before landing with a small splash.

They stared at each other for a moment; Manning's breath was labored, as if even he was shocked by what he had done.

"Damn you!" She pounded his chest with her fists.

He stood holding her in his arms, impervious to her pummeling. She tried to wrench free of his hold and head for the path that led home, but the tree root that had tripped her before sent them both sprawling onto the turf.

She lay gasping, the wind knocked out of her.

"Emma, are you hurt?" Manning lay beside her, one arm still around her.

She rolled onto her back, her cloak protecting her from the dewy grass. "No. Just ... winded. Leave me ... be!"

Manning bent over her, kissed her gently. "Is that really what you want?"

He untied the laces of her cloak, parted it and kissed her throat.

"Damn you! What ... what are you ... doing?"

"Hoping you'll stay and let me pleasure you."

He nipped ever so gently at her neck, making it difficult for her to catch her breath. "Have you ... gone mad?"

He lifted his head. His face was shadowed; she wished she could see him more clearly.

"I know I'm not—not who you wanted," he said. "But I want to make you happy, at least tonight. I won't do anything to hurt or dishonor you. Will you trust me?"

He kissed her, his tongue curling round hers. It was too lovely, too tempting. Perhaps, just this once . . .

"Yes," she whispered.

She thought she saw the gleam of his smile as he pushed down the sleeves of her gown, then freed her breasts from her bodice. As the cool air touched her skin, she turned her face, hoping the darkness hid her blushes.

Then he leaned in to kiss her breasts, and it was all she could do not to cry out. She tried to hold back her pleasure even as he circled each nipple before taking it into his mouth and gently sucking on it. With each hot breath on her skin, with each cooling breeze, the exquisite pulling sensation inside her grew.

He stopped kissing her breasts and shifted. For a moment, she wondered if that was all he planned to do; it was all she could do not to moan with disappointment. Then he began to pull up her gown and petticoat, cotton and silk whispering along her legs. His hand brushed along her stockings, then he stroked the bare skin above them, causing her to draw in a sharp breath.

"Don't be afraid. I won't hurt you," he murmured.

She held her breath as he stroked upward, finally meeting tender flesh that only she had ever touched before. She'd given up that guilty pleasure two years ago, first because she had felt dead inside and then because she decided it was best to remain numb. Now it all came back to her: the secret fantasies, the dreams of a lover's touch, the sweetness of release. The moans she'd stifled into her pillow.

How could she make such a shocking display of herself with Manning?

She made a half-hearted attempt to roll onto her side, but he held her fast, stroking her folds with a feather-light touch. She yearned for him to touch the sensitive bud of flesh between them; soon, she'd be begging. He moved over her, placing a knee between her legs. She was hopelessly entranced, the turf soft and cool under her cloak, Manning's breath hot on her breasts, his hand a wicked hair's breadth from where she longed to be touched.

She cried out as he flicked a finger across the bud. Devil that he was, he circled it again, increasing his pressure but avoiding the most sensitive spot, bringing her half to tears with frustration. Again, he brushed it and though she tried to remain silent, another moan escaped her. He varied his caresses, so she never knew where or how he would next touch her. It was different than pleasuring herself. Unpredictable. More intense.

He stopped to look down at her. Heat flared through her; she was caught between embarrassment at his frank gaze and the desire for more. He bent his head back down to her breasts, kissing and nipping at them, adding to the torment between her legs. She put her arms around him, but fought the wanton urge to move her hips in time to his caresses. Finally, she gave in, no longer caring what he thought.

It came over her like a flood: sensation so intense she could not keep from crying out and thrashing. Time seemed to stop. She floated, slowly catching her breath. Then something softened inside her, like the loosening of a tight knot. She buried her head in Manning's shoulder and her breaths became deep, gusty sobs.

His arms came around her, while pent-up emotions wracked her body and tears flowed down her cheeks. It seemed as if she would never stop, but finally she relaxed into his embrace, feeling drained and peaceful.

"I am sorry. I do not know what came over me," she said, faintly embarrassed.

He laughed softly, then shifted onto his back, pulling her up to lie against him, her head cradled in the dip of his shoulder. "You needed to cry."

"I suppose I did. Thank you."

"It was . . . my pleasure."

She noticed his breath was nearly as labored as hers. He must have wanted to take his pleasure, too. He could have taken advantage of her aroused state, and he hadn't.

"And thank you for—for—"

"For not yielding to my baser instincts? I was tempted." He cleared his throat and shifted slightly away from her. "So much that I deserve a medal for my self control. No, I ought to be sainted for it. St. Gilbert the Gallant—how does that sound?"

She laughed out loud. Then the nightingale resumed his warbling. His liquid trills enchanted her. She looked up and saw the stars twinkling through gaps in the leafy canopy overhead. She hadn't even seen them before. She stared up in wonder. It was all real, and achingly present and beautiful. A different sort of reality would intrude soon enough, but for now she would allow time to stand still.

She let out a sigh.

Manning stroked her shoulder. "I know life hasn't treated you kindly, Emma. Miss Grimshaw told me your history, how your brother fell ill and you lost your father, not long after Hartley must have departed for the Continent. I can only imagine how alone you must have felt."

She surreptitiously brushed away a few more tears.

"You're one of the bravest women I've known. Listen to me. You deserve to be happy. You will never forget, but you can love again. You will, I promise."

She didn't know how to tell him that her tears were no longer for Charles alone. Truth be told, she grieved for her younger self, the one who'd dreamed of love and romance. The younger self who was still there, inside her, at risk of falling in love with yet another man who would leave her.

All the more reason to take advantage of what time they had left together.

She snuggled deeper into his shoulder, hugged him with the arm that lay across his chest. It felt so comfortable.

She hoped he wouldn't take offense at the request she was about to make.

Chapter Fifteen

"Tell me about Maggie. Please."

"How do you know about Maggie?" Gil wondered if his men had said anything to Emma.

"You spoke her name, when you were waking from a bad dream. It was not long after your accident."

Now he remembered that she'd asked about Maggie before. "Are you sure you wish to hear the tale?"

"If you are willing to tell me." Her voice was soft with the kindness born of grief.

He drew a long breath, and began. "When I first met Maggie, she was the wife of a sergeant in the 74th Highlanders."

"Your old regiment." Her voice held only warm concern, no criticism for his association with a woman not of his own class.

"Yes. I was in the 95th by then but I still had friends in the 74th. I'd gone to dine with some of them while we were encamped on the northern frontier of Portugal, in ... the autumn of 1811. On my way to the officers' mess, I caught Sergeant Ross beating Maggie. Of course, I put a stop to it and reported him to his superiors, but I didn't give it much thought afterwards." He drew another long breath, and continued. "It wasn't until the following spring that we met again. Do you know anything of the storming of Badajoz?"

"Very little."

"The losses were severe." Faces came before him: Cary, Stokes, Croudace. Major O'Hare, who'd said to George Simmons 'A Lieutenant-Colonel, or cold meat in a few hours'.

Afterwards, Gil was promoted to captain, one of many who advanced due to deaths of their fellow officers. But O'Hare ... they'd buried him the next morning.

Emma stroked his arm, bringing him back to the present.

"I was fortunate. I came through with just a ball in my shoulder. I caught a fever and was in a bad way for a time, until Maggie found out and came to nurse me. Ross was killed during the siege, though I didn't know that until later. I barely remembered how we'd met, but Maggie must have cherished the memory. She said she wanted to repay my kindness. At first I was too feverish to protest. I was just happy to have someone caring for me. She was cheerful and pretty and I enjoyed her company. Later, we became lovers. Are you shocked?"

She was slow to answer, but her voice was steady. "I couldn't know what it was like for you. I cannot judge."

"Fellow officers thought it bad form, as she was a sergeant's widow. But it would have been thought stranger had I married her."

"You didn't?"

He shook his head. "God forgive me, no. I didn't think much past the next battle. She followed me through the campaign of 1812 until winter, when we were quartered in a village called Alameida. We stayed there until May. Our cottage was overgrown with ivy and honeysuckle and a nightingale sang to us every night. Until then, we'd been careful not to bring a babe into the world, but it was so pleasant, we ... forgot." He remembered it: the one bright morning he'd been so lost in contentment that caution seemed unnecessary. "In June, Maggie told me she was increasing."

He remembered how she'd looked: blooming yet uncertain of his reaction. "She didn't expect me to marry her. But I told her I would not father a nameless child. It was the eve of the battle of Vittoria, too late to arrange anything, but I vowed to marry her as soon as I could." He looked away.

"What happened?" She cupped his chin and drew his head back so he could see her looking at him, her face solemn and steadfast.

"We were outside a village called Ariñez. The French were defending it with artillery fire: grape and round-shot. Some fool told Maggie I'd been hit. It was a mistake; it was another officer who'd been wounded. She came running, despite orders to stay behind the lines."

He couldn't continue; there was no way he could describe seeing Maggie caught in the cannon-fire.

"I am so sorry." She leaned closer, her body warming his side. She understood.

"No one spoke of it." Except Dryburn, just arrived at the regiment with his newly purchased commission. He'd had the gall to tell him that it was for the best. Gil had punched his lights out for it. Dryburn wanted to call him out, but fellow officers stopped him.

"In August," he continued, "We celebrated the anniversary of our regiment. Two trenches were dug in the ground to create tables of earth and we picnicked there. The sound of our cheers kept the enemy standing at arms the greater part of the night."

"I am glad you had friends with you."

"Brothers, more like," he said. "All the family I've ever had. But what a stupid clunch I was! I should have married Maggie and sent her back to England when I had the chance. I didn't value her as I should have. She was so humble, always acting as if she were the lucky one. I didn't know how happy I'd been until she was gone."

Emma just nestled in the hollow of his shoulder, listening and stroking his arm in quiet sympathy. He tipped his head to look at her. In the moonlight, a tear streaked a silver ribbon down her cheek. He kissed it, tasting the salt on her skin. He wished he could keep basking in her warmth. He wished this night would not end, that the sky would stop revolving mercilessly around them.

She murmured something he could not quite catch.

"What was that?"

More loudly, she said, "Learn, that the present hour alone is man's."

The present hour... To enjoy her soft breathing, to hold her, to watch her face, serene in the moonlight, her hair tumbled over his shoulder. If only he could bury himself inside her and bring her to another peak of pleasure. He'd make love to her all night if it were possible.

But while he'd never regret it, she would.

When he said nothing, she continued, "It's from a play by Samuel Johnson." Her voice was husky, a little nervous. Did she know what he was thinking?

"I haven't read it." His voice came out hoarse. Strained. "I've not had much leisure for reading, or play-going," he said, trying to sound more natural.

She nodded. Her hair brushed his cheek. "One rarely has the opportunity to—to do all one would like." She tipped her head away, as if absorbed in the moonlight's reflection on the lake. "I wish ..."

"What do you wish, Emma?"

Her eyes were wide, her lips parted. Slowly, she whispered, "I wish we could make love. *Truly* make love."

Damn.

"You know that wouldn't be wise," he murmured. He kissed her, meaning to console her. But she curled a hand around his neck and held him there, making a yearning sound deep in her throat. He broke off the kiss, but not before he'd hardened to the point of pain.

"I know. But for once, I wish I didn't have to be wise."

"Don't tempt me, Emma."

He tried to tuck her breasts back into her bodice but fumbled, entranced by the softness of her skin. Her eyes closed; her mouth parted in a sigh of pleasure. All he'd done was to arouse her further.

"I know it would be a foolish risk. I know we cannot."

"There is a way, but—"

"You know of a way to prevent . . . consequences?"

"There is always a risk, Emma." He smoothed her skirts down, swallowing hard as his hand skimmed the velvet of her exposed thigh.

"We shall never have another chance." She sounded heartbroken. Was she thinking of another night out here by the lake, another good-bye, another man?

He'd be a fool to consider what she was offering.

"You would regret it," he said.

"I would not, I promise," she said. "Just this one time, Manning. I want nothing more. No tomorrow. Just . . ."

She raised herself on one elbow, looking down at him. A strand of hair fell across her shoulder; her eyes gleamed in the moonlight. She leaned down to kiss him and he could not help gathering her closer. He couldn't think, only surrender to hungry kisses, the need to stroke and touch her breasts. He rolled them both over, kissing her breasts while stroking her intimately. She was wet and eager. Ready, so ready . . .

"Are you sure, Emma?"

"Yes."

He'd be a fool to believe her in her distraught state.

When she began to fumble at the buttons on his breeches, the same desperate need took hold of him. He'd wanted it all night. Lord, he'd wanted it ever since she'd pulled back the folds of his balloon and found him amongst the wreckage.

She drew down the fall of his breeches, releasing him to fall heavily against her. So close, but he did not want to rush.

"Not so fast." He struggled for a measure of control, caressing her again with his hand, watching her face contort with longing.

He was a fool.

When she pulled him close again, he thrust inside her. She stifled a cry; he felt tender flesh resist. He pulled out, but not before the damage was done.

"Emma! I'm sorry. I thought . . ."

"... I'd done this before? No, no, we didn't! He said we should wait. He promised he would come back to me."

He held her close. "I'm sorry, Emma."

"I don't want your sympathy, Manning! I want you to make love to me."

She kissed him hungrily, her hands linked over his back, pulling him back down to her. He was hard as ever, wretched fool, even knowing she pined for someone else. But he knew what she wanted, or what she thought she wanted: release, a temporary obliteration of grief.

"You won't ... regret this later?"

"No! Never." Her hands touched his buttocks, hesitantly at first, then taking hold and urging him back inside her.

It was all he could do to move slowly, easing into her, watching her breath rise and fall, her eyes widen in a sort of delighted surprise as he filled her. No, he wasn't hurting her. He began a slow rhythm, trying to be gentle and prolong their pleasure. She wrapped her strong arms around his back and kissed him deeply. Then she lifted her hips sharply. She dug her hands into his back, inviting ever harder strokes, each time lifting to meet him more fiercely. She wrapped her legs around him. He thought he might die of ecstasy.

I love you. He wanted to say it, but she did not want to hear it from him. He was but a dream lover, standing proxy for a ghost.

God help him, he was her slave.

Her moans became more desperate. She shuddered and let out a high, keening cry. He pulled free and withdrew, just in time, allowing his seed to spill onto the cold grass.

Emma closed her eyes, savoring the tremors that still shook her, less sharply, more deeply than the first time. How strange and wonderful it had felt to have him inside her. But Manning had withdrawn, protecting her—both of them—from anything that might make this more than a sweet memory. Ready tears welled up in her eyes but she kept them closed. She didn't want to cry again. She couldn't let Manning think she expected any more from him.

He moved closer. Warmth radiated from his body as he tucked her cloak up and around both of them.

"Warm enough?"

The tenderness in his voice nearly broke her composure. All she could do was nod.

He brushed her cheek with one finger, wiping away a tear that had escaped. Lord, he'd noticed. She opened her eyes. He lay on his side, propped up on one elbow, watching her.

"Thank you," she said, and thought what a silly thing that was to say. But it was all she could think of.

He sighed and pulled her back into his arms. The nightingale resumed his trills; she thought she would always link that sound with beauty and loss. Then she heard the less welcome sound of carriage wheels on gravel, the murmur of distant voices. Guests were leaving the ball.

It was time she went home, too.

With a wrench, she sat up and started to put herself to rights. She hoped sharp-eyed Becky would not guess what had happened. Manning buttoned his breeches; she could not read his expression. She tried to pin her hair back up but knew she was making a botch of it.

"Let me help." Manning came closer, his hands warm against her skin as he helped her with her hair.

He stood and reached down a hand to help her up. Her legs shook as she rose; he steadied her. Still kind, still gallant. She couldn't bear it. She couldn't keep him, any more than she could keep Charles.

He offered her his arm but she shook her head. "There's no need for you to go with me."

"Are you at that again?" he said, a rueful laugh in his voice. "No, I'm coming with you."

To argue would be making too much of it. She'd maintain her composure a little longer. So she accepted his arm and they moved toward the gap in the woods near the end of the lake, slowly and in silence. Perhaps he wanted to talk as little as she. This way they could still pretend to be lovers, walking through moonlit woods together.

They walked past drifts of bluebells, breathing in their delicate fragrance. The moonlight cast shadows of the trees along the path; patches of starlit sky winked in and out of the canopy above. A clear night, foreboding a clear day for tomorrow's flight. She had to accustom herself. It was his choice to put himself in danger again.

As they approached a small clearing, he stopped. She looked up at him and he drew her back into his arms.

"Emma, I know this may seem sudden to you. But . . ."

He paused and her mind raced. She knew what was coming, and knew how little he wanted to say the words. "Are you planning to offer for me?"

"Yes. Emma—"

"There is no need to be noble about it!" she interrupted. "I know you've no wish to be married. I gave my virtue willingly enough. I don't expect I shall miss it." She pulled free of his embrace and started to walk on.

He grasped her arm; she stopped but did not turn to face him.

"I'm not being noble," he said. "I've come to—"

"Don't pretend you love me. I am touched, but there is no need for it," she said. "What we did was . . . was beautiful and I thank you for it. But you had no wish to ask me earlier. And it would be folly to think of making a life together. I have Kit to think of. Do you think we could live hand-to-mouth, following you around the country and watching as you risk your neck in that balloon?"

He was silent, his face grim. Had she offended him with her refusal?

She put an arm around him. "It does you credit that you offered, Manning. Now let us forget about it, shall we?"

He exhaled, put an arm around her waist. "As you wish, Mistress."

Her heart ached. But they walked on, arms entwined around each other, each step taking them closer to daybreak. To sanity.

There, the lane was in sight. The cottage was just a few more steps away. A light glimmered faintly through the trees. The kitchen lamp.

They reached the lane and he swung her into his arms for a final, hungry kiss, molding her up against him. She yielded for a moment, a wild pulse coursing through her body. Then stifling a sob, she pulled free.

"Good night, Emma," he called softly as she ran toward the gate. He watched as she passed into the garden and walked toward the kitchen door.

He turned back toward the Manor, blood still churning from their kiss. Lord, how he wanted her. He could have made love to her all night. But he was not the right man; the way she had dismissed his offer had made that abundantly clear. She obviously didn't believe his clumsy attempt to declare himself. Just as well. Perhaps, in time, some lucky gentleman might win her, perhaps even that damnably eligible Mr. Newhall. All as it ought to be.

And for him? A beautiful memory. Memories ought to be cherished. He came to a halt. That damned nightingale resumed its warbling.

Yes, memories ought to be cherished.

He quickened his pace, knowing there was something he still had to do.

Chapter Sixteen

"Miss, wake up! You have a visitor!"

Emma groaned and rolled over. She must have imagined Becky's voice. It was too early. She felt strange: tired, different somehow ... Lud! Memories flooded through her. Manning kissing her, his fingers bringing her a blessed release. Their mad, sweet love-making. His proposal, which he'd made out of a sense of duty. Their parting kiss, which made her wonder if she had misread him after all ...

"Miss, you must get up!"

She sat up. Becky had said something about a visitor.

"Who is it?" she asked eagerly.

"It's that Mr. Blodgett, Miss."

Dear God. She hugged her knees to her chest. Stupid, stupid, stupid! To have thought it was Manning. He was still at the Manor, probably relieved that she refused his proposal. She ought to be relieved, too, for what sort of life could he offer her and Kit?

"He's sitting with your brother," Becky added.

Blodgett. Why did *he* choose to visit, this morning of all mornings? Perhaps he had come to talk about that beastly book. She gritted her teeth and swung her legs over the side of the bed. "Then you must help me dress, quickly."

"I told him you were sleeping, but he wouldn't go away."

"No, you did right. We cannot leave him alone with Kit for too long."

Becky nodded and helped her dress in wordless sympathy. Mercifully, she hadn't asked any questions last night, though she probably had some idea of what had happened. Emma prayed Becky's loyalty would outweigh her temptation to gossip.

"The black gown. Yes, that one, thank you."

A dress she'd dyed for mourning, now faded to a dusty gray, respectable and steadying, a reminder of her situation. Becky helped her pin up her braid into a prim coil. Surely no one would take her for a ruined woman now. She glanced in the mirror; her cheeks were suspiciously pink, but there was no help for it.

She left Becky to tidy up and descended the stairs in time to hear Blodgett lecturing Kit.

"And so, dear Christopher, you will see that all of nature demonstrates the workings of the divine, if only you strive properly to understand it."

Her father had spoken similar words, but on Blodgett's lips they sounded hollow and hypocritical. Kit was scowling as she entered, but he seemed to have kept his tongue.

Blodgett came to his feet as he saw her. She made him a curtsey. "How kind of you to visit again so soon. Kit, I believe it is time for Becky to take you for your airing. It looks to be a lovely day."

"Yes, and there's very little wind, so it should be perfect for the balloon ascension!" he replied.

Blodgett's lips thinned with disapproval.

"Did you like the ball, Emma?" Kit continued.

"Very much, dearest. I danced many, many dances."

Blodgett was silent; perhaps he hadn't noticed the color in her cheeks.

Becky came down and Emma bade her take Kit out into the garden. Reluctantly, she sat down in the wing chair while Blodgett settled back onto the sofa.

"I am sorry to have kept you waiting. I assure you I am not in the habit of sleeping late," she said.

"Your good maid informed me you attended a ball at Chesmore Manor." His voice held a delicate hint of censure.

"Sir George and Lady Chesmore were kind enough to insist on my presence."

His smile seemed frozen. "You may be forgiven for succumbing to the temptation presented by such an event."

Forgiven? For dancing? What might he do if he found out what she'd really done last night! Manning would be discreet, but there still might be rumors. How could she have taken such a risk?

"I trust it was a pleasant occasion," he continued.

"Everyone was most amiable."

"I was relieved to hear that Captain Manning removed to the Manor. Even with the good Miss Grimshaw present, I could not but feel his presence was a grave imposition."

"It was brief enough."

"I hear there is a balloon ascension planned for today. Captain Manning's health must be much improved."

"I believe him to be completely recovered."

"Christopher told me you intend to view the ascension. I must urge you to reconsider; no good can come of such an outing."

"I do not believe it will harm Kit."

"The excitement could be injurious to his system, let alone the frivolous tone of such a gathering." He sighed. "At least promise me you will do nothing so dangerous as to allow Captain Manning to take you up with him."

"I assure you I have no intention of doing so," she said coolly. "In fact, I have the most cowardly fear of heights."

He laughed politely. "One might say you are suited for even more *elevated* pursuits."

She said nothing, wondering again why he had come.

"You are suited for more elevated company as well." An odd gleam shone in his eyes. She remembered Manning's warning, that Blodgett was infatuated with her. Ridiculous!

"That is what I have come to talk to you about," he continued. "I have long felt that your present duties are too heavy. It is my desire to offer you a position of greater ease."

He paused, perhaps for dramatic affect. She clasped her hands in her lap, her mind reeling. Perhaps Manning was right. Was Blodgett about to offer for her? Surely not. She doubted he'd given up hope of the heiress he'd been courting.

"What sort of position?" she asked, keeping her voice neutral.

"As you know, my mother recently suffered a decline in her health and is no longer able to move about in Bath society as she once did. She has a maid to attend to her needs, but she would benefit from the companionship of a respectable female, one who could be a support to her spirits. I trust you will be pleased that I can offer you one hundred pounds per annum, in compensation for acting as her companion."

She exhaled in relief. It was *not* marriage he offered.

Then she caught her breath, realizing the magnitude of his offer. It was twice the pay of many governesses and many times her current wages, yet all she could feel was dismay.

"Your brother would of course be welcome in my home," he added. "You must consider the many advantages to him of living in Bath. He would have the benefit of regular visits from Dr. Procton and of drinking the waters. The hot baths might prove beneficial to his diseased limb."

"You—you are very kind. I do not wish to seem ungrateful, but there is much to consider."

Could she and Kit be happy living in Blodgett's household? Yet if she might consult with other physicians in Bath ... She thought of Manning and his offer to send them to London to seek alternate opinions, and wondered what he would say about this offer. But why should she care what he thought? He had nothing but a passing fondness for her. He'd taken pleasure in their lovemaking, but his offer of marriage had been prompted by pity.

She did not want his pity!

Blodgett cleared his throat. "I see I have surprised you," he said. "If you are concerned about your present duties, I can assist Sir George in finding a suitable replacement."

"Your offer is most kind, most flattering," she stammered. "Do not imagine me ungrateful, but—but it is very sudden. Would you be willing to grant me some time to think about it?"

He gave her an indulgent nod, seeming confident that a hundred pounds per annum would sway her in the end. It probably would.

"Very well, Miss Westfield. I shall be staying at the Hare and Hounds until tomorrow. Be so good as to send word there when you have come to a decision."

He rose and she jumped up to hand him his hat and cane from the small stand near the door. He clasped her hand for a moment. Surely it was her imagination that he held her hand a little too long. It was a relief when he released it, gave her a quick bow and left the cottage.

She closed the door behind him and returned to the parlor. He passed by the window, taking slow, measured steps as restrained as everything else about him. Could she and Kit bear to live with such a man? She sat down in her usual chair, vowing she'd think it through like a rational woman. But a moment later, she sprang up and began to pace the room.

Blodgett was often in London on business; perhaps they would not have to deal with him too much. To accept his offer would be the prudent thing to do.

She paused at the opposite end of the room, by the bare patch of plastered wall near the doorway. Unbidden, the memory rose up in her mind of Manning the day he'd left to go to the Manor. He'd pressed her against just that spot, kissing and caressing her until she could think of nothing else. Last night he'd finished what they had begun there. She'd wept with bliss at his lovemaking and lain peacefully in his embrace as if there were no tomorrow.

She strode across the room again and stared out the window at the hedge across the now empty lane. Tomorrow was here, Manning would be leaving soon, and she had a decision to make.

Emma was still pacing when Birkin arrived to take her and Kit to the balloon ascension. She came to the door and watched him hop down from the wagon and come up the path, whistling and moving jauntily enough on his wooden leg. There was an air of excitement about him, no doubt on account of the curst balloon ascension.

Men were such fools!

"Good morning, Miss," he said as she met him on the doorstep. "The Captain wanted me to give you this."

He handed her a small pouch made of faded dark green cloth. The color of the 95th regiment, it looked as if it had been fashioned from a scrap of a ruined uniform. She stared at it for a moment, then hastily thanked Birkin and bade him sit down while she and Kit readied themselves for the outing.

Clutching the pouch, she ran out into the garden. She asked Becky to make Kit ready, then darted back into the cottage and up the stairs to her room. A pulse beat in her throat as she sank onto her bed. She loosened the drawstring and reached in, her fingers trembling. She found a slip of paper and drew it out.

Dearest Emma,

Memories ought to be cherished. Please keep these, with my apologies and my thanks. The perfume case belonged to my mother. She would have liked you to have it.

Gil

Good God, what did he mean? She slipped her hand back into the pouch and her fingers touched several items, one of them hard and flat. She drew it out. It was the locket

Charles had given her! She wondered how long it had taken Manning to fish it out of the lake. It couldn't have been an easy task.

Was it his way of saying he did not want to supplant Charles in her memory?

"Emma! Emma! Are you ready to go?" Kit's voice wafted up the stairway, through her open door.

She sucked in a breath. There was still something else in the pouch, something that had belonged to Manning's mother. "In a moment, dearest!"

She pulled it out and looked at it. It was a perfume case, just a few inches long, the sort that could fit easily into a reticule. Made of silver, it was decorated with simple bands of cut decoration like rows of leaves.

The perfume case belonged to my mother.

She blinked back a tear. If she remembered his tale correctly, he'd been just five years old when his parents had been buried together in Jamaica. She opened the case and carefully removed the tiny cut glass bottle hidden inside. She removed the stopper and held it up to her nose. Pierced by wonder, she inhaled the faint scent of roses long dead.

"Emma! When will you be ready?"

"I—I cannot find my shawl," she said, though it hung on a peg near the door.

She thought of the young woman who'd followed her husband to Jamaica only to join him in an early grave. Of the small son who'd somehow held onto this keepsake through all his campaigns. She covered her face with her hands. She could not keep it.

What the devil did Manning think to give it to her?

"Emma!"

Damn him for making this so difficult! For tearing away the cold comfort she had taken in thinking their lovemaking meant nothing to him. It would have been so much easier to dismiss him as a carefree rogue, but now that was impossible.

She couldn't forget what he'd told her of his life, of his parents, of Maggie. She couldn't forget that he too had suffered. She must hold some place in his heart, though he clearly had no intention of ever taking a wife, else he would never have given her something so precious.

"Is anything wrong, Miss?" This time it was Becky, from the bottom of the stairs.

"Not at all. I shall be down in a trice!" Emma thrust everything back into the pouch and jumped up to place it inside her trinket box. She would have to find a way to return it later. She snatched her shawl from its peg, flung it around her shoulders and then wiped her eyes with a corner. Somehow she would manage to meet Manning in front of everyone. She would smile, as if unmoved by their parting.

She could do it. She'd had practice.

"Have you taken ill, Miss?" Becky gave her a worried look when Emma came downstairs.

"Not at all," she said, heading toward the open door and the sunshine streaming in. Birkin had already settled Kit up on the box next to him.

Becky gave her a doubtful look but followed as Emma led the way down the path. She said nothing more when they took their seats behind the box. Birkin and Kit were already deep in conversation about the upcoming ascension and balloons in general. At least *they* didn't notice anything.

For a while Emma just held on to the seat, staring at the hedges on either side. Manning was leaving and she owed Blodgett an answer. She needed to be calm, but all she felt was panic and a wish for the world to slow down. Twenty more minutes and they'd be at the Manor. She would see Manning, perhaps for the last time.

Her brother laughed out loud. Emma raised her head to see Becky blushing and giggling behind her hand.

Birkin turned around. "I'm sorry, Miss! I get a bit carried away with m' tales."

"I—my attention was elsewhere. I am sure it is no matter."

Kit turned to stare at her. "How could you miss it, Emma? Birkin was telling us how he was flying with Captain Manning, and—"

"Now I'm sure your sister doesn't wish to hear this," said Birkin.

"—and they got too low and were going to get caught in some trees, and they had no more ballast to throw overboard. Can you guess what they did?"

"I cannot," she said. Then she remembered how Manning arrived, half-naked, and she'd thought him mad . . . "Perhaps they threw off their coats?"

"No, they'd done that already. They pissed over the side!"

He collapsed in giggles. Birkin renewed his apologies, but a bubble of laughter rose in Emma. How disgusting it was, and just the sort of humor little boys—and grown men, she supposed—enjoyed. She covered her face and laughed until the tears came, sobs that had nothing to do with the silly story. She pulled a handkerchief from her reticule and hid behind it until she felt more composed.

Soon the Manor came into view.

Chapter Seventeen

They passed through the gate and trundled past the house and stables. Birkin took the wagon as close as he could to the south lawn, where a crowd of villagers and local gentry were already assembling. Two tall poles stood in a roped-off enclosure in the center of the lawn, a rope suspended between them, from which hung netting and folds of blue and yellow cloth: the balloon in position for filling. Several colorful pavilions were set up just outside the enclosure; the largest Emma recognized as one Sir George and his family sometimes used for picnics.

Manning was probably in the thick of preparations, no doubt eager to fly again, just weeks after the crash that nearly cost him his life. Her heart turned over, and she reminded herself it was only a tethered ascension. He would not kill himself today. If it happened, it would be on some other flight, and she would read about it in the newspapers.

He emerged from the crowd and headed towards them. Her heart turned over yet again. She clasped her hands tightly in her lap.

"Captain Manning! Are you going to fill the balloon now?" Kit asked.

"Yes, you're just in time," Manning replied, as Birkin reined in his horse and jumped down off the wagon.

Emma would have climbed out by herself, but Manning was there, reaching out his arms to her. His blue-green eyes were alight with something: excitement, concern, questions. *Are you well? Are you angry with me?*

"I trust you slept well, Miss Westfield."

"Quite well, thank you." She avoided his gaze as she slid toward the edge of the wagon. His hands were firm around her waist, holding her for a moment before setting her down. Warmth rushed through her; a pulse beat in her throat, between her legs. Good God, she was hopeless! She hurried out of the way so Becky could dismount from the wagon. As she turned, she caught Manning looking after her, his jaw tight as she'd never seen it before.

An instant later, he shook off the frown and helped Becky down from the wagon. He went to the back and assisted Birkin in unloading Kit's wheeled chair. He seemed his usual smiling self as he came back to the front, lifted Kit down from the box himself and set him gently down in his chair. Emma moved to push it, but Manning waved her aside with a concerned look.

Let me at least do this for you.

"The ground is uneven; it will be easier for me," he said.

So she just walked alongside, aching, afraid everyone would guess her folly. Fortunately, the crowd's attention focused on what was going on in the enclosure. Lund was arranging a series of casks and bottles around the suspended balloon. Sancha appeared to be loading the newly made car which stood beneath.

"Has Reed come back?" Birkin asked as they walked.

"Not yet," Manning replied.

"What's the matter?" Kit asked. "Is Reed missing?"

"He went to the village on an errand. He'll be back soon." Manning's voice was light but Emma sensed a thread of worry in his tone. It set off a vague disquiet within her, a sense that something was not as it should be.

"You *can* manage without him?" Kit asked.

"Of course," said Manning in a reassuring tone.

He brought them to one of the pavilions a few yards from the enclosure, where Emma saw the Squire sitting with his ladies, in their best walking dresses and bonnets, all sipping lemonade. Lady Chesmore and Lydia looked up sharply as she approached. She raised her chin, wishing she could be anywhere else. Sir George rose and offered her a chair, which she was forced to accept.

"Emma dear, I am so relieved to see you!" said Lady Chesmore. "You gave us quite the fright, walking home while you were unwell."

Manning maneuvered Kit's chair to a position next to her, his face impassive.

"Thank you, I was merely a bit warm," she replied.

"Poor thing, you are not accustomed to so much dancing, are you?" asked Lydia.

"She danced quite handsomely with Captain Manning," said Lady Chesmore.

Emma flinched. Had Lady Chesmore guessed something?

"Yes, I consider myself fortunate to have been one of her partners," said Manning. "Now if you will all excuse me, I must attend to the preparations." He bowed and left them.

At a signal from Lady Chesmore, a servant offered lemonade and biscuits, first to Emma, then to Kit. Emma forced herself to accept, realizing she had eaten nothing since last night and had better do so, unless she wished to faint and draw more attention to herself.

Meanwhile, Lady Chesmore continued, "What a shame you had to leave early. And that Captain Manning decided he was excessively tired, such a little while later . . ."

Good God, had Lady Chesmore seen something? Or was she trying to provoke her into a revelation?

"Perhaps his head pained him," said Emma as coolly as she could manage.

Sir George left them, mumbling some excuse about wishing to speak to a tenant.

"I am so excited about this ascension!" said Lydia. "Arabella says she shan't go, because she is in the family way.

But I vow I cannot wait for my chance to fly with Captain Manning. And how I wish I could go up with him afterwards!"

"Afterwards?" Emma asked.

"Oh, did you not know? He plans to make a proper flight after the tethered ascents."

Emma's stomach clenched. So he might kill himself today after all. Conscious of Lady Chesmore's scrutiny, she said, "Then I trust all will go well this time."

"How I wish I could go with him, but he said it would be improper!" Lydia tittered. "I shall have to content myself with the tethered ascension. Of course I know *you* will remain sensibly on the ground, Emma. But *I* am not too old to enjoy an adventure!"

"Of course not," Emma murmured.

She was never more grateful when Kit asked if they could go closer to the enclosure. "I want to see *everything!*" he pleaded.

"If you will all excuse us," she said and quickly rose.

She pushed the wheeled chair toward the enclosure. Though her muscles strained to push the chair over the uneven turf, it was a relief to be away from the Chesmores.

A moment later Manning spotted them and hopped over the ropes. He came over and took over the chair from her, pushing it to a position just outside the enclosure.

"Thank you," she said with a shaky smile.

He nodded and was off, as quickly as he'd arrived. She followed him with her gaze and saw him talking to some of the other children who were running about. He came back, accompanied by Tom and several others of her students.

"Now attend to Kit!" he told them. "He can explain everything to you."

Kit beamed up at him. Watching them, another pang went through Emma. Her brother looked so happy; he did not feel the shadow of parting, not yet. She'd have to help him bear it, but for now they might as well enjoy what they could.

"What are those?" Tom pointed to some large casks.

"Those three casks on the outside have iron shavings in them, for making the gas," said Kit. "Do you see those tin tubes? The vapour passes through them into the next cask, where water cools it off. Then it goes through the next tube into the mouth of the balloon."

"But how do they make the gas?"

"See all those bottles?"

The children nodded.

"They're full of vitriolic acid. It's amazing stuff but you have to be very careful with it. If you spilled just a drop on yourself, you'd get a terrible burn!"

"What's it for?"

"They pour it into the casks and it will all start bubbling like a witch's cauldron," said Kit, with relish. "Then you'll see the balloon start to fill."

"Oh, look! What are they doing now?"

Interested despite herself, Emma watched as Manning and his men filled a tub with the acid. A stick protruded from the tub, which they removed, allowing the acid to flow into one of the casks. And it was just as Kit had described: no witch's cauldron could bubble more furiously. A slight breeze brought an odor to them, something like bad eggs, no doubt the result of the reaction going on inside the casks. Already the top part of the balloon was swelling, where it was suspended between the two poles. Manning and his team poured acid into the other casks, doubling and tripling the noise and effervescence. The crowd let out a cheer.

Manning came out from the center, smiled and bowed to the crowd, clearly in his element. She shuddered, looking away when his eyes met hers.

"Papa says I can go up!" Tom said. "Will you fly too, Kit?"

Kit looked up at her, doubt and hope mingled in his blue eyes.

She shook her head. "I am sorry. It would not be wise."

The children all looked at her, then turned their attention back toward the slowly filling balloon. Kit was blinking in an effort to hold back tears.

She felt like a dragon. The sun was bright above them in a quiet sky. Wisps of clouds drifted almost imperceptibly. It was hard to imagine anything could go wrong on such a day. Was she wrong to hold her ground?

Gradually the top of the balloon swelled out, giving it the shape of a mushroom. After ten minutes or so of silent watching, the children drifted off to run about the field, leaving Kit and Emma alone. She ventured a few questions to Kit, but he returned short answers, keeping his face averted.

She should have known better than to bring him, when all he could do was observe others enjoying themselves. She'd allowed herself to be weak, and she was still weak, because she longed to give in and do what was assuredly against his physician's advice. She was weak, because her eyes couldn't stop straying towards Manning, moving around the enclosure, directing his men to adjust the netting over the balloon as it swelled to something like an inverted tear-drop.

Eventually, the balloon was full enough to support itself and the rope from which it was suspended was taken away. The surrounding crowd grew noisier, pressing closer around the edges of the enclosure. Several of the children came back to Kit.

"Is it nearly full?" one of them asked.

"They won't fill it completely," said Kit. "The vapour expands as the balloon rises. They'll leave a little room, otherwise it would burst when it got too high!"

All she needed, another image of disaster from her clever little brother. But she couldn't be angry with him; he'd mastered his disappointment and was behaving far better than she deserved. The jut of his chin signaled his resolve to act as if nothing was amiss.

Just as Kit had said, Alcyone now floated, a near-perfect oval but a little loose at the bottom, held down by a number of mooring ropes attached to sandbags. Manning and his crew disconnected the tubing. A mounting block was set near the car, to help passengers enter. On a signal from Manning, a group of Sir George's servants, along with several sturdy villagers, entered the enclosure. Under the direction of Lund, they took up positions around two sturdy ropes on either side of the car.

"Those are the tethers," Kit said, pointing to them. "There are two, in case one should break."

Emma shuddered.

"Captain Manning is going to go up first," Kit continued, "to make sure all's well, and those men will hold onto the tethers."

"What if they let go?" Tom asked.

"They won't. But if they do, he'll fly off." Kit looked up at the sky, shading his eyes. "Maybe into Surrey, and who knows where else? But it would be too bad if he didn't take someone with him!"

Emma's stomach rolled over again.

Shouts and clapping assaulted her ears. She turned her gaze back to the enclosure and saw Manning bowing and smiling to the crowd. *Fool.* Did he enjoy danger so much?

He climbed into the car and turned to face the crowd again. His crew held onto the sides of the car as others detached the mooring ropes. Lund returned to direct the men holding onto the tethers.

"All ready?" she heard Manning shout.

A chorus of aye's echoed over the hubbub.

"Let go!"

The crowd roared as the balloon began a gradual ascent. Manning waved, grinning from ear to ear. *The devil.*

"Birkin said he'll go to about five hundred feet."

Emma could not take her eyes off the sight. In the still air, the balloon ascended nearly straight upwards, until it floated high above the lawn.

"Isn't it grand?" breathed Kit, his face as rapt as the children's around her. She felt strange, like a skeleton at a feast. From her position, she could not even see Manning, but the car of the balloon seemed dangerously high above them. She wished he would come down already.

Which he did, soon after. The men on the tethers hauled him back to the ground, to more bursts of applause. Emma exhaled, realizing her shoulders had stiffened somewhere about her ears.

But there was more to come. Sir George and his sister entered the enclosure. As patrons, they had the honor of the first ride. Lydia giggled and blushed as Manning handed her into the car of the balloon. Sir George scrambled in after and they sat down in the seats built into each end of the car. Once again the balloon arose; this time they could hear Lydia shriek with terror as it did so. Then she began to giggle again. Emma thought she saw Manning grimace as they rose.

Soon she could no longer see their faces. They rose to a height she could not guess, though perhaps it was five hundred feet. Perhaps ten minutes later a pennant was waved over the side. Apparently that was the signal for Lund and the rest of them to bring the balloon down to earth again, for they began hauling on the tethers.

A few minutes later, Manning jumped out and handed Sir George and his sister out. Both were beaming. Lydia gave Emma a triumphant look, but she was beyond caring, too conscious of Kit's slumped shoulders and disconsolate face. She put a hand on his shoulder but he hunched away from her touch.

More passengers were brought into the enclosure, in some order of precedence that must have been established beforehand, the gentlefolk riding first. Even the vicar and Miss Grimshaw ventured a flight, exiting the car with bright eyes and pink cheeks, as if a few minutes aloft had somehow taken a decade from them.

Now more than ever she felt an ogre for not allowing Kit a ride. It really looked quite safe . . .

Next Manning took up the surgeon, Hollis, and his children, whose excited cries could be heard even above the crowd's chatter. As they climbed out, Manning glanced towards her. Their eyes met, a question and an invitation in his. His gaze shifted and she knew he was looking at Kit. She knew he was hoping to give her brother a treat he would remember all his life.

She wavered, then nodded.

Manning smiled. He jumped out of the car and came toward them.

Kit straightened and looked up at her with questioning eyes. "Emma ... You don't mean? ..."

"Yes, Kit. We shall go up in the balloon."

"Hurrah!"

Manning crossed the ropes and lifted Kit into his arms. Turning to go back, he gave Emma a grateful look. She followed him to the enclosure, suddenly weak-kneed. She hadn't lied when she'd told Blodgett she disliked heights. For a moment, she thought about asking Manning to take Kit up without her, but then she felt an equally strong compulsion to remain with her brother. Silly, because there was nothing she could do if anything went wrong.

By this time, Manning had lifted Kit into the car of the balloon and established him in one of the seats. She set her feet onto the mounting block and climbed up. Manning gave her his hand and held onto her until she dropped, flustered, into the car. A cheer rose from the spectators. She took the seat opposite to Kit's. Like the old, ruined car, this car was constructed of basketwork with an embellished cloth covering. Around the inside, sandbags were slung at intervals as ballast, but somehow this safety precaution was no comfort. Manning stood between her and Kit, just inches away. She repressed the urge to cling to him.

"I'm afraid of heights," she blurted out, feeling foolish.

"I'll catch you if you swoon," Manning promised.

Her flush intensified, then she glared at him.

"Are you both ready?" Manning asked them.

"Let us go!" said Kit and Emma reluctantly nodded.

"Very well then. Let us go!"

More cheers and clapping erupted from the crowd, but Emma gripped the sides of the car as the balloon began to rise.

Chapter Eighteen

Emma stifled a scream as the balloon continued to ascend, surely much more quickly than it had with its previous groups of passengers. No, it was just her imagination. What a coward she was!

"You're not scared, are you, Emma? Just look!" Kit was peering eagerly over the edge of the car. Emma bit her lip on the verge of telling him to sit back. He was really in no danger of falling out.

She glanced up at Manning, wondering if he was silently laughing at her. His smile was warm and reassuring. *I want very much for you both to enjoy this.*

"Would it harm you to take a look?" he asked. He shifted so that his leg just brushed her knee. She suspected it was a comforting gesture, but it sent a little, guilty thrill through her. She was hopeless.

She looked down. The balloon had already risen far above the Manor. She could see the rooftop and all the details of chimneys, the upturned faces of people below. They were so high, and still rising! She had that mad feeling she'd had once, having climbed to the top of the church steeple. She was going to fall and since she was doomed anyway, she might as well leap. She fought the urge, gripping the sides so tightly it hurt.

"There. It's not so bad, is it?"

She realized Manning was speaking to her. The balloon came to a stop; she felt the pull of the tethers on the car, which swayed a bit as it halted. Her stomach lurched and the sour taste of lemonade rose in her mouth. She closed her eyes, praying she would not embarrass herself. "It's horrid! When can we go down?"

"How can you say that?" Kit protested. "Look at the church! See, there's our cottage!"

She reopened her eyes, determined not to ruin Kit's fun.

"If you look out, rather than directly down, it might be better," Manning suggested.

She ventured to peek out again and realized he was right. She studied the landscape and magically, the vertigo receded. She took in the Manor, the shimmering surface of the lake, the shore where they'd made love last night ... The woods she'd walked through so many times, where she had rejected Manning's proposal. And there was the thatched roof of their cottage. To the north, she saw the stone spire of the church rising amid the wood that bordered that side of the village.

"Not so horrid now?" Manning asked.

"No," she admitted. "It is lovely."

"I want to go higher. Can we?" Kit asked.

"We've got a little more play in the line," Manning replied. "We could, if your sister permits?"

"Very well, let us go higher!" she said stoutly.

He shouted orders over the side and Alcyone began to ascend. More of the village came into view as their perspective changed. Emma drank in the vista of surrounding fields, striped with rows of wheat, beyond them the sloping Downs. A stream glistened in the sunshine. The air was delicious, not too cold. The horizon beckoned, green and bright in the sunshine. She could almost understand why Manning enjoyed flying.

Almost.

She shifted her gaze to closer sights. "See the bluebell wood!" she said, pointing to drifts of blue peeking through the still sparse, pale green canopy of leaves. Her breath caught as she remembered how she and Manning had walked there last night.

"And there's the stream where I caught that trout!" said Kit. "Do you remember how you lost hold of it and it wriggled all over the bank?"

"I rather wish I didn't!" She laughed.

"Oh, and there's Bow Hill. I see the barrow mounds! Remember how we flew our kites up there the ... the summer ... before ..." Kit's voice faltered.

The summer before he'd taken ill. A cold hand seemed to squeeze Emma's heart.

"I suppose I shall never go there again." Kit continued, his tone flat. She saw him holding back tears and cursed herself. She hadn't thought this through properly. She'd worried about whether the flight would injure Kit's health. She should have thought about how he would feel, seeing his earlier haunts—places he'd never be able to visit again. She'd been too busy thinking about herself and Manning.

Should she have held firm to her original decision? Which was worse—the pain of having to forego the adventure, or the bitterness of knowing it had to end?

"Thank you for showing it to me," Kit said solemnly to Manning.

Manning put a hand on Kit's shoulder. "Do you wish to go down?"

"No, not yet," said Kit after a pause. "Unless we must?"

"There is no hurry," Manning replied, though there were others eager for a flight.

She too was glad to wait. Manning kept his hand on Kit's shoulder; his leg against her knee. It felt as if they were a *family*. She looked up at him and saw the same awareness in his eyes. If only ... But it was impossible.

All they could do was bask in the present moment. She could no longer regret *anything*. At least they would have memories.

Kit cleared his throat. "Captain Manning?"

"Kit?"

"I will miss you."

"I will write to you," Manning replied, and Emma didn't doubt he intended to follow through.

"Might you visit us sometimes?"

Once again her eyes met Manning's. Her heart clenched.

He forced a smile as he turned back toward Kit. "I can't promise to visit often, but I will try."

His leg brushed her knee again, as if by accident, and they exchanged another glance. How impossible it felt to meet again as mere friends! She couldn't imagine how they would bear it, but for Kit's sake, she was grateful.

Glancing at Kit, she saw a tear leak out of his eye. Perhaps it was time to end this.

"Shall we go down now, dearest?" she asked him.

Her brother composed his face and nodded.

"I think it would be best for us to go home directly," she said to Manning.

"Very well." He shouted the order and they began to descend. Emma held tight to the side of the car again but the descent was smooth and shorter than she expected.

The crowd cheered again as they landed. Emma felt her heart would burst. Manning, his face impassive, directed one of Sir George's grooms to drive her and Kit home. He lifted Kit out. As he carried him toward the awaiting wagon, Kit buried his face in Manning's shoulder. Emma followed, explaining to anyone who inquired that her brother was not sick but merely fatigued by the excitement.

"Has he taken ill, Miss?" Becky asked.

"He's tired and must go home. You may stay here if you wish. I can manage."

"I'd better go along with you," said Becky.

"Thank you," Emma replied, as they reached the wagon. As the groom climbed up and offered Becky a hand onto the box, Emma directed Manning to set Kit onto the seat behind it. Then he lifted her up, his hands lingering briefly on her waist, perhaps the last time he would touch her.

She put her arm around Kit, feeling him shake with the effort not to sob. She sensed that Manning was watching them, but as the groom drove off, she did not look back.

Gil hurried through the woods toward Meadowcross Cottage. He didn't know how he'd endured the rest of the tethered ascents. It was a relief when everyone went off to gorge themselves on roast beef and ale. His crew held Alcyone in readiness for a free flight, but he could not take off without seeing whether Kit and Emma were all right.

There was still too much unsaid between them.

He redoubled his pace, leaping over tree roots as he ran. His chest ached, not with the effort of running, but the feeling of being ripped apart somehow. He burst out onto the lane and nearly collided with Becky, who was hurrying in the opposite direction, towards the village.

She let out a shriek and rocked back on her heels. He saw her clutch a folded paper to her chest. "Lawks, sir! You startled me, running out of the woods like a gypsy!"

"I am sorry, Becky," he said. "Why are you in such a hurry? Has Kit taken ill?"

"No, sir. Miss gave him some chamomile tea and he fell asleep." She looked anxious. Why?

"And Miss Westfield? She is well?"

"As well as always." He sensed a reproof in her words.

"Then where are you going?"

"Miss Westfield asked me to deliver this note to the Hare and Hounds. It's for that Mr. Blodgett."

"What can *he* be doing here? Let me see that note."

"I'm not sure I should, sir."

"You know I mean Miss Westfield no harm. That can't be said of Blodgett, can it?"

"It's not my place to say," she said, but she frowned.

"Please let me see the note."

She hesitated, then handed it to him. He opened it up.

Dear Mr. Blodgett,

I am writing to inform you that I have decided to accept your kind offer. I am at your disposal to discuss arrangements. Please believe me to be most deeply grateful.

Your very obedient
Emma Westfield

What did it mean—*your kind offer?*
He crumpled the paper in his hand.
"Sir, you mustn't! Miss will be angry!" Becky reached for the note. "But what's in it to make you as mad as a bear?"
He swallowed his anger. Becky might be an ally. "Read it for yourself."
She smoothed out the paper and read through, frowning. "Miss is going to marry that—that pompous ass? Begging your pardon, sir, but it doesn't seem right, does it?"
"Not at all. Will you help me put a stop to it?"
Becky gave him a skeptical look. "And just what are your intentions, Captain Manning?"
"I mean to marry her."
"And take good care of her and Master Kit?"
"Yes, on my honor."
Her expression cleared. "Then let me know what you wish me to do."
"Can you mind Kit for several days?" Without waiting for a reply, he set off down the lane at a run.
"You don't mean to be abducting her?" she called out behind him.
"If that is what it takes to keep her from marrying Blodgett!"
He left Becky behind to follow as well as she could. Moments later, he reached the cottage and entered, not bothering to knock.

Emma was not in the parlor or the kitchen. He found her outside, wearing a smock over her old gray gown and fiercely pulling weeds in the vegetable garden.

"Emma!" he called.

She straightened up. "Why are you here?" she asked, her voice tight as a whiplash.

"To save you from making the biggest mistake of your life." He moved forward.

"How do you know my plans? Did Becky tell you?"

"It doesn't matter how I found out. I won't allow you to go through with it."

"What right have you to dictate what I do or do not do?"

"The right of one who loves you." He put his arms around her and kissed her fiercely.

She tipped her head back. "If it were a lasting passion, you'd have said something before. I think you still feel sorry for me. And don't think you can just delude me with kisses!"

"No, I've a better idea than that." He changed his grip and hoisted her up into his arms. She gave an incoherent cry of protest. At the same time a bubble of joy rose up in him, a sense that for once he was doing the right thing.

"Have you gone mad?" she shouted. "Put me down!"

He carried her back toward the cottage, fiercely relishing the solid, warm weight of her. She was quiet at first, perhaps with shock, then she began to struggle.

"Put me down! You'll hurt yourself. It's just weeks since you were an invalid in my parlor."

She couldn't know what she was doing to him, squirming in his arms so deliciously.

"After last night, you know I'm completely recovered!"

She went still for a moment. "Manning, please . . ."

"Call me Gil."

"Gil . . . last night was . . . lovely . . . and I will never forget it. But whatever you are doing now, please stop."

He stepped over the threshold into the kitchen, where Becky had just arrived, a little out of breath but with an excited look on her face.

"Becky! Stop this lunatic!" Emma called out.

"He's no lunatic, Miss. He's just sweet on you, that's all." Becky, bless her, moved aside to let him pass. "Better trust him than that fat fool, Blodgett! Now don't you fret about Kit. I'll take good care of him."

He carried Emma out through the parlor and out of the cottage and onto the path. She began to struggle again, not realizing how her movements aroused him. He turned onto the lane.

"For heaven's sake, where are you taking me?" Emma cried.

He just laughed.

Chapter Nineteen

"Put me down! You will ruin everything!" Emma pushed her hands against Manning's chest, but he held her tight.

"I mean to keep you from ruining everything."

"You lunatic, Mr. Blodgett has offered me a position! If we are seen like this, he'll have no choice but to withdraw his offer."

"Let him. You'd never be happy with him."

"*What?* Did you think he offered *marriage?*"

"What else?"

"He asked me to be his mother's paid *companion!* And he is offering me five times my current wages. So there is nothing to be jealous about."

He turned onto the path through the woods that led back to the Manor.

"Good God! You are not planning to— You are not going to take me up in that curst balloon of yours?"

He only grinned.

"Do you wish to kill us both? Have you forgotten what happened the last time you flew without a tether?"

"It was windy, I had run out of ballast, and the springs in the valve were worn out. Today we have perfect weather and plenty of ballast. The new valve is working perfectly."

"Unlike your brain! Put me down!"

"If I do, you'll go off to live with Blodgett. Can't you see he has designs on you?"

"Erasmus Blodgett is a gentleman. Only a besotted, jealous fool would think anything else."

"That would be me." He laughed merrily.

"You cannot wish for marriage. You are just feeling sorry for me. You pity me, because of last night, but—"

He halted and kissed her. Startled, she yielded for a moment, then averted her face, but not before a wave of treacherous heat spread through her.

"That's what you'll get from me, anytime you start speaking nonsense," he said, moving forward again at a quickened pace. Each step made her acutely aware of him, his long stride, his laughter, his hands on her. Every secret place he'd touched last night tingled with awareness. She struggled for sanity.

"But what shall we do? How shall we live?"

"I'll take care of you and Kit, I promise."

She heard voices and the music of fiddles. She smelled roasting meat. They were getting close. They left the wood and reached the lake. They passed the spot where he'd made love to her the night before. God help her, she longed for him to do it again.

No one saw them at first, as almost everyone was busy eating and dancing at the other end of the lawn. Lund, Birkin and Sancha were sitting at a trestle table set up in the enclosure, eating and watching over the balloon to make sure no drunken merrymaker tried to take her up.

As Emma and Manning approached, the crew got up.

"Your Captain has gone mad!" she shouted. "Tell him to set me down!"

"Make ready. Miss Westfield and I are going up," Manning said.

Lund nodded, though he looked concerned. "Reed's still missing, sir."

"You can look for him once I'm gone."

Emma looked toward Sancha in desperation. "Please tell him not to do this."

"Go with him, you pale English fool! Can you not see he loves you?" said Sancha. "I shall put in some food for you."

"Sancha's right. The Captain won't let you come to harm," Lund said reassuringly.

Manning set her down into the car of the balloon and vaulted in beside her. He put his arms around her, shouting orders while his crew loaded the car with several blankets and a covered basket with food for the journey.

A few of the revelers turned their heads, noticing the renewed activity near the balloon. They started towards the enclosure. A cry rose up and like a building wave, the crowd began to move towards them.

Meanwhile, Birkin and Lund had taken positions on either side of the car, holding it down while Sancha ran about, releasing the sandbags. The front runners in the crowd were just outside the enclosure.

"Manning..." Good God, he really planned to go through with it!

"Emma." His eyes blazed down at her. "Fly with me. I want you to know what it's like up there."

He was giving her a chance to say no. She ought to be sensible. She ought to be practical. The words she ought to have said stuck in her throat.

He pressed her closer. "Look me in the eye. Tell me you and Kit won't be happier with me than with Blodgett."

She looked up and found she couldn't lie to him.

"Will you fly with me, Emma?"

A wild, irrational joy rose inside her, as if she were exchanging a bleak, dreary future for one that was bright, even though she could not see it clearly. Perhaps she'd lost her mind, but it suddenly felt right to go with him.

She nodded.

"Let go!" he shouted.

As the balloon began to rise, he pulled her close and gave her another quick kiss. A cheer rose from the crowd. She laughed, feeling as mad as he.

When she looked out, she saw they were rising swiftly. Manning kept an arm around her while he checked the instruments slung on a cord along the side of the car: a barometer and a compass. He made some sort of adjustment, tugging briefly on what she guessed was the valve-rope. She remembered Kit saying how the gas in the balloon expanded as they rose and could cause it to rise too high, or even burst. Manning nodded and smiled. It seemed everything was going as it should. She let go the breath she hadn't realized she was holding.

"How high are we?" she asked, seeing how much higher they'd risen this time. The people below them were mere specks.

He looked at the barometer and paused, as if doing some mental calculations. "A few thousand feet, more or less."

"Good God!"

"Afraid?" he asked.

"A little."

"Don't worry. We could not ask for better conditions."

He released her and turned his attention back to his instruments. She saw that the barometer was steady and they were heading in a northwestern direction, the land passing slowly beneath them.

Apparently satisfied that all was well, Gil pulled her back up against him. As they stood in the center of the car, he kissed her, then began to untie the strings of her bonnet.

"What are you—"

He set the bonnet aside and kissed her throat.

"You cannot be thinking—"

"Of course I am." He stripped off her gloves, one by one, kissing each hand. He pulled her gardening smock over her head and flung it somewhere behind him.

"That's better," he said, a wicked look in his eyes.

"Are you mad?" she gasped. "You cannot make love to me in a balloon!"

"Never fear. You will enjoy it."

Manning released the buttons that held the front of her bodice closed. He pushed down the bodice and petticoat to reveal her shift and corset, the latter made to fasten up front. A convenience for a woman living alone . . . or for a lover.

She dared not move, for fear of unbalancing the car. Manning only grinned as he unfastened the corset and peeled down her shift, revealing her breasts to the open air. He stared at them in open delight. Her cheeks burned; it felt shocking to let him watch her so, in broad daylight. She gripped the sides of the car as he bent to kiss her breast.

"L-lunatic! Are you in the habit of taking ladies up only to—to ravish them?"

He raised his head. "Never. You are the first."

She moaned as he kissed her breast again. He caressed her legs as he drew her skirts up past her stockings until her dress was rucked up around her waist. He kissed her lips, cupping her bare bottom with his fingers. He sought and found the hidden places he'd pleasured last night. He flicked a finger against her folds, then the sensitive knot between them. His tongue raked hers, then he lowered his head to kiss her breasts again.

Still holding the sides of the car, she arched back to welcome his caresses. The sight of the open sky sent a frisson of shock through her. Her nipples tingled deliciously with each exchange of cool air and his hot mouth. Fear left her. Something in her gloried in being so wanton. She let go of the sides of the car. Manning was driving her to the brink. It was time to retaliate.

She reached down and began to unbutton his breeches. He moaned against her breasts as she unfastened one side of the fall. She unfastened the other side. Blushing at her own boldness, she touched and found him firm and hot. He gasped, and she stroked him again, exploring the softness of his skin, the hardness beneath.

His eyes grew dark, frantic. "God . . . Emma!"

So he was not the only one who could drive a lover to madness! She took him into her hand. He drew a rough breath and thrust several fingers inside her. Her knees buckled. He settled to kneel on the floor of the car, bringing her down with him, so she felt him against her opening.

"Emma . . ." he breathed, his eyes beseeching her.

She lowered herself further. He gripped her with both arms, pulling her down as he penetrated deeply, piercing her with sharp pleasure. He held her in place, nearly motionless, so she was keenly aware of him inside of her. She remembered how they had moved together last night and yearned to recapture that rhythm. He kissed her slowly, thoroughly, until she could not wait any longer. When he relaxed his hold, she lifted her hips and bore down, drawing a groan from him.

The next time, she raised herself higher and hovered. His eyes were closed with the effort of holding back. She lowered herself in a little teasing motion, and rose again without quite taking him in. The next time she bore down on him swiftly, taking in all of him, and it seemed to break his control. He began to thrust harder than before, reaching deeper than she'd imagined possible.

"I love you, Emma," he said, with a thrust that went straight to her core.

She paused, remembering the tokens he'd sent this morning.

His cocky impudence, the abduction, his wicked lovemaking . . . were all a guise for a passion she could not doubt anymore. This was not pity, but a need so great it almost frightened her.

He loved her!

A rush of tenderness came over her. She kissed him again as she came down in one more powerful stroke. As she met him, her body shook with a sudden ecstasy. They cried out and clung to one another. She knew he'd found his release, deep inside her, and that nothing would ever be the same again.

Part Two

"Indeed, the whole scene before me filled my mind with a
sublime pleasure of which I never had a conception.
I had soared from the apprehensions of the Artillery Ground,
and felt as if I had left behind me all the cares and passions
that molest mankind."

— Vincent Lunardi,
An Account of the First Aerial Voyage in England, 1784

Chapter Twenty

Gil held Emma as she relaxed in his arms, spent and happy—at least he hoped she was happy. He certainly was. He stroked her hair, which had come uncoiled, and noticed that her cheek was damp. The sense of rightness that had swept him along thus far deserted him.

"Tell me what is wrong, Emma. I'll do anything to make it right." Fool! As if she needed to tell him. As if he could undo *this*.

She lifted her face and gave him a shaky smile. "I am sorry," she said. "I don't know what came over me. I promise I won't always cry when we make love."

His shoulders sagged with relief. If she spoke of making love again, it followed that she didn't hate him. But that brave smile struck him in the heart. Did he seem such a bad bargain?

Perhaps he ought to count himself lucky she hadn't thrown herself out of the balloon.

"Thank you for returning my locket," she said, surprising him.

"I was wrong to throw it away. I am sorry."

"You were right. Memories should be cherished," she said. "There will always be a part of me that grieves for Charles, but I no longer feel bound by that grief. You understand that, I think."

He nodded. She guessed he was thinking of Maggie.

"And thank you for that perfume case. I had been telling myself that our—our lovemaking was nothing but a—a brief diversion—for you, but once I saw that I knew it was more."

He pulled her closer. "It was always more with you, Emma. I'll take care of you. You're not alone anymore."

She rested her head on his shoulder, and he wondered what she was feeling. Relief? Dismay? It would be natural for her to want someone to share her concerns, but he might not be that someone. Perhaps she was wondering who would take care of whom.

He continued to hold her, stroking her hair. Villages, fields and woods passed lazily beneath them. It was as if he and Emma were still and the earth turned beneath them. He checked his instruments and saw that they'd ascended a few hundred feet as the sunshine warmed the balloon.

Then he became aware of fluttering. They'd entered a previously unseen stream of white-winged butterflies. He gazed at them in awe.

It seemed like a good omen.

"Emma, look up," he said softly.

She lifted her head. Her eyes widened as she gazed around her. "Can this be real?"

"Very real," he replied. "Durand told me he once encountered butterflies at a few thousand feet. But I wasn't sure I believed him."

"It seems like something out of a fairy story, or a dream," she murmured.

He said nothing, afraid to disturb the dream, if dream it was. She too seemed to want to just enjoy the moment. They flew on for a time, nestling together and drinking in the sight of fragile wings in concert around them.

He could not ask for a greater gift.

"I thought flying would be exciting, or perhaps terrifying," she said, after a time. "I had not thought it could feel so very peaceful."

"I might have gone mad after Waterloo, had Durand not bequeathed Alcyone to me. He could not have guessed what she meant to me." Immediately, he regretted saying it. He'd not meant to reveal what might make her doubt his strength, or his sanity.

"I understand now. I can see why you would not wish to give it up."

"I don't know anything else, besides soldiering. Now that we have peace, there is less opportunity for advancement."

"I do not think you should return to that life."

"No," he said.

She said nothing more. Perhaps she was remembering his laudanum-inspired raving on her parlor sofa. But he feared there was more behind her solemn look. Perhaps she understood why he loved flying so, but she would worry about him every time he did it.

They flew on, silent by mutual agreement. As the balloon began to cool, they began to gradually descend, leaving the swarm of butterflies. The sky was the deep blue of afternoon, empty of all but a few streaks of cloud.

"Where are we?" Emma asked.

He checked his pocket-watch and looked down. They were passing to the west of a modest market-town. "Somewhere in Hampshire. I think that town over there is Bordon."

She straightened up. "Bordon? We have flown nearly thirty miles! How far do you mean to go?"

Did she sound concerned? In the heat of the moment, he'd thought to dissuade her from accepting Blodgett's offer. More than that, he'd wanted to show her that life could still be full of joy and wonder. He hadn't thought how ruination might feel to her.

Perhaps she would forgive him.

"Not too much further," he said. "When we land, we shall find an inn. I'll tell them we are married. We will be, soon enough. My crew should catch up to us by tomorrow evening, or Monday at the latest. I can take you home and then as soon as possible, I'll take you to my friends, Colin and Susan."

"The Stansteads? The ones you asked me to write after your accident?"

"The very same."

"He is an army friend?"

He nodded. "So is Susan. They married after her first husband was killed in a skirmish. Now they make their home in Richmond, where Colin is busy with plans to convert the powder mill he inherited from his father to other purposes. They have three children, so no need to fear they will not welcome Kit. I think you'll like them. We can get a special license and be married at their home."

"Ought we to write to them first? I expect they will be very shocked."

"I'll write to them. But after all the adventures we've had, it would take far more than this to shock them. They'll welcome you with open arms."

"And . . . afterwards?"

"We can talk about that later."

After a moment, she nodded. He didn't doubt that at some point they would revisit the subject of his relatives in Norfolk, but he did not want to sully this precious time with talk of them.

Emma shifted, stretching her shoulders. He too had gone stiff from holding her so long in one position. Slowly, they disengaged themselves and took seats at either end of the car and began to rearrange their clothing. Soon, Emma looked almost like a prim schoolmistress again, if one could ignore sweet color in her cheeks and the fullness of lips that had been thoroughly kissed.

She reached for her smock and began to fold it into a tight ball. He tucked it and her gloves into his small valise.

"Are you hungry? I'll see what Sancha has packed for us." He opened the basket. It held several sandwiches made with the roast the Squire had provided for the ascension, along with a bit of cheese. There was also a flagon; he opened it up and smelled apples. "Ah, cider. Do you wish for some?"

She nodded. He offered it to her first then gave her one of the sandwiches. He drank deeply of the sweet potent cider, then ate his sandwich. Emma ate heartily; he was glad to see she had not lost her appetite. As they ate, the sun sank lower, shading the sky from gold to rose, outlining the few wispy clouds in silver.

Emma looked about her in renewed wonder. "Must we land soon?"

So she wasn't too upset about the distance they'd gone!

"I'm afraid so," he said, giving a short tug on the valve-rope. A short brief whistle above them indicated the valve had released some of the vapour and then closed, just as it should. "I wish I could stay up here with you longer."

He watched the barometer. If they descended too rapidly, he could empty one of the sandbags, but at present there was no need. When he looked up he saw Emma watching him.

"Are you frightened?" he asked.

"It seems so safe . . . while we are up here."

He decided to take her words at face value. "This will be nothing like my last landing. For one thing, there is little wind below us. See, the tops of the trees are not even moving. We also have plenty of ballast. We shall do very well. I promise."

He hoped he was right. Despite the ideal conditions, he'd never had so much at stake on a landing.

She still looked grave. He suspected she was still thinking about what would happen afterwards.

They had left Bordon—if that was what it was—behind and were moving slowly over open farmland. It was time to start looking for a good spot to land. They passed over several fields of growing corn, but he sought further, looking for a pasture, or a field left fallow for a season; he would not trample crops, except in an emergency. Just ahead there was a village with some dense woods beyond it, but there was some good open land beyond the woods.

All looked well, except for the furrow on Emma's brow.

He gave another quick tug on the valve. They approached the village, flying low at about five hundred feet. They had left the current of air in which they'd been traveling; the balloon was slowing in its progress. A few villagers looked up, pointing and shouting a welcome. Gil waved a pennant in response.

They passed over a squat church, near the edge of the village and north of the dense woods.

He pointed. "I'll land in that meadow, just ahead."

Emma's knuckles were pale as she gripped the sides of the car. But her voice was steady as she asked, "Is there anything I ought to do?"

"No. Just hold on as we land. There may be a bit of a bump." No more, not if he could help it. "Just don't get out until I tell you."

She gave him a steady look. "Without me as ballast, you'd go flying off again, wouldn't you?"

"Which is why I beg you not to get out early. I'm looking forward to sharing a real bed with you tonight."

Her shoulders eased a little. "Like ordinary gentlefolk?"

"I cannot always be making love to you in the woods or in the air," he said. "A bed might be a pleasant variation."

She let out a gurgle of laughter. He thanked God for her bravery. She might be nervous—which was entirely natural, given the last landing she'd witnessed—but there would be no hysterics.

They approached the meadow over a stand of trees, the balloon descending a touch too quickly for his liking. He spilled part of a sandbag over into the trees; they continued to descend, but at a slow, regal pace. If he was any judge, it would be a perfect landing.

"Shall we need that?" Emma pointed to the grappling hook. "Is it for anchoring the balloon?"

"Yes, but it's only a precaution today. We'd need it more if there were high winds." Normally, he might not have bothered with it on such a flight, but he would take no chances with Emma aboard.

They reached the meadow, still slowly descending. Gil cast out the grappling hook. Their descent slowed as the weight of the hook reached the ground, lightening the load. They halted when it caught on a rocky outcropping. The car tilted slightly but nothing to cause concern.

"All's well," he assured Emma as he reopened the valve briefly. As Alcyone began to descend again, he took up the slack to the anchor.

She remained pale but calm during the rest of the descent. Her eyes widened in surprise as they landed with the lightest of thumps.

He grinned. "Not so bad, was it?"

She kept her mouth prim, but her eyes were glowing. "Shall I kiss the ground now?"

He tugged at the valve rope again, releasing more of the vapour, ensuring that no unexpected breeze would move them. Out of the corner of his eye he saw several farm laborers crossing the stile into the pasture. "No, kiss me instead."

He leaned forward to snatch his reward as the men came running up.

Chapter Twenty-One

Her lips still warm from his kiss, Emma sat quietly while Manning ordered the grinning laborers to hold onto the mooring ropes dangling from Alcyone's netting. Gradually, he began to release the inflammable air from the canopy. Emma watched his face, bathed in the golden light which mirrored her feelings. Grateful as she was for their safe landing, she would always treasure the memory of their flight.

More people arrived and helped to secure the balloon.

"Where are we?" Manning asked the crowd, pulling out the small notebook and pencil he carried in his coat pocket.

"Between Selborne and Faringdon, sir," said one of them.

"Selborne?" she echoed.

Manning glanced up from his writing. "Do you know it?"

She smiled. "It is where Mr. Gilbert White lived. He was a famous naturalist and a friend of my father's. I never knew him—I was very young when he died—but Papa used to talk about him, and of course we read his *Natural History and Antiquities of Selborne.*"

"We can take a look about us tomorrow, then."

He finished recording the time and place of landing. After a few more minutes, he deemed it safe for them to exit the car. He asked a few of the onlookers to hold it steady, climbed out and then helped Emma, his hands caressing her waist briefly as he handed her out.

The crowd gave them a cheer; Manning bowed and Emma made them a curtsey. In his showman's voice, he introduced them as Captain and Mrs. Manning, and she smiled, feeling less embarrassed than perhaps she should have. They were already betrothed, with the heavens as their witness.

Manning secured promises of a farm wagon to collect the balloon and then inquired about nearby inns. The onlookers directed them to the Rose and Crown in Faringdon, being the closest inn suitable for gentry. A young woman amongst the crowd introduced herself as Nell Brown, the landlady's daughter. Offering her a coin, Manning asked her to conduct Emma to the inn and secure them the best bedchamber. Then he handed her the small leather valise Sancha had stowed in the car.

"Make yourself comfortable, darling," he murmured to Emma, putting an arm around her. "I'll come as soon as I can get everything folded up and secured. No need to order dinner unless you wish for it; I'm not hungry. Not for food, anyway."

He winked and then released her. Blushing a little, she walked off with the landlady's daughter.

The sun hung low in the sky; trees adjoining the pasture cast long shadows over the field, banding the sunny golden green of the grass with darker emerald.

"What's it like to fly, ma'am, if I might ask?"

Emma smiled at the eager look on Nell's face but found it difficult to reply. "It seems as if it ought to be very exciting," she said. "Parts of it, like taking off, are thrilling. But once one is high above the earth, it feels very peaceful."

"As if your troubles were far away?"

Emma nodded. It had seemed so; and even now she could not—or did not want to—summon up worries about the future.

"That does sound lovely." Nell seemed content to say no more as they walked down the lane. Emma was glad of it; she felt as light and new as a child and wanted to drink everything in. It was as if she'd never before seen a sunset that tinted the sky with salmon and gold, never walked beside a hedgerow and studied the intricacy of the foliage or inhaled the scent of flowering brambles that hinted at succulent berries to come. And the thought of sharing a bed with Manning filled her with unreasoning delight.

The sun was just setting as they reached the village. They passed several cottages and a shop, long closed. Emma stifled a laugh as she remembered she was without a change of clothing or even a toothbrush. At least she and Manning had the one valise to lend them some slim respectability. She hoped everyone would assume they could not carry much with them in a balloon and not be surprised when she wore the same gown tomorrow. Surely Manning would not care if she slept in her shift.

The Rose and Crown turned out to be quite a modern brick building. Nell told Emma it had been built just a few years before by a Mr. Knight of Chawton. The landlady greeted Emma kindly but with obvious curiosity, asking a number of questions as she conducted Emma to a room on the upper floor. Emma did her best to reply but was happy when they reached the room, neatly appointed and with a view of a small garden. She approved the room but declined dinner, asking only for water for washing up.

Once Nell had started a fire in the grate and lit several candles about the room, she and her mother left. Emma took a longer look about her. There was a large four-poster bed, covered in a quilt, and a small dressing-table. A wing chair stood by the fire. She went to the window and looked out. The garden below was all in shadows. In the darkening sky stars were beginning to appear.

She wondered how long it would take Manning to pack up his balloon. He would wish to do it carefully, she supposed, to avoid damage to the varnished silk. Wonderful as today's flight had been, an uneasy shadow passed over her heart. He would fly again. It felt like tempting fate, yet to try to stop him might do more harm than good. She pulled the curtains closed, shutting out the sky.

Nell came back in with hot water, and although she wanted to linger, Emma smiled and dismissed her. Manning's valise stood on a side table where Nell had left it. He'd told her to make herself comfortable, so Emma decided he wouldn't mind her borrowing what she needed from it. She opened it up and rummaged through until she found a dressing case containing a brush.

She removed her bonnet and undressed down to her shift. After washing up, she sat down to work on her hair, pulling out the pins and brushing until it lay in loose, gleaming waves over her shoulders. Her reflection in the mirror hardly looked like the same person who had set out for the Manor this morning. She looked like a woman who was loved, whose lover was coming for her.

She decided not to braid her hair as she usually did for sleeping. She guessed Manning would enjoy seeing her like this. Ought she to climb into bed? Or should she sit about in just her shift? She did not know how these things were done. She decided to wait up for him and sat down by the fire. Her legs shook a little. Ridiculous! They'd already made love twice, so why was she such a fool now?

Because then they'd been swept up in the moment by currents of desire that had nothing to do with reason. This was different. This was deliberate.

I'm not hungry. At least not for food.

She curled her legs up onto the chair and stared into the glowing coals, reliving everything that had happened. Now she understood how serene and glorious flying could be, and what it meant to Manning. Not that she was at ease with his occupation; conditions would not always be as perfect as today. It was still dangerous. To argue about it would only cause a rift between them, but perhaps in time he would find the serenity he sought in the skies within himself. And in her arms . . .

Sometime later she woke from a doze, hearing voices below. One of them was Manning's, although she couldn't quite make out his words. She straightened up, heart pounding a rhythm that matched the swift footsteps coming toward the room.

There was a scratch on the door. "Emma?"

"Come in," she tried to say, but her voice was husky with sleep. She cleared her throat and repeated her welcome.

Manning came in and closed the door behind him. He paused for a moment and stared at her, taking in the sight of her curled up in the chair, wearing only her shift. She tried to smile, though she felt as if her heart had leapt up to her throat. She rose from the chair, finding her legs had gone numb as she stumbled towards him. He crossed the room in two strides and pulled her up against him, kissing her as if they been parted for days, not hours.

He crushed her up against him, kissing first her mouth and then her neck. He backed away for an instant and gazed at her again with darkened eyes, his hands on her shoulders. A delicious fever gripped her as he pushed her shift down off her shoulders, baring her breasts. He pulled the shift down further, past her hips and let it fall to the floor. He brought her close again and boldly caressed her back, cupped her bottom and lifted her up against him. She returned his kiss, breaking it only to unbutton his coat. She pulled it off and caught him staring at her again, as if she were the most beautiful thing he'd ever seen.

"Emma ... You are ... paradise itself."

She blushed but resisted the urge to cover herself. "No, you are good to say that, but I am far too muscular for true beauty!"

"You're a goddess!" His voice was rough. "Ever since that night you helped me back onto the sofa, I've been dreaming of those strong arms and legs wrapped around me."

He picked her up and carried her toward the bed, already turned down. He laid her onto the snowy sheets and she moved to make room for him. As he pulled off his waistcoat and cravat, his eyes never left her. The bed shifted as he sat down at the edge to remove his boots and breeches.

Still in his shirt—perhaps too impatient to remove it—he swung himself into the bed and onto his side to look at her again. She heated, knowing the light of the bedside candle fell full upon her, while he remained in the shadows. She sensed his gaze rove over her face, her breasts, her belly, the triangle of curls between her legs. He leaned over her to kiss one breast and then the other, his hair brushing against her skin. She stroked his head with one hand as he teased her nipples to ever more exquisite tightness. He shifted again, claiming her mouth, and as he reached down for a more intimate caress, she parted for him. He made a hungry, inarticulate sound and moved over her. She put her arms around his waist and drew him in. He paused, his breath noisy over the crackle of the fire, reflections of the candles in his eyes.

"What's wrong?" she asked.

"Emma, I want you to the point of madness. But I don't want to hurt you."

Did he doubt she was just as aroused?

She smiled up at him. "Do your worst." And she pulled him down towards her.

He plunged in and she stifled a cry of joy. In case he misunderstood, she wrapped her legs up around his waist, holding him in a tight embrace of arms and legs. Then he pulled back and stared hungrily at her for a second before plunging in again, deep inside her. Driven by some wanton inspiration, she tightened her inner muscles to embrace him intimately. He practically growled in response. Drawing back, he stared down at her again.

"Emma, what you do to me . . ."

"Do you wish me to stop?"

In answer, he thrust again and she met him, catching his rhythm. As in a dream, she sensed the rocking of the bed, heard the sound of their breathing. A deep pleasure flooded her; her insides clenched, no longer under her control. Manning tensed and cried out and she held him tightly, shuddering with the force of their climax.

His passion spent, he tried to roll off of her, but she continued to hold him, relishing the weight of him, the gradual slowing of his breath. The next time he moved, she released him long enough to let him extinguish the candle. He turned back and gathered her up next to him.

She found the nook in his shoulder where she'd rested last night on the grounds of the Manor—was it only last night? She did not even feel like the same person. Perhaps she was not. But if she had changed, it was to become softer, gentler, and yet stronger than she'd been before. It seemed they were floating together on the bed, as they'd floated in the skies. She drifted into dreams of sunsets and warm embraces.

A slanting beam of sunlight teased Gil's eyes open. The room was shaded but birds were beginning to sing outside. Joy stole over him as he remembered the previous day. Then he realized he was alone in the bed.

Emma stood near the window, looking out through the gap in the curtains. Her hair hung down her back in loose waves; she wore nothing but his coat, the tail of which just covered her sweet bum. The sight of her bare legs brought his usual morning arousal to an exquisite throb.

He wanted to make love to her again. But what was she thinking, standing there with her back to him?

"Good morning," he called out softly.

She turned around and gave him a slow smile. She didn't seem angry, or even worried, and yet he couldn't tell what that smile boded.

"I always wake early, even when it is not a school day," she said. "I'm sorry if I woke you."

He cleared his throat. "Then come here and apologize properly. You look very fetching in my coat, but I would rather you took it off."

She shed the coat as she neared the bed. His eyes had adjusted to the light and he drank in the sight of her gloriously muscled body and full breasts.

He gathered her into his arms and pulled her on top of him. Her breasts fell against his chest like soft pillows; her

215

hair spilled down to brush his neck. He hardened against her belly and sucked in a slow, cooling breath. If he wasn't careful, he'd go off like a rocket and miss giving her the slow, thorough pleasuring she deserved. If she was ready for more . . .

"Did you sleep well?"

"I'm the hardy sort. An Amazon, remember?" She chuckled deep in her throat, sending another surge of desire through him.

"*My* Amazon. I'll grapple with you any day."

She hugged him back but a moment later, she lifted herself up onto her arms, watching him with a thoughtful expression. "Are you not warm in that shirt?"

He tensed. Her hands brushed his hips as she pulled up the hem of his shirt. His pulse quickened, half in arousal, half dismay. Hastily, he pulled her down for a kiss. But she would not be deterred. She broke the kiss and sat back, straddling his legs. He tried to reach for her but she arched back, distracting him with the sight of her full breasts, the delicious curve of her waist. Before he could protest, she grasped the hem of his shirt and pulled it up to his neck, exposing him to the open air. God, he longed for her to touch him again.

But she was looking at his chest. At his scars. She must have seen them earlier, of course. Still, he did not want her to examine them now. They had better things to do.

He tried to pull her back down toward him, but she resisted. She grasped the back of his shirt and pulled it over his neck. Resigning himself, he lifted his arms, allowing her to pull the sleeves off. She anticipated his next attempt to snatch her close, rolling away from him. Propping herself up on one elbow, she touched the faint scar on his left arm.

"Gil . . . How did you get *this*?"

At least she was accustoming herself to his Christian name.

"An unfortunate accident while shaving," he replied.

"Tell me the truth!"

"An elephant bit me."

"Liar! *Tell me.*"

"Stubborn woman," he muttered. "Very well. It was in the Peninsula, in a village called Barba del Puerco. We were posted to guard a bridge over the Agueda at the end of a steep mountain pass. The French attacked at about midnight while we were asleep, but we were able to repel them."

"And then?" She brushed the scar, sending shivers down his arm and elsewhere. God, how he hungered for her.

"A graze from a musket ball. Nothing, really. We lost about twenty men that night. I was lucky."

She continued to stroke the scar, pleasuring and tormenting him all at once.

"Satisfied, Mistress?" Before she could react, he pulled her back on top of him.

But she pulled away again. This time her quiet gaze moved to his other arm, the one that bore a long, white slash, long healed but never forgotten. He did *not* want to talk about that one.

"And this? Was this nothing, too?" She asked, reaching to touch his right arm.

He gave her a sheepish look. "You see, there was this Marquesa. A proper Spanish beauty, with flashing eyes and the most magnificent figure I ever saw—before I saw yours, of course." She stuck her tongue out at him at that. Much better. "Her husband was rather irate, and—"

"And challenged you to a duel, where you received that scar." She made a sound like a growl, about as menacing as a kitten. "I don't believe a word of it. Tell me the truth."

"No, I've had enough of this interrogation. I have a better idea." He leaned over and kissed her breast.

She sighed and rolled back towards him. But just as he was congratulating himself on his strategy, she straddled him, adding to his torment. There was a stubborn jut to her chin. God help him! Pinned beneath her so, he'd tell her anything.

She touched his arm again. "How did you get this?"

"You don't want to know, love."

"Yes, I do. If we're to be married—"

"We *shall* be married."

"Then I want to know everything about you."

"I love you. Isn't that enough?"

She leaned forward to kiss the long scar, her lips warm against his skin.

"It happened at Assaye." He swallowed, forcing the images back, the memory of the heat, the noise, the carnage.

"I remember. You were in India and you were just sixteen. Your friend Captain Forsythe died there, didn't he?"

"It was a damned stupid blunder!" he spat. "Orrock—the East India Company *officer* in command—failed to follow Wellington's orders. The idiot brought us too far to the right, straight into direct fire from the Mahratta artillery." He swallowed, his rage still fresh after so many years. "We were pounded. Those of us who survived formed squares as the Mahratta horsemen circled and attacked with their long swords."

She kissed his arm again. "How did you ever survive?"

"Colonel Maxwell charged in with the cavalry to rescue us. He died doing so. I'll never forget it."

"Once you had your command, you took good care of your own men."

"We had our losses. But the Duke never wanted us to take foolish risks."

"If I didn't say it before, I know you were right not to support—what was his name? Dryburn?—at Waterloo."

He thrust back those memories. He'd dwelt in them long enough. "It would just have been more lives lost, darling."

"I know. I cannot imagine how awful it must have been to watch his company fall."

"Enough! It's all past."

"Perhaps, but I still wish to understand." She touched the round scar on his shoulder. "And this?"

"Do you really wish to know?"

"I think you told me you were hit in the shoulder at Badajoz."

He nodded.

"I am glad Maggie was there to care for you."

"You would have done the same." The next words burst from him. "I didn't value her as I should have!"

A mistake he wouldn't make again.

He clenched his jaw as Emma kissed the spot.

"I am sure you made her very happy." She kissed him again and a sharp, sweet memory shot through him: how Maggie had smiled that morning when she'd told him she was with child. And then it struck him: Emma might already be carrying his child now.

He'd not fail her, he told himself. She kept stroking and exploring with strong, gentle fingers as he strove to remain still. It was only fair, this questioning. Since she'd bravely decided to take him on—he was no longer under any delusion that he was just rescuing her—she deserved to know all. But every soft touch seared him like fire. Anger, grief and longing roiled in him. He didn't want her to pity him. He longed to stop the talk, to just bury himself inside her and put it all behind them.

"This ... this was from Waterloo." She brushed the scar on his chest, the one that had nearly done him in. "It happened after ..."

"After the debacle with Dryburn and his men," he said. "The farm was taken; we were about to be overwhelmed. I was hit while ordering the retreat; Lund and a few others carried me back behind the lines."

He would never forget the carnage. The screams of the wounded, the memory of Dryburn raving as the surgeons worked on him. His friends ... Some had survived unscathed, like Johnny Kincaid. Others had recovered from grievous wounds, like Simmons. But so many friends were gone. Charlie Eeles, Smyth. Molloy.

And Emma's first love, Charles Hartley.

He willed himself back to the present.

Emma leaned over to kiss the wound, her hair brushing over his chest. It was too much; he couldn't bear it. He pulled her down against him.

Pity was the last thing he wanted from her now.

"It's all right, love. I was lucky. Sancha nursed me, and later Susan—Colin Stanstead's wife. It's all healed."

"Perhaps," she said, lifting herself to smile down upon him. "I think it is a miracle you held together and that you are here now."

Yes, it was a miracle and he wanted to celebrate it in the best way possible. He reached for her breasts, feeling their firm weight in his hands, catching at her nipples with his thumbs. She gasped as he reached to draw a finger through the slick fold between her legs. He could have taken her right there, but he would not rush, not until she was as aroused as he was. He toyed some more, watching until her face contorted with the effort to contain her pleasure. He put his hands around her waist and repositioned her.

Her eyes widened as she realized what he wanted. "Ah . . . I didn't know we could— It seems so wicked . . ."

"Ride me, Emma."

Light slanting through the window caught the blush in her cheek. She straightened up and lowered herself, slowly taking him in. She embraced him with her inner muscles in that cunning trick she'd learned last night. Breathing hard, he struggled not to go off half-cocked. She pulled herself up, caressing him every inch of the way, before lowering herself again in a heady plunge. She learned quickly. He was losing command of himself, leaking into her. He gritted his teeth and tried to hold back. She rocked up and down with deliberate slowness. He caressed her buttocks, focusing on the softness of velvet skin over the firm muscles, trying not to give way.

But he could not bear her teasing rhythm much longer. He pulled her down onto him and rolled them both over, still deep inside her. She bucked as he thrust again and again. She tightened around him and cried out. His own climax was upon him; his whole body clenched. There was no holding back now. He filled her with his seed, then came to rest on top of her.

She held him close, and he rested there for a moment before rolling to his side and pulling her into his arms.

"I love you," she murmured.

Gratitude flooded him as she nestled against him, sweaty and trusting. It brought back memories of another time, in that honeysuckle-covered cottage in Alameida: a warm bed, birds singing outside and a sweet, loving woman in his arms.

This time, he vowed it would end differently.

Chapter Twenty-Two

Emma woke up, her head still pillowed on Gil's shoulder. He was smiling at her. Sunshine filled the room.

She shifted onto one elbow. "What time is it?"

He rolled toward the side table where his pocket watch lay. "A little after nine."

Not so very late, then. She sat up, aware of his gaze as she held the covers around her. "I should like to go to church."

"Whatever you wish. Shall I help you dress?" he asked, grinning.

"No, then we will never get there! Besides, I am famished." She gave him a shove. With a loud sigh, he swung himself out of bed.

"Very well, Mistress. We must keep up your strength."

They dressed as promptly as two lovers could. Gil went down to inquire about breakfast while Emma finished brushing out and pinning up her hair.

Although they'd spent the night and early morning like heathen, she felt eager to attend church. Not out of guilt—she still had no sense of wrongdoing. Quite the reverse; their lovemaking felt like a gift. It was not guilt that drew her to church, but a feeling that she wanted to start this new life aright.

Somehow, over the past few days, she'd regained a sense of hope. Not that the sorrows of past years had been erased—she suspected now that they would always be a part of her, and she would not wish it otherwise. Nor had she recaptured her old trust in a divine Protector who would keep her from harm; that would be a child's thinking. But now she trusted that whatever came, she would be sustained.

She came down to the private parlor feeling light and peaceful. She feasted on eggs and toast, savored her coffee, and managed to keep her countenance when the landlady asked, with a kind but knowing look, how long they'd been married. Wondering just how much sound carried through the inn, Emma blushed while Gil, with a glint of amusement in his eyes, told Mrs. Brown it had not been long.

They walked off to church soon afterwards, arms linked, enjoying every step. Inside the ancient building, the elderly vicar mumbled an incoherent sermon, but it was no matter. The cool stone surrounding them and the light slanting in through the windows exactly suited Emma's mood. She hadn't come for any doctrinal lessons, only a quiet place to contemplate the most important commandment of all.

She was deeply aware of Gil beside her, quiet and sober but—she sensed—as content to be there as she was. She thought of Kit, back at Meadowcross Cottage. No doubt Becky was taking good care of him, but Emma looked forward to seeing him again. He'd be overjoyed by the news of her engagement.

After the service, the local gentry surrounded them, asking questions about their flight and inviting them to dine. Gil politely declined, saying they needed to return home soon.

The crowd finally dispersed and Gil suggested they go for a ramble before returning to the inn. Emma put an arm over his, noticing a certain determined look on his face. She guessed he, too, realized it was time to discuss their future.

"They showed me how to reach a bridle path to Selborne," he said. "Would you like to go there?"

She nodded. They walked past an enormous yew in the churchyard and down the lane heading out of the village. By the time they reached the path that led to Selborne, they were alone. They walked in silence for a few more minutes, through an open field where swallows flew low, catching insects in mid-flight.

"Gil—" she began, hearing him say her name at the same time.

They both laughed, a little awkwardly. She let him begin.

"You're wondering what sort of mess I've landed you into, but I promise you it will be all right. My men should arrive by tomorrow. Once they take charge of Alcyone, we can return to Tichbury."

She thought of the gossip that must be raging there. How would they be received on their return? Friends like the Grimshaws would be shocked but sympathetic. She didn't want to think about Arabella or Lydia, or the jealous reactions of those who perceived Gil as a Good Catch.

"I know I've exposed you to gossip and I'm sorry for that," he said. "But I promise the Stansteads will welcome you. We'll be married as soon as possible and I'll look for a place for us to live. I have a lodging in Richmond for myself and the men, but you deserve better."

"I don't expect life to be all balloon rides and lovemaking," she protested. "Kit and I are accustomed to living in a cottage. I have some money too, that I've been putting by in the hope of taking Kit to university someday. I can write more books and I can draw. Mr. Blodgett will have no further wish to deal with me, but there are others who might."

"I will provide for you, Emma! I can't promise you luxury, but we shall manage. I've made arrangements for ascensions at Greenwich, Deptford and other fairs." His jaw was tight, as if he expected an argument.

She was prepared for that. "Very well," she said mildly.

"You don't object?"

Good. She'd thrown him off balance. "I don't *wish* you to put yourself in danger, but I also cannot imagine you seeking employment as a clerk at a bank or some such thing."

He stared, baffled by her meekness. She looked away so he would not see her smile.

They walked for a few minutes in silence. There *was* another occupation she thought would suit him, but she had to broach the subject carefully.

"Gil, I'm sorry I spoke so harshly to you the night of the ball."

"The ball?"

"You don't remember? I accused you of neglecting your responsibilities regarding your uncle's estate."

"Don't worry about it," he said stiffly. "You didn't know the circumstances."

"I would like to."

"There's nothing much to tell. I'm not welcome at Lynnford Abbey and since my uncle has the constitution of an ox, there's no chance of my succeeding him there any time soon."

"But you are his heir. It is his duty to teach you everything you will need to know when he is gone."

"Emma, there's bad blood between us. Very bad." There was a warning in his voice.

"Tell me what happened," she said as gently as she could. "Whatever it is, I would like to understand. Was there a disagreement between your father and your uncle?"

"Disagreement? I suppose you might call it that." They continued onto a bridle path, following the signpost to Selborne. "If it were not for my uncle, my parents might be alive today."

She flinched at the raw anger in his voice.

"No, it was not murder," he said. "But it might as well have been."

"Tell me how it happened."

"The story goes that my mother was the only daughter of the vicar, but so beautiful that all the young men in the neighborhood were mad for her, even those who might have

225

looked for a bride with greater fortune and connections. My uncle never forgave my father for winning her heart. It is said he wanted her for himself."

They passed into the shade of a line of trees.

"My father had little money of his own; my grandparents must have expected my uncle to help him to a profession. He made a pretense of accepting my parents' marriage and offered to use his influence to help my father to a commission in the army. But rather than arranging a more advantageous posting, my uncle had him sent to the West Indies."

"You're certain that was not a mistake?"

He shook his head. "It was no mistake. They all must have known how many Englishmen perished there, far more from disease than military action. But according to Captain Forsythe, who was a friend of his, my father felt honor-bound to follow through. He desired my mother to remain behind, in England, but she followed on the next ship. I was born in Jamaica." He stopped and briefly closed his eyes. "They lasted longer than most, nearly six years. But there was an epidemic of yellow fever. They died within a few days of each other."

"Yet you survived." She leaned close to him, squeezing his arm.

"My father had sent us to live at a station high up in the hills, where the air was cooler and disease was not so rife. But when we had word that he had taken ill, my mother left me with servants and went to nurse him."

Somewhere a cuckoo called mournfully.

"I was sent to Lynnford Abbey to live with my aunt and uncle and my cousin George, who was a year or so older."

"I know. Miss Grimshaw's cousin wrote about it. From her letter, I am guessing they were not kind to you."

He looked away. "Oh, I was happy enough. My relations didn't care for me, but when they were out of sight the servants cosseted me no end. They must have liked my father. And I was forever running away to the river and the marshes."

She guessed there was more to it than that. They passed out of the woods into another open area.

"And what did you do when you ran away?" she asked.

"There was an old man who let me go out on the Bure with him and taught me to fish. Other times I stole away to one of my uncle's farms. My aunt complained of my preference for low company, but I didn't care. I was never happier than when I was trailing after Farmer Colby. He seemed like a magician to me, turning dirt and manure into wheat and barley and turnips. I must have been an annoying brat, but he never lost patience with me. As for Mrs. Colby, somehow she'd got the idea they didn't feed me at the Hall and she had to make up for it." He let out a small laugh.

"They sound like good people," she said.

"I thought about them often. We were supposed to be fighting for the King, but *I* was fighting for the Colbys and others like them. When I saw how Boney's troops had ravaged Spain and Portugal, laying farms and fields waste, it was a comfort to know all was right back in Norfolk."

Several clouds drifted over them, their shadows passing over the green corn.

"Perhaps you could visit them," she suggested.

He shrugged. "It was so long ago. They may have forgotten me."

"I doubt that. When did you leave?"

"When I was nine. Captain Forsythe came to visit and decided to befriend me."

"Perhaps he noticed you were not being treated kindly?"

He shrugged. "He offered to take me with him to India and bring me up in the army. Everyone was happy with that arrangement."

"Did your aunt and uncle at least write to you?"

He shook his head. "I believe Captain Forsythe occasionally sent them reports of my progress. But after Assaye ..."

Where Captain Forsythe fell, she remembered. "But you were only sixteen. They ought to have sent for you."

"Grant, the Quarter Master, took it upon himself to write to my uncle and ask if he wished me to be sent home. There was no reply. I was glad of it. I was an ensign by then and there was talk of sending me to the newly forming Light Brigade. Soon, I was transferred from the 74th and sent to Shorncliffe in Kent, where I joined the 95th under Sir John Moore."

His voice had warmed. She sensed his loyalty to the famous commander who founded the new brigade and died later after the disastrous retreat to Corunna. Then he'd formed a life and a family of sorts in the army.

The question of his real family continued to trouble her.

"What happened when your cousin died? It would have been natural for you to go home then, surely?"

"That was late in 1812. I had my company by then. And I had Maggie." His jaw tightened. "I didn't hear of George's death until some chance gossip brought it to Colonel Barnard's ears. He urged me to return to Norfolk and look into affairs there. When I told him I'd no desire to return, he wrote to my uncle. A good man, Barnard. He was shocked when my uncle wrote back saying he'd rot in hell before seeing me at Lynnford Abbey. Just as well. I can imagine his and my aunt's reactions if I'd returned with Maggie, a mere sergeant's widow, on my arm. No, I was happier where I was."

"Perhaps your uncle was still beset by grief. You have not heard from him since?"

"If you're thinking that he may have repented, all I can say is you don't know my uncle. He probably regards my continued survival as a personal insult."

Seeing the set of his jaw, she decided not to press him further. Norfolk still had a hold on him. In time, he would see that he needed to return.

Chapter Twenty-Three

The next day, Emma clutched the strap as the post-chaise wobbled around the turn to Meadowcross Lane. Gil's crew had arrived in Faringdon in the morning and would return with the balloon once the horses had a chance to rest. It felt so strange to be coming home again. Everything looked the same, but she felt so different.

Gil consulted his pocket-watch. "We've made good time," he said.

"Then I should visit Sir George and Mr. Grimshaw to-day." It was not a task she looked forward to, but it had to be done.

"Wait for me. Once I've settled up at the Hare and Hounds, I can go with you. They won't speak ill of you with me present."

"They won't be unkind," she said. "They are probably shocked, and now they must find a new schoolmistress. I feel sorry that I was not there today, but Miss Grimshaw may have taken over. She did so once before, when I was ill."

"I'd wager she'll be happy to continue until they find a re-placement," he said. "How soon might you and Kit be ready to leave?" There was no mistaking the eagerness in his voice.

"A day or so," she said. The cottage's furnishings would be left for the next schoolmistress. Besides that, they had little: clothing, some books and pictures. It felt strange to be thinking of packing up and leaving their home, not knowing where their next one might be.

Based on all Gil had told her, she looked forward to meeting the Stansteads. But more than anything, she was eager to see Kit again.

The carriage slowed and stopped.

Gil helped her down. "Trust me. All will be well." He gave her a quick kiss. "I'll be back soon."

The door was open but the cottage was quiet. Emma felt a spurt of anxiety—what if Kit had fallen ill while she was gone? But it was a fine evening. Kit and Becky were most likely in the garden. She ran through the kitchen and out the back door, slowing as she saw Kit sitting on the bench and Becky hoeing the vegetables.

Kit's face lit up. "Emma!" he called.

She ran across the bit of lawn and bent over to hug him. "I've missed you," she murmured, stroking his hair.

He withdrew a little, his face reddening.

She took the hint and straightened up. "How are you feeling, dear?"

"Well enough," he said impatiently. "So are you going to marry Captain Manning?"

"Yes, Kit."

"Famous!"

Becky joined them. "I'm happy for you, Miss! It is just what I have been telling everyone."

"Is there much talk then?"

"You know how people are. But everyone likes you—at least everyone who matters—and they wish you to be happy."

"Where will we live?" Kit asked.

"I don't know. As soon as arrangements can be made for someone to take my place, we shall go to Elmwood Lodge, in Richmond. Captain Manning's friends, Sir Colin and Lady Stanstead, live there. He says they will be happy to have us visit. They have three children of their own."

She turned to Becky. "You could have a place with us, if you wish, but of course I understand if you wish to remain closer to your family." *And a certain footman.*

Becky paused for a moment. "That's very kind of you, Miss. I should like to go talk to my parents about it. Would that be all right?"

"I must go speak to Mr. Grimshaw and Sir George, but after that, you must go home. I am grateful you have stayed as long as you have."

"I was glad to help, and so happy for you and the Captain!"

They chatted a bit more, then Emma went back into the cottage, hoping Gil would be back soon. Although she dreaded the visits they would have to make, she would rather get them over as soon as possible. The sooner everyone knew of their betrothal, the better.

As she entered the parlor, Pandora came to greet her, rubbing alongside her and purring. She bent to pet her and realized with a pang that she'd have to leave her behind. Pandora belonged with the cottage; she'd lived there all her life. With the thatched roof, the place needed a good mouser.

So many good-byes to make ... But a new life also beckoned.

She straightened up, hearing a knock on the door. She hadn't thought Gil would stand on ceremony. She went to the door but instead of Gil, Mr. Blodgett stood there, his mouth pursed with disapproval.

She stared for a moment. "Mr. Blodgett! I thought you were going back to Bath."

"I could not leave until I knew your fate. I suppose I must be glad to see you alive."

"Thank you, I am very well." She decided to take the bull by the horns. "Captain Manning has asked me to marry him and I have accepted."

Something—a gleam, something like fury, but surely it could not be—flashed in his eyes. Gil had warned her against Blodgett, but it was nonsensical to think he was jealous.

"I know you do not like Captain Manning, but—"

"Excuse me for not expressing the usual sentiments on such an occasion," he interrupted more sharply than he'd ever spoken to her. "As your friend, I must urge you to reconsider your decision."

He would prefer her to be ruined than married?

"I am sorry to give you pain, but my mind is quite made up."

"You must allow me to speak with you about this. Has our friendship meant so little that you will not allow at least that much?"

"I am sorry, but I have much to do. There is nothing you can say that will change my mind," she said, hoping he would take his leave.

Blodgett held his ground. "Are you certain it is marriage he offered?"

"Of course. I thank you for your concern, but—"

"At least allow me to offer you an alternative!" he said.

"You cannot still wish to employ me as your mother's companion?"

He coughed. "I am afraid that my mother's constitution is not strong enough for her to endure the gossip that would ensue from taking you into her household."

"Then what are you suggesting?"

"I know of a cottage in a quiet village, in the vicinity of Bath. With my assistance, you and your brother could remove there. You could live there in peace and seclusion, away from both temptation and censure."

She stared, knowing exactly what Gil would make of this offer. "And of course, you would visit us upon occasion?"

His face reddened. "My many charitable activities would preclude frequent visits. But . . . it is my hope I would be . . . welcome . . . now and again." He reached to grasp her hands; his grip was sweaty and trembling.

She stepped backward, avoiding his grasp. "There is no way on heaven or earth that I would accept such an offer. I must ask you to leave. *Now.*"

"You mistake me! You must know I have the greatest regard for your virtue! I merely wished to offer you a safe haven ... Emma ..."

"What's this?" Gil called sharply from the doorway.

"Mr. Blodgett is just at the point of leaving," she said.

Blodgett spun sideways, his eyes bulging.

"Perhaps he needs some help." Gil grasped Blodgett by the cravat, dragging him toward the door.

"Unhand me! I insist!" Blodgett spluttered.

"Don't hurt him!" she shouted. "There's no need."

"There's every need to rid your cottage of such vermin!" He shoved Blodgett out, closed the door behind him and turned to face Emma. "What the devil was he doing here?"

"Nothing I couldn't manage."

"He won't trouble you anymore."

"There was no need to throw him out that way!"

"You still can't see what that worm wants from you?"

"I do now; I am not a complete fool! But he's done no harm, and he did pay Dr. Procton to attend Kit."

"No harm? What has all that medicine and mollycoddling done for your brother? He needs fresh air and more to do than lie about worrying about his health."

He released her and strode toward the kitchen.

She raced after him. "What are you doing?"

By the time she'd caught up with him he was reaching for the shelf where she kept Kit's medicine.

"No! Please, Gil, don't—"

She tried to snatch the bottle away from him, but he turned, uncorking the bottle and then pouring the contents out through the open window.

"Good God! How could you do that?" She stared at the empty bottle, her stomach knotting with fear.

Gil dropped the vial and put his arms around her. "Don't worry, love. Kit will be the better without this rubbish, you'll see."

"Idiot! You've no idea what you've done!"

"It's only a quack nostrum and you know it!"

"No, it isn't!" She shuddered. "Do you think the same notion hadn't crossed my mind already?"

Now he looked worried. Damn him!

"A year ago, I questioned Dr. Procton about the medicine," she continued, forcing her voice to be steady. "He warned me there would be dire consequences if Kit did not receive regular doses. I could not afford to consult another physician, yet in my heart I still doubted him. I tried the experiment of withholding the medicine for a day, just to see what would happen."

"And?"

"First Kit had the headache, then he became violently ill. I gave him his dose and in a little while he began to feel better. I dared not try the experiment again."

"There's an apothecary in the village. Could he not compound some more of the medicine?"

"No, it is Dr. Procton's own formulation."

"I'll go after Blodgett. I'll apologize. I'll beg. I'll do whatever is needed to get him to send for more. Better yet, I'll go to Bath myself to fetch it."

She shook her head. "That would take three or four days at best. If it is the same as last time, Kit will be ill by tomorrow evening!"

"Then we go to Richmond. Colin and Susan must know of a good physician. We'll get the best one in London, if we have to. If I can hire a chaise today, there is enough light to do several stages, stay at an inn and reach Richmond by noon tomorrow. Will that do, do you think?"

She swallowed her anger and nodded. "I will write to the Squire and the Vicar and begin packing. And now I must tell Kit our new plans."

"I am sorry," he said. "I'll do whatever is necessary to make this right again, I promise you!"

From the stricken look on his face, he was as anxious as she was. It was no use berating him.

All they could do is head for Richmond and hope for the best.

Chapter Twenty-Four

A hard rain drove against the windows of the postchaise.
Gil frowned at the dark gray blur outside, then looked
back at Kit. The boy sat between them, leaning against
Emma, his eyes closed, his face paler than usual. Emma
looked up and as he met her eyes, he saw the same worry
reflected in them.

"Emma?" the boy said faintly.

"What is it? Are you unwell?" she asked.

"I ... I think ..."

"Get the basin!"

Gil snatched up the basin stowed near his feet, which
Emma had brought for just such an emergency. As the boy
continued to retch, Gil shouted for the postboys to stop, but
the carriage continued to bound along. Emma took over the
basin and he opened the window, shouting as loudly as he
could.

This time they heard him. The chaise slowed and eventually stopped. Kit seemed done, for the moment at least; Gil
took the basin from Emma and opened the door.

He leaned out the door and dumped out the contents of
the basin. Then he turned it upright, allowing the rain to rinse
it out a little. He leaned further out and shouted to the
postboys, asking how they still had to go on the stage. When

he returned to his seat, Kit lay in Emma's arms, his eyes closed.

"Do you think he can endure any more travel?" he asked her.

"Could we not stop soon?"

"There is an inn about two miles off. We could make for it and see if there is a physician nearby who could attend Kit."

She nodded, but her face was wracked with worry. He almost wished she would berate him. So far, he wasn't doing well in his new role. Everything he'd done had gone awry. Yesterday, there had been no postchaise to be had at the Hare and Hounds. Instead, they'd set off this morning, hoping against hope that Kit would not fall ill, or that they could cover the fifty-odd miles to Elmwood Lodge before he did so. The weather had not cooperated, turning the road into pudding and slowing them to a snail's pace.

The sky was too dark to guess the hour, or read his pocket watch. They were still several stages away from Richmond. They would have to stop for the night.

Gil hoped to heaven they could find a physician to help Kit.

As the chaise slowly plowed through the mud, Kit fell ill one more time, necessitating another stop to clean up and empty the basin. He lay back in Emma's arms, exhausted. Gil read the signs of strain in her face but there was nothing he could do to speed their progress.

Rain was still pouring on their arrival at the inn. Several other carriages and a stagecoach stood in the crowded yard. With a sense of foreboding, Gil carried Kit into the inn, Emma holding the umbrella over them both, to little effect. The public rooms were crowded with bedraggled travelers seeking shelter from the storm. Gil shouted for the landlord, who emerged from the crowd to inform them there was one small room left.

"We shall take it," he replied. "I am Gilbert Manning. This is my wife and her young brother, who is ill. Is there a physician in the village?"

"Dr. Wilson. His house is just outside the village, but he won't come out at this hour, not on a night like this."

"We'll see about that. Is there a private parlor to be had?"

"I'm sorry, sir, they are all taken."

"Be so good as to send a dinner up to our room, then. Is there anything you need for Kit?" he asked Emma.

"Some cloths and vinegar, and a pot of boiling water. *Please*," she said with a look of entreaty toward the busy landlord.

"I'll do my best, ma'am," he said gruffly, then called for a servant to take them to the room.

They followed the maid up the stairs and down a passage to a small back room furnished with a bed, a wing chair and small table in the corner. Emma turned down the bed and Gil set Kit down in the middle. The boy looked frighteningly thin and pale.

"My head hurts," Kit murmured, wriggling as if trying to find a more comfortable position.

"I'll see if I can do something about that, dearest." Emma smoothed the covers over her brother, her face as pale as his. She hadn't slept well last night for worrying, he guessed, and tonight would prove a far worse challenge. Gil hoped she wouldn't fall ill, too.

"I'll go find that physician," he said. "Do you think you can manage for now?"

"Of course. Go!"

While Gil was gone, the maidservant came and went several times, bearing trays with dinner and the other items Emma had requested. She coaxed Kit to eat a crust of bread while she prepared a decoction of bark. She hesitated to give it to him, in case the physician would suggest some other medicine, but after he moaned again, more loudly, and there was still no sign of Gil or the physician, she decided to just give it to him. Kit cast the medicine back up within a very few minutes. Swallowing her fear, she cleaned him, settled him into bed and began to bathe his forehead in vinegar-water. Eventually, he quieted and fell into an uneasy sleep.

She wondered why Gil had not returned. Her own head had begun to ache, so she ate a little bread and cold roast chicken and felt a little better. But where was Gil?

Another half hour passed before she heard his voice outside the door. He staggered in, his greatcoat dripping and his face ashen.

"The doctor would not come out?"

"By the time I'd found his house—some fool of an ostler gave me wrong directions—he was not only sitting down to dinner, but he'd already broached his third bottle. He wasn't happy that I barged in on him and he refused to come out." He flung off his greatcoat, hanging it on a peg near the door. "I would have dragged him here by his heels if I'd thought he was in a state to do any good. How is Kit?" He looked anxiously toward the bed.

"A little better. I gave him a decoction of bark for the pain. It made him ill again, but he is sleeping, so perhaps it did him some good anyway."

"What should we do? Should we try Dr. Wilson in the morning?" He made an expression of distaste.

"I don't like the sound of that man. If Kit is well enough tomorrow, I think we should press on to Richmond and see if we can find a proper physician to attend him." She got up from the chair. "Now that you are here, I shall see if I can get them to make some barley-water, or let me do so. That might be a good thing to give Kit if he wakes. And there is some dinner here for you."

"Did you eat?"

"I'm not a fool; I know I must keep my strength up," she retorted.

"What shall I do if he awakens?"

"If he's in pain, bathe his forehead. If it's very bad, just come fetch me. Now eat while you have the chance."

He sat down at the small table in the corner, looking so drawn and anxious she regretted her sharp manner. But she needed to get to the kitchen.

When she returned with the barley-water, Kit had awoken and was retching again, though he'd little left to bring up. After the episode passed, Gil helped her tidy up, then she poured some of the cooled barley-water into a glass. Gil propped her brother up so he could drink. Kit made a face as he tasted it, but he drank it all down. He shivered; the room had gotten colder as evening went on.

Gil went to build up the fire. She removed her shoes and climbed into the bed, curling around Kit and hugging his shaking body next to hers. She might as well stay in her dress; she doubted any of them would sleep much tonight.

Having gotten the fire going, Gil settled down in the chair. She watched him stare into the fire, his expression so remorseful that she could not remain angry with him.

"Come here," she said. "There is room enough and you can warm Kit from the other side."

A spasm of emotion crossed his face, but he removed his shoes and coat and climbed into bed.

She touched his shoulder and gave him a faint smile. Between them, they held Kit until he stopped shaking. She fell asleep praying he'd be better by morning.

Gil woke suddenly, with the sense of having overslept. Dim light filtered through the curtains. He looked at Kit, still curled up in his sister's arms. Breathing gently, thank goodness. Kit had woken several more times in the night with heart-wrenching bouts of nausea. Gil and Emma had done all they could to make him comfortable, sharing unspoken fears of what would happen if this continued any longer. But judging by the sun, Kit must have slept longer this time. He looked more peaceful. Even Emma's face was serene in her slumber.

Perhaps the worst was over.

If so, he'd gotten off easily for his blunder. He'd taken his new responsibilities far too lightly. He'd thought his life would go on much as it had, just with the added pleasure of having a beautiful wife and a plucky young brother. Now he knew he had to make bigger changes.

He would do anything—*anything*—to ensure their security and happiness.

"Emma, wake up. We're nearly there."

Emma roused and looked down at Kit, lying in her arms. His color was good, for him. She was glad he'd managed to sleep despite the rocking of the chaise. He certainly needed it—they all did—after such a dreadful night.

Back in the inn, he'd woken with a slight headache, but seeing the breakfast tray, he'd demanded some tea. She'd allowed him to drink a cup and it seemed to do him good. He'd managed to keep down some toast, so they'd decided to continue their journey. When they'd stopped to change horses, he'd drunk a little more tea and eaten a biscuit. It really did seem that the worst was over.

"How are you feeling?" she asked him.

He nodded, frowning slightly.

"Still a bit of a headache?"

"Much better," he said, though she guessed it still pained him.

"We'll be at Elmwood Lodge soon and arrange for a physician," Gil said.

Kit scowled. "I'm perfectly well now. I don't need a physician!"

"You shall see one anyway," said Emma. "You know we are all in league to torment you!"

Kit snorted and shifted to look out the window. Emma exchanged glances with Gil. He smiled at her, but there was a little constraint in his manner. Perhaps he feared she was still angry with him over Kit's medicine. He *had* behaved foolishly, but he'd done much to atone for it last night, helping her through an exhausting and most unromantic night.

She gave Gil a quick smile, then followed Kit's gaze. They passed through a gate and through lightly wooded grounds to a rambling white house fronted by a classical portico. She straightened her bonnet, though no doubt she looked a mess. Gil, on the other hand, was looking quite cheerful.

The carriage had not even come to a halt when the doors opened. A stream of people poured out: a tall gentleman with dark hair, a fair-haired girl who seemed somewhere around Kit's age, and a small boy who looked much like her. A footman followed close behind, then a lady bearing an infant.

"Captain Manning! Captain Manning!" the two older children cried out.

The tall gentleman who must be Sir Colin held the boy with one hand, to keep him from coming under the carriage wheels. Emma saw that his other sleeve was folded and pinned neatly to his coat.

The carriage came to a halt. Gil jumped out and the children besieged him. He detached himself, laughing, and turned toward Emma. She slid toward the door with Kit in her lap and handed the boy to Gil. She climbed out and saw that the lady with the infant had come down the steps to join the group by the chaise.

"Welcome to Elmwood Lodge," the gentleman said, bowing. "I am Sir Colin Stanstead. This is Mary and here is Edward. And there is Lady Stanstead, with William." His face, which had seemed a bit harsh in repose, softened into a smile as he looked at Emma and Kit.

She curtseyed. "It is so kind of you to take us in on such short notice. It must seem very sudden . . ."

"Not at all," said Lady Stanstead, a fair-haired woman of about Emma's height. "We were so delighted when Gil wrote us about you. You must tell us the whole story, but first let us take your brother to the nursery."

Gil set off with Sir Colin and the older children. Lady Stanstead hung back a little, smiling at Emma. She was very beautiful, though faint lines around her eyes hinted at her years of following the drum. Emma could only imagine what that must have been like.

"I am afraid you've had a wretched journey," said Lady Stanstead. "Did your brother fall ill?"

"He was very sick last night, but he seems better today," Emma replied, as they climbed the stairs to the entrance, where the footman held the door for them.

"Do you think we ought to call for a physician right away? Gil wrote that you wished him to see a physician, so we have arranged for Sir William Knighton to come tomorrow."

"Knighton? The same one who—"

"Who is one of the Prince Regent's physicians? Yes, it is he. We wanted to consult the best. He has children of his own, so he should deal well with your brother. Do you wish us to inquire if he can come to us sooner?"

"Thank you, but as Kit seems better, I think we can wait."

They entered a hall. Emma followed her hostess toward a flight of stairs, her nerves calmed by Susan's kind welcome.

The house had a pleasant, unpretentious feel to it. There was a well-worn look to the furnishings which hinted at straitened circumstances. She remembered Gil telling her that Colin had heavily invested in converting the poorly run and dangerous gunpowder mill he'd inherited to produce some new sort of building material.

They climbed up a flight of stairs and turned toward what Emma guessed was the nursery wing. She could hear Sir Colin introducing the nursery staff. Lady Stanstead turned and paused before the door.

"After we have made your brother comfortable, tell me what you would like best. Some food, or a bath perhaps?"

"A bath would be lovely," Emma admitted. "Thank you for your kindness. It must seem quite an imposition to have to take us in on short notice."

"Rubbish! And please call me Susan. As Gil is like a brother to us, you are to be our sister." She settled the baby on her hip and gave Emma a warm, one-armed embrace. "I know you have had troubles, Emma. I can see it in your face. But believe me when I say we will do all we can to help."

Emma nodded, feeling some of the anxiety drain from her. She sensed challenges ahead, but for now, she welcomed the chance to rest among friends.

Chapter Twenty-Five

E mma and Gil watched as Sir William Knighton bent his head to Kit's chest. The nursery seemed unnaturally quiet; the Stansteads had gone for a drive so as not to intrude on the examination. She and Gil had exchanged little private conversation since their arrival at Richmond, both reluctant to discuss anything important until they knew for certain that Kit was out of danger.

He was still a bit out of sorts, scowling at the prospect of seeing yet another physician. But at least he hadn't embarrassed her in front of one of the most famous physicians in the country.

For her part, Emma liked Sir William. Unlike Dr. Procton, he'd spoken respectfully to her, without a hint of condescension. He also struck her as more competent. It made her all the more nervous to hear his report.

"There, I am done. I trust it was not so bad?" Sir William smiled at Kit.

"No, sir. Am I going to be sick again, sir?" Kit asked.

"I see no reason to think so. I expect you will be feeling quite yourself within a very few days." He looked toward her. "Shall we return to the library?"

She nodded. They left Kit in the care of a nursery maid and went back downstairs, to the library. It was a mild day,

Elena Greene

sunny and bright. The windows were partially open, letting in the breeze and the sound of birds singing in the elms that lined the drive. But Emma knew she could not enjoy any of it until she felt more at ease about her brother.

"You seem distressed, Miss Westfield. I assure you I have nothing alarming to report," said Sir William, once they'd seated themselves.

"You believe my brother is on the mend?"

"I do," he replied. "Without knowing precisely what was in Dr. Procton's recipe, I cannot say exactly why your brother fell ill. It is likely that the sudden withdrawal of the medicine proved a shock to his constitution. Did you say he has been drinking a good deal of tea?"

She nodded. "It seems to make the headache a little better."

Dr. Knighton looked thoughtful. "Perhaps Dr. Procton's medicine had a stimulant effect and that is why tea has proven beneficial. In any case, it is usually preferable to wean a patient gradually from a medicine that has been given over an extended period. It ought not to be done without consulting the physician."

"Miss Westfield is blameless," said Gil. "I was the one who destroyed the medicine."

"It was a mistake, but no serious harm was done," Dr. Knighton replied.

"What do you recommend now?" Emma asked. "Does he not need some medicine for his heart?"

Sir William paused, then spoke carefully, as if picking his words. "Dr. Procton has an excellent reputation. However, I must ask you, when did he last examine your brother?"

"It was over a year ago."

Again he hesitated. "Perhaps there was a lingering weakness in the heart after the illness that caused your brother's deformity. However, I detect no problem now. All I recommend is a strengthening diet and plenty of fresh air to tempt his appetite."

"But—but that is the reverse of what Dr. Procton recommended. He warned against overexertion and exposure to infections. I must confess I have not always obeyed his

245

instructions. I have thought it good for Kit to be out of doors and with other children as much as possible."

"I see no reason to treat your brother as an invalid. In fact . . ." He paused for a moment.

"What is it?" Gil asked with a touch of impatience.

"Nothing to distress you, I promise! As I was examining the boy, I observed that he has not lost all feeling or capability in his bad leg. I do not wish to raise false hopes, but—"

"What? Do you think he might be able to walk again?" Gil asked, voicing the question Emma almost feared to ask.

Sir William nodded. "I have seen good results in cases of infantile paralysis where a brace was used to correct and support the affected limb. We do not often see this malady in older children. However, I do not believe the case to be hopeless. I recommend you visit Mr. Timothy Sheldrake, in the Strand. He is experienced in the construction of various braces or trusses to correct distortions of the limbs. He has achieved good results in many cases."

"We were told . . . we were told that Kit would never be strong enough, even for crutches. That it would be dangerous to even try . . ." She raised a hand to her cheek. "Forgive me, but I never thought—Good God! I should have known! I knew Dr. Procton was too strict, advising us to keep him abed and not to tax his strength in any way. I ought to have sought another opinion sooner!"

Gil pressed her hand. "It's not your fault."

"Do not punish yourself, Miss Westfield!" said Sir William. "During your brother's recovery from such an illness it was no doubt correct to keep him quiet. Had Dr. Procton examined your brother again after a suitable interval, I am certain he would agree with my recommendations."

Emma bit her lip. Sir William was being diplomatic, but she felt sure now that Dr. Procton was a quack.

"Tell us what we must do," said Gil.

"Of course. I shall write out Mr. Sheldrake's direction for you. You must call upon me if you have any further concerns about the boy's health."

Somehow, Emma managed to croak out a few words of thanks.

After they'd seen Sir William out, they returned to the library. Gil sat down on the sofa and pulled her into his lap, wrapping his arms around her.

"Gil! What if the Stansteads return and find us like this?" she asked.

"They'd think nothing of it. But they won't be back just yet." He lowered his face to kiss her, but she averted her face.

"Are you still angry with me about that medicine?"

"Of course not! You were quite right about it, and everything else."

"So you haven't forgiven yourself." He pressed her head back against his chest and began to gently stroke her hair.

"How can I? I was so stupid!"

"You'd lost your father and your home. You had limited means and few friends. You did as well as anyone could in such a situation."

She sighed and shifted in his arms. It felt wrong to allow him to comfort her, but it felt so good to have him stroking her hair. Then he began to stroke her neck and knead the tight muscles in her shoulders. "Sir William seemed hopeful. I think he knows his business."

"I think so too. But—but what if it is too late? What if we raise Kit's hopes only to have them dashed again?"

"Kit is stronger than he looks. I'd wager anything he'll do the trick."

"I wish we could be sure." Gil's caresses were having their effect; she sagged into his arms, giving in to the relief he offered.

"One can never know for certain what life will bring. So why not enjoy it anyway?" He kissed her neck and something inside her let go, tightness giving way to arousal. She shifted around and kissed him. He made a satisfied sound in his throat. His hand slid to her thigh where he continued his gentle caresses.

"What are you doing?" she protested.

"Trying to stop you from worrying," he murmured, drawing up her skirt.

"You haven't even shut the door! What if the Stansteads return? Or a servant comes in?"

"Makes it more exciting, doesn't it?"

Lud! His hand was between her legs. She choked back a whimper; he kissed her again. "Beast!"

He laughed and held her tight, plying his fingers in a devilish pattern. "Do you wish me to stop?"

"No ... I mean yes. Is that the carriage?"

She thought she could hear the crunch of wheels on gravel. Nevertheless, Gil continued to pleasure her. She was so close, so wickedly close to release.

Voices sounded in the hall. The Stansteads were home.

"They're going up to the nursery," Gil whispered. "We have a few minutes. Let go, Emma." He brought a finger inside her, bringing her closer to her peak. Desperately, she kissed him, in an effort to muffle the sound as the ecstasy came upon her.

Not a moment too soon, for now they heard footsteps coming down the stairs.

"Ah, there you are."

Emma slid off Gil's lap just as the Stansteads appeared in the doorway. Colin and Susan exchanged quick, amused glances before seating themselves across from Gil and Emma.

"So tell us. What did Sir William have to say about Kit?" Susan asked.

Emma was too mortified to speak, but Gil relayed Sir William's conclusions as if they'd just been drinking tea.

"That is excellent news," Colin said. "We can take your brother to see this Mr. Sheldrake tomorrow, if you wish."

"Thank you," said Emma.

"Then perhaps we could hold your wedding the following day?" Susan asked eagerly.

"We can procure a license tomorrow," said Colin. "You may be married here, if you wish. I am quite certain our good vicar will accommodate you."

"I shall give orders for a wedding breakfast," said Susan. "Gil told me you have been in mourning, Emma. I would be delighted to lend you a gown. I think we are much the same size."

"Thank you, you are so kind."

"Not at all. I am looking forward to planning it all. Colin, will you tell them what else we have been thinking?"

Her husband nodded. "Bordering our land there is a property on which there is a cottage ornée built some fifty years ago by a duke for his mistress. The present owner is seeking a tenant, but in the meantime he would be happy to let me hire it for you for your honeymoon."

"Consider it our wedding present," said Susan. "It is a charming place. You could be quite alone there, and we can take care of your brother. What do you think?"

Emma blinked. It was a lovely gift, and generous given what Gil had told her about the Stansteads' circumstances. But it seemed strange to be married before they even knew where they would live, or how they would manage.

She realized they were all looking at her. Gil's hand tightened around hers.

Susan jumped up to come sit beside her. "Oh, here we have been rushing and making all your decisions for you. Perhaps you wish for something quite different?"

"No, not at all," she said. Things would sort themselves out in time, she was sure. Meanwhile, it was foolish to delay. She might already be carrying Gil's child.

The Stansteads smiled, the sudden tension dispersing.

"Since Gil has been lucky enough to find a woman of character willing to marry him, we must try to do justice to the occasion," said Colin.

Everyone laughed, but then the Stansteads exchanged some glances Emma could not understand.

Susan lifted her chin as she looked at Gil. "You must forgive us for meddling. But we must ask you this. Do you still mean to fly at Greenwich and all those other fairs?"

Gil's expression turned sober, but Emma saw none of the defiance she'd expected. Her heart began to race. Had he had a change of heart, or did he have some new scheme in mind?

"I have a different plan," he said. "I shall go to Norfolk and see if I can make peace with my uncle."

Chapter Twenty-Six

A moment passed before anyone could reply.

Emma looked stunned. "Are you in earnest?"

"I am. I can't promise any good will come of it, but I know I must try."

A slow smile came to her face. He was torn, glad that they were finally in accord, but afraid she would get her hopes up too high.

"I am relieved to see you've come to your senses," said Colin.

"Yes," said Susan. "We've been hoping you would do this ever since we all returned to England."

"I must warn you all, my uncle is not likely to welcome me," he cautioned.

"Time has passed since your cousin's death," said Susan. "Perhaps he will relent. After all, you are all that remains to him of his brother."

"A brother he sent to his death in the West Indies."

"Keeping the feud between the two of you will not bring your parents back," Susan retorted. "In the meantime, you have a family to care for now."

He nodded. "I'll do my best to make my uncle see sense."

"You said he is a good landlord," said Colin. "He should see the merit in training his heir."

"I hope so. But I shan't bring Emma or Kit to Lynnford Abbey until I know they'll be treated with respect. May they remain here until I return?"

"You are not going to go alone," said Emma, before the Stansteads could reply.

"You don't know what my relations are like, Emma," he said. "I'd rather you stayed here."

"I'm not afraid of them. I want to be with you and help if I can."

"I know you're more than a match for that blackguard and his harridan of a wife. But—"

"I recommend you not argue with Miss Westfield," Colin interrupted, a rare smile lurking in his eyes. "Just be grateful she's willing to throw in her lot with yours."

"Exactly," said Susan. "We will be happy to take care of Kit. Now Emma, it is time we dealt with some more pressing matters. Shall we go look at some gowns?"

Two days later, Gil waited with Colin and the vicar in the flower-bedecked drawing room. What could be keeping the ladies?

Nearly twenty minutes had passed since the vicar arrived, ready to perform the ceremony. The Stansteads' governess was doing her best to keep the children occupied, aided by Sancha, who had a way with the young ones. Lund and Birkin stood by quietly, looking rather as if they were on parade. Only Reed was missing. A thorough search of every inn and hedge tavern within miles of Tichbury had failed. If he'd fallen to drinking, as they feared, it seemed as if he'd fled some distance before doing so. Gil hated having his men go missing; in some ways it felt worse than losing one in battle.

But there was no use fretting about that. The vicar was here, but where was Emma?

"Manning, you look awful." Colin grinned. "You'd better stop scowling or you'll frighten Miss Westfield into crying off."

"I just want her here already," he muttered.

"The ladies are just making sure every curl is in place and every bit of lace is placed just so," said Colin, "as if we did not think them beautiful no matter what they did!"

He grumbled under his breath.

"It is not unusual for a bridegroom to be anxious," said the vicar kindly.

He forced a smile for the vicar. Emma would not cry off now; she was not like that. And everything was going well. They'd taken Kit to Mr. Timothy Sheldrake's establishment to be fitted for a brace and Mr. Sheldrake seemed optimistic. Although he didn't look forward to confronting his uncle, it was high time he did so. With Emma by his side, he might even succeed.

He jumped up, hearing voices in the doorway.

Finally, Emma was there, lovely in a pale blue borrowed gown. Her cheeks were flushed and the narrow lace trim around her neckline fluttered with her breath. He'd reined in his temptation to steal into her room these past few nights. Now he wished he could just have her to himself in that elegant cottage the Stansteads hired for them.

She met his eyes, looking excited but happy, and he knew he was the luckiest of men.

The vicar quickly arranged everyone and began the ceremony. When it was time for Gil to promise to love, comfort and honor Emma, he put all the passion of his intentions into his voice. As she spoke her lines, she watched him with love in her eyes.

Once again, a woman was ready to give her heart and her life into his keeping. God help him if he failed this time.

After the ceremony had ended and they'd shared a wedding breakfast on the terrace, Emma said her goodbyes and joined Gil to walk to the cottage. She sensed that everyone was watching them as they walked across the lawn;

it was a relief to reach the gate in the hedge that separated the properties. The cottage stood atop a small hill. Gil took it at an increased pace; she could not match his long strides and released his arm.

"I did not know we were racing!" she protested.

"I'm sorry, Emma." He pulled her close and bent down for a hard, hungry kiss.

She gave a breathless laugh. "Since you are so very eager, then let us run!"

She picked up her skirts and charged up the hill at her best pace, but he caught up quickly. He beat her up the shallow steps of the entrance and opened the door before her. When she reached him, he swept her up into his arms and swung her in, pulling the door closed behind them. Then he pressed her up against the wall for another greedy kiss.

He pulled down the small sleeves of her gown and leaned to kiss the tops of her breasts. She shivered with pleasure when he drew her skirt up around her waist and his fingers sought out her pleasurable spots.

"Gil, you madman! Shall we not go to the bedchamber?"

"I can't wait. I've wanted to do this ever since I kissed you at Meadowcross Cottage."

"So have I." She was mad too, for she wanted him to take her, right there against the wall. Now.

He released her to work at the falls of his breeches. And then he was back, nudging her legs wider and then entering with a thrust that caused her to gasp with pleasure. "When we're done, we can rest on that sofa over there."

He had her pinned against the wall, while he was tantalizingly still.

"Then we can go upstairs. See the landing?"

She nodded.

"I'll make love to you there, in a few hours, when the setting sun streams in through that window. After I remove every last stitch of your clothing and feast my eyes on the sight of you bathed in the light."

Then he began to move, with deliberate slowness. "I promise I'll have you in bed by nightfall."

"There it is. Swanham."

Emma noted the strain in Gil's voice. She wasn't surprised; to revisit scenes from his childhood was bound to stir up all sorts of mixed feelings. She wished they could talk freely. But Colin and Susan had offered them not only the use of their traveling carriage and coachman, but also the services of a maidservant and a footman to act as Gil's valet. Since Anna and Stephen rode with them, intimate conversation was impossible.

The carriage rounded a bend. A row of flint cottages came into sight. Although they appeared well-built, some had broken window-panes. Where there ought to have been small gardens, there were weeds.

"Some of these cottages appear to be empty," she observed.

Gil nodded grimly. "This is not how I remember it."

"Things have been difficult since the war."

They headed on in silence, past the stone church and the yard with its mossy gravestones. Across the green they saw an inn, signposted the Swanham Arms, which at least appeared to be open.

"It used to be accounted a good inn," Gil said. "We can come back here if we must."

Lord Manning had not replied to the letter Gil had sent indicating their intentions. The Stansteads were disappointed, but Gil hadn't seemed surprised. They'd decided to go on with their plans anyway.

"Should we stop and make some inquiries?" she asked. "Perhaps they could give us news of your uncle here."

Gil's expression lightened. "No doubt they could, but I've a better idea. Let us stop and see Farmer Colby. He'll tell me what I need to know. We are almost there."

She nodded. Gil shouted instructions to the coachman. They drove on, past more partially deserted cottages and into a small wooded area which soon gave way to open fields. The first one they encountered was full of weeds. Not just weeds, Emma noted, but rather substantial shrubs and even small saplings.

"This field looks as if it has not been worked for several years," she said. "Surely they would not leave it fallow for so long?"

Gil shook his head.

They passed the field and turned down a deeply rutted lane.

"There's the barn," said Gil in a tight voice. "Good God!"

Even from a distance, she could see there were tiles missing from the roof. As they approached the farmyard, more outbuildings came into view, all showing signs of disrepair. There was no one about.

Even the dilapidated outbuildings did not prepare them for the sight of the farmhouse. Its roof was also damaged. The window and door frames, originally painted white, were faded and peeling. A huge crack scarred the chimney.

Emma took hold of Gil's hand, but he just stared out the window, remembering, she guessed, how the place had looked in his childhood. Before the carriage even came to a complete stop, he flung the door open and jumped out.

With a motion to the servants to wait, she scrambled after him as fast as quickly as she could.

Chapter Twenty-Seven

G il headed for the door, which hung crookedly off one
hinge.

"Be careful!" Emma shouted, running after him. "It may
not be safe in there."

But he disappeared inside, as if he'd not heard. She
frowned and followed him through the doorway. She found
him in the middle of a large main room. Its whitewashed
walls were stained; there was a smell of damp. Cobwebs hung
in every corner. Every cupboard and shelf was bare. A large
oak table stood in the middle of the room. He stared at it,
perhaps remembering happier times spent around it.

She put her arms around him from behind and tried to
murmur some words of comfort, though she did not know
what to say.

She wished she knew what could have happened to cause
this desolation. The estate comprised a number of farms.
Were they all in the same abandoned state?

Gil cleared his throat. "Back in the Peninsula, whenever
the French retreated before us, they would lay the countryside waste so there'd be nothing left for us when we got
there. I never thought to see anything like that *here*."

She hugged him harder. Eventually he turned around, his
face hardened from despair to a controlled rage.

"My uncle shall answer for this." He turned to leave the farmhouse.

She followed, her mind whirling. No landlord in his right mind would leave a farm to waste this way. Surely Gil was relying too heavily on childhood memories of his uncle's coldness. How could he believe this devastation was intentional?

Emma sat silently beside Gil as gaps in the hedgerows revealed more neglected fields full of weeds, gorse bushes and saplings. His whole body was taut with anger; she knew better than to question his suspicions in front of the servants. They would all know the truth soon enough.

They rounded a bend and turned up a long drive. The house came into sight. Built of the same local flint as the cottages they'd seen, it was a mix of architectural styles, several gables of varying sizes interrupting the rectangular facade, an octagonal tower in the corner. She guessed it had evolved over time.

As they approached, she saw that the lawn was overgrown. Several rhododendron bushes were blooming, but looked to be in need of pruning. A closer view of the house revealed crumbling stonework. All of it strengthened her conviction that some disaster had befallen the family. But surely someone—a solicitor, perhaps—would have sought out Gil had his uncle died.

"Is there even anyone there?" Anna asked.

"There is. Look." Gil pointed to wisp of smoke coming from a chimney.

They came to a halt in front of the house. Stephen jumped out to let down the steps. Gil leapt out, then handed Emma and Anna down.

It seemed there were no servants on the watch for visitors, as was the usual practice in a country house of this size. But there was that plume of smoke.

"Drive round to the stables," Gil told the coachman. "I don't know what you'll find, but at least rest the horses. We'll probably return to the Swanham Arms in an hour or so."

He climbed the stairs two at a time and struck the large knocker. There was no response. He cursed under his breath and knocked again. He waited a bit, growing more tense by the moment. Then he tried the door. It creaked open. They entered a musty, dimly lit entrance hall just as a stooped individual in the garb of an upper servant hobbled in.

"Barnes?" Gil asked.

The old man bowed and straightened back up. His face was like wrinkled parchment; his eyes squinted in a valiant attempt to focus.

"Master Gilbert! That is, I should say, Captain Manning. I am glad you are here."

"You remember me," Gil's voice softened.

"You have a great look of your father."

Gil nodded and looked toward Emma. "This is my wife. Until recently, Miss Westfield of Tichbury, in Sussex."

"My felicitations on your marriage," said Barnes, creaking a little as he bowed to Emma. "I wish we could make you a better welcome, Mrs. Manning."

"How many of you are there?" Gil asked. "Is Mrs. Wycke still here?"

"Yes sir. She now serves as cook as well as housekeeper. There's a housemaid and a scullery maid, besides your aunt and uncle's personal servants."

"Just the four of you, to manage this awful pile? You ought to be comfortably retired by now!" The rage was coming back into his voice.

"Most of the rooms are closed up. We do not entertain, as you see."

"But my uncle is still here?"

"Yes, he is in the drawing room with your aunt. But I am afraid . . ."

"You have been directed to send us away?"

"I am sorry, sir."

"We will see them. If necessary, I'll tell them I forced my way in. In the meantime, perhaps you could make our servants comfortable."

"Yes, of course. But I should warn you—"

But Gil was already on his way; in her hurry to follow, she missed whatever Barnes was trying to tell them. They practically ran down a dusty corridor, passing rooms full of furniture shrouded in cloths, finally approaching a room near the back of the house.

He paused on the threshold. "This will be ugly. Are you sure you wish to come with me?"

"Of course."

They crossed the threshold together. This room was only slightly less dismal than everything else they had passed. The walls were mostly bare, although there were outlines on the wallpaper where pictures had hung. A small fire burned in the hearth; a large wing chair had been drawn up close next to the fire, facing away from them. A woman Emma guessed was Gil's aunt sat at a writing desk facing the window.

She turned around; her eyes were dark in a pale, angular face. "You! Go away," she said in a loud whisper. "You are not wanted here."

She glared at them as they came further into the room.

"I have the right to know what has been—" Gil broke off, as they both saw the man huddled over in the chair.

A blanket covered his legs. His sparse hair was gray, but not grayer than his gaunt face. His pose made it difficult to judge his height, but Emma guessed he had been a tall man. He snored, making a horrid gurgling sound. He seemed nothing like the big, hale man Gil had described to her.

"I told you to go away," Lady Manning hissed again.

Lord Manning stirred. He opened his eyes and stared blankly at them for a moment.

"James ... Diana? Good God ..."

Horror and pity overwhelmed Emma. He'd just named Gil's parents. So the poor man was wandering in his mind.

No wonder the estate had gone to waste. Although there ought to have been a steward to manage things ...

"You fool!" Lady Manning got to her feet and came near the chair. "It is your scoundrel of a nephew. And this young woman must be the wife he wrote about."

Lord Manning blinked several times and his eyes seemed to focus. With a visible effort, he straightened up. A twisted smile came to his lips.

"*You*. So that curst balloon didn't kill you, after all."

Emma started. No, he could not have ... it was insane to even think that he might somehow have been involved in Gil's crash.

"I remember reading about it in the newspaper," Lord Manning continued.

Emma shook off her lurid suspicion.

"But afterwards, he wrote to us, so of course he didn't die," said Lady Manning, looking exasperated.

"Yes, he does seem to have a charmed life," Lord Manning said. His eyes seemed huge in his sunken face as he looked at Gil. "You think I haven't been paying attention? I read all the lists. Badajoz, Toulouse, all the others ... Waterloo ..."

Gil's voice was tightly controlled. "I have come to present my wife and to discuss matters which concern us all."

His uncle turned his gaze towards Emma. "So you are married. She looks English, at least. Better than that Scottish trollop you'd taken up with on the Peninsula."

Gil's fists clenched, but he kept them by his sides.

"Sudden, isn't it?" asked Lord Manning.

"*Very* sudden," echoed Lady Manning, looking pointedly at Emma's belly. "Clearly some scrambling affair! You've caught yourself the heir to a barony, Mrs. Manning, but soon enough you'll wish you'd let him off your hook!"

Gil took a step toward his aunt. "If you say one more word against my wife, I'll—"

Emma put a hand on his arm. "Let her be! We have more important things to discuss."

His expression was grim, but he contained himself. "Yes, we do. I saw the Colbys' farm has been abandoned. What the devil has been happening here?"

"It's none of your business," Lady Manning replied.

"As the heir, I have the right to know."

His uncle made an effort to straighten up in his seat. "You'll learn what you've got coming to you once I'm gone, and not a day sooner!" He ended in a hollow, choking sound.

"Yes, begone with you!" his wife added. "You are not wanted here."

"Then I'll find out what I need to know elsewhere," said Gil, turning to leave.

But Emma had been thinking quickly. "Are you quite sure you don't wish to talk to us?" she asked Lord Manning and his wife. "The alternative could be quite painful."

"What do you mean?" asked Lady Manning.

"We would not like to do this to you, but my husband has it in his right to lay suit against you for waste of the estate."

"Impudent, grasping hussy!" Lady Manning looked daggers at Emma. "But your scheme won't work. We are under no requirement to maintain the estate in good order."

"I believe entailed land is supposed to be maintained in its original use," she replied. "Am I right?" She gave Gil a warning look.

He caught on. "You're quite right. So what shall it be? Will you cooperate with us or must we seek legal recourse?"

"It's an idle threat," said Lady Manning. "You cannot afford a lawsuit!"

"I just won a rather large wager," said Gil.

Lady Manning seemed taken aback. "What do you want?"

"A full disclosure of what has happened, and a promise to cooperate in whatever course of action I decide."

"You wish to turn us out of our home! Carrion-birds, the pair of you!"

Lord Manning raised his head and gave his wife an ironic look. "You've been begging for us to remove to Bath. Why do you care now?"

"Because they want to beggar us!"

"I want to know what is happening on the estate. Are the other farms in the same state as the Colbys'? How did that happen?" Gil seemed at the limits of his patience.

"We don't wish you to be beggared," said Emma, looking straight at Lady Manning. "Tell us what we need to know and whatever happens, you'll be provided for."

Lady Manning's face twisted for a moment, then she composed herself. "Very well," she said stiffly. "About six years, ago we began to have some ... pecuniary difficulties."

"Why tiptoe about it?" Lord Manning interrupted. "Our good-for-naught son ran up gaming debts in London and fell into the hands of moneylenders."

"It was just youth and high spirits," retorted Lady Manning. "He would have settled down in time."

"You spoiled him like a lap-dog! It's no wonder he raced that curricle in his cups and broke his neck. Damn him! If only I'd had the forethought to sire more sons." He glared at Gil. "But after she bore him, I never went to her bed again. Who would want to? But I wish I had. I wish I had!"

There were bright spots on Lady Manning's thin cheeks. Emma felt a surge of pity for the woman, married for decades to a man who still yearned for his brother's wife.

"But then why are the farms deserted?" asked Gil. "What became of Colby and the others?"

"That was your uncle's doing." Lady Manning's voice was full of loathing. "After our son died, he swore you'd never see a penny from this place. He dismissed the steward and then when the tenants' leases were ending, he refused to renew them. When the estate was already shockingly encumbered!"

"That is madness," Emma said.

"Of course it is!" Lady Manning concurred. "Some of the tenants tried to stay, but when he refused to do his part in keeping the buildings and ditches and I know not what else in good repair, they gave up. Everyone tried to reason with him. All our neighbors, *everyone*! But he would not listen. Perhaps he was already ill, only he seemed of sound mind at the time. But no one visits now. As you see, we have descended to living in squalor."

"And there'll be nothing left for you to pick off this carcass!" Lord Manning laughed and descended into another coughing fit.

Emma saw despair shadow Gil's face. She had to do something. "Do you mean you prefer to face legal consequences?" she asked.

Lord Manning descended into another coughing fit, but Lady Manning looked frightened.

"If you don't want a lawsuit, you must relinquish control of the estate to me," said Gil. "We'll make sure you're not left destitute. Write to your solicitor and he will draw up the necessary papers."

"I'm afraid *he* won't sign them," said Lady Manning, looking at her husband.

Lord Manning had fallen silent. Emma wondered if he'd fallen asleep again, but he raised his head and stared at her and Gil again, with that same combination of longing and horror. Perhaps his diseased mind was once again throwing up an image of Gil's parents.

She came forward and knelt next to the wing chair. "Will you help us? It would do your conscience good."

"You ought never to have followed him to Jamaica. I would not have lost you . . ."

Gil came to kneel beside Emma and looked his uncle in the eyes.

Lord Manning stared back, as if struggling to make sense of what was happening. "What do you want from me?"

When Gil spoke, she sensed the effort it cost him to speak calmly. "I'm your nephew, Gilbert. You sent my parents to their deaths. You've scattered our people. Let there be an end to it. Sign over the estate to me."

Lord Manning shuddered and looked away. "Oh, very well. My curst physician tells me I won't last more than a few months anyway."

"But what of me?" Lady Manning demanded.

"You'll have your widow's jointure. You can go off to Bath, to live with that sour sister of yours, as you've been threatening the past few years." He turned his gaze back to Gil. "Don't think you've won! With no experience and no capital, you've no chance of salvaging matters."

He slumped down in his seat and closed his eyes. Lady Manning bent down to pull the blanket, which had slipped, back over him. Unexpectedly, a tear ran down her cheek. She gave Gil and Emma a defiant look. "I have tried to be a good wife to him, but . . ."

"It has been a trial," said Emma. "But it is nearly over."

Lady Manning straightened up. "I will write to our solicitor in London. All shall be as you wish. Please leave us now."

Unexpectedly, Lord Manning lifted his head. He stared wildly at Gil and Emma. "Yes, go!" he begged.

"I would damn you to hell," said Gil. "But I think you are already there."

He took Emma's arm to lead her out. Outside the door, they nearly ran over Barnes. The butler looked delighted.

"Forgive me, sir, I took the liberty of listening. I could not be happier, now that you are going to set matters to rights."

Emma's heart ached at the butler's optimism; if it only were that easy. Gil looked close to some breaking point. They needed to talk. More than that, they needed to get out of this awful house.

"We shall go outside and walk a bit," she said to Barnes.

"Very well, ma'am. Perhaps Master Gilbert can show you the abbey ruins; he used to enjoy playing there. I can take you to the back entrance."

"I remember the way," Gil said.

G il crossed the terrace, leapt down the steps, strode past untended flower beds and through the shrubbery, heading towards the abbey ruins. He knew Emma was following, ready to support him in any way possible. But he could not bear to speak now, not even to her.

He reached the ruins. Years ago, sheep used to graze here, keeping the turf short. Now the crumbled arches and piles of rubble were surrounded by high grass threaded with daisies, cheery among the devastation. He leaned his forehead against the cold stone wall and drew in a breath of the fragrant air.

Barnes was right to direct him here. It had been a childhood refuge of sorts. He'd led George many a merry chase here. Although his cousin was bigger, Gil was always quicker. The arches and low walls, the piles of rubble that lay strewn around, afforded him many hiding places.

George had never managed to catch him here.

But there was no running away now. So many depended on him, not only Emma and her brother, but Barnes and Farmer Colby and the rest of them . . .

Emma had caught up to him and sat down on a pile of rubble. Bless her, she knew enough not to try to say anything.

"Damn him. *Damn him!*" He pounded a fist against the stone, almost relishing the pain.

Emma just watched him in mute sympathy.

"You were right," he said. "I ought to have come back sooner. When my cousin died, I ought to have followed Colonel Barnard's advice and come back, whatever my uncle said."

She got off the rubble and waded through the high grass to stand beside him. "You could not know what he would do. Who could have guessed? Don't blame yourself."

He turned to meet her. She put her arms around him and he pulled her tight. "You were magnificent back there. Thank you. But I never meant to bring you into such a horrible mess."

"We shall manage."

"I've no experience of managing an estate. No knowledge of farming except what I learned as a boy."

"In your years as an officer, haven't you learned how to judge character, how to lead men, how to command respect and loyalty? You will learn the rest." She stood on tip-toe to kiss him.

For a moment, he forgot his anger in the sweetness of her kiss. He didn't deserve her generosity, but he could not resist the comfort she offered. He molded her against him. She moaned into his mouth and he flared into sudden arousal. He wanted to bury himself inside her, feel her strong legs wrapped around him. He reached to lift her skirts but before he could do so, she dropped to her knees and began unfastening the fall of his breeches. Soon, she had him in her hands and began to toy with him as she'd learned to do on their honeymoon. When she took him into her mouth, he groaned and stiffened against the wall, struggling for control. He pulled her hair out of the coil on top of her head and caressed it.

She continued to pleasure him, his wanton angel, driving him half-mad with desire and out of his despair. He was nearly there; close to the rapture that would drive everything else out of his head.

It was time he took care of her, too. With an effort of will, he gently pulled her up and held her against him. She looked up at him with questioning eyes. He shifted his grip and lifted her up. He carried her several paces and set her to perch on the very edge of a low wall.

Her eyes widened as he unbuttoned her spencer, then pulled down her bodice to bare her breasts, rosy nipples crinkling in the cool breeze. He kissed them in turn, treasuring her sighs of pleasure. He reached up her skirt; she was already wet, nearly ready if her moans were any sign. But he made sure, tickling her until she murmured an incoherent plea he could not resist. He positioned himself and entered in one swift, satisfying stroke. She sighed and wrapped her legs around his waist, just as he longed for her to do.

He hoped she would enjoy what he planned to do next.

He widened his stance and lifted her off the wall. She cried out in surprise and tightened her arms and legs around him. Her inner muscles squeezed him in a hot caress; he almost couldn't bear it. Then she began to move, working against him as he braced to meet her movements, seeing his passion mirrored in the strain on her face. She cried out. He stopped struggling and released himself into her tight, pulsing warmth.

He moved back to the wall, perching her there again, still inside her. She leaned her head onto his shoulder and he held her close, filling his lungs with fresh air.

Gradually, he became aware of the sunshine on his neck, the smell of grass and flowers. Sweet Emma, taking care of him as if he hadn't brought her into this predicament. Somehow he'd manage to take care of her and Kit, and all of the others. It was the devil of a mess, but he would surmount the challenges his uncle had warned them about.

His lack of experience could be remedied, as Emma had said. But as for capital . . . he knew only one way to solve that problem.

Emma shifted and looked up, searching his face. "You're planning to fly again." She said it calmly, but he could see the effort it cost her.

"It's the only way. With the estate so encumbered, no honest banker would lend us anything. I can't ask Colin; he's in deep on this mill conversion. I promise I'll be careful. It will only be until we can begin collecting rents again."

"I understand."

Perhaps she still hoped for some other solution. Or she was putting a brave face on it. He knew she would suffer through each flight until she knew he was safe. He couldn't deny that accidents occurred, especially in bad weather. He hated to put her through this, after the losses she'd already suffered.

For now, it was the best he could do.

Chapter Twenty-Eight

Emma couldn't speak. She could only hold Kit in a tight hug, holding back tears that would embarrass him. She'd known the Stansteads would take good care of him over the weeks she and Gil had been gone. She'd never imagined that he would greet them on their return by taking a few tottering steps from his wheeled chair into her arms.

"Well done!" Gil exclaimed.

Kit beamed as the governess brought his chair up behind him so he could sit back down.

She exchanged a smile with Gil, enjoying the brief moment of pure happiness.

They'd had few of those over the past weeks, which they'd spent searching out his uncle's old land steward and finding the dispersed tenants. Luckily, his old friend Farmer Colby had moved to his oldest son's farm on a neighboring estate. He and his second son, along with some of the other tenants, were eager to return to their farms. There had been some bittersweet reunions. They only strengthened Gil's determination to fly at Greenwich and the other fairs.

"I wish you would reconsider," said Susan.

Emma watched Gil. The children having gone to bed, he had related the details of their findings to the Stansteads, along with his current plans.

"There's no other choice," Gil replied. "Before I can collect any rents, buildings and fences must be repaired, ditches cleared, equipment replaced..."

He glanced around, appealing to their understanding. His gaze met hers and rent her heart. Of course she understood. They all did.

"What did your solicitor say?" Colin asked.

"He advised me not to apply for further loans. He said it was best if the bankers did not know quite how matters lay." A bitter note crept into his voice.

The Stansteads exchanged glances.

"Don't even think of offering to lend us money," Gil said before the others could say anything. "I know your circumstances. I can't let you take on the risk."

"I know you would make good on a loan," Colin said.

"And we would all rather know you were safe," said Susan.

"I won't keep it up for long," Gil replied. "Just until the autumn. Greenwich Fair will reopen on Whitsunday; that's probably the busiest. Then Deptford Fair begins Trinity Sunday; it's been growing in popularity and I don't doubt will attract a good crowd. Then there's the Cherry Fair in Croydon, others in August and September."

Emma suppressed a shiver, attacked again by the suspicion that had crossed her mind while talking to Gil's uncle.

"Are you quite well, Emma?" Susan asked. "You look pale."

She straightened up. "I shall do." There was no need to say anything; they would think she was indulging lurid fears. Flying was dangerous enough; there was no need to suspect foul play.

"I know you're worried," said Gil. "But I promise I won't let anything stop me from coming back to *you.*"

He slid an arm around her waist, but it gave her little comfort. She'd heard promises before.

Emma woke with a start, her heart pounding. She opened her eyes, but there was nothing to be seen. She heard a rushing sound. There was something she had to do, but she couldn't remember what. A moment later she recalled her surroundings. They were in Greenwich. The sound she heard was rain. Gil would fly again tomorrow, and there was nothing she could do about it.

She'd tried to put a brave face on her fears, especially for Kit. Gil knew how worried she was, though they didn't talk about it. She knew she couldn't change his mind; he knew better than to try to convince her that what he was doing wasn't dangerous.

She listened to him softly snoring beside her. She was glad she hadn't woken him; if he had to fly, at least he ought to be well rested. But she could not fall back asleep; she had stiffened into one position. Gingerly, she rolled over onto her other side.

Gil murmured something incoherent, and then "Are you all right?"

"Of course. The rain woke me," she lied.

"You're worrying."

"I can't help it," she replied. "It's in my nature."

He gave a sigh and rolled closer. He curled his arm around her, brushing fingertips against her breast. A quick rush of heat spread through her and she stifled a moan. What an odd feeling, for her nipples to be so sensitive. She'd been feeling faintly queasy at times, but she had set it down to nerves. Her courses were a little late. It was too early to say anything to Gil, but perhaps it was not anxiety that made her feel so strange. And so hungry for his touch ...

She rolled to face him. Running a hand along his shoulder and neck, she found his face and kissed him. He opened his mouth eagerly, joining her in a play of tongues and stroking her hip. Her breasts ached to be caressed; she felt a hot pulse deep inside her, also longing for his touch.

But she remembered his plans for the day and ended the kiss.

"I am sorry. I ought not to keep you awake."

He laughed. "I'll trade sleep for *you* any day." He pulled her up onto him. Her nightdress caught between them; she loosened it around her shoulders and let it drop below her breasts. He kissed them and she shivered as flashes of heat seemed to radiate from her breasts to her insides.

It was their last chance to make love before he flew again. She might never become accustomed to the risks he took, but that was no reason not to take pleasure in the moments they could share. He had taught her that much.

She changed her position and discovered that he was more than ready. She rearranged the bed clothes and lowered herself onto him, her breasts tingling anew as she rocked back and forth, bringing them both to a peak of pleasure.

Praying this would not be their last time.

Afterwards, she lay for a while with her head in the hollow of his shoulder, wondering if she should voice the fears that lovemaking hadn't driven away.

"Please, Gil," she murmured a moment later. "Don't go up today. I have such a bad feeling about it."

"Don't be foolish! You sound like Sancha."

She sighed, unable to think of any new argument to stop him. "Well then, we had better get some sleep."

Soon his breathing slowed and she knew he slept again. But sleep did not come as easily to her. For a long time, she lay listening to the rain on the rooftop.

When she awoke, it was no longer raining. Sunshine streamed in through a gap in the curtains. The bed beside her was empty and cold. Gil must have been gone for some time, but Anna sat in a chair near the bed, busy darning a shirt Kit had torn the day before.

She bade Anna a good morning.

"Good morning, ma'am. Captain Manning has gone to fill his balloon. He didn't want to disturb you, so he sent me up to help you when you were ready."

"And my brother...?"

"He's with Stephen in the parlor, getting his breakfast."

She sat up, her stomach churning a bit. She hoped a cup of tea and some toast would set her to rights. She dressed and joined Kit and the footman in the private parlor Gil had hired for them, where she helped herself from the sideboard.

"*Must* Stephen carry me about the fair?" Kit whined, resuming a plea he'd begun the day before. "I'm walking pretty well now. I hardly even need the cane."

She sat down and bit into the toast. "You are coming along famously, dearest, but Gil and I told you we are concerned about the crowds and all the jostling. You will find it much pleasanter to ride up on Stephen's shoulders."

And Gil had insisted they go with the footman. Even during the day, fair-goers could be a bit unruly.

They left the inn and joined the throng. Emma glanced up at her brother. His complexion was rosy and his eyes were bright; he would never admit it, but she suspected he enjoyed the vantage point of riding on tall Stephen's shoulders. At least he hadn't caught her anxiety.

Although most of the attractions of the fair were set up around the principal street, Gil would ascend from the Park, just below Greenwich Hill, where there was open space for an enclosure and surrounding crowds. He planned to make a number of tethered ascents, accepting passengers who paid a modest price for a ticket. At three o'clock he would take off for a free flight, with a wealthy adventure-seeker who'd paid handsomely for the opportunity for a longer ride.

The skies were clear and there was little wind. Everything seemed perfect but Emma still felt uneasy.

They reached the main thoroughfare and found it lined with booths and stalls selling foodstuffs and various types of merchandise. They bought some toys to bring back to the Stansteads and then they took in a Wild Beast show. After some gingerbread, Kit asked if they could go up the hill to see the famous Observatory.

They skirted the crowds around the balloon enclosure, where Gil was still giving tethered rides, and climbed up the long hill. The crowds thinned as they went; most people seemed to be either watching the balloon or enjoying the attractions back on the main street of the Fair.

As they approached the Observatory, Emma caught sight of a man among the trees to their left. Though thin and wearing shabby clothing, he seemed vaguely familiar. A breeze lifted the cap off his head. She could see his face more clearly. It was Reed!

From his shabby clothing and haggard face, Emma guessed he had fallen into another drunken melancholy. She knew Gil would wish to see him, but she was too far away to call out. Reed was behaving strangely, furtively passing from tree to tree as if he feared to be seen. Perhaps he was ashamed of having succumbed to drink again and did not want any of them to see him.

"Stephen, I see someone I must speak to. Please take Kit to the Observatory. I'll join you there in a few minutes."

"Are you sure you wish to do that, ma'am?"

"I'll be safe. See, there are very few people about." She could not imagine poor Reed presented any danger. "Come look for me if I am not back in fifteen minutes."

"Very well, ma'am."

She headed off toward the trees.

"Reed! It is I, Miss Westfield," she said as soon as she was in earshot.

This time he turned around. His face was gaunt, but he did not appear to be drunk. He seemed frightened. But why?

"Mrs. Manning now, actually," she amended. "We were worried about you. Why did you leave?"

"I can't tell you that now," Reed said. "I must stop the Captain from flying!"

A chill crept over her. "And why is that?"

He seemed about to say something, then his expression changed, as if he saw something over her shoulder that frightened him. An instant later, a large man appeared at her left and felled Reed with a heavy blow with the butt of a pistol. She would have screamed, but the ruffian grabbed her and held her close.

"Ye're too pretty to hit. I'll just take you with me."

He squeezed her; she smelled gin on his breath. She kneed him in his tender parts.

He bellowed with rage, but when she tried to run past him, he shoved her so she landed on her back. He laughed and rolled Reed down into a shallow gully, where he would not be seen by casual passersby.

She scrambled to her feet, but the ruffian took hold of her again, this time holding his pistol against her side.

"Ye'll come with me. No tricks. Scream, and I'll shoot."

He put an arm around her, so that from a distance they would look like a courting couple. Still holding the pistol to her side, he walked her quickly toward the back end of the Park. Feeling sick, she realized there was nothing she could do now, though she vowed to try to escape as soon as she had the slightest chance.

She had to discover what Reed wanted to warn Gil about.

He led her into a wooded area. She saw a herd of deer in the distance. Something passed overhead. It was a small red balloon. Gil had told her he would set some off to judge which way Alcyone would go once they began free flight.

Further in, she saw a man leaning against a tree, also watching the pilot balloon as it passed. Seeing them approach, he straightened up, leaning on a cane.

"Hodges!" he said sharply. "Who is this? And what happened to Reed?"

He came forward with a pronounced limp. He was tall, thin and dressed like a gentleman, but his face was pale, his brow sweaty. Emma wondered if he was ill.

"Mrs. Manning. She came runnin' into the woods to talk to Reed."

"Mrs. Manning!" The man sounded dismayed.

"Who are *you?*" she asked. "Why did Reed think my husband was in danger?"

"You'll find out soon enough," he said, then looked toward the ruffian. "Hodges! I told you to bring Reed back if you could!"

"I just popped 'im on the head. Quiet-like, no noise."

"Fool! I don't want anyone raising the alarm. What did you do with him?"

"Rolled 'im into a gully. Nobody'll see 'im there. He won't wake soon."

"I hope not." The gentleman wiped his brow again. "Do you think anyone will come looking for her?"

"Didn't see no one."

"You'd better go look. But first bind her up. Over there, under that tree."

The strange gentleman pulled a pistol from his pocket and pointed it at Emma. Hodges pushed her to a spot under a tree near the edge of the woods. While his master continued to cover her with his gun, Hodges bound her wrists together.

"Sit down," the gentleman commanded.

She lowered herself onto the damp ground. Hodges knelt down in front of her and leered as he pushed up her skirt.

"Stop that. She is a lady. Just tie her up. And hurry!" the gentleman hissed.

Hodges grunted, but made short work of binding her ankles together.

"Now go! If anyone is looking for her, train your pistol on them and bring them here. Do not raise an alarm, do you understand? I want no gunshots and no more bodies!"

Hodges headed off. Emma felt sick again, remembering she'd told Stephen to look for her if she did not meet them at the appointed time. She doubted he'd be prepared to deal with an armed ruffian. And he would have Kit with him.

She turned her attention back to the strange man in charge of this scheme, whatever it was. He'd hobbled about ten feet back, to the edge of the woods. He fidgeted with something she hadn't noticed before: a metal framework shaped like a ladder on two legs, supporting a long pipe or tube of some sort. Then the man stopped to look at something hidden in the grass.

"What are you doing?"

"Don't worry. You are safe enough. I'll release you when it is all over."

"When *what* is all over?"

"You'll see." A strange note of elation came into his voice.

"Who are you?"

He stood up and limped back to her. He made her an awkward bow, and suddenly clutched his stomach as if in pain. A moment later he straightened up. His hand trembling, he drew a flask from a pocket in his coat and took a few sips from it.

He smiled at her then, but there was no mirth in his eyes.

"Forgive me for not introducing myself earlier. I am Captain Dryburn."

Chapter Twenty-Nine

Emma stared at Dryburn. "But we heard you were—"

"Dead?" His laugh had a hollow ring to it. "It's easy enough to feign suicide when people think you have nothing left to live for. But they are wrong."

She stared at the man responsible for Charles's death, who was now plotting against Gil somehow. He did not seem well, or perhaps not quite in his right mind. She had to learn what he intended.

She licked her lips. "And what is it that you live for, Captain Dryburn?"

"Justice. I shall avenge the death of my men."

"So you caused Gil's earlier crash?"

"Quite right," he said. "I planned it. All Reed had to do was cut through the right springs, and the valve would have stuck shut and caused the balloon to burst as soon as it rose too high. But the fool either forgot which springs to cut or he began to have regrets. Either way, he botched the job. Weakling! He was probably ashamed to tell you what he'd done, but I couldn't take chances. I sent Hodges to Tichbury to deal with Reed, but he escaped and came back to spy on us. Damned turncoat!"

"But why would he even do such a thing in the first place?"

"Loyalty to me and to the memory of his brother. Reed was my bâtman—my personal servant—at Waterloo. His brother was also in my company. His younger brother, whom he'd sworn to take care of, slaughtered in the mud like so many others."

"He regretted it. I am certain of that. You will too, if you continue. You know you will!"

"Never! I'm"—he looked away from her—"sorry if it gives you pain. That scoundrel must have cozened you into thinking him a hero, just like everyone else."

"That charge was a mistake. If Gil had joined you, more would have died needless deaths."

"No!" He wiped his brow again, his hand trembling. "If Manning's company had joined us, we would have been able to hold the farmhouse. We would not have had to retreat as we did!"

"You are wrong. In your heart, I think you know that. Admit it to yourself and then you may see if there is anything you could do to redeem yourself. Perhaps you could help some of soldiers who have been living in hardship since the war."

"I don't need redemption! I need justice. I need them all to see what happens to their bloody hero!"

He took another sip from his flask; Emma noticed his eyes looked strange somehow. Then she remembered the Squire's grandmother, who had become addicted to laudanum during a prolonged illness. Dryburn looked just the same.

Appealing to his reason was useless. But perhaps his impaired state might make it easier to foil his plan.

"What is it you are going to do?"

His expression changed; he looked at something beyond where she was lying. His face twitched; he seemed dismayed by whatever he was seeing.

She twisted, trying to see what he was looking at, and could not help crying out.

It was Stephen, with Kit in his arms, followed by Hodges, who held a pistol to his back. Kit was pale and he was struggling not to cry.

"I couldn't help it, ma'am," said Stephen as they got closer. "He threatened to shoot your brother if we didn't do as he said."

Dryburn lifted his pistol and trained it on Stephen, his hand trembling. "Set the boy down, then move toward that tree," he said, gesturing with his cane toward a spot several yards from Emma.

As soon as Kit was set down, he staggered and fell. He struggled to get up, but Emma gave him a warning look and he stayed down.

Dryburn watched him, scowling, then turned back to Hodges. "Bind them up."

Hodges shoved Stephen down near the indicated tree. He bound him up and then hit him with the butt of his pistol for good measure. Stephen slumped down. Although she could see he was still breathing, she doubted he'd rouse in time to help.

"I didn't say you should hit him!" Dryburn said.

Hodges gave an exasperated grunt and went to tie up Kit.

"My brother is crippled," she said to Dryburn. "Please don't tie him up. This is frightening enough for him without that!"

Kit did his best to look even more terrified than he was. It worked.

"Oh, very well," muttered Dryburn.

She guessed Dryburn had had little experience working with ruffians like Hodge. Gil had described him as rather straitlaced. His dismay at hurting those he believed to be innocent made her wonder if she could turn his conscience to good use. Perhaps she could persuade him to give up his plan.

She glanced again at Kit, hoping he would not try to run off until she signaled that it was safe to do so. He was alert and looking about him. His eyes widened as he saw the strange object Emma had noticed before.

"It's a firing-frame!" he exclaimed. He turned towards Dryburn. "You're not planning to shoot rockets at Gil, are you? Because it won't work. Those Congreve rockets aren't good for much but making a scary noise. That's what Gil told me."

"Perhaps he did not know there have been improvements in the design," Dryburn retorted. "In any case, I don't need to actually hit the balloon. If a rocket passes close enough, it will ignite the vapour escaping from the balloon and there will be a fireball such as no one here has ever seen!"

Emma had no idea whether Dryburn's scheme could work or not, but she remembered how careful Gil and his crew were to avoid the slightest spark anywhere near the balloon enclosure.

Dryburn cleared his throat. "Hodges! Go make sure no one else comes near."

Hodges left; Emma wasn't sure whether to be relieved or not. It must be getting close to time for the final ascension. Would Gil think they were just tarrying at the Observatory or would he send someone to look for them?

Meanwhile, Dryburn continued to mop his brow, pacing about near the firing-frame. Kit was watching, with a calculating look in his eyes. Emma hissed to catch his attention, then made a slight shake of her head. *No, it is too dangerous.*

He lifted his chin defiantly. *Damn.* There was no way she could stop him if he tried to escape.

Dryburn checked his pocket-watch and muttered something under his breath. Then she heard "almost time."

Another pilot balloon drifted slowly by. She cursed the clear day. She cursed the low winds. But there was no use wishing for a storm. Gil would take off as scheduled, and moreover, he planned to fly low at the start, to give everyone at the fair the best possible show.

"Captain Dryburn!" she said.

He looked toward her, scowling. "Don't think you can change my mind, Mrs. Manning."

"I know you're suffering, but revenge will not make you feel better. I can see you are unhappy that Hodges hurt Reed and poor Stephen here. Do you truly wish to hurt or kill more innocent people?"

"I need justice!"

"My husband will not be alone in his balloon. He has a passenger, someone who has never done you any harm! Do you want to kill him too?"

"Can't be helped." He fumbled in his pocket for the flask, took a sip, muttered under his breath and put it away, with an obvious effort. Perhaps he dared not take too much until he'd succeeded in his scheme.

"Gil has an estate to manage. It's been in a bad way for a number of years. You would be wreaking vengeance not only on him, but upon all his tenants and laborers. Do you really wish to do that?"

"Be quiet!" There was a shrill note in his voice; perhaps she'd managed to touch his conscience.

"And what of my brother and me? Do you wish to make us destitute? And what of the soldiers my husband has in his employ?"

"You are fools to place your trust in him. I'm doing you all a favor!"

"I don't think you wish to hurt so many who have done you no harm."

His face twisted; he came toward her, cane raised as if he might hit her.

As he passed near, Kit stuck out his good leg and tripped him. Dryburn fell over, cursing. Kit grabbed Dryburn's cane and scrambled to his feet. Dryburn struggled to get up. Kit staggered off in the direction of the balloon enclosure, moving with surprising speed despite his awkward gait and a cane that was too long for him.

Emma remembered that Hodges was in the lightly wooded area ahead of them. "Kit! Go toward the Observatory! Find someone you can send to warn Gil!"

He swerved. Emma glanced back towards Dryburn. He was still on the ground, but he had drawn his pistol.

"Run, Kit!" she shouted.

But Dryburn's hand shook, and he seemed either unwilling or unable to pull the trigger.

Kit disappeared in the woods to their left. A slender hope entered Emma's heart.

Dryburn pulled himself up against a tree, but even in his maddened state, he could see he had no chance of catching Kit. "Your brother is a brave lad," he said, "but it's no matter; he cannot make it in time."

He limped as quickly as he could back towards the firing-frame.

"Please, I beg you to reconsider!" she shouted after him. "You will be caught!"

He growled under his breath. He took another drink from his flask and she knew he was beyond even appeals to his conscience. She could only pray he was too far gone to follow through with his plan.

So she sat against the tree, rubbing her wrists against the trunk and hoping the rope would wear through. Another pilot balloon floated by; it might be the last one before the ascension.

She hoped Dryburn was wrong and that Kit would be able to get a warning to Gil. But it was likely half a mile to the Observatory. Kit had not gone so far since the onset of his illness. But though he was lame, her brother was no weakling.

Meanwhile Dryburn loaded a rocket into the tube on his contraption. He stood, looking toward the lower part of the Park.

Emma lost track of time. Was there some sort of delay, or had Kit managed to send a warning? She had almost convinced herself that all would be well when Dryburn cried out, "There it is!"

Alcyone came up over the ridge, flying low and presenting all too clear a target. Emma could see two figures in the car, silhouetted against the brilliant sky. Kit had failed.

Fear pierced her. *Please, let him miss.*

Dryburn repositioned the frame, making some sort of adjustment to the angle. He stepped back and pulled on a long lanyard attached to some sort of firing mechanism. The rocket erupted from the tube with a shrieking sound, trailing smoke as it spiraled off into the air. Nowhere near Alcyone.

She let out her breath. He had missed. *He had missed!*

Cursing, Dryburn stuck a sponge on a stick up into the tube, his movements jerky but unnaturally fast. He loaded another rocket into the tube and set it off. It flew past Alcyone, closer than the previous rocket. Too close?

There was a sound like the loudest thunder-clap she'd ever heard. Flames engulfed the balloon. A hot wave of air struck her as she watched the car fall, bits of the fiery envelope drifting down more slowly to the wet ground.

It was all over so quickly, it hardly seemed real. But it was. The gaily striped balloon was gone. All she could see were barely identifiable pieces of the car and scraps of smoking varnished silk. She could not see Gil or his passenger, but no one could have survived the fire or the long drop.

Dryburn watched for a moment. Then he lifted a fist to the sky and shouted, "Hurrah! And may you burn in hell!"

She curled up, heaving with sobs, her stomach roiling. She thought of the life growing inside her, how Gil would never see their child. And last night, she'd given up trying to warn him. She'd sensed a plot but not trusted her instincts. Perhaps, had she insisted ... Pain wracked her, a feeling that something inside was being ripped open. He couldn't be dead; she couldn't bear the pain, not again.

Despair opened up before her, but she couldn't afford to succumb. She had Kit and her unborn baby to think of. She sat back up, rage against Dryburn giving her a measure of strength. "It is you who will burn in hell, for taking two more lives!"

He staggered towards her, letting out a hoarse laugh. The flask fell from his hands. Empty. How much had he just taken?

"No ... I have ... have avenged my men," he said, slurring his words. "I can die in peace."

His eyes looked stranger than ever; he swayed and fell. He lay on the ground, his muscles jerking involuntarily.

He was dying, but it would not bring Gil back to her.

Horror and grief threatened to crush her. She wanted to die but she had to live. She needed to escape before Hodges returned. Tears clouding her vision, she resumed rubbing her bound wrists against the tree trunk.

"Emma! Emma!"

Her heart turned over again. It was Gil's voice. She saw him running towards her, Lund behind him. Somehow, he was alive!

She let out a sob of relief.

Gil fell to his knees beside her and put his arms around her. He looked at Dryburn, writhing on the ground, then back at her. "Did he hurt you?"

She shook her head and then just feasted her eyes on the sight of him. He was alive! Her roguish, loving husband, his eyes full of concern for her. "Thank God! So Kit was able to warn you in time?"

He pulled out a pocket-knife and started to cut through her bonds. "Yes, he reached the Observatory, where he met Sancha, who'd come to look for you. She ran down the hill, or rather, tumbled down it, and told us what was happening."

"But I saw you... I thought I saw you and your passenger in the balloon."

"Piles of sandbags, wearing our hats. The best we could do on short notice, but it must have fooled Dryburn."

"But... why?"

Having freed her, he pulled her back into his arms and held her close. "I knew if Dryburn got what he wanted, he would not hurt you. I was afraid of what would happen if he became desperate. I couldn't risk losing you."

She relaxed in his arms for a moment, then she remembered Hodges. "There's a ruffian about in the woods! You must—"

"Don't worry. We met Reed as we were coming. He told us how Hodges had hit him and warned us he might still be about. We took care of him," he said.

"Manning!" Dryburn croaked.

They turned to see Lund standing over Dryburn, who had rolled over to stare at them. His muscles continued to twitch. His hands were blue. He struggled to draw breath but his gaze was focused on Gil.

"Why are you here? Is this ... hell?" He averted his gaze, staring up at the canopy of leaves. "But how can it be? It is so ... beautiful."

Gil stared in horror.

Dryburn twitched violently. "So ... beautiful," he said, between labored breaths, then he went still, his eyes still staring up at the sky.

Emma shivered. Her stomach heaved.

"He *did* hurt you!" Gil asked, his voice harsh and urgent.

"No," she gasped, retching, though she'd little enough in her stomach.

"Then what is wrong?"

"Nothing. I'm increasing!"

"Increasing?"

Despite her nausea, she laughed. "In the family way!"

He exhaled sharply and held her closer. "Are you sure you're all right?"

"I am, I promise. Only a little queasy."

She saw that Lund had just helped Stephen up. The footman held a hand up to this head, but otherwise seemed unharmed.

"Stephen!" Gil called. "Are you all right?"

Stephen nodded. "Just sorry I wasn't able to stop that blackguard, sir." He stared down at Dryburn.

"If you can manage it, I want you to help Lund take his body and hide it somewhere on Blackheath. We should try to spare his family any further disgrace. Let everyone keep thinking he died last winter."

"What about the balloon?" Lund asked. "People will talk about that."

Gil paused for a moment. "An accidental discharge of fireworks."

"But there're no fireworks planned for tonight."

"Canceled due to the accident," Gil said.

"Ye're the Captain." Lund shrugged. "It may work."

The two other men headed off to the south, bearing Dryburn's body.

Gil turned his attention back to Emma, gathering her close again. "I'll take you to the Observatory. Kit's waiting for us there. Shall I carry you?"

"No, just let us sit here for a bit. I'll be better soon, now that I know you're alive."

He shifted to sit with his back against the trunk, still holding her.

"I had such a bad feeling—earlier, and again last night—that someone wished you harm," she said. "I should have tried harder to stop you!"

"Don't blame yourself. It's a lesson to me to be more obedient, darling."

"I shall remember you said that," she said.

They sat in silence for a bit and she began to feel better, happy just to lean against him, to feel the rise and fall of his breath, his hands tenderly stroking her.

"So I'm to be a father," he said slowly, wonder in his voice.

"It is a surprise to you? You *do* know how babies come about?"

He laughed and caressed her belly. "I suppose we *have* been rather busy."

"Rather," she said, smiling. "I'm better now. Let us go join Kit and the others."

He helped her up and would have carried her, but she insisted she was well enough to walk.

As they headed off, she gazed at Alcyone's remains, glad there were no greater losses but still a little sad. "I'm so sorry. Your balloon . . ."

"You and Kit are safe. That's all that matters. I'll think of another way to raise the funds. All will be well, I promise."

Something inside her softened, like a tiny heartbreak she willingly accepted. She smiled at him. "You don't have to make promises. Nothing in life is certain."

"At least I promise to love you, and do my best to care for you and Kit and this scamp growing inside you. He or she *will* be a scamp, you know."

"I know." One more soul to love and worry about. She could bear it; no, she welcomed it.

"Kiss me," she commanded. "*Now.*"

Epilogue

Norfolk
December, 1817

E mma looked up as a gust of wind rattled the windows of the drawing room at Lynnford Abbey. Winters in Norfolk were infamous for their severity, but she was warm enough. She'd moved the writing desk closer to the hearth, where a substantial fire burned. She and Gil had become quite fond of sitting here. Once she'd rearranged the furnishings and filled the bare walls with some of her sketches, it had begun to feel like their home.

She finished sharpening her pen and began a long over-due letter.

Dear Miss Grimshaw,

I am happy you and Mr. Grimshaw are enjoying your usual health. I must apologize once again for being such a poor correspondent.

Our circumstances have improved a great deal since the summer. As I mentioned in my previous letter, the gentleman who wished to ride with my husband at Greenwich offered to pay for the construction of a new balloon, and it became quite the fashion amongst wealthy adventure-seekers to pay for rides. This proved to be much safer than Gil's original plan for ascensions at the fairs, for all were in agreement not to fly unless conditions were perfect. All has gone well.

We have begun repaying the mortgages and also started many of the repairs necessary in order to make the estate once again suitable for tenants.

I'm happy to say I will soon be in a position to help. Mr. Blackwood of Edinburgh has agreed to publish Papa's book about birds. He has offered me a tidy sum for it and he will allow me to complete it as Papa would have wished. Now I must work quickly to finish, for as you know I expect to be confined in a few months. I have grown quite enormous but I am feeling as robust as always.

I have been striving to make Lynnford Abbey more homelike. We are still keeping many rooms under Holland covers. We do not entertain on a great scale, though we have been warmly welcomed by our neighbors. No doubt they are pleased to see the improvements we are undertaking.

You may be interested to know that Gil's crew, whom we once mistook for gypsies, are faring well. Lund and Sancha were married a few months ago, having finally overcome their religious differences. They are now happily established on one of our farms. Birkin is busy repairing one of our windmills, as he is quite clever in all things mechanical.

Gil is well as always, learning the business of the estate and becoming accustomed to being called Lord Manning. Kit is thriving and would send you his love, were he given to expressing such sentiments!

I wish you and Mr. Grimshaw a happy Christmas and hope you will consider visiting us in the summer.

Yours affectionately,
Emma

Elena Greene

Norfolk
February, 1818

"Look! It's working!" Kit bounced with excitement. "Birkin's done the trick!"

Gil let out a sigh of relief. They all stood on the bank of the channel, watching the windmill's new sails turn, hearing the sound of the repaired scoop-wheel as it began the work of pumping water out of fields that had begun to return to marshland.

Windmills like this one were the key to farming the black, soggy soils of this region of Norfolk. He was more than glad to see this one working again, and to know that he'd helped to recreate the magic he remembered from his childhood. In its own way, it was no less exciting than any of his adventures abroad or in the air.

Beside him, Emma smiled, huddled in her cloak against the cold wind.

"Warm enough?" he asked, putting an arm around her waist.

She nodded. Norfolk winters were severe, but she never complained, saying the baby growing inside her kept her warm enough.

A strange spasm crossed her face. Had her time come? But a moment later, her brow was smooth again. The midwife had said it would be soon, but no lady about to be confined could have spent the last few days as Emma had, turning the house upside down in early spring cleaning and helping the new gardener restore order to the kitchen garden. Or could she?

"Tired?" he asked.

"Just a little," she said. "I would like to go home now."

Home. He'd never thought he'd ever have a real home and he'd never imagined Lynnford Abbey would ever feel like one. Now he looked forward to returning, to having a quiet dinner with Emma and Kit, perhaps playing some chess or backgammon afterwards.

He gave her a kiss first. Her mouth parted sweetly to him; her round, hard belly pressed against his side. Even through all their warm clothing, he felt the baby kick.

He laughed. "Very well then. Let us go home."

They had about a half an hour's drive ahead of them, passing through the village on their way. They spent the time talking about all the changes taking place around them: ditches being cleared, cottages repaired. Emma spoke a little less than usual; he set it down to fatigue. He'd try to persuade her to rest a little before dinner.

But as they approached Swanham he noticed that odd spasm cross her face again. "Gil," she said. "Before we go on, we should see if Mrs. Stokes is at home."

She wanted to see the midwife? "Do you mean . . .?"

She nodded, with a reassuring smile.

Excitement, dread, every joy and fear he'd felt watching the baby grow inside her, all surged through him now. But the baby would not wait and he could not let Emma or Kit see his rising panic. He called out the order to the coachman, stifling the urge to order him to drive faster.

Kit looked anxious. "You'll be an uncle soon," Gil told him, trying to sound calm but not even fooling himself.

"Don't worry, either of you," said Emma. "The pains aren't strong. I'm sure we have enough time to get home."

As they drove through the village, Emma quietly endured another wave of pain. He knew not to ask how bad it was; she wouldn't say anything to distress him or Kit. He prayed he wouldn't have to help her give birth in the carriage!

It was a relief when they reached Mrs. Stokes's cottage and found her there. She readily agreed to come with them. Although he'd tried to convince Emma to go to Norwich, or better yet, London, to be attended by a reputable accoucheur, Emma had stubbornly insisted that she wished to be confined at home and that she liked Mrs. Stokes. Well, he liked the midwife, too, and found her capable, motherly air comforting. Perhaps it would all go well.

During the rest of the trip—a mere ten minutes which seemed an eternity—the two women chatted about gardening and other commonplace subjects. At intervals, Emma stopped talking to suffer through pains which were coming more closely together.

"Are you all right, Emma?" Kit asked, as she relaxed after what seemed like the strongest pang yet.

"Perfectly, dearest," she replied. "Everything is just as it should be."

"Indeed it is," echoed Mrs. Stokes. "Your sister has a strong constitution. I'm sure she will come through as easily as anyone and better than most."

Somehow it was not enough to reassure Gil. However, he kept his fears to himself until they reached the Abbey. Once he'd gotten Kit settled down with a book, he ran back to his and Emma's bedchamber. The fire was burning brightly; the room felt almost too warm. Emma sat on the old birthing chair she'd found in some odd corner of the house, dressed in her nightdress. Mrs. Stokes sat in a chair nearby. Emma's maid was on her knees, cleaning the floor.

"Her ladyship's water just broke," said the midwife. "It won't be long now."

"Good God," he muttered. He wasn't ready, but he didn't want Emma to suffer for too long either.

"Come here," Emma said, smiling. "I want you to be with me."

He advanced slowly into the room, looking at the midwife. "Are you sure I should be here?"

"If her ladyship wants you here, then you should be," said the midwife. "You can stand behind her and put your arms around her. It can be a comfort."

He did as he was told, glad to be given a task he could manage. He put his arms around Emma and felt her relax.

"Thank you," she murmured.

"I'll reckon you've not been present at a lying-in before,

my lord," said the midwife.

He swallowed. "While I was campaigning in the Peninsula, there were many births in camp. One can't help hearing what goes on in nearby tents, but I was never actually there. All the women crowded around and helped. I wish Emma had some female relative to support her."

"You'll do well enough," said Emma. "I—oh ..."

"A big one, my lady?"

Emma nodded, moaning softly. "I never thought... it would be so strong," she said when it was over.

The midwife examined Emma and gave a satisfied nod. "We're almost there. Next time, cry out if you wish. Whatever helps, I say."

"Yes, do what you must," he said. "Don't mind me."

"You won't faint?" Emma asked.

"I didn't say that. Just don't mind me if I do."

She and the other women laughed at him. He prayed it would be over soon.

A few minutes later, Emma said, "I feel ..."

"Yes, the baby is coming!" said the midwife.

During the next few pains, Emma made a sound like a determined growl and strained with all her might, and then, suddenly, it was over. Mrs. Stokes held a wet infant in her hands. They held their breaths while she worked to clear its nose and mouth. A high-pitched, insistent cry filled the room.

Gil felt Emma relax again, heard her sigh of relief. "Thank God," he breathed. "You were magnificent, Emma."

"Well done," said Mrs. Stokes. "You have a fine boy."

"Oh, let me hold him," said Emma.

"Soon, my lady."

Not long after, the midwife and maid had tidied matters up and helped Emma to her bed. They placed the swaddled baby in her arms. Gil, who'd stood quietly out of the way, came around to look at her. Sweaty and disheveled as she was, her eyes were glowing. She'd never looked so beautiful. Then he took a better look at his son. A little muffin-faced thing, like most infants he'd seen, the baby was already rooting around and seeking Emma's breast.

"A greedy little scamp," he commented, feeling ridiculously proud.

"What will you name him?" asked the midwife, helping Emma to position the infant for suckling.

"James William," he and Emma said in unison, then laughed.

They'd chosen the names to honor his father and Captain Forsythe. Gil prayed he'd be a good father, just as they'd tried to be. He prayed his son would live in more peaceful times.

He looked at Emma and saw the same hopes mirrored in her eyes. They were embarking on a new adventure, greater than any that had come before, and there was no certainty. Only hope.

And love.

THE END

Author's Note

While writing this book, I found myself researching a lot of odd questions. How did the process used to create hydrogen for balloons in the 19th century smell? How did one shoot a Congreve rocket? And so on. I can only share a few of the interesting things I learned, along with some of my sources, for any fellow history geeks.

Before I talk about anything else, I have to confess that I slightly altered the history of Waterloo. I replaced the real Captains Leach and Chawner, who were in charge of the two companies of the 95th Rifles stationed at the sandpit near the farm of La Haye Sainte, with my fictional hero, Gil, and the unfortunate Captain Dryburn. The idea of going to the aid of those defending the farmhouse was discussed and dismissed as hopeless. Captains Leach and Chawner sensibly maintained their positions until forced to retreat. Captain Dryburn and his ill-fated charge are entirely my own invention.

I've tried to be as accurate as possible on all other matters regarding the Riflemen and the battles in which Gil fought. Although I've read Bernard Cornwell's Sharpe series and watched the adaptations starring Sean Bean (how I suffer for my craft!) I've also consulted many other references.

Two excellent starting places for a study of the Riflemen are *Wellington's Rifles* by Mark Urban and *Military Illustrated's Rifleman* by Phillip Elliot-Wright. However, my favorite resources are accounts written by the officers themselves, since they convey personal impressions of battles and army life that are only touched on in the higher level histories.

I based a lot of Gil's military backstory on the experiences recounted in *Captain of the 95th Rifles*, by Captain Jonathan Leach (the same Captain Leach mentioned above). *A British Rifleman* by Major George Simmons was also very useful. Simmons knew how to administer first aid on the battlefield and was also wounded himself a number of times. He was severely wounded by a musket ball that pierced his chest at Waterloo and, like Gil, was fortunate to survive.

In addition to these sources, I want to include what is probably the most popular and readable personal account by a Rifleman: *Adventures in the Rifle Brigade*, by Sir John Kincaid. Here's an example of his writing style:

"...I found myself all at once within a few yards of one of their regiments in line, which opened such a fire, that had I not, riflemanlike, taken instant advantage of the cover of a good fir-tree, my name would have unquestionably been transmitted to posterity by that night's gazette. And, however opposed to it may be the usual system of drill, I will maintain, from that day's experience, that the cleverest method of teaching a recruit to stand at attention is to place him behind a tree and fire balls at him..."

The other main subject I researched for this book was the early history of ballooning. The first manned and untethered balloon flight occurred on the 21st of November, 1783. The scientist Jean-François Pilâtre de Rozier and the Marquis François d'Arlandes ascended in a hot air balloon built by the brothers Joseph-Michel and Jacques-Etienne Montgolfier, members of a family of paper manufacturers. On December 1st of the same year, the scientist Jacques Charles and Nicolas-Lewis Robert completed the first flight of a hydrogen balloon. Since there was no compact fuel source at the time, hot air balloons could go only on very short flights. Hydrogen balloons were capable of much longer flights, depending on weather conditions and how heavily they were loaded, and were thus more popular during the Regency.

One of my favorite references on the history of ballooning is *The Romance of Ballooning: The Story of the Early Aeronauts*, from the Viking Press. It's a copiously illustrated collection of letters, articles and excerpts from period books recounting the adventures of the early balloonists.

I also delved further into a number of full-length personal accounts of 18th and 19th century ballooning. I especially enjoyed reading about the adventures of the aeronaut Vincent Lunardi in his *An Account of the First Aerial Voyage in England* (1784) and *An Account of Five Aerial Voyages in Scotland* (1786).

Although its accounts of ballooning are Victorian, I also found a lot of interesting anecdotes and tidbits in *Travels in the Air* by James Glaisher, F.R.S., Camille Flammarion, W. de Fonvielle, and Gaston Tissandier. Flammarion reported encountering butterflies at high altitudes; having read that, I couldn't resist giving Gil and Emma the same experience.

The early aeronauts sometimes had to resort to desperate measures to avoid landing in trees or water. If they ran out of ballast, they were obliged to discard whatever they could in order to keep their balloons aloft.

In 1785, Jean Pierre Blanchard and Dr. John Jeffries made the first crossing of the English Channel in a hydrogen balloon. They were about five or six miles from the French coast when the balloon began to descend. Here's an excerpt from Dr. Jeffries' account:

> "...yet still approaching the sea very fast, and the boats being much alarmed for us, we, though unwillingly, cast away first one anchor; then the other, after which my little hero (Blanchard) stript, and threw away his coat. On this I was compelled to follow his example. Then he stript and cast away his trowsers."

When Gil arrives at Emma's village half-naked, it is purely in the interest of historical accuracy. That's my story and I'm sticking to it.

Excerpt from
Lady Dearing's Masquerade

"Ah, there you are! You shan't run away now!"
Livvy turned to see the Turk coming their way
from the opposite end of the ballroom. Her escort glanced
back, then took her arm and began to lead her on a crooked
path through the milling revelers.

The Turk's loud voice boomed again. "I'll see your face
before the night's done, you jade!"

The stranger steered her ever faster through the crowd,
then pushed her gently against one of the pillars that lined the
sides of the ballroom. Shielding her with his body, he pressed
her head to his shoulder and draped his cloak around her.

Her heart galloped as his muscular form pressed against
hers. First in fear, then, as he did nothing more, an old,
familiar heat flowed through her, stoked by the sharp intake
of his breath, the betrayal of his unmistakable masculine
reaction to their closeness.

It was wonderful and terrifying.

And all he did was hold her. He made no attempt to kiss
or fondle her, merely hiding her under his cloak, his body
subtly vibrating with his restraint. Nothing more. He demanded nothing more.

Elena Greene

Desire flushed her body, and she stiffened. She couldn't allow this, didn't want to feel anything like it again. But she didn't wish to run away either. So they stood for long moments, pressed so close that she could barely distinguish his labored breathing from her own, while desire ebbed and flowed with her fears.

Then he shifted. "I think . . . he is gone," he whispered.

She looked up at him, but it was too dark to see his face. His ragged breath spoke of arousal. The heat rose inside her again, like a madness. Recklessly, she stretched upward, on tiptoes and raised her face to him. Another tortured breath, and he lowered his face to hers.

His kiss was shockingly sweet: shy, hesitant, as he pressed his lips almost chastely against hers and stilled his body. As if he guessed what she wanted when she herself had not known. Dreamily, she succumbed to pleasure; she parted her lips and kissed him back, relishing the firm roundness of his lips, the taste of him, the merest hint of wine on his breath.

She gasped as the stranger's tongue curled around hers. Shocked, she submitted to his slow, tentative exploration, sensing she had but to say the word and he would stop. But she didn't wish to stop him. She lifted her arms to embrace him, ventured to flick her tongue against his. A shudder ran through his body; he let out a low groan, yet did nothing but kiss her.

Her late husband had never kissed her like this; she had not known that anyone *could* kiss so.

Then thoughts of Walter fled. The stranger deepened his kiss; she let out a little moan of pleasure. He pressed against her more closely and she tightened her embrace, whimpering, returning each flutter of his tongue. She felt safe yet lost, feasting yet hungry, helpless with longing for more.

A chill came over her. She froze, then pulled her face away.

She had vowed never to be helpless again.

"I cannot . . . I am sorry. Let me go," she whispered.

For a moment Death continued to press her against the pillar, the rhythm of his breath harsh, his body hard.

"Please," she begged, terror constricting her throat. "Let me go. I should never have come!"

Then he backed away, slowly releasing her. As she slid out from under his cloak, she nearly wept with relief. He was a gentleman after all.

"Forgive me," he said in one shuddering breath. "Please don't be frightened. I won't touch you again if you don't wish, but please let me—"

His eyes were dark, full of desire and remorse; his voice low and caressing. She was touched, but it was wrong to stay. It was terribly wrong of her to have encouraged him.

"I must go," she interrupted before she changed her mind. "Please don't follow me!"

Books by Elena Greene

Regency Romance

The Wedding Wager
(a traditional Regency novella)

Lord Langdon's Kiss

"The Three Disgraces"
The Incorrigible Lady Catherine
The Redwyck Charm
Saving Lord Verwood

Historical Romance

Lady Em's Indiscretion
(an erotic Regency novella)

Lady Dearing's Masquerade

Fly with a Rogue

Elena Greene grew up reading anything she could lay her hands on, including her mother's Georgette Heyer novels. She also enjoyed writing but decided to pursue a more practical career in software engineering. Fate intervened when she was sent on a three year international assignment to England, where she was inspired to start writing romances set in the Regency. Her books have won the National Readers' Choice Award, the Desert Rose Golden Quill and the Colorado Romance Writers' Award of Excellence. Her Super Regency, *Lady Dearing's Masquerade*, won *RT Book Club's* award for Best Regency Romance of 2005 and made the Kindle Top 100 list in 2011. When not writing, Elena enjoys swimming, cooking, meditation, playing the piano, volunteer work and craft projects. She lives in upstate New York with her two daughters and more yarn, wire and beads than she would like to admit.

Find Elena online at **www.elenagreene.com**
Write to Elena at 2520 Vestal Parkway East
PMB #173, Vestal, NY 13850

www.ingramcontent.com/pod-product-compliance
Lightning Source LLC
Chambersburg PA
CBHW051519260626
47170CB00003B/689